THE ATTACKS OF SEPTEMBER 11, 2001

PHOTOS ©: 154 TOP: NEW YORK DAILY NEWS ARCHIVE/GETTY IMAGES; 154 BOTTOM LEFT: ANDREW LICHTENSTEIN /GETTY IMAGES; 154 BOTTOM RIGHT: 2001 THE RECORD (BERGEN CO. NJ)/GETTY IMAGES; 155 TOP: AP IMAGES; 155 CENTER: PETER HERMES FURIAN/SHUTTERSTOCK; 155 BOTTOM: STOCKTREK IMAGES, INC./ALAMY STOCK PHOTO; 156 TOP: WIN MCNAMEE/GETTY IMAGES; 156 CENTER: JUSTIN LANE-POOL/GETTY IMAGES; 156 BOTTOM: FRANCOIS ROUX/ALAMY STOCK PHOTO; 157 LEFT: PETER J. ECKEL/LIFE IMAGES COLLECTION/GETTY IMAGES; 157 RIGHT: FRANCOIS ROUX/ALAMY STOCK PHOTO.

SPECIAL THANKS TO KEVIN FLYNN

LIBRARY OF CONGRESS CONTROL NUMBER: 2021936105
ISBN 978-1-338-68048-5

10 9 8 7 6 5 4 3 2 1   21 22 23 24 25
PRINTED IN THE U.S.A.   40
FIRST EDITION, AUGUST 2021

EDITED BY KATIE WOEHR
LETTERING BY JANICE CHIANG
INKS BY COREY EGBERT
COLOR BY CHI NGO
BOOK DESIGN BY KATIE FITCH
CREATIVE DIRECTOR: HEATHER DAUGHERTY

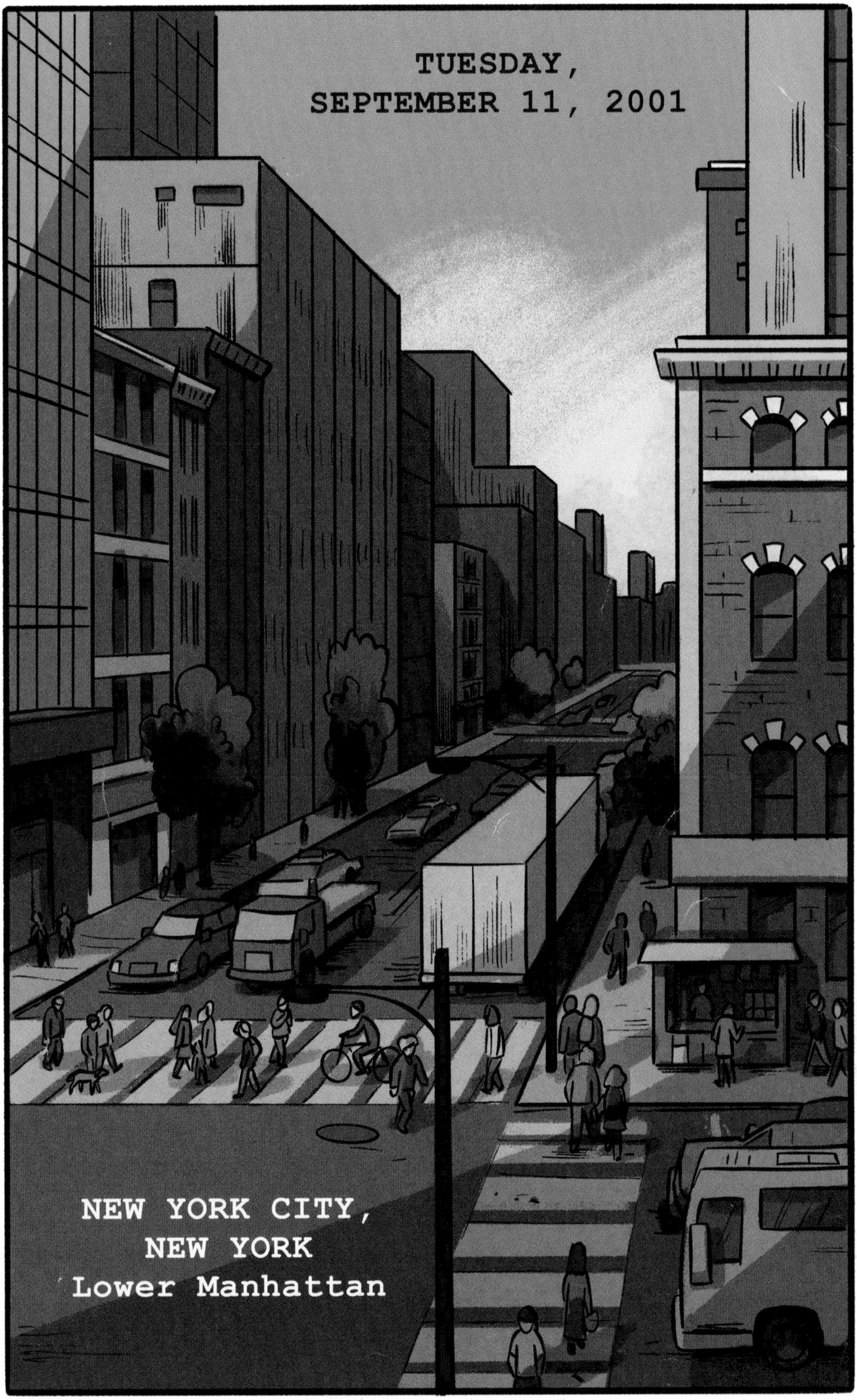
TUESDAY,
SEPTEMBER 11, 2001
NEW YORK CITY,
NEW YORK
Lower Manhattan

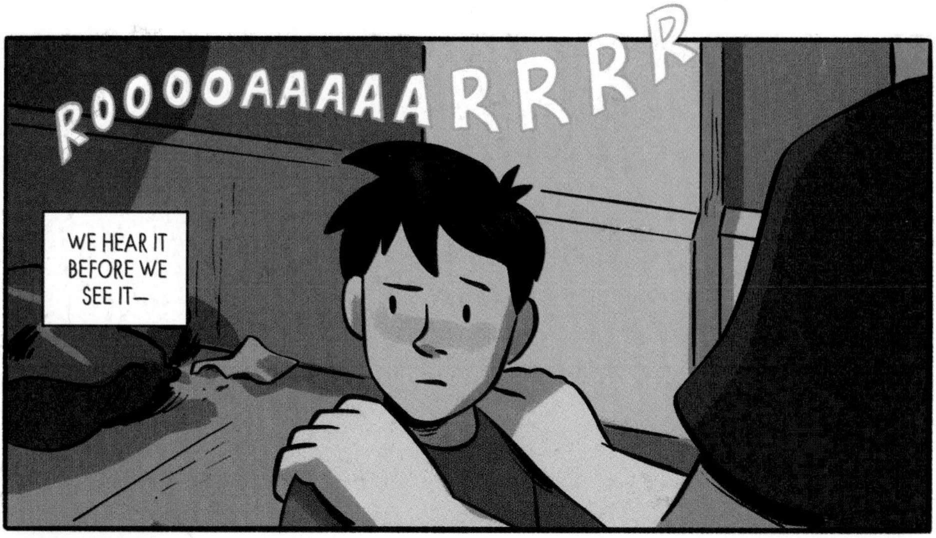
ROOOOAAAAARRRR
WE HEAR IT BEFORE WE SEE IT—

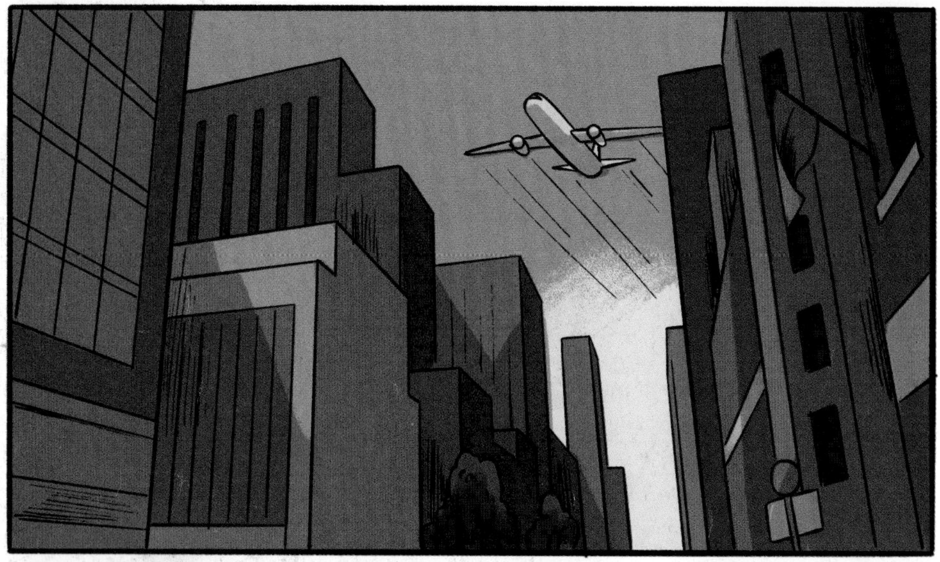

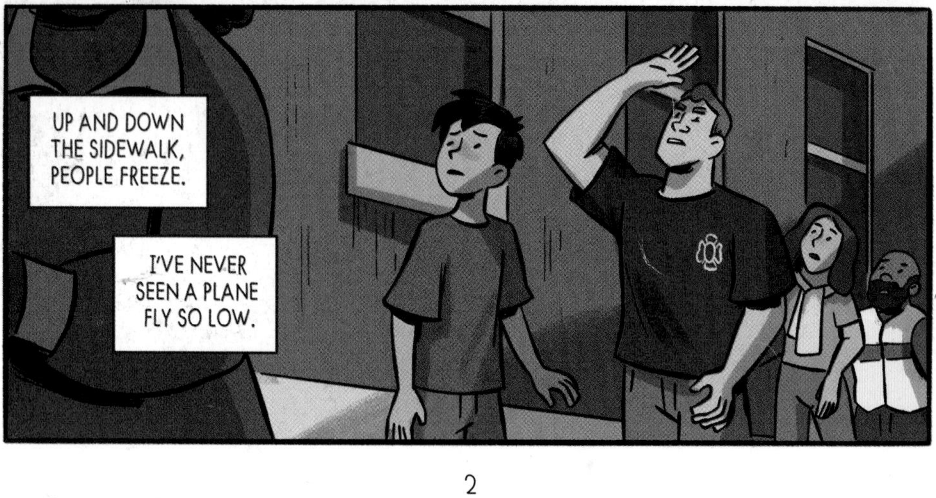
UP AND DOWN THE SIDEWALK, PEOPLE FREEZE.
I'VE NEVER SEEN A PLANE FLY SO LOW.

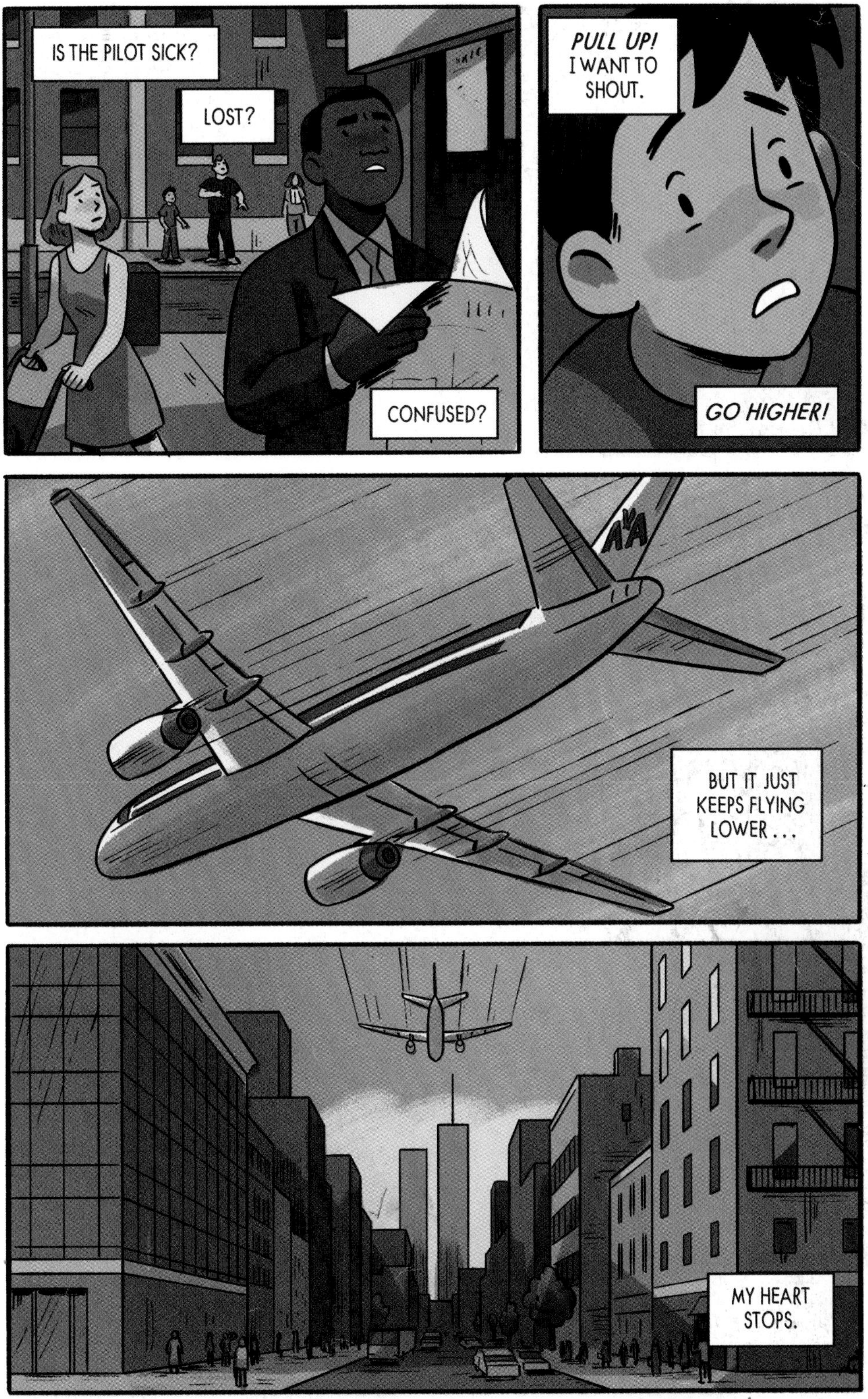
IS THE PILOT SICK?
LOST?
CONFUSED?
PULL UP! I WANT TO SHOUT.
GO HIGHER!
BUT IT JUST KEEPS FLYING LOWER . . .
MY HEART STOPS.

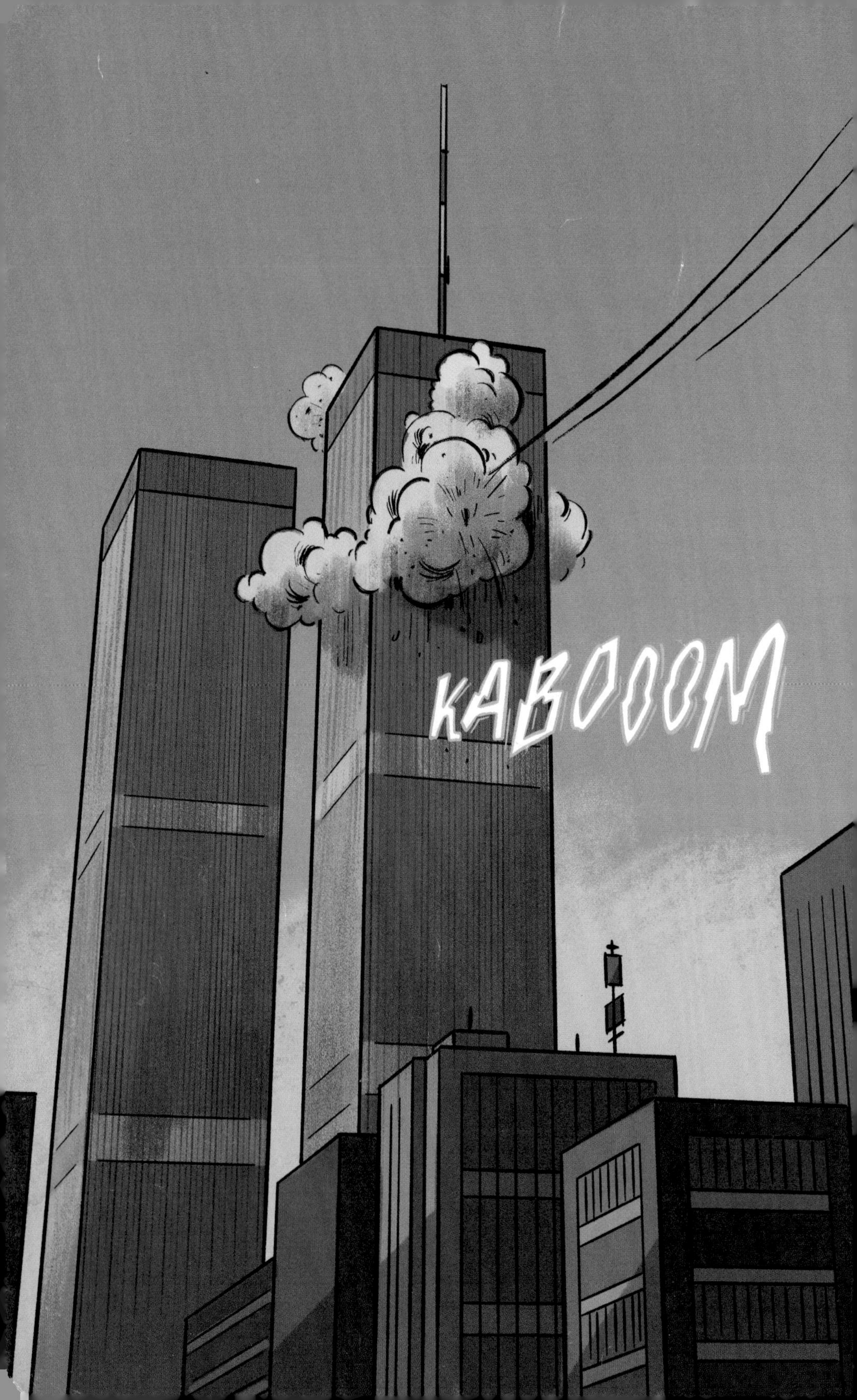
KABOOOM

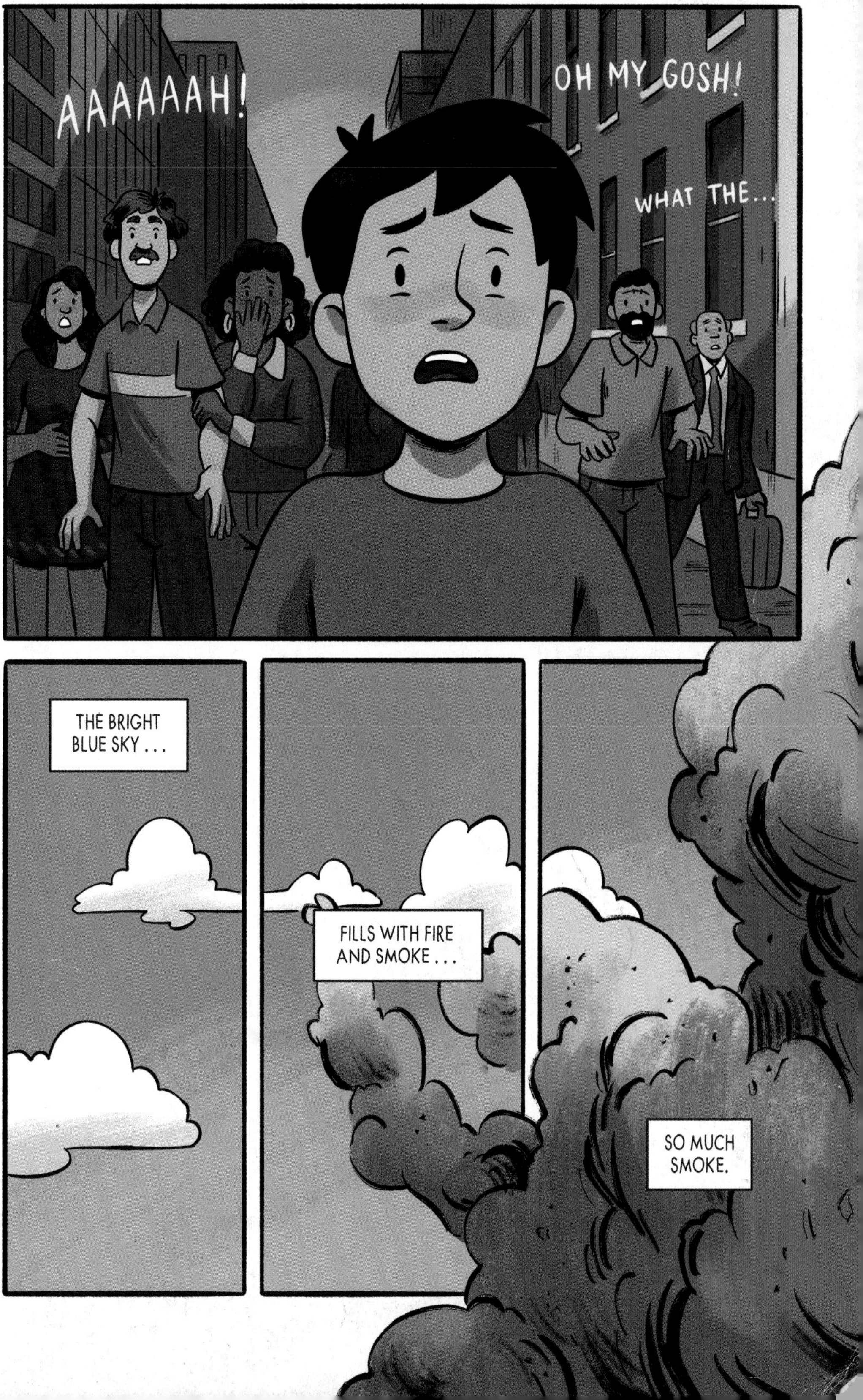
AAAAAAH!
OH MY GOSH!
WHAT THE...
THE BRIGHT BLUE SKY . . .
FILLS WITH FIRE AND SMOKE . . .
SO MUCH SMOKE.

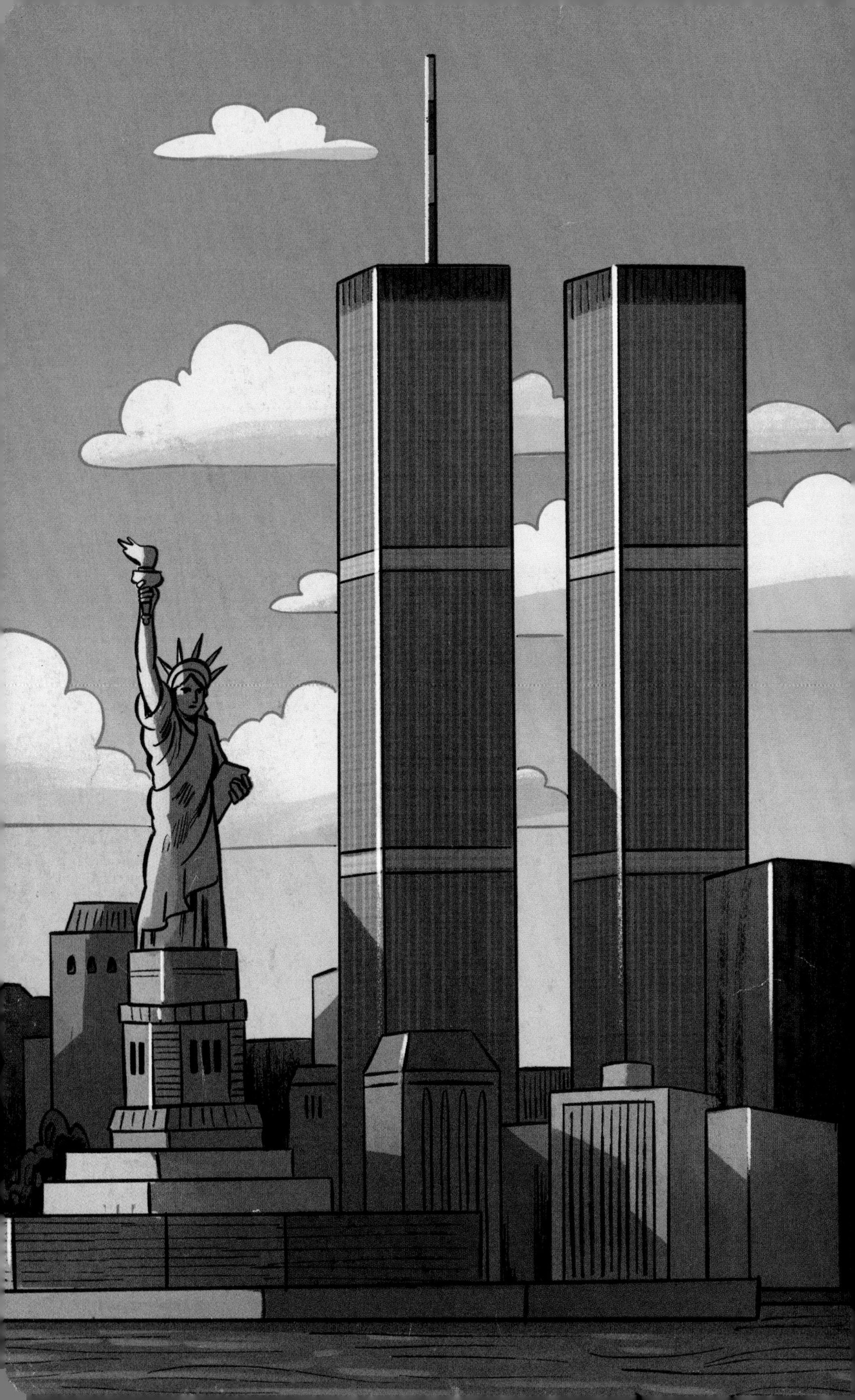

I SURVIVED

THE ATTACKS OF SEPTEMBER 11, 2001

BASED ON THE NOVEL IN THE *NEW YORK TIMES*
BESTSELLING SERIES BY LAUREN TARSHIS

ADAPTED BY GEORGIA BALL
WITH ART BY COREY EGBERT
COLORS BY CHI NGO

graphix
AN IMPRINT OF
■SCHOLASTIC

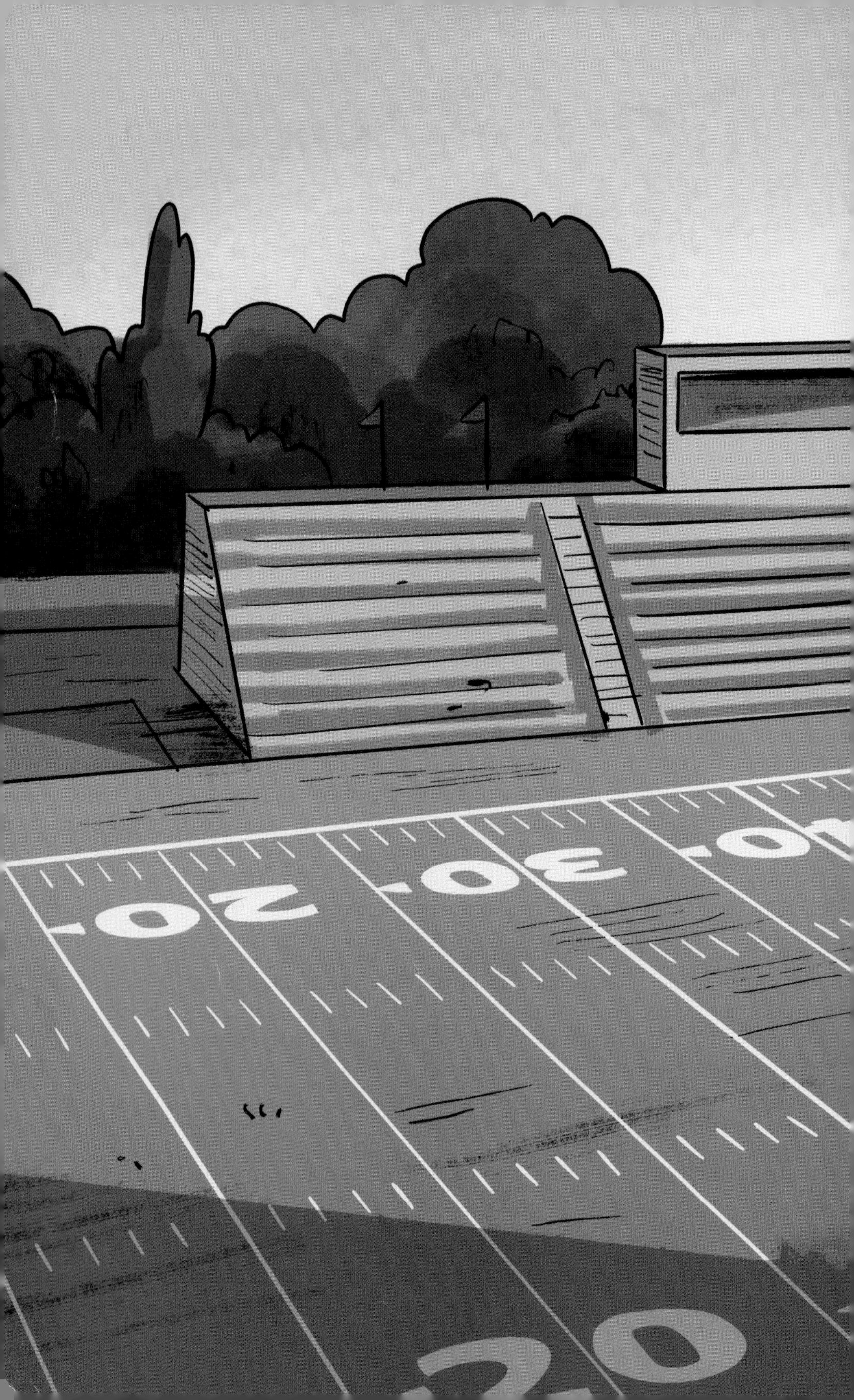

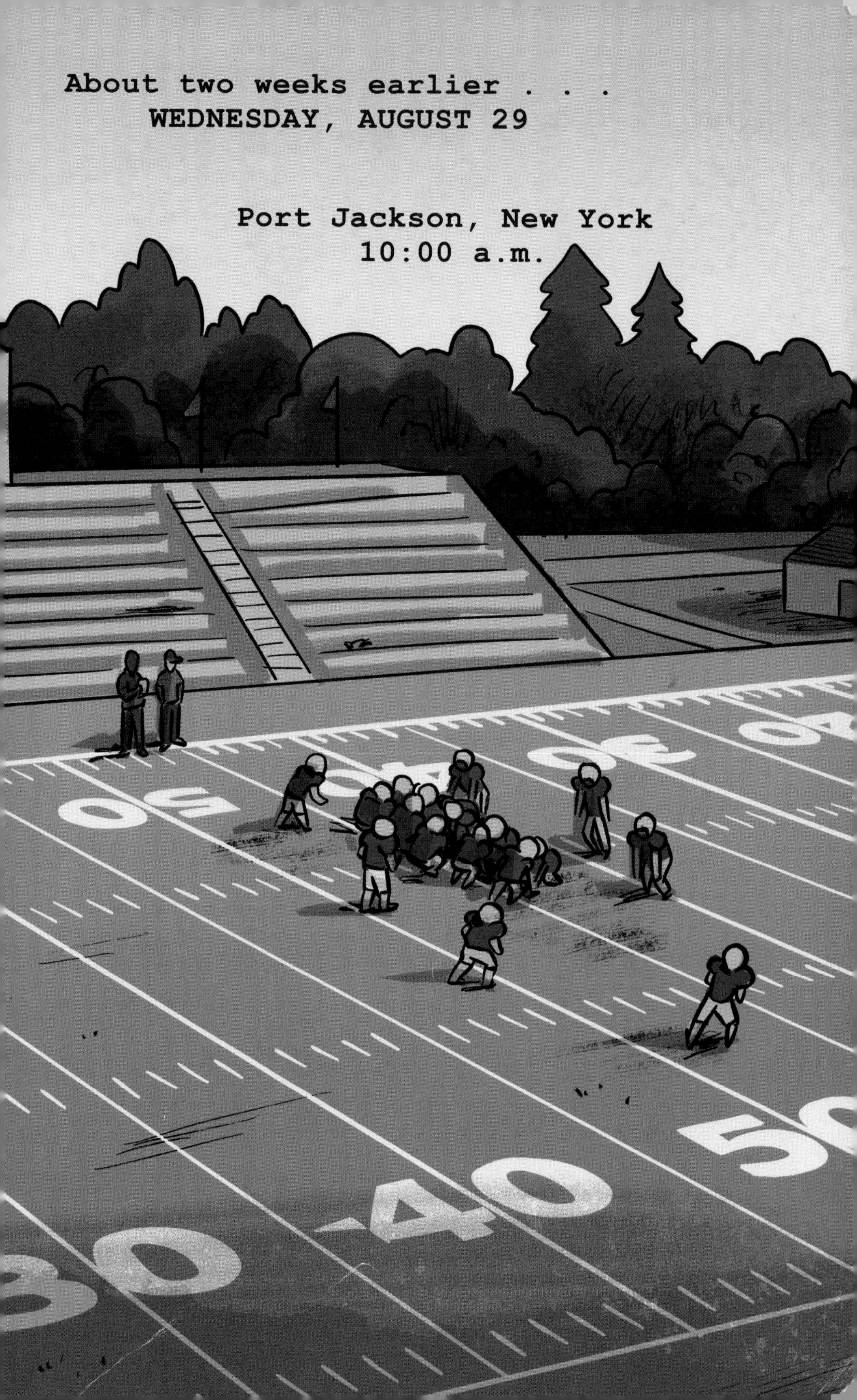
About two weeks earlier . . .
WEDNESDAY, AUGUST 29
Port Jackson, New York
10:00 a.m.

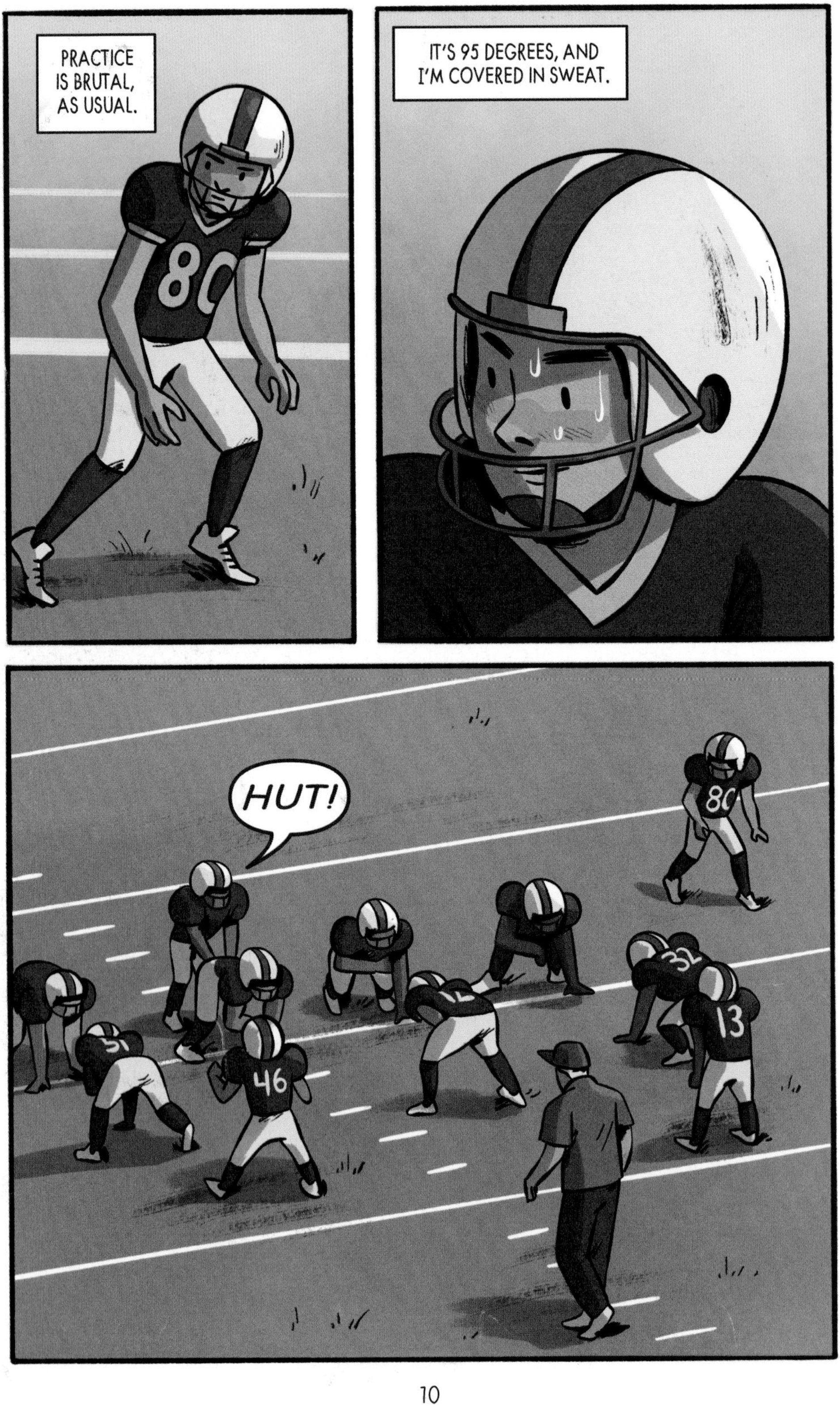
PRACTICE IS BRUTAL, AS USUAL.
IT'S 95 DEGREES, AND I'M COVERED IN SWEAT.
HUT!

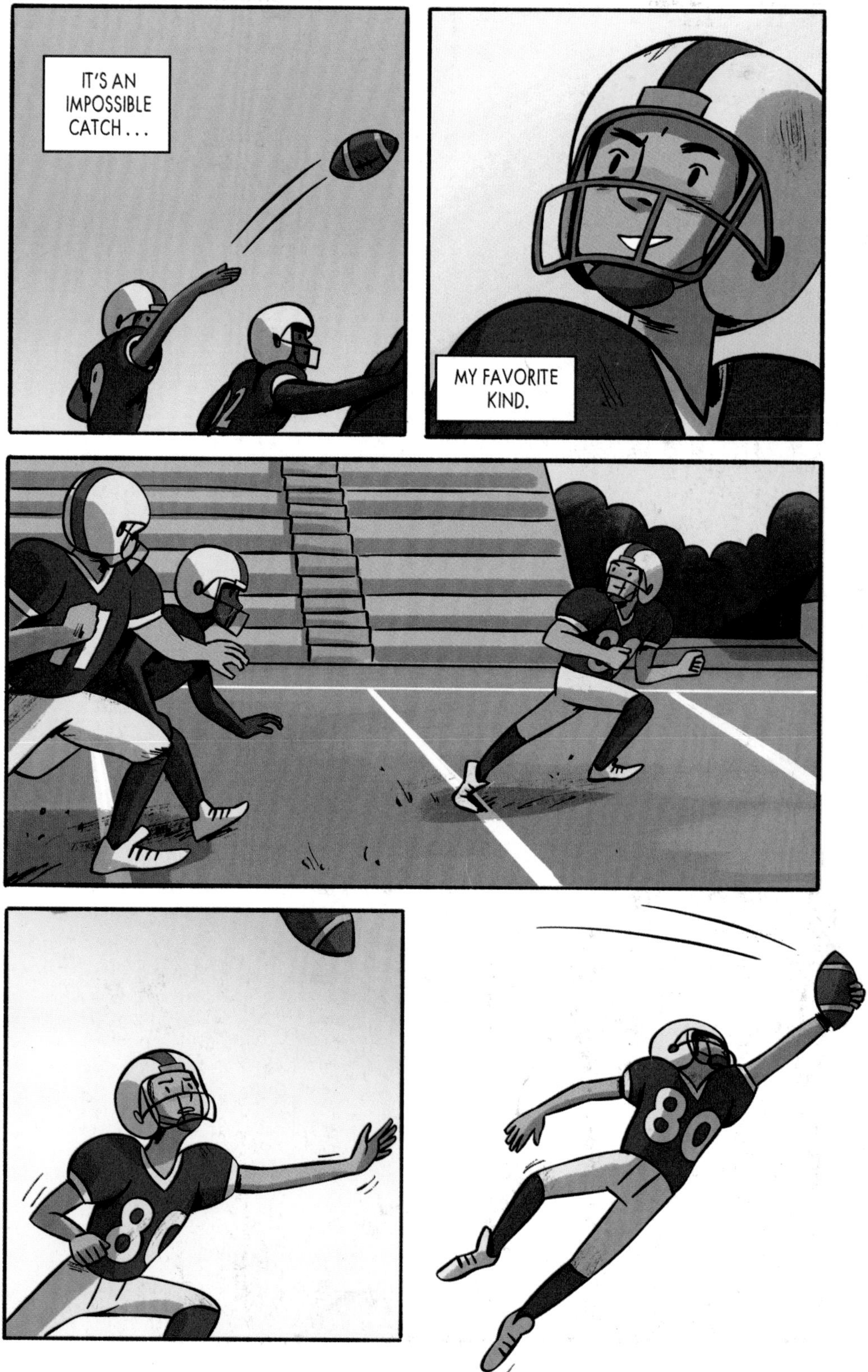
IT'S AN IMPOSSIBLE CATCH . . .
MY FAVORITE KIND.

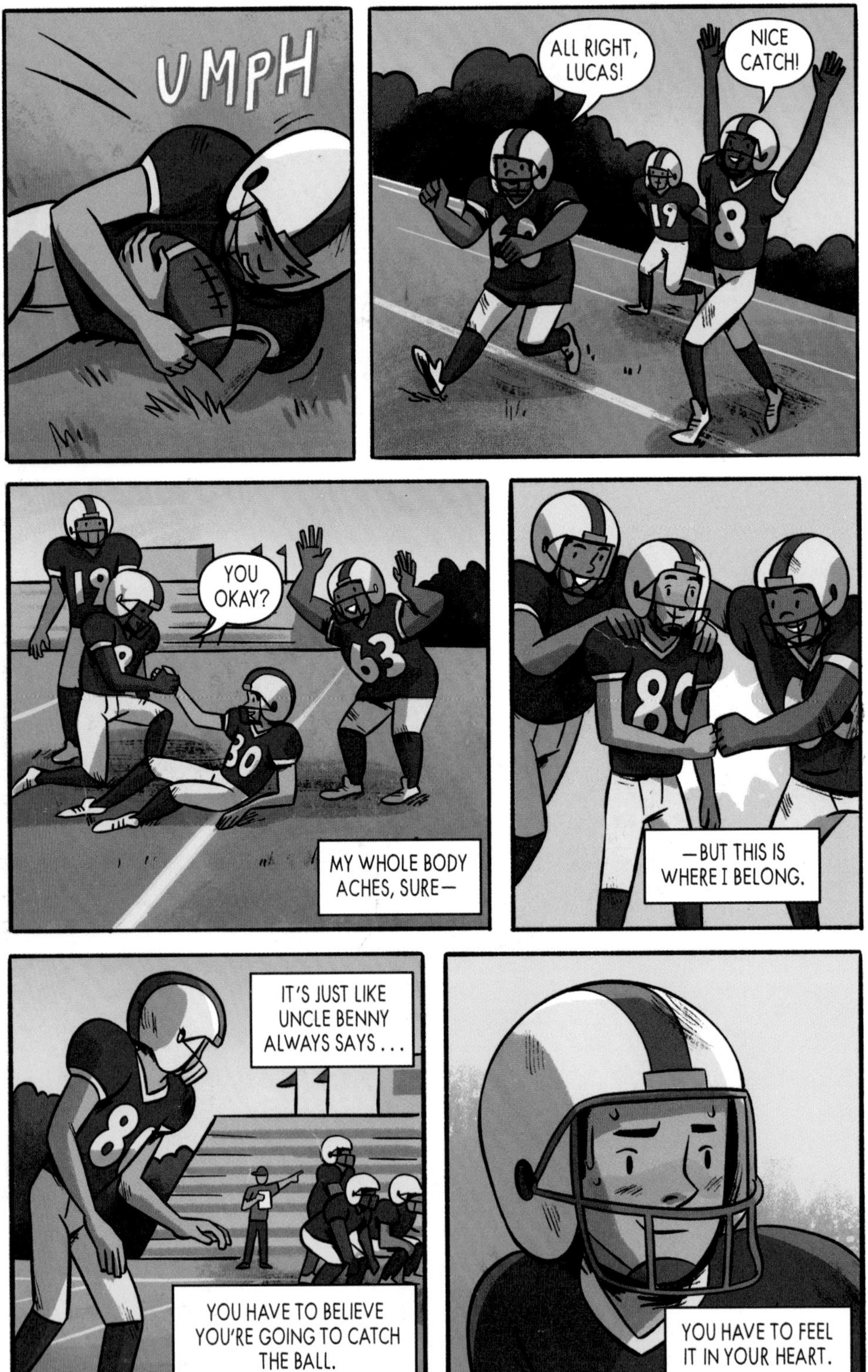
UMPH
ALL RIGHT, LUCAS!
NICE CATCH!
YOU OKAY?
MY WHOLE BODY ACHES, SURE—
—BUT THIS IS WHERE I BELONG.
IT'S JUST LIKE UNCLE BENNY ALWAYS SAYS . . .
YOU HAVE TO BELIEVE YOU'RE GOING TO CATCH THE BALL.
YOU HAVE TO FEEL IT IN YOUR HEART.

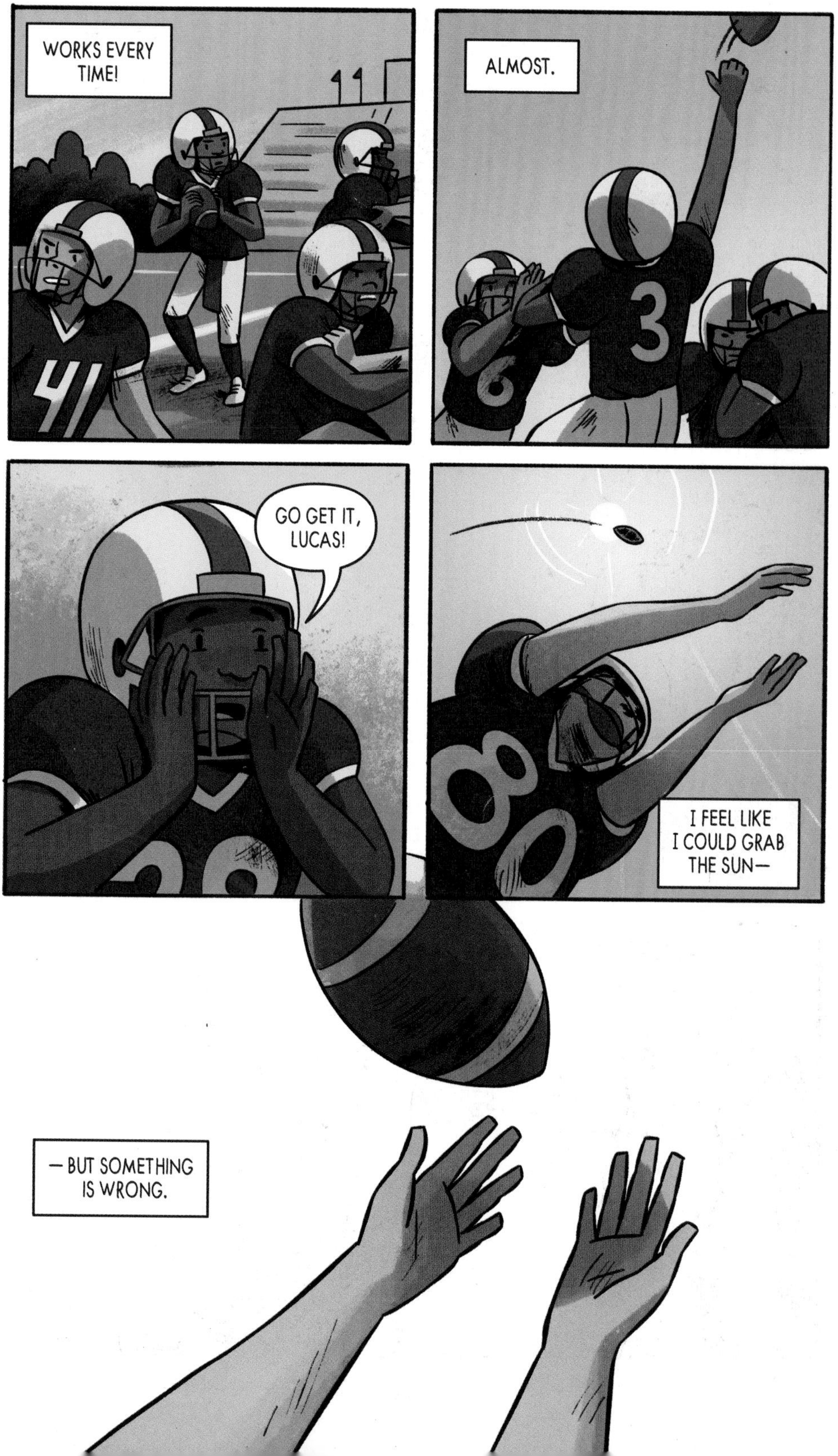
WORKS EVERY TIME!
ALMOST.
GO GET IT, LUCAS!
I FEEL LIKE I COULD GRAB THE SUN—
—BUT SOMETHING IS WRONG.

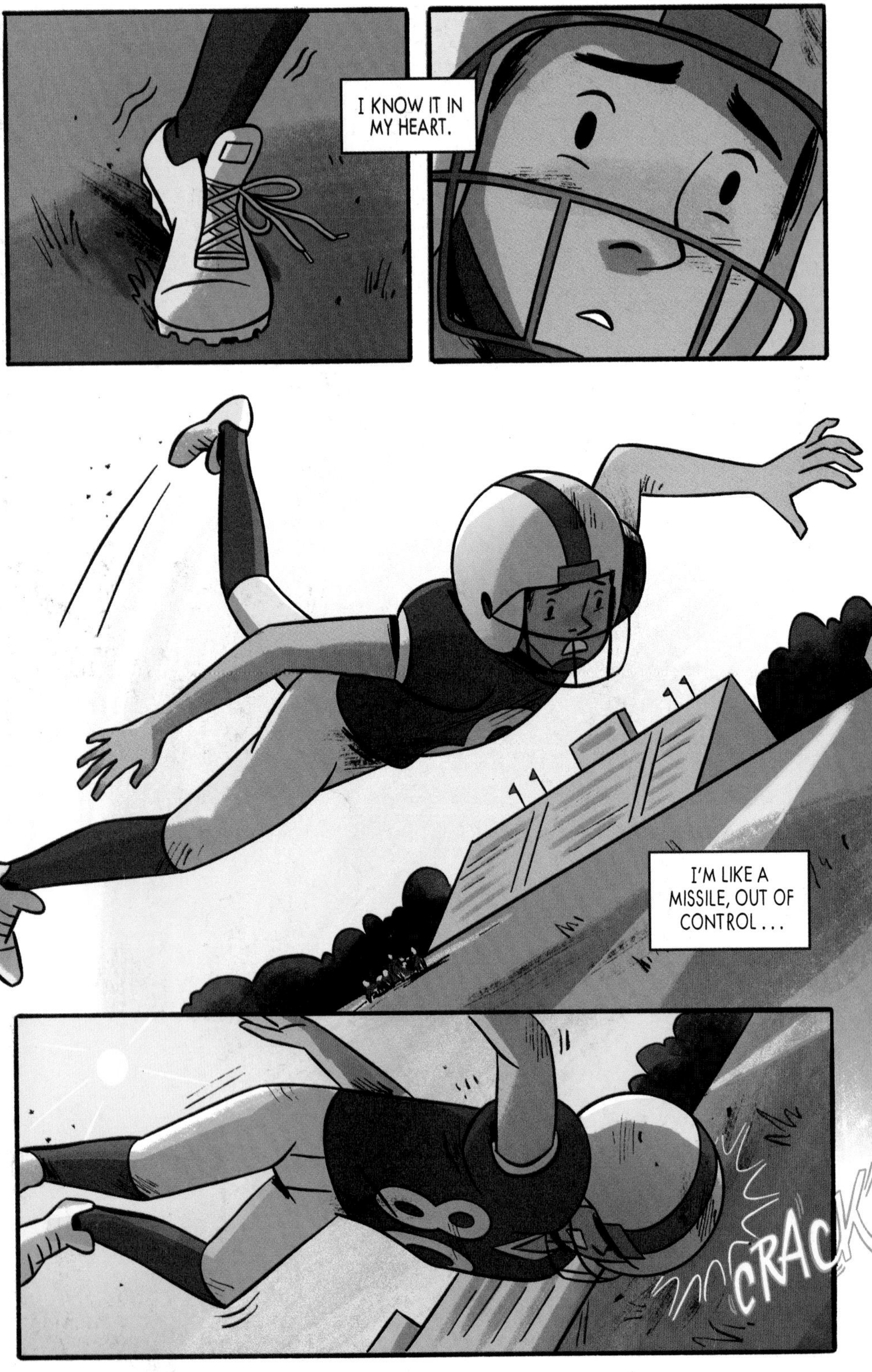
I KNOW IT IN MY HEART.
I'M LIKE A MISSILE, OUT OF CONTROL . . .
CRACK

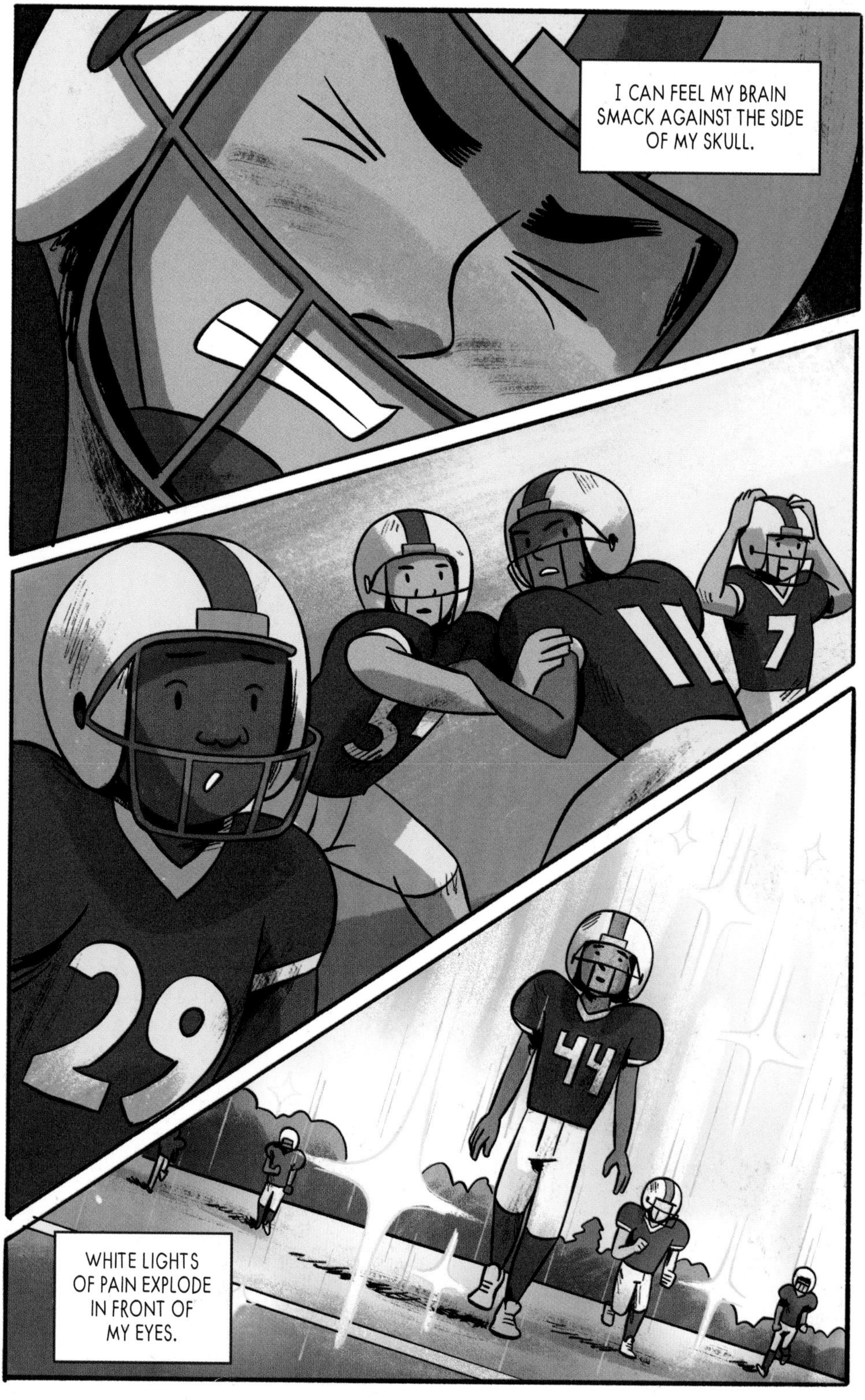
I CAN FEEL MY BRAIN SMACK AGAINST THE SIDE OF MY SKULL.
29
11
7
44
WHITE LIGHTS OF PAIN EXPLODE IN FRONT OF MY EYES.

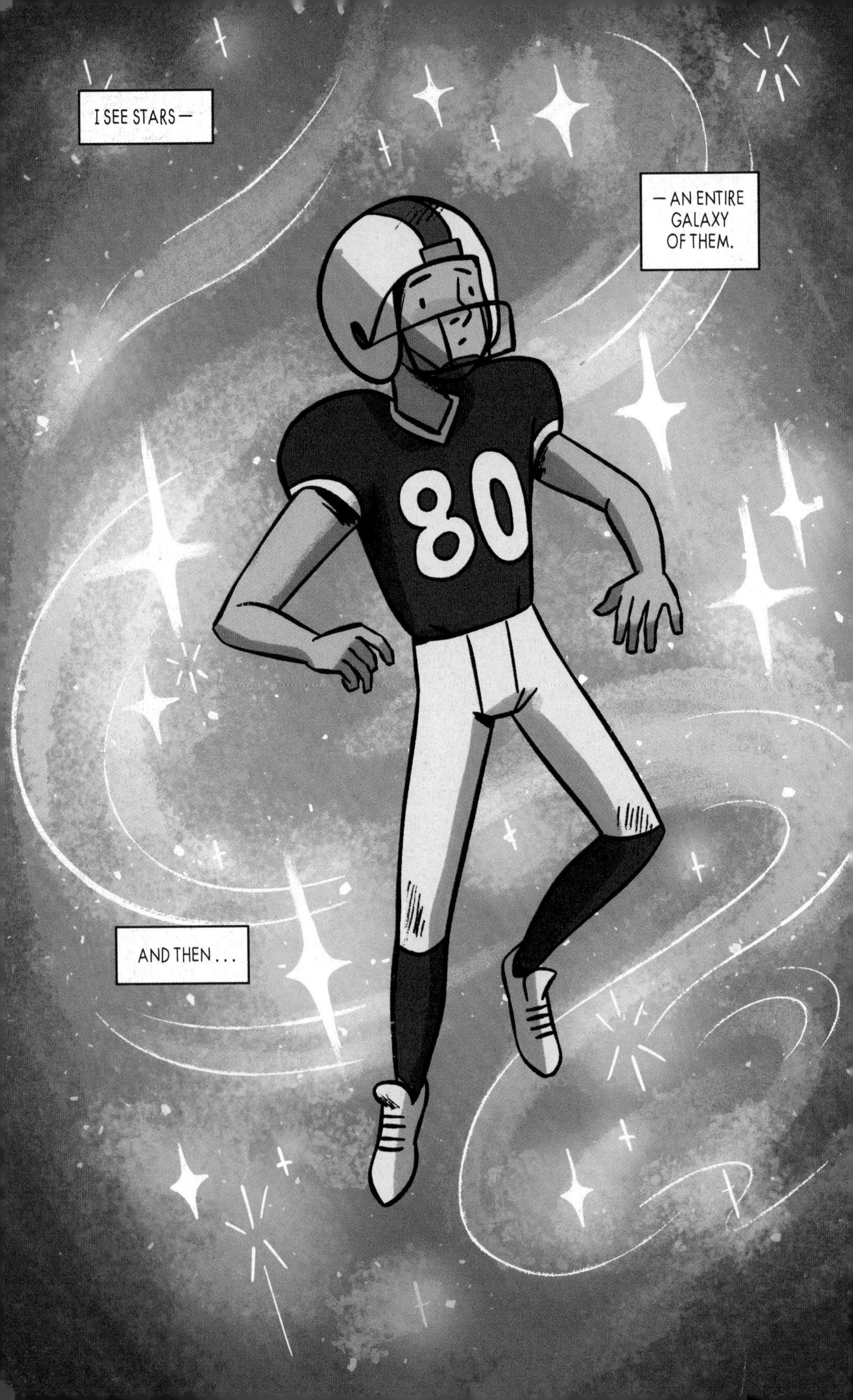
I SEE STARS —
— AN ENTIRE GALAXY OF THEM.
80
AND THEN . . .

I BLACK OUT.

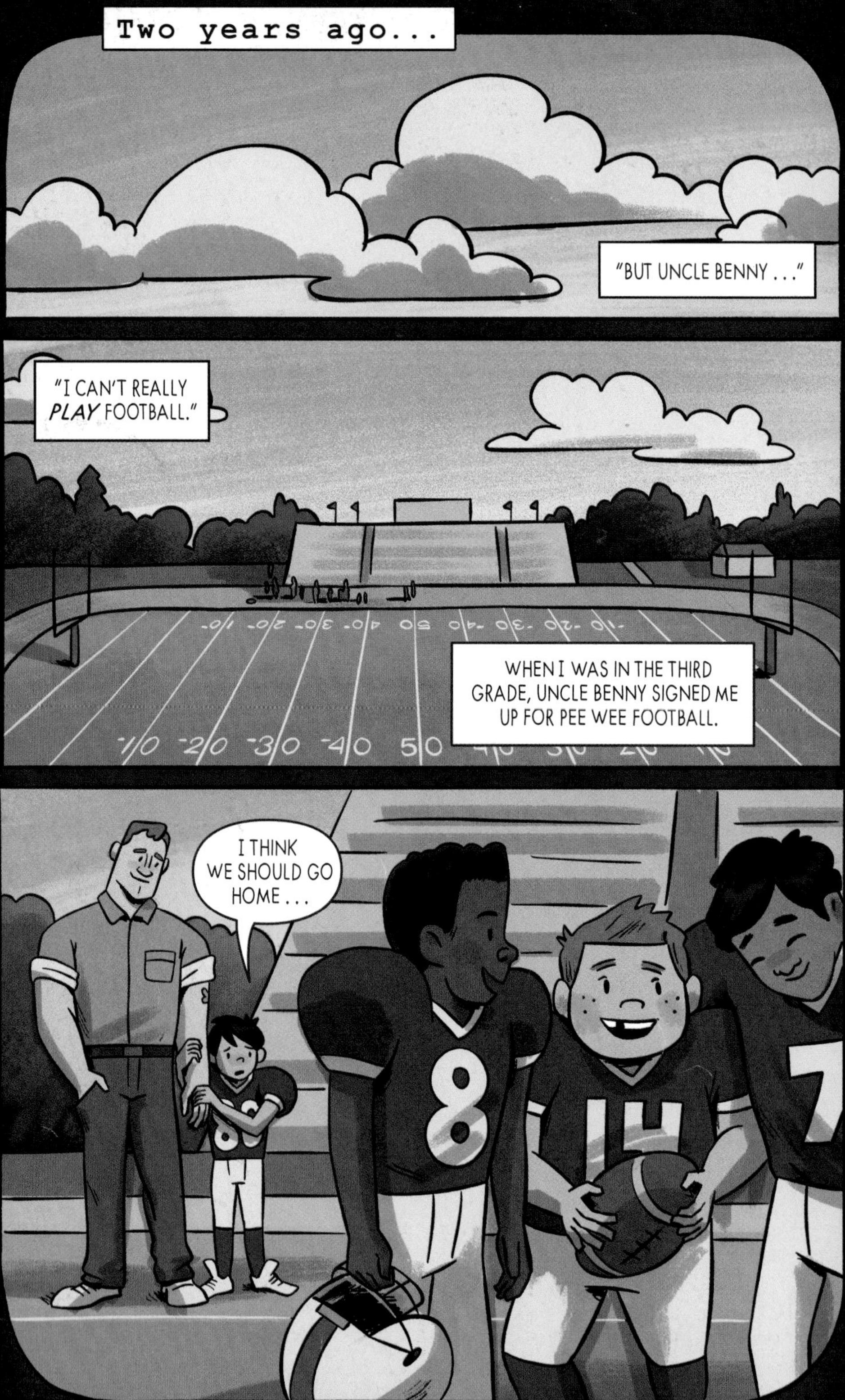
Two years ago...
"BUT UNCLE BENNY . . ."
"I CAN'T REALLY *PLAY* FOOTBALL."
WHEN I WAS IN THE THIRD GRADE, UNCLE BENNY SIGNED ME UP FOR PEE WEE FOOTBALL.
I THINK WE SHOULD GO HOME . . .

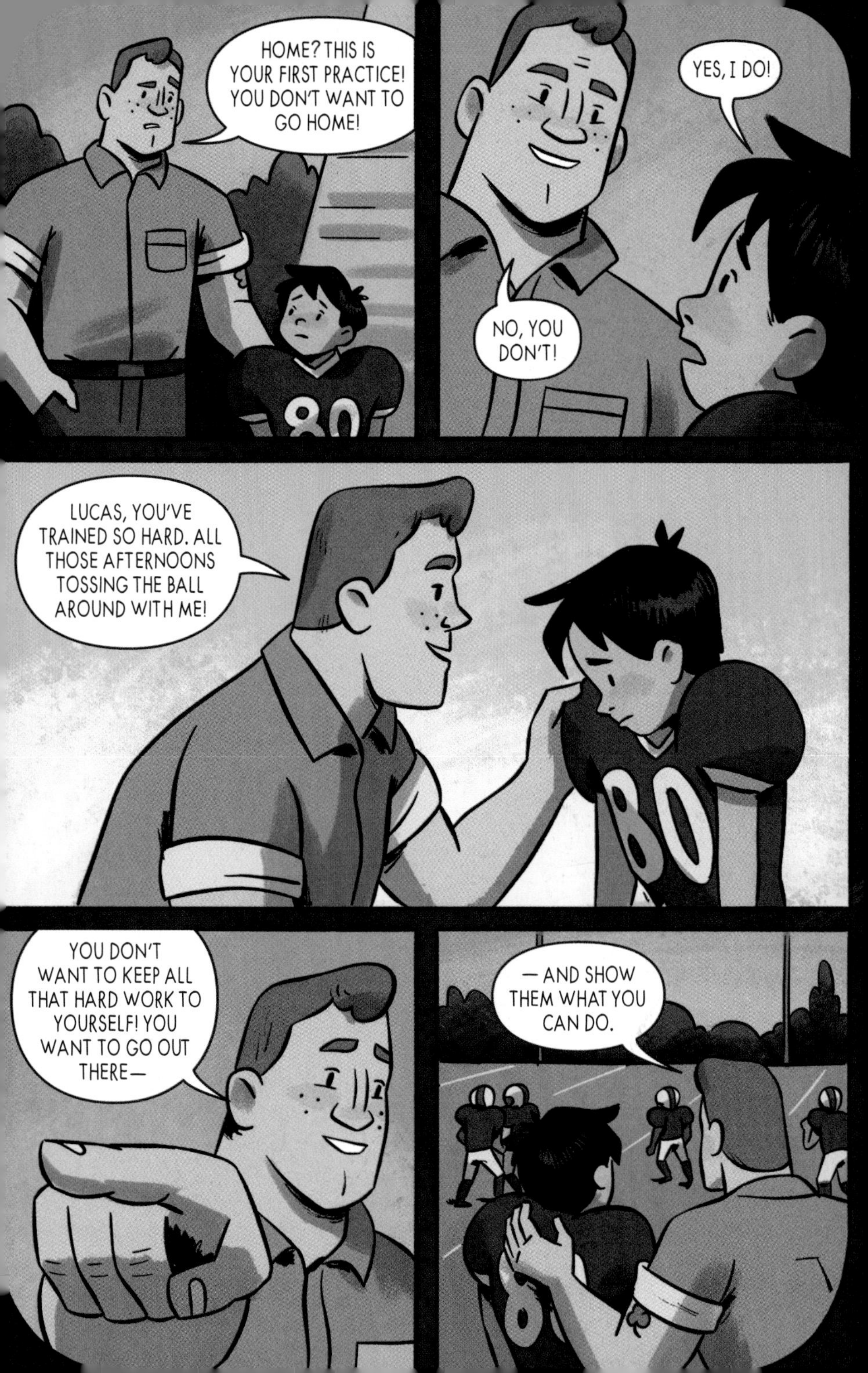
HOME? THIS IS YOUR FIRST PRACTICE! YOU DON'T WANT TO GO HOME!
YES, I DO!
NO, YOU DON'T!
LUCAS, YOU'VE TRAINED SO HARD. ALL THOSE AFTERNOONS TOSSING THE BALL AROUND WITH ME!
YOU DON'T WANT TO KEEP ALL THAT HARD WORK TO YOURSELF! YOU WANT TO GO OUT THERE—
—AND SHOW THEM WHAT YOU CAN DO.

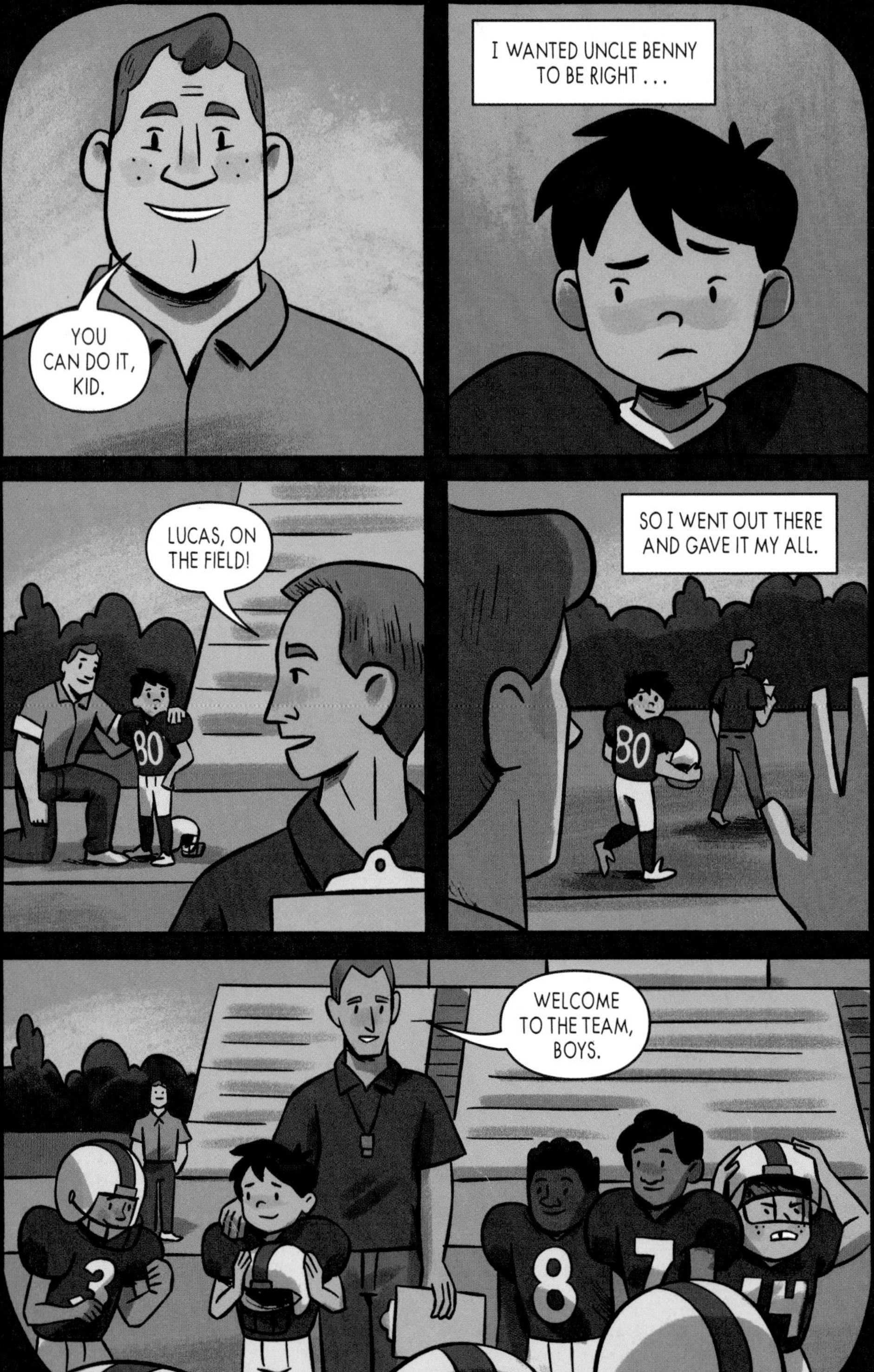
YOU CAN DO IT, KID.
I WANTED UNCLE BENNY TO BE RIGHT . . .
LUCAS, ON THE FIELD!
SO I WENT OUT THERE AND GAVE IT MY ALL.
WELCOME TO THE TEAM, BOYS.

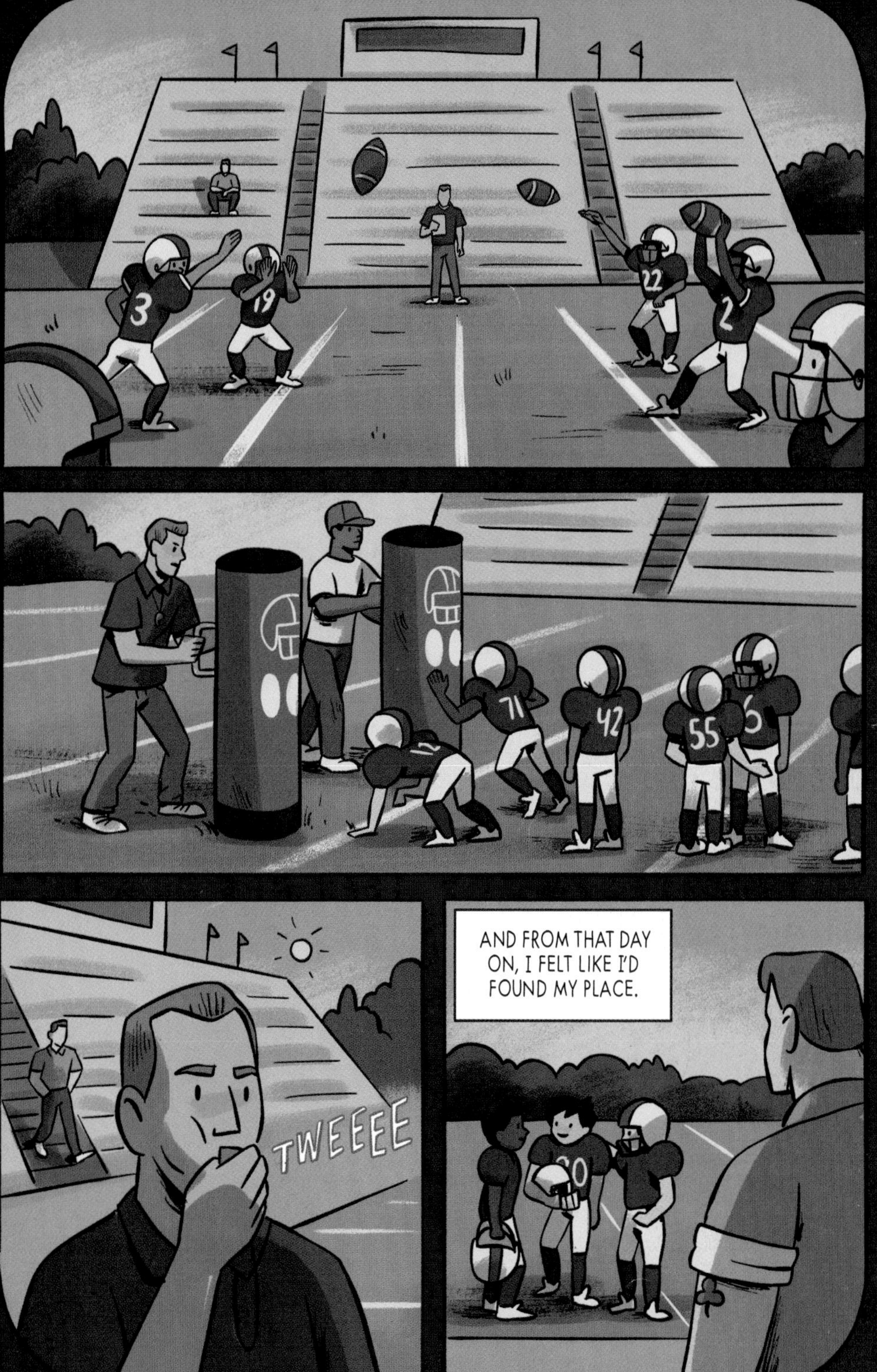
TWEEEE
AND FROM THAT DAY ON, I FELT LIKE I'D FOUND MY PLACE.

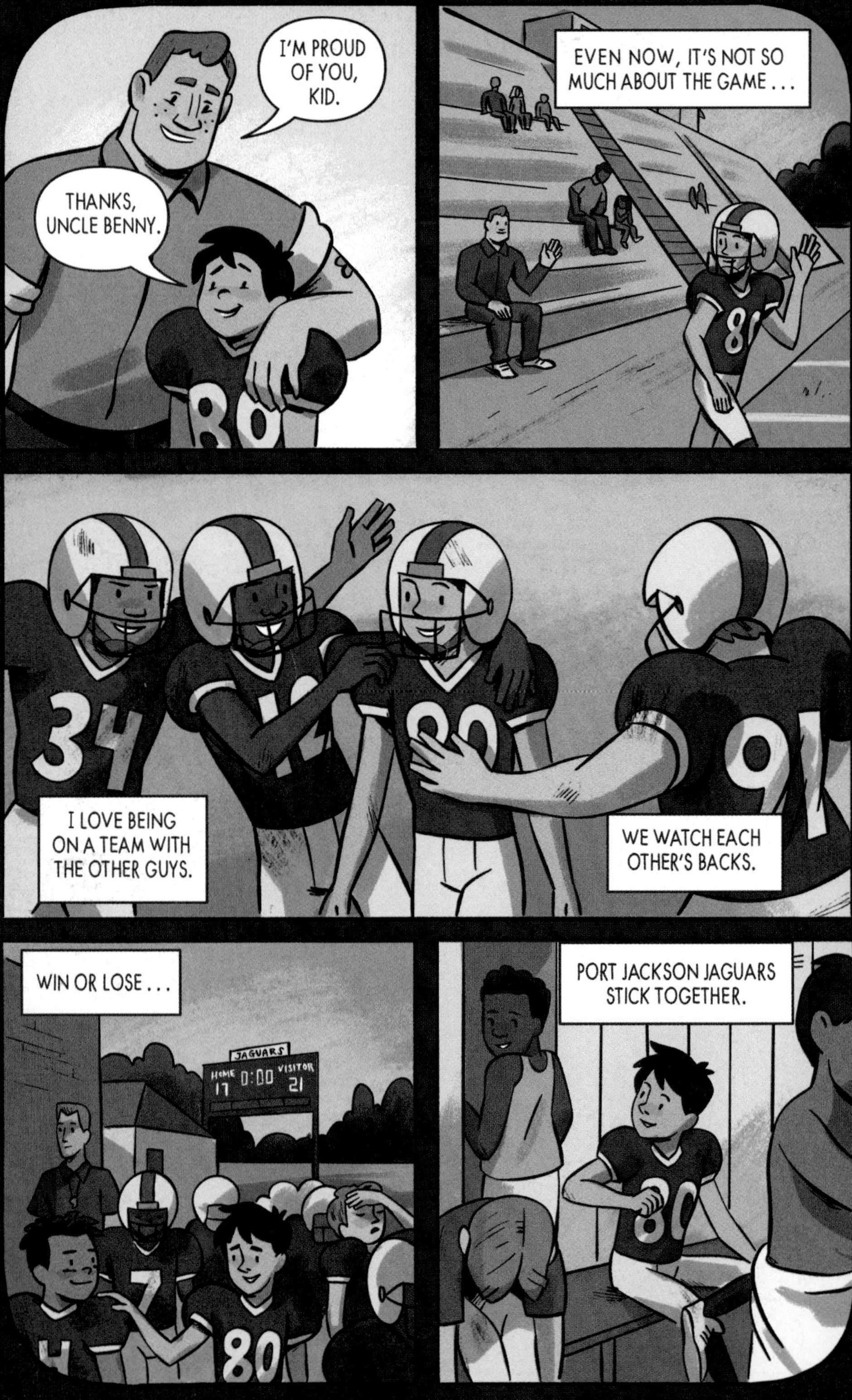

I'M PROUD OF YOU, KID.
THANKS, UNCLE BENNY.
EVEN NOW, IT'S NOT SO MUCH ABOUT THE GAME . . .
I LOVE BEING ON A TEAM WITH THE OTHER GUYS.
WE WATCH EACH OTHER'S BACKS.
WIN OR LOSE . . .
JAGUARS
HOME 17 0:00 VISITOR 21
PORT JACKSON JAGUARS STICK TOGETHER.

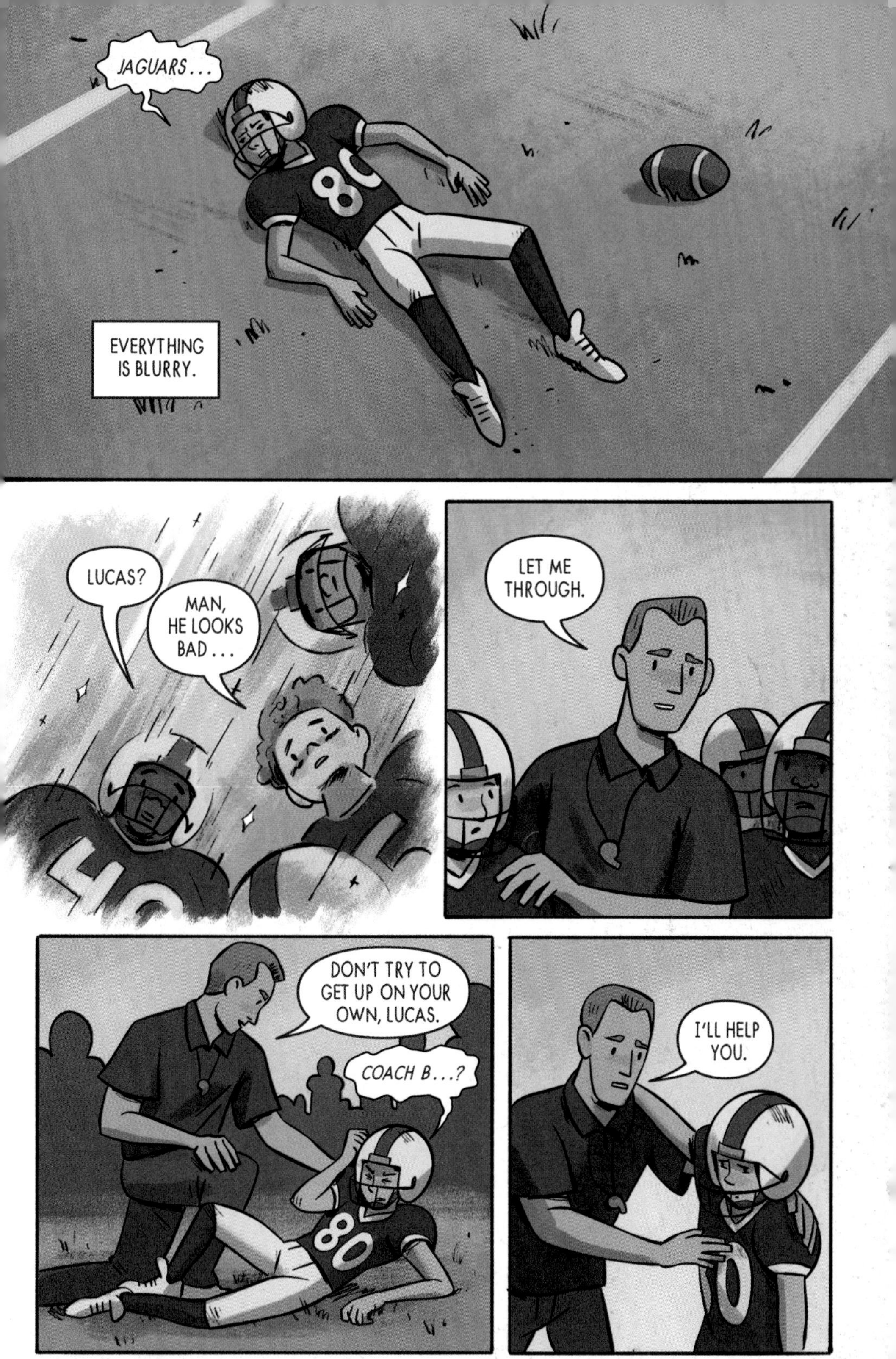
JAGUARS . . .
EVERYTHING IS BLURRY.
LUCAS?
MAN, HE LOOKS BAD . . .
LET ME THROUGH.
DON'T TRY TO GET UP ON YOUR OWN, LUCAS.
COACH B . . .?
I'LL HELP YOU.

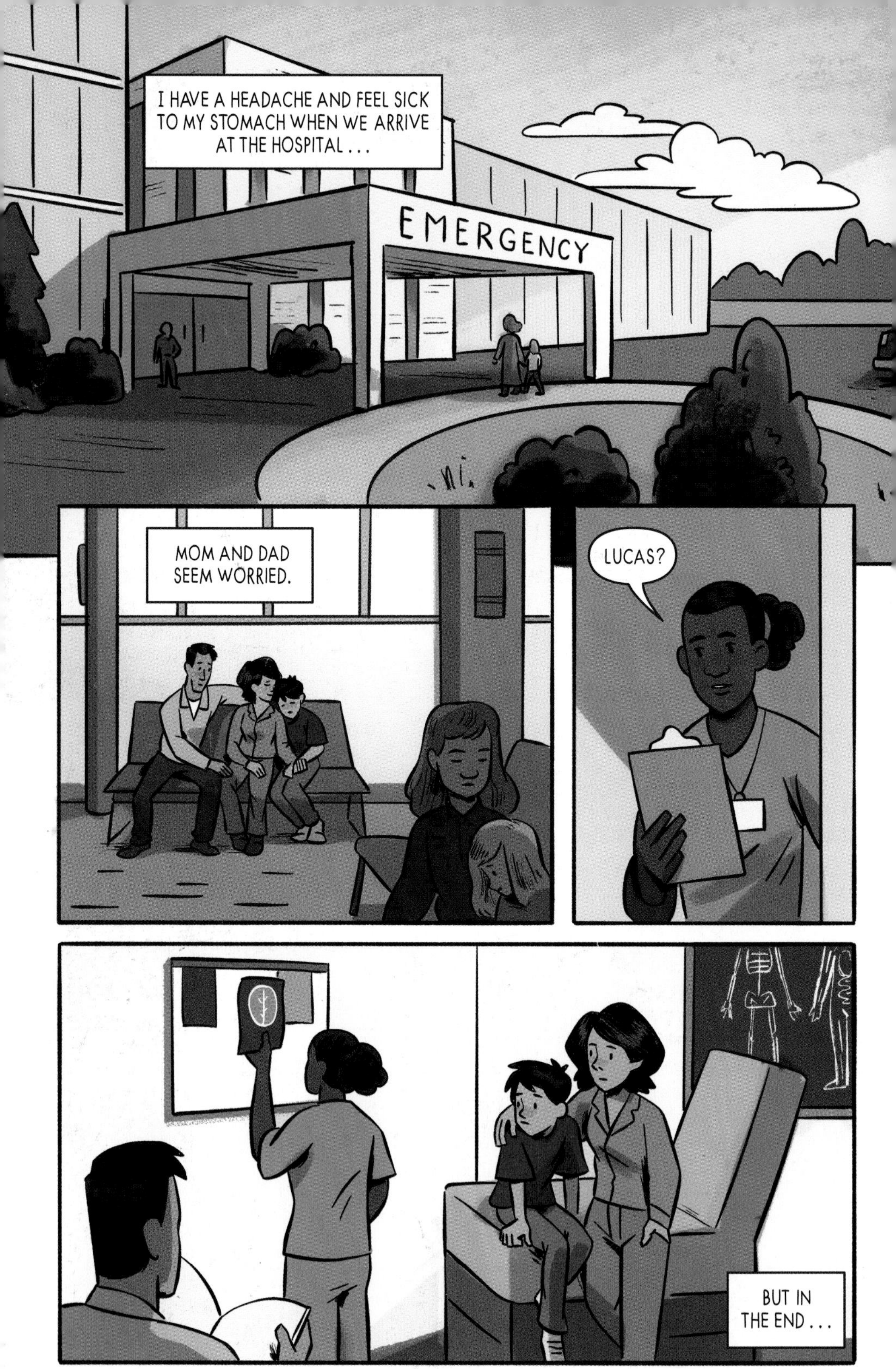
I HAVE A HEADACHE AND FEEL SICK TO MY STOMACH WHEN WE ARRIVE AT THE HOSPITAL . . .
EMERGENCY
MOM AND DAD SEEM WORRIED.
LUCAS?
BUT IN THE END . . .

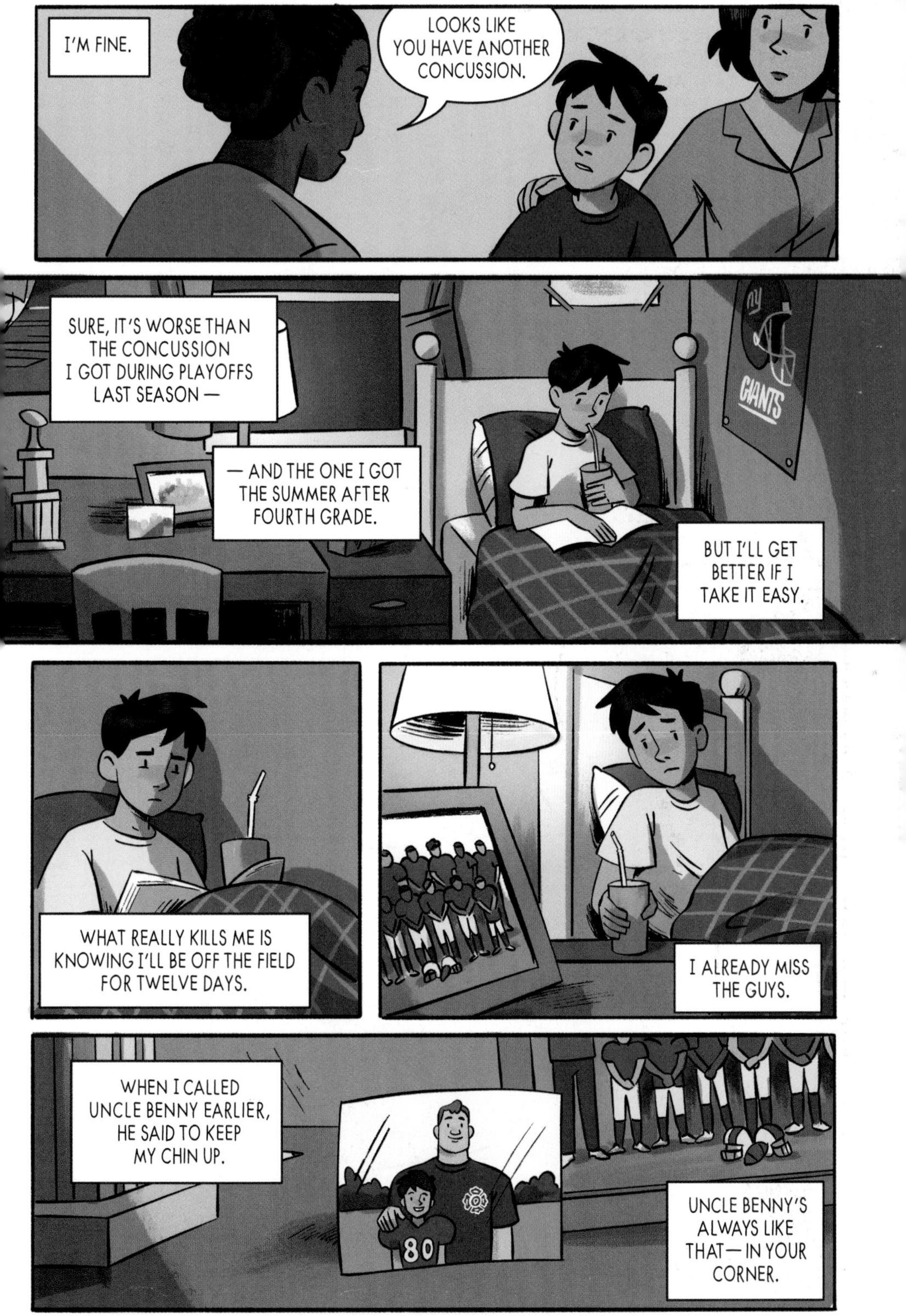
I'M FINE.
LOOKS LIKE YOU HAVE ANOTHER CONCUSSION.
SURE, IT'S WORSE THAN THE CONCUSSION I GOT DURING PLAYOFFS LAST SEASON —
— AND THE ONE I GOT THE SUMMER AFTER FOURTH GRADE.
GIANTS
BUT I'LL GET BETTER IF I TAKE IT EASY.
WHAT REALLY KILLS ME IS KNOWING I'LL BE OFF THE FIELD FOR TWELVE DAYS.
I ALREADY MISS THE GUYS.
WHEN I CALLED UNCLE BENNY EARLIER, HE SAID TO KEEP MY CHIN UP.
80
UNCLE BENNY'S ALWAYS LIKE THAT— IN YOUR CORNER.

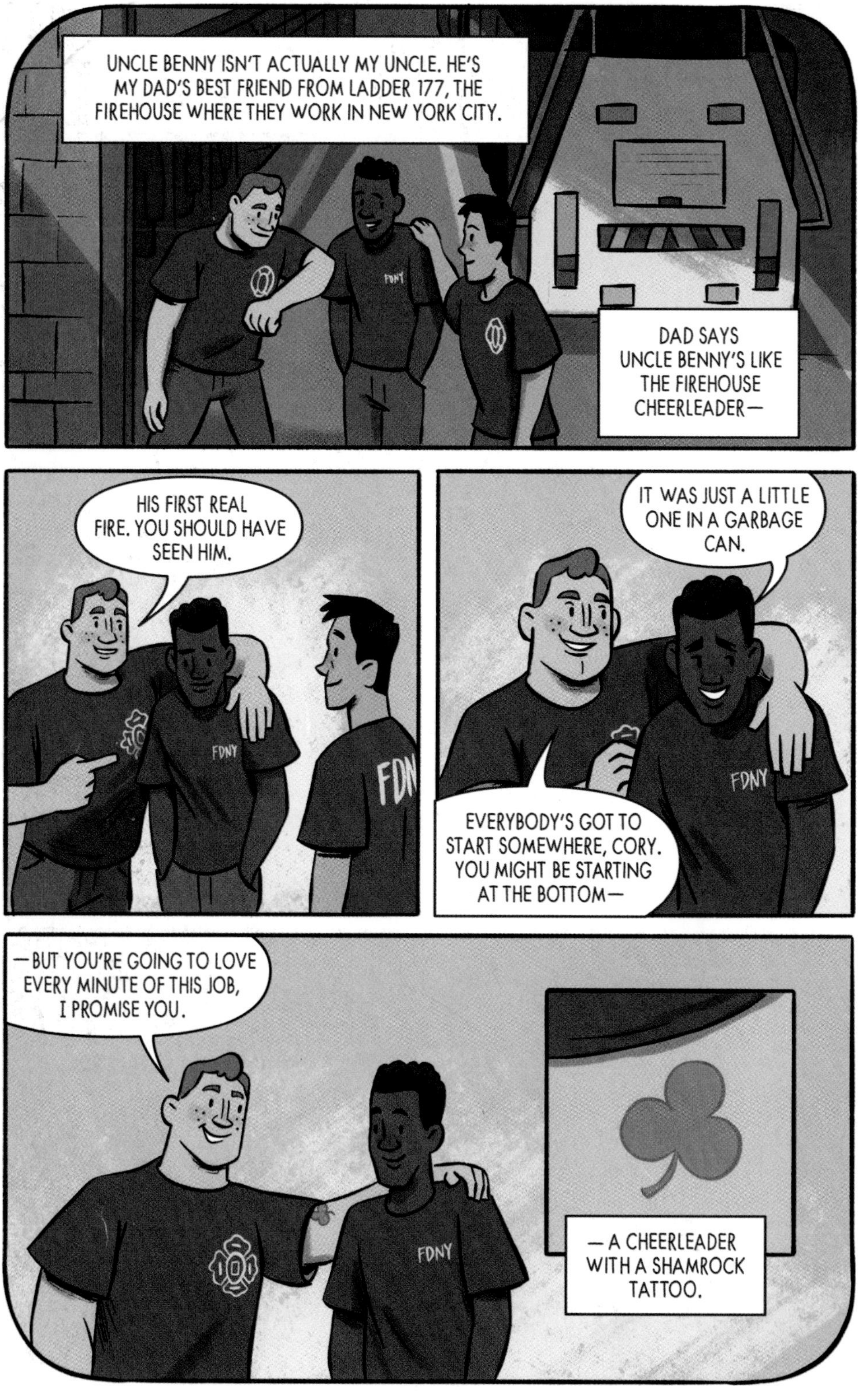
UNCLE BENNY ISN'T ACTUALLY MY UNCLE. HE'S MY DAD'S BEST FRIEND FROM LADDER 177, THE FIREHOUSE WHERE THEY WORK IN NEW YORK CITY.
FDNY
DAD SAYS UNCLE BENNY'S LIKE THE FIREHOUSE CHEERLEADER—
HIS FIRST REAL FIRE. YOU SHOULD HAVE SEEN HIM.
FDNY
FDN
IT WAS JUST A LITTLE ONE IN A GARBAGE CAN.
FDNY
EVERYBODY'S GOT TO START SOMEWHERE, CORY. YOU MIGHT BE STARTING AT THE BOTTOM—
—BUT YOU'RE GOING TO LOVE EVERY MINUTE OF THIS JOB, I PROMISE YOU.
FDNY
—A CHEERLEADER WITH A SHAMROCK TATTOO.

I GOT TO KNOW UNCLE BENNY WHEN DAD WAS HURT IN A WAREHOUSE FIRE.

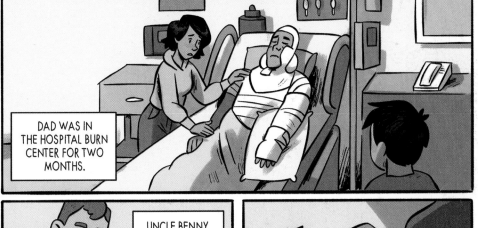

DAD WAS IN THE HOSPITAL BURN CENTER FOR TWO MONTHS.

UNCLE BENNY PRACTICALLY MOVED IN WITH US UNTIL DAD WAS BETTER.

I USED TO WAKE UP AND FIND HIM READING THE SPORTS PAGES IN THE NEWSPAPER.

27

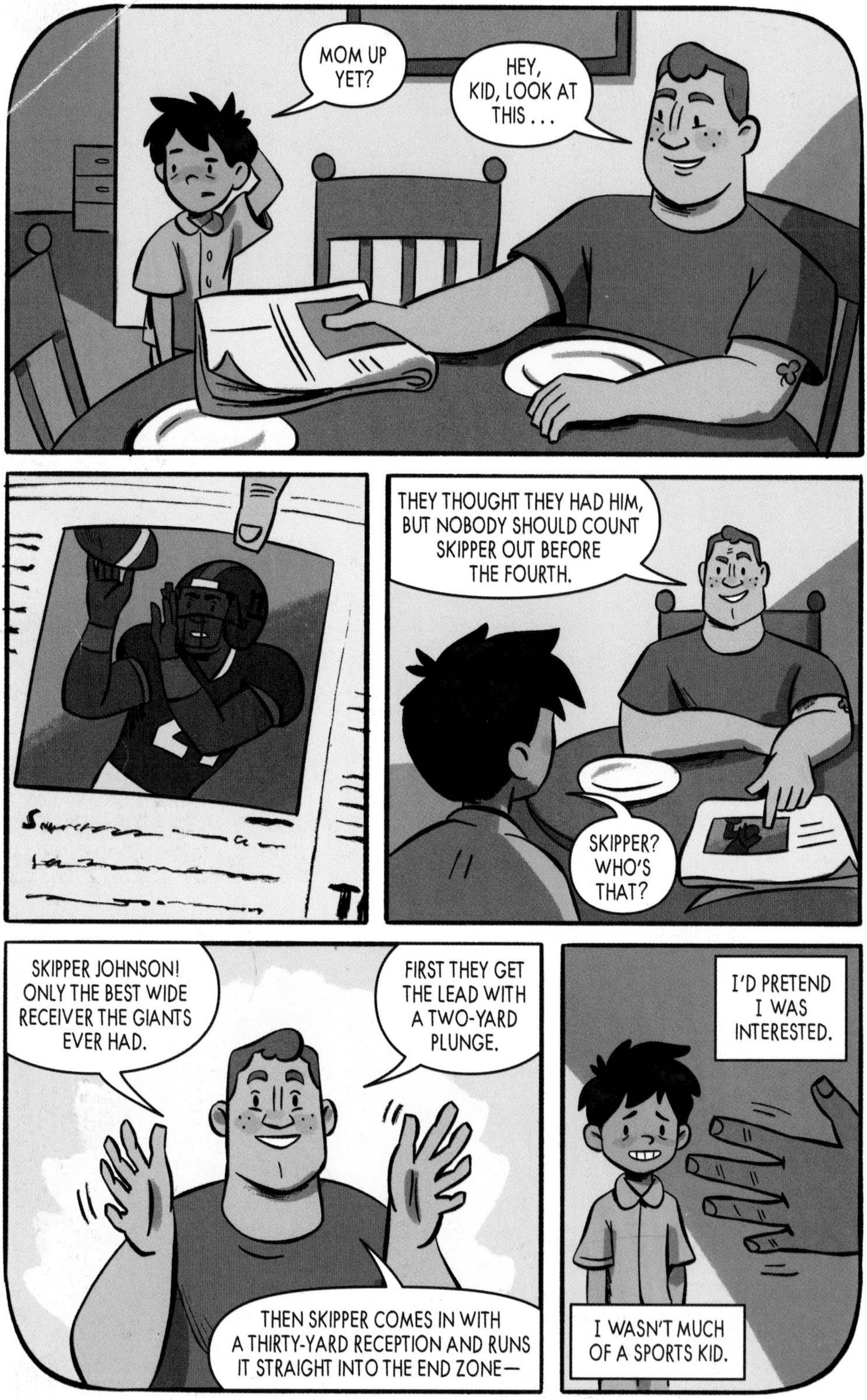
MOM UP YET?
HEY, KID, LOOK AT THIS . . .
THEY THOUGHT THEY HAD HIM, BUT NOBODY SHOULD COUNT SKIPPER OUT BEFORE THE FOURTH.
SKIPPER? WHO'S THAT?
SKIPPER JOHNSON! ONLY THE BEST WIDE RECEIVER THE GIANTS EVER HAD.
FIRST THEY GET THE LEAD WITH A TWO-YARD PLUNGE.
THEN SKIPPER COMES IN WITH A THIRTY-YARD RECEPTION AND RUNS IT STRAIGHT INTO THE END ZONE—
I'D PRETEND I WAS INTERESTED.
I WASN'T MUCH OF A SPORTS KID.

DAD AND I WERE TOO BUSY FOR SPORTS.

BEFORE DAD GOT HURT, WE SPENT EVERY WEEKEND IN THE BASEMENT WORKSHOP.

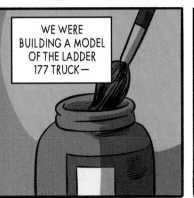

WE WERE BUILDING A MODEL OF THE LADDER 177 TRUCK—

—THE SEAGRAVE 75.

UNCLE BENNY ISN'T INTERESTED IN TRUCK MODELS.

HE LOVES FOOTBALL.

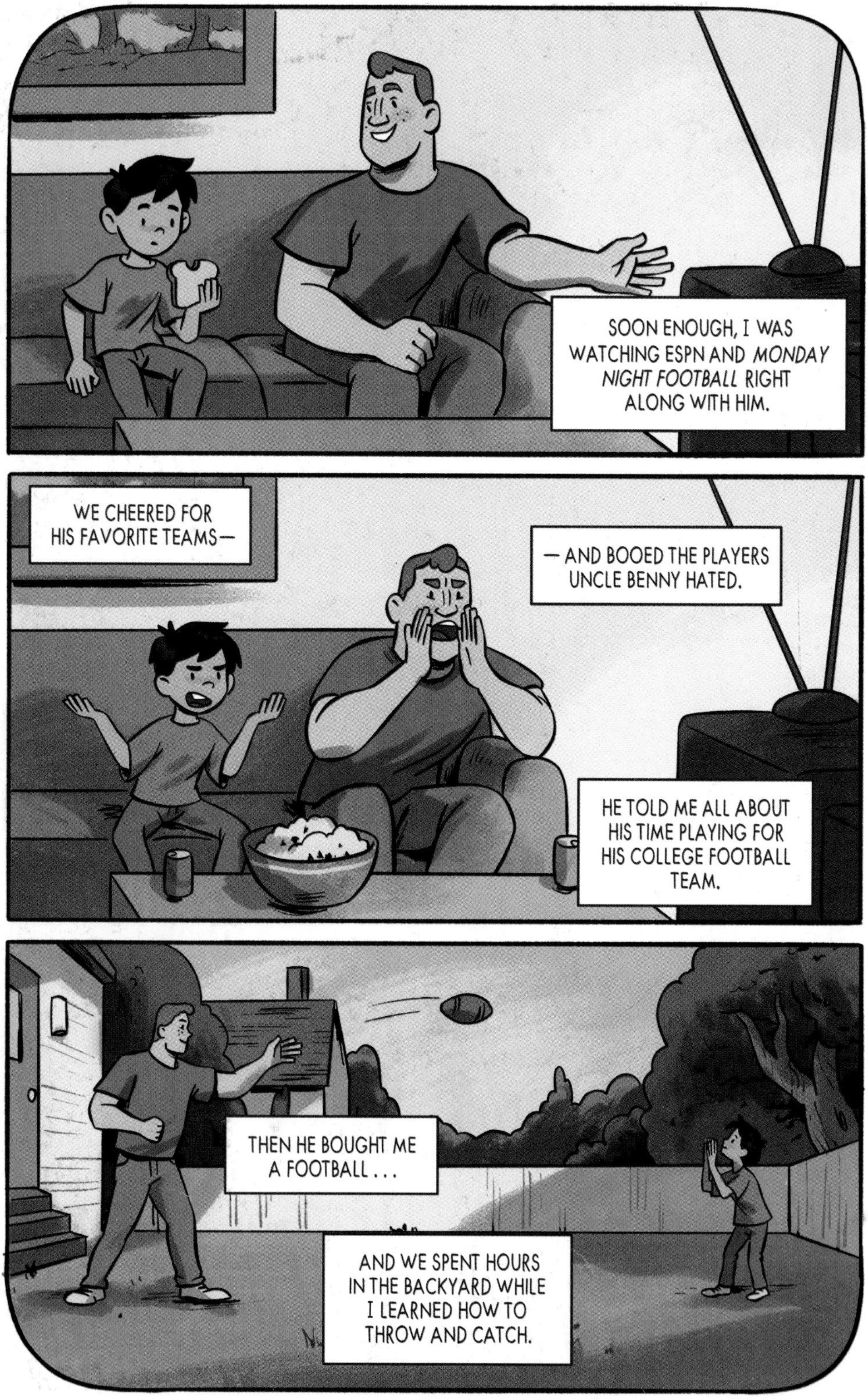
SOON ENOUGH, I WAS WATCHING ESPN AND *MONDAY NIGHT FOOTBALL* RIGHT ALONG WITH HIM.
WE CHEERED FOR HIS FAVORITE TEAMS—
—AND BOOED THE PLAYERS UNCLE BENNY HATED.
HE TOLD ME ALL ABOUT HIS TIME PLAYING FOR HIS COLLEGE FOOTBALL TEAM.
THEN HE BOUGHT ME A FOOTBALL . . .
AND WE SPENT HOURS IN THE BACKYARD WHILE I LEARNED HOW TO THROW AND CATCH.

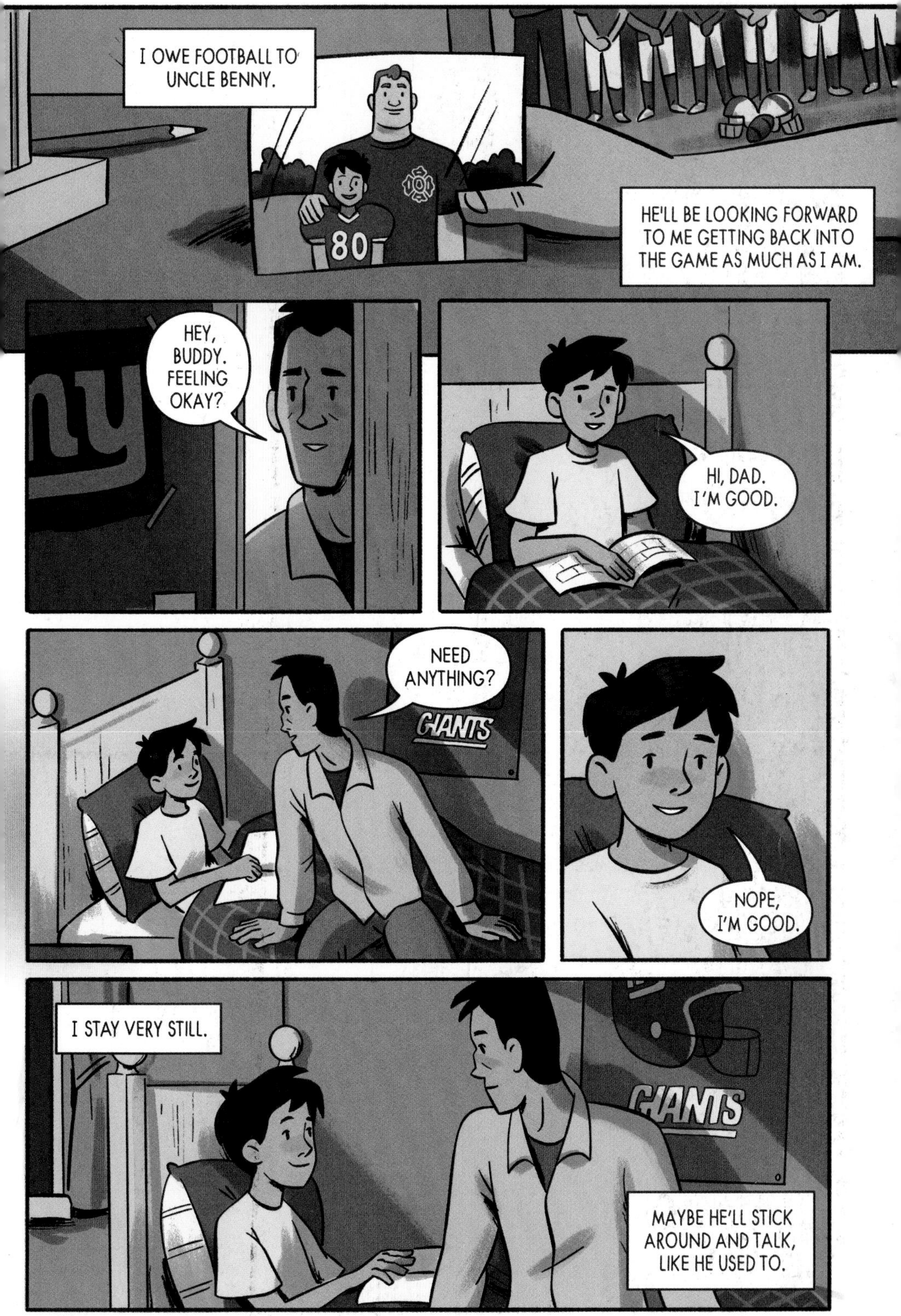
I OWE FOOTBALL TO UNCLE BENNY.
80
HE'LL BE LOOKING FORWARD TO ME GETTING BACK INTO THE GAME AS MUCH AS I AM.
HEY, BUDDY. FEELING OKAY?
HI, DAD. I'M GOOD.
NEED ANYTHING?
GIANTS
NOPE, I'M GOOD.
I STAY VERY STILL.
GIANTS
MAYBE HE'LL STICK AROUND AND TALK, LIKE HE USED TO.

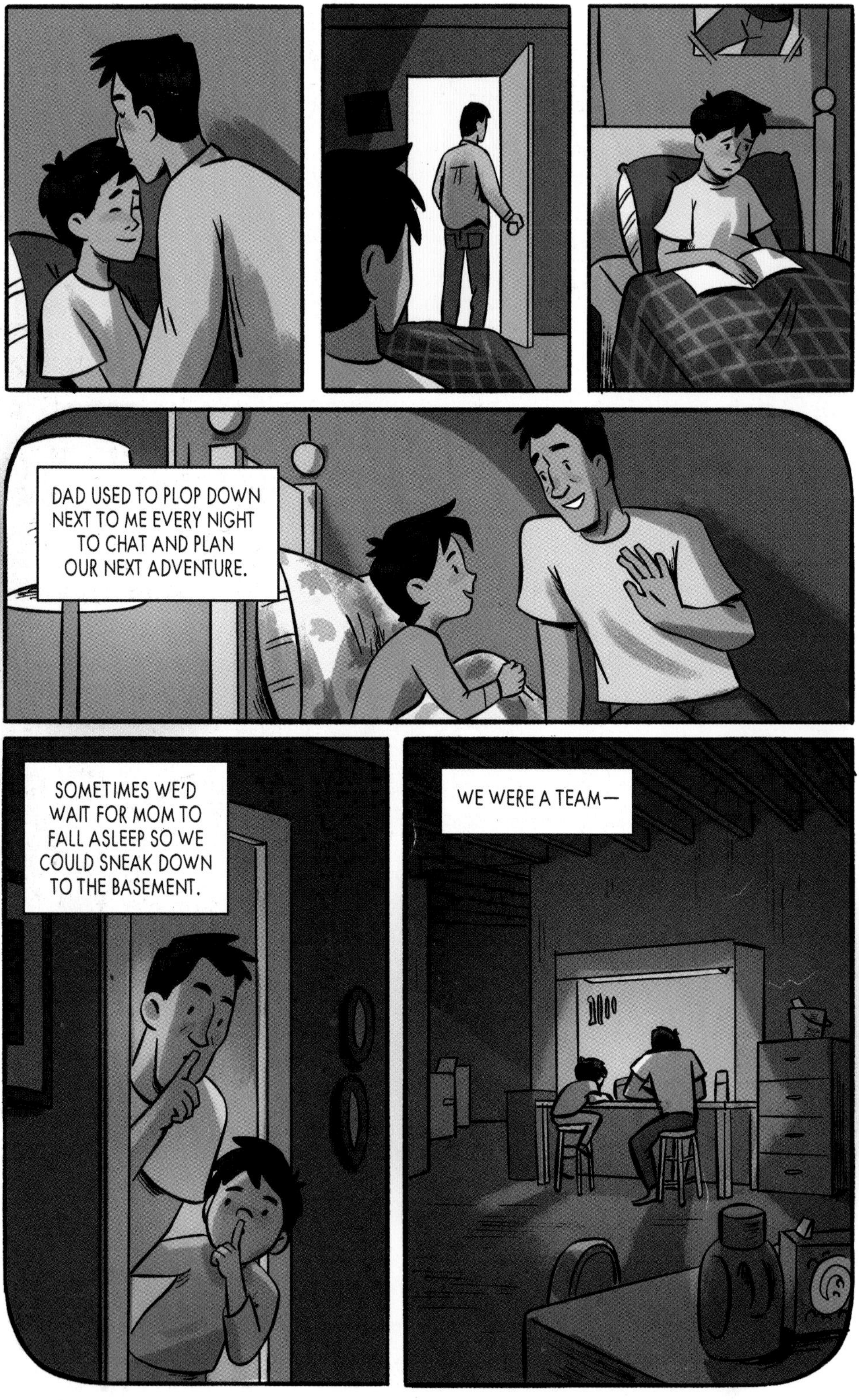
DAD USED TO PLOP DOWN NEXT TO ME EVERY NIGHT TO CHAT AND PLAN OUR NEXT ADVENTURE.
SOMETIMES WE'D WAIT FOR MOM TO FALL ASLEEP SO WE COULD SNEAK DOWN TO THE BASEMENT.
WE WERE A TEAM—

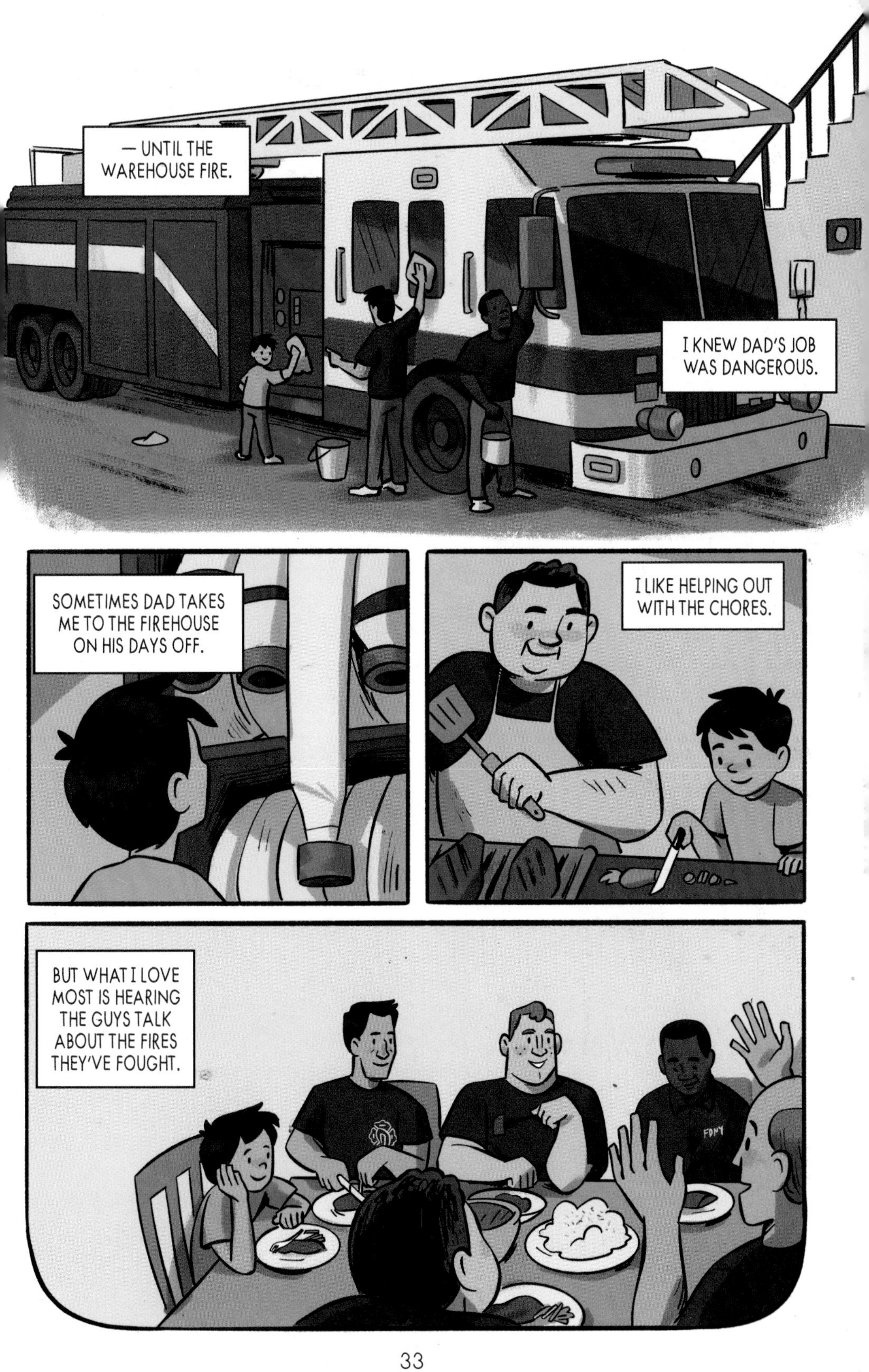
— UNTIL THE WAREHOUSE FIRE.
I KNEW DAD'S JOB WAS DANGEROUS.
SOMETIMES DAD TAKES ME TO THE FIREHOUSE ON HIS DAYS OFF.
I LIKE HELPING OUT WITH THE CHORES.
BUT WHAT I LOVE MOST IS HEARING THE GUYS TALK ABOUT THE FIRES THEY'VE FOUGHT.
FDNY

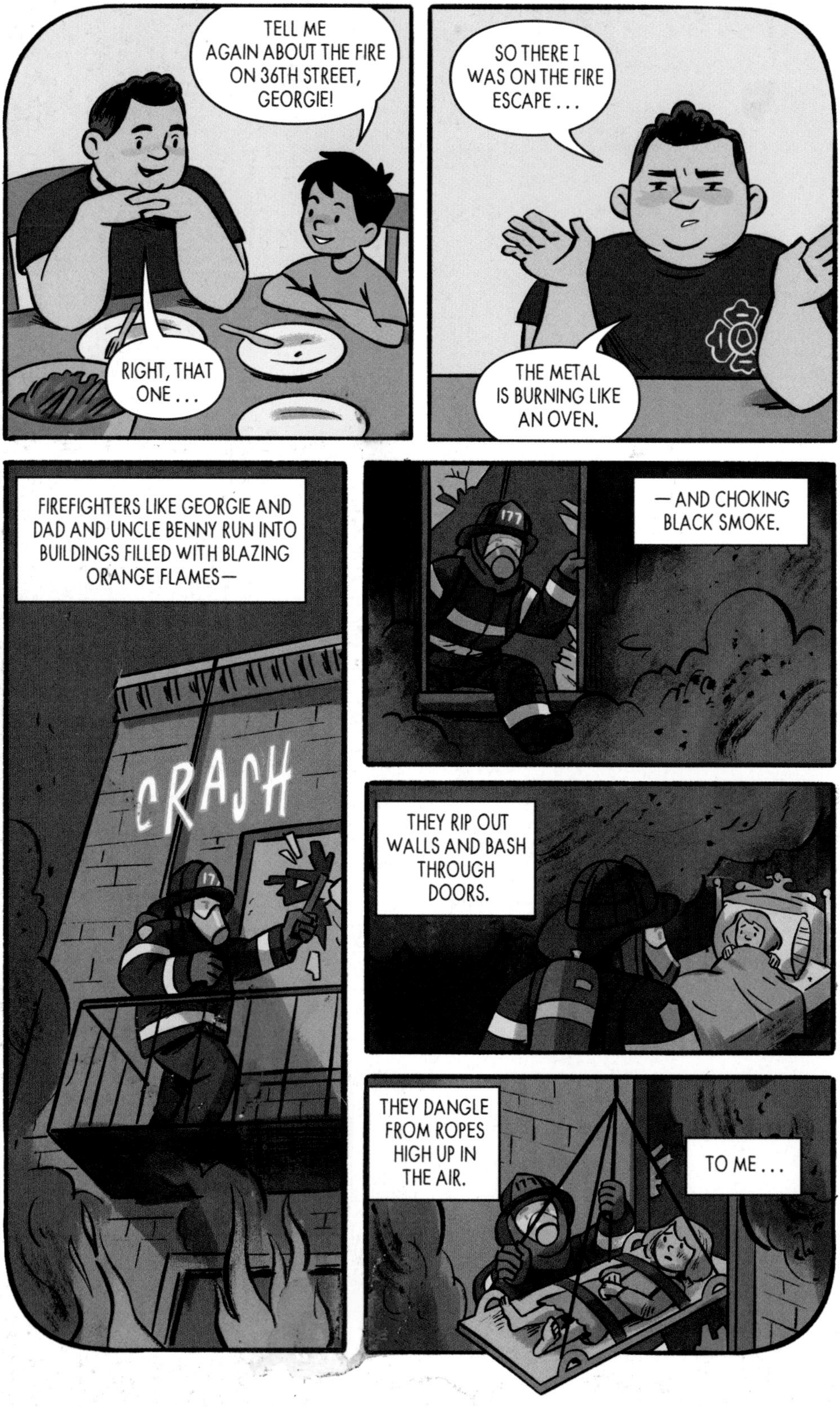
TELL ME AGAIN ABOUT THE FIRE ON 36TH STREET, GEORGIE!
RIGHT, THAT ONE . . .
SO THERE I WAS ON THE FIRE ESCAPE . . .
THE METAL IS BURNING LIKE AN OVEN.
FIREFIGHTERS LIKE GEORGIE AND DAD AND UNCLE BENNY RUN INTO BUILDINGS FILLED WITH BLAZING ORANGE FLAMES—
CRASH
—AND CHOKING BLACK SMOKE.
THEY RIP OUT WALLS AND BASH THROUGH DOORS.
THEY DANGLE FROM ROPES HIGH UP IN THE AIR.
TO ME . . .

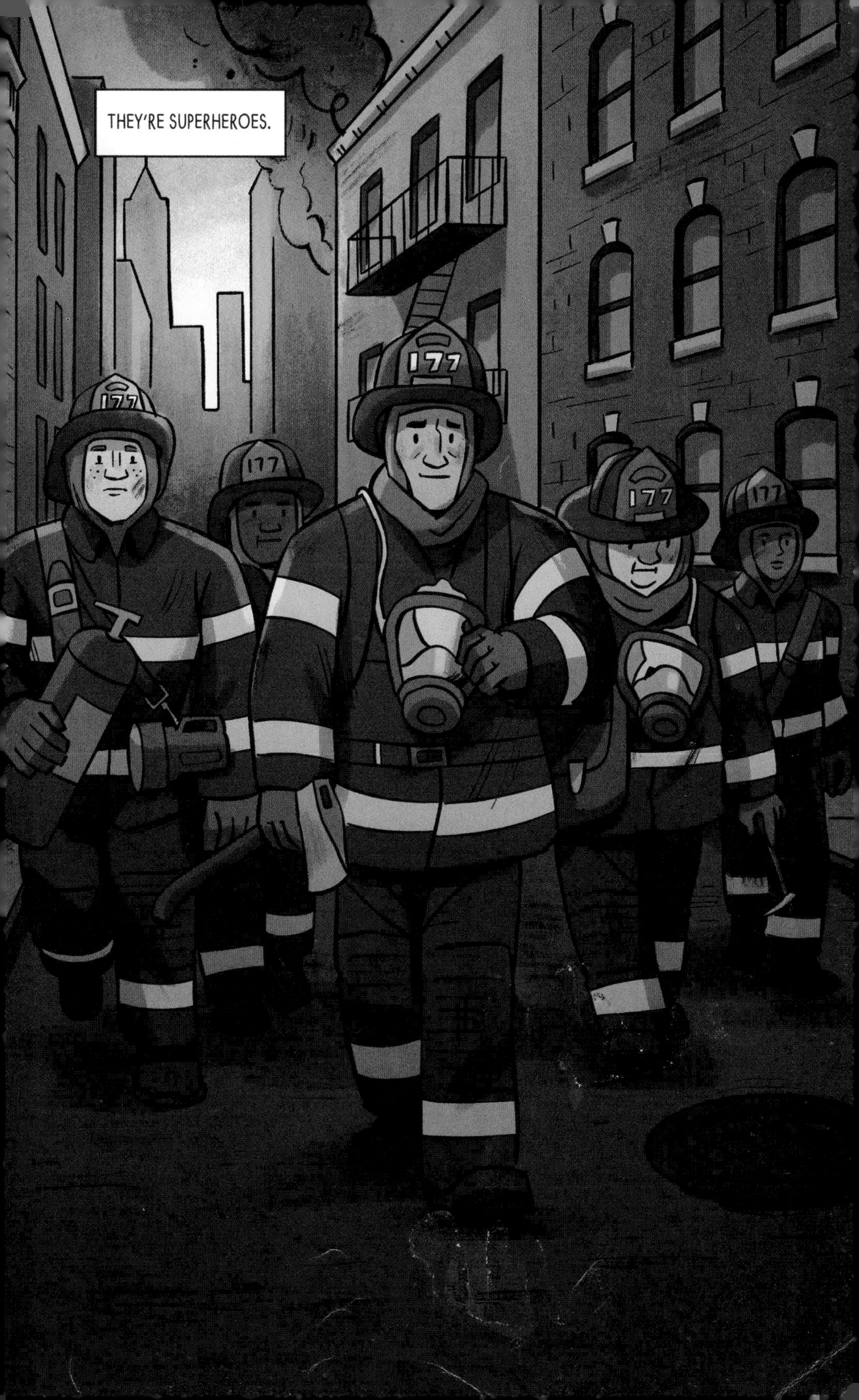
THEY'RE SUPERHEROES.

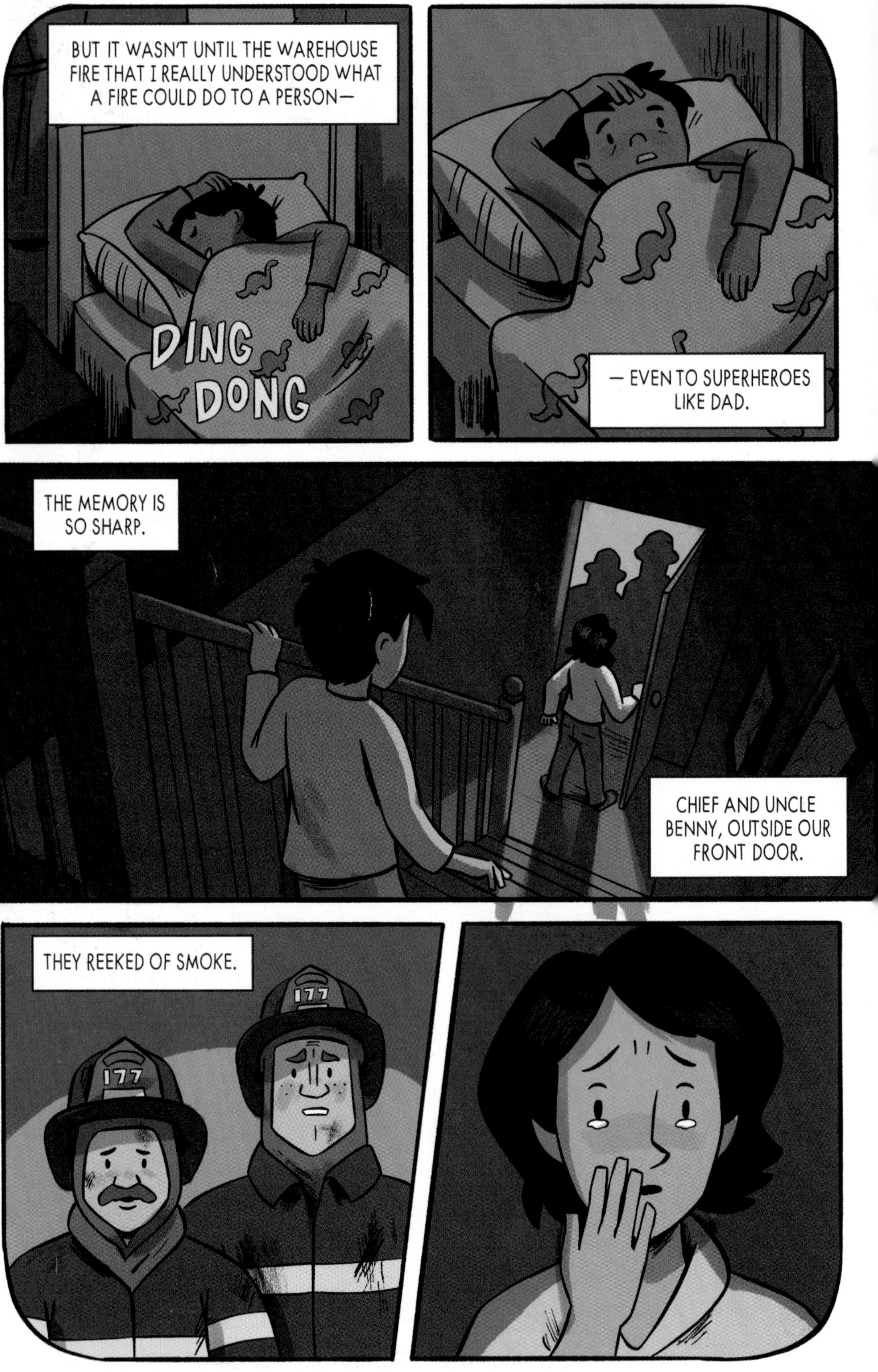
BUT IT WASN'T UNTIL THE WAREHOUSE FIRE THAT I REALLY UNDERSTOOD WHAT A FIRE COULD DO TO A PERSON—
DING DONG
— EVEN TO SUPERHEROES LIKE DAD.
THE MEMORY IS SO SHARP.
CHIEF AND UNCLE BENNY, OUTSIDE OUR FRONT DOOR.
THEY REEKED OF SMOKE.
177
177
177

THAT WAS THREE YEARS AGO.

DAD NEVER TALKS ABOUT WHAT HAPPENED THAT NIGHT.

ALL I KNOW IS THAT FOUR FIREFIGHTERS DIED IN THE EXPLOSION THAT BURNED HIM.

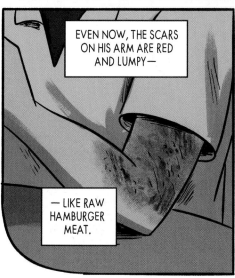

EVEN NOW, THE SCARS ON HIS ARM ARE RED AND LUMPY—

— LIKE RAW HAMBURGER MEAT.

BUT THE BURNS AREN'T THE WORST THING THE FIRE DID TO DAD.

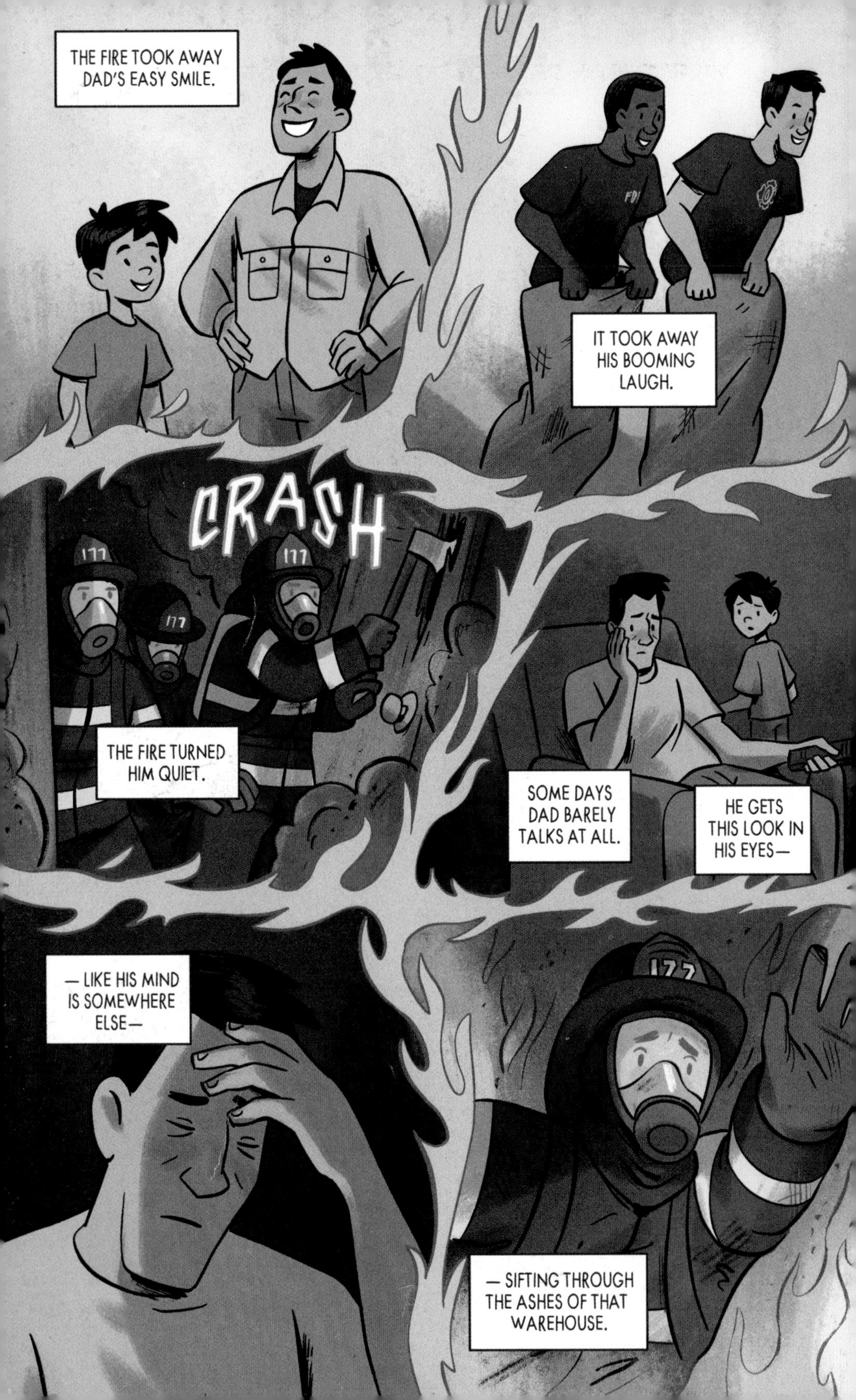
THE FIRE TOOK AWAY DAD'S EASY SMILE.
FDNY
IT TOOK AWAY HIS BOOMING LAUGH.
CRASH
177
THE FIRE TURNED HIM QUIET.
SOME DAYS DAD BARELY TALKS AT ALL.
HE GETS THIS LOOK IN HIS EYES—
— LIKE HIS MIND IS SOMEWHERE ELSE—
177
— SIFTING THROUGH THE ASHES OF THAT WAREHOUSE.

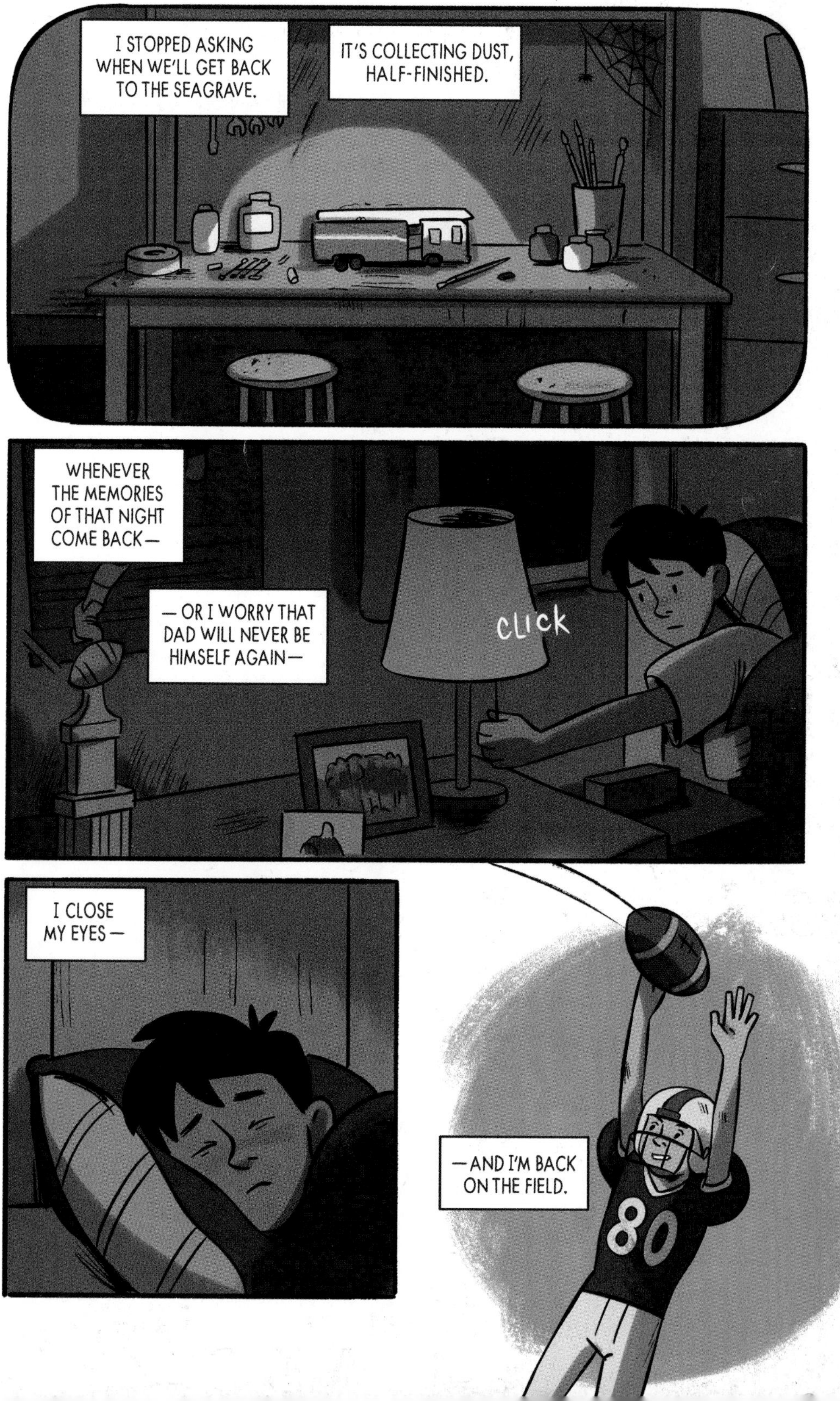
I STOPPED ASKING WHEN WE'LL GET BACK TO THE SEAGRAVE.
IT'S COLLECTING DUST, HALF-FINISHED.
WHENEVER THE MEMORIES OF THAT NIGHT COME BACK—
—OR I WORRY THAT DAD WILL NEVER BE HIMSELF AGAIN—
CLICK
I CLOSE MY EYES—
—AND I'M BACK ON THE FIELD.
80

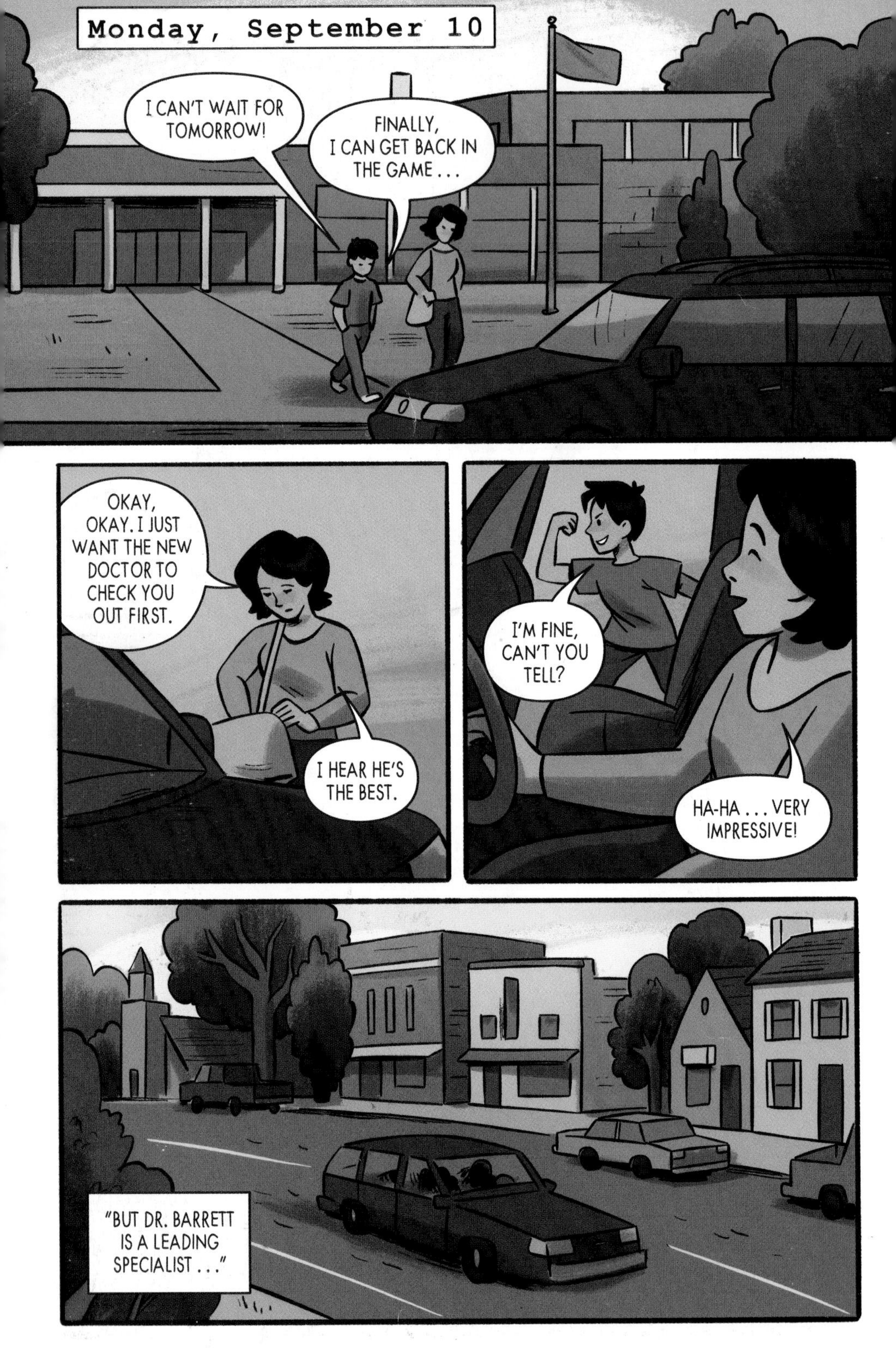
Monday, September 10
I CAN'T WAIT FOR TOMORROW!
FINALLY, I CAN GET BACK IN THE GAME . . .
OKAY, OKAY. I JUST WANT THE NEW DOCTOR TO CHECK YOU OUT FIRST.
I HEAR HE'S THE BEST.
I'M FINE, CAN'T YOU TELL?
HA-HA . . . VERY IMPRESSIVE!
"BUT DR. BARRETT IS A LEADING SPECIALIST . . ."

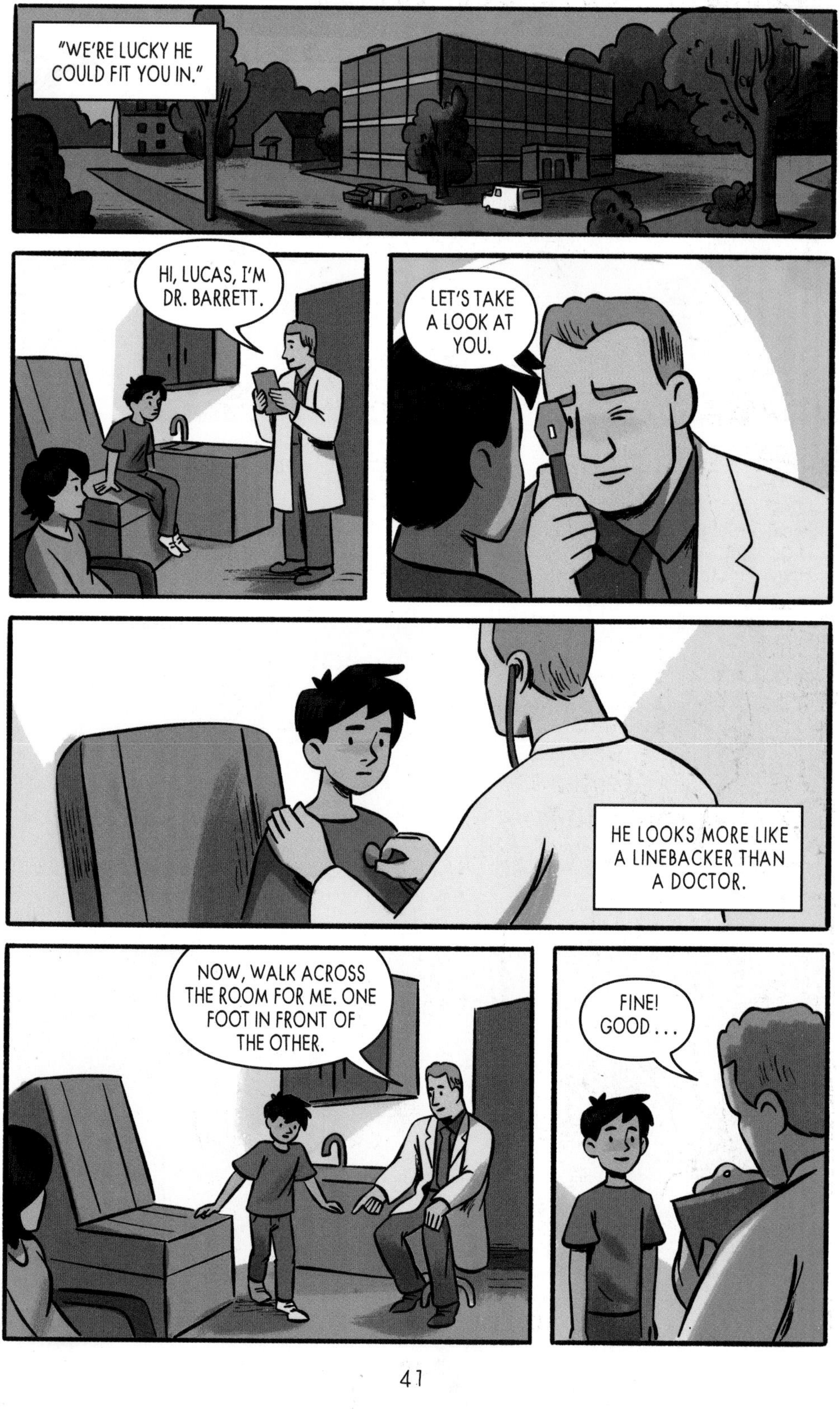
"WE'RE LUCKY HE COULD FIT YOU IN."
HI, LUCAS, I'M DR. BARRETT.
LET'S TAKE A LOOK AT YOU.
HE LOOKS MORE LIKE A LINEBACKER THAN A DOCTOR.
NOW, WALK ACROSS THE ROOM FOR ME. ONE FOOT IN FRONT OF THE OTHER.
FINE! GOOD . . .

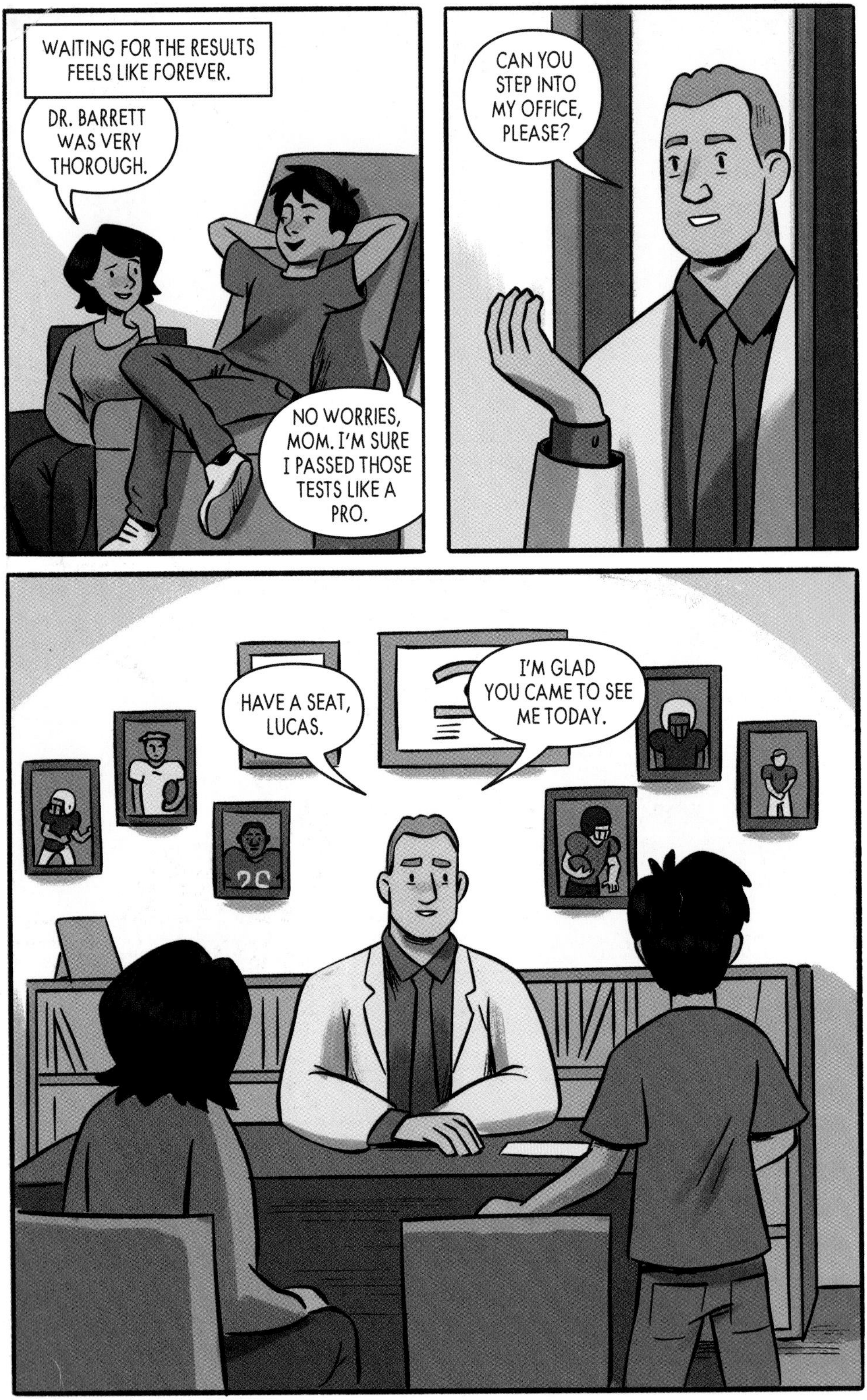
WAITING FOR THE RESULTS FEELS LIKE FOREVER.
DR. BARRETT WAS VERY THOROUGH.
NO WORRIES, MOM. I'M SURE I PASSED THOSE TESTS LIKE A PRO.
CAN YOU STEP INTO MY OFFICE, PLEASE?
HAVE A SEAT, LUCAS.
I'M GLAD YOU CAME TO SEE ME TODAY.

I SEE YOU'VE NOTICED MY WALL OF FAME.

THAT'S DAN BROCK. HAVE YOU HEARD OF HIM?

I THINK SO.

THE NAME SOUNDS FAMILIAR, BUT I'M NOT SURE WHY.

HE WAS ALL-AMERICAN AT THE UNIVERSITY OF WISCONSIN AND A THIRD-ROUND PICK FOR THE NFL.

THAT'S TYRUS VALLONE . . .

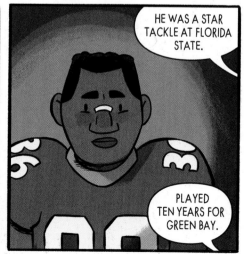

HE WAS A STAR TACKLE AT FLORIDA STATE.

PLAYED TEN YEARS FOR GREEN BAY.

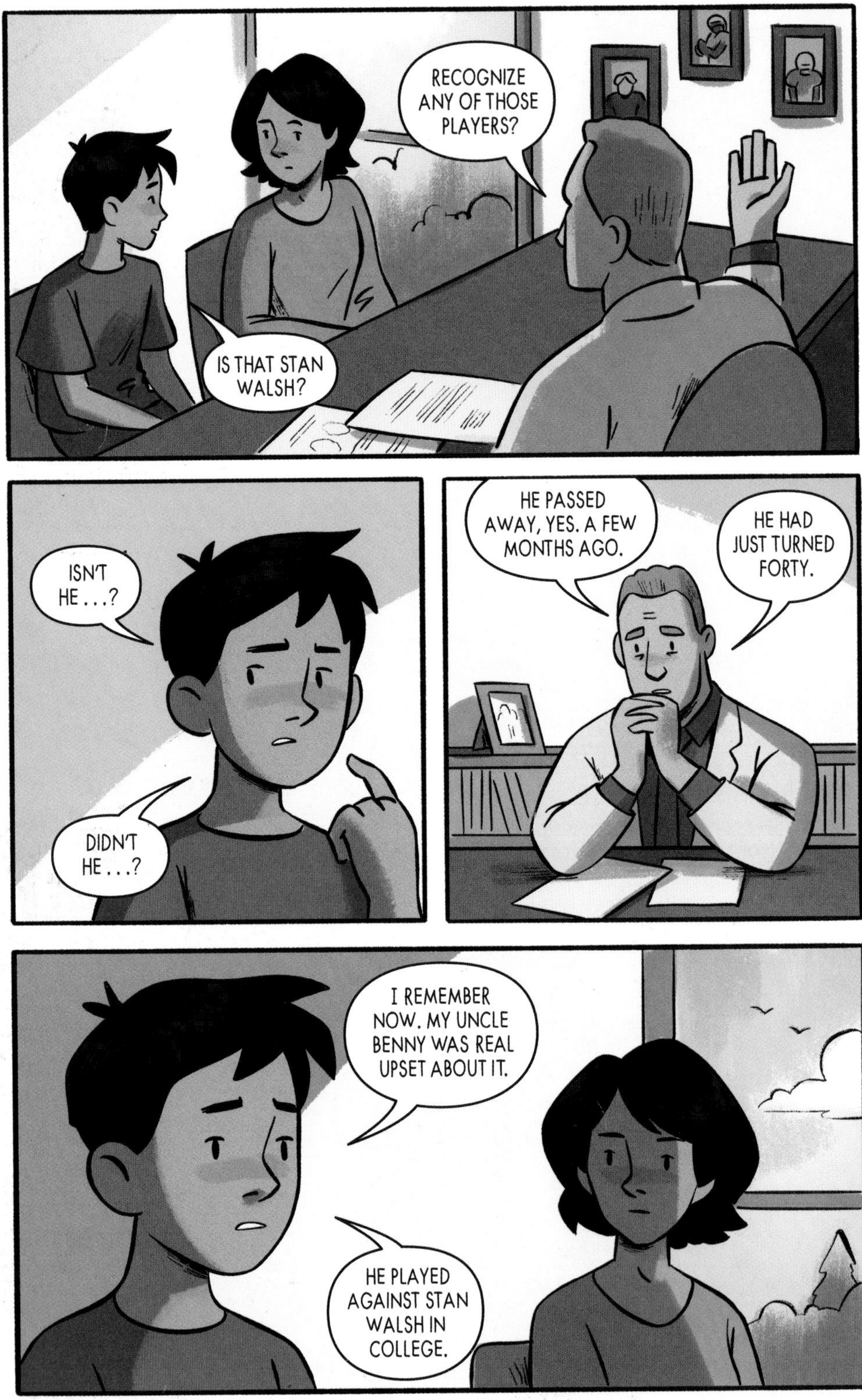
RECOGNIZE ANY OF THOSE PLAYERS?
IS THAT STAN WALSH?
ISN'T HE . . .?
DIDN'T HE . . .?
HE PASSED AWAY, YES. A FEW MONTHS AGO.
HE HAD JUST TURNED FORTY.
I REMEMBER NOW. MY UNCLE BENNY WAS REAL UPSET ABOUT IT.
HE PLAYED AGAINST STAN WALSH IN COLLEGE.

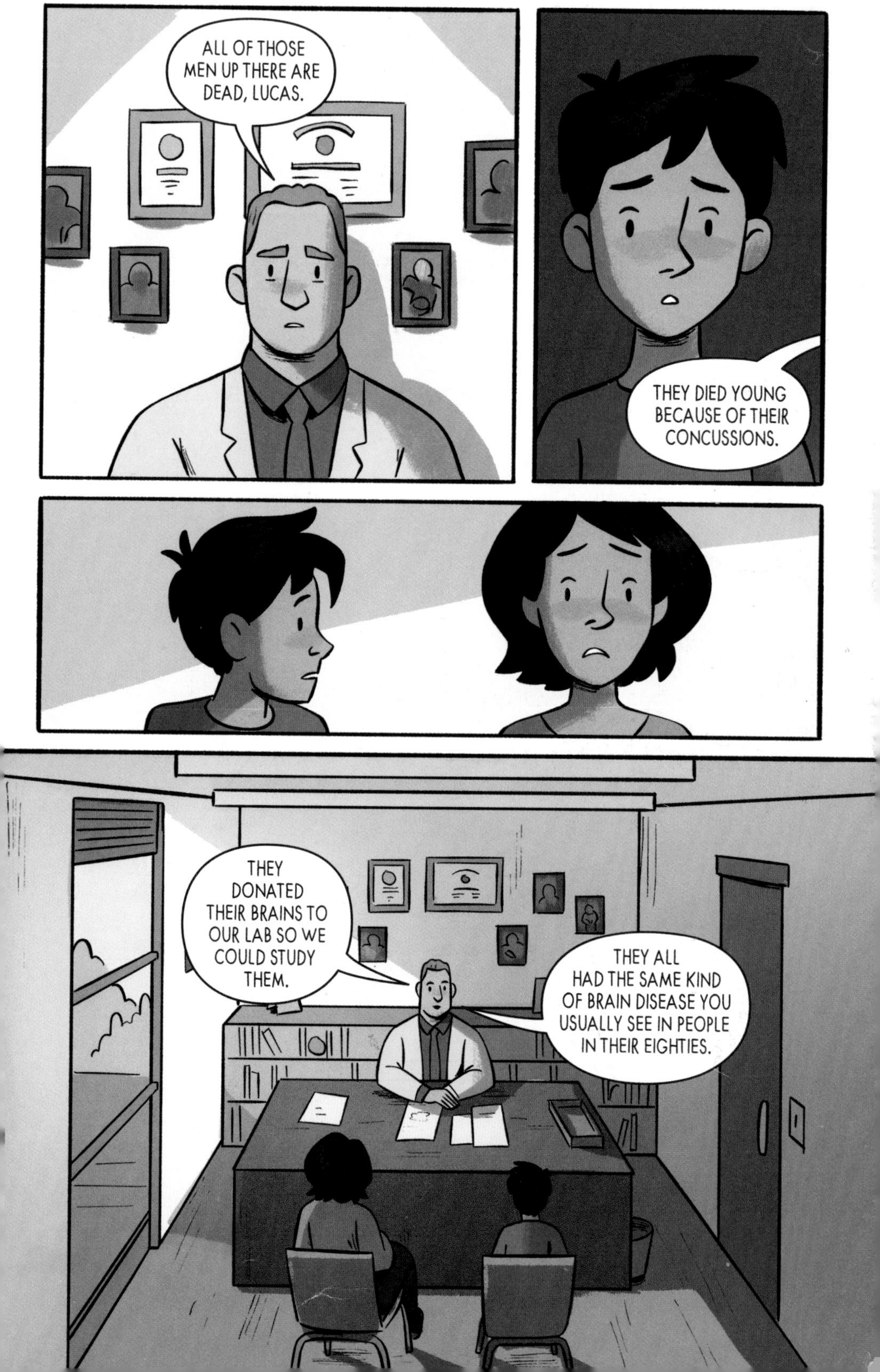
ALL OF THOSE MEN UP THERE ARE DEAD, LUCAS.
THEY DIED YOUNG BECAUSE OF THEIR CONCUSSIONS.
THEY DONATED THEIR BRAINS TO OUR LAB SO WE COULD STUDY THEM.
THEY ALL HAD THE SAME KIND OF BRAIN DISEASE YOU USUALLY SEE IN PEOPLE IN THEIR EIGHTIES.

WE USED TO THINK CONCUSSIONS WERE LIKE SPRAINED ANKLES...

YOU GET DINGED, YOU LET IT HEAL, YOU'RE GOOD TO GO.

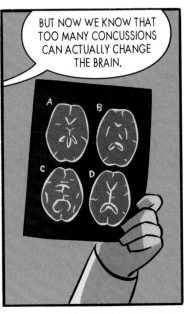

BUT NOW WE KNOW THAT TOO MANY CONCUSSIONS CAN ACTUALLY CHANGE THE BRAIN.

HOW MANY CONCUSSIONS IS TOO MANY?

I HOLD MY BREATH.

I DON'T THINK I WANT TO HEAR THE ANSWER.

I WOULD SAY THAT IN AN ELEVEN-YEAR-OLD BOY...

THREE CONCUSSIONS IN TWO YEARS IS TOO MANY.

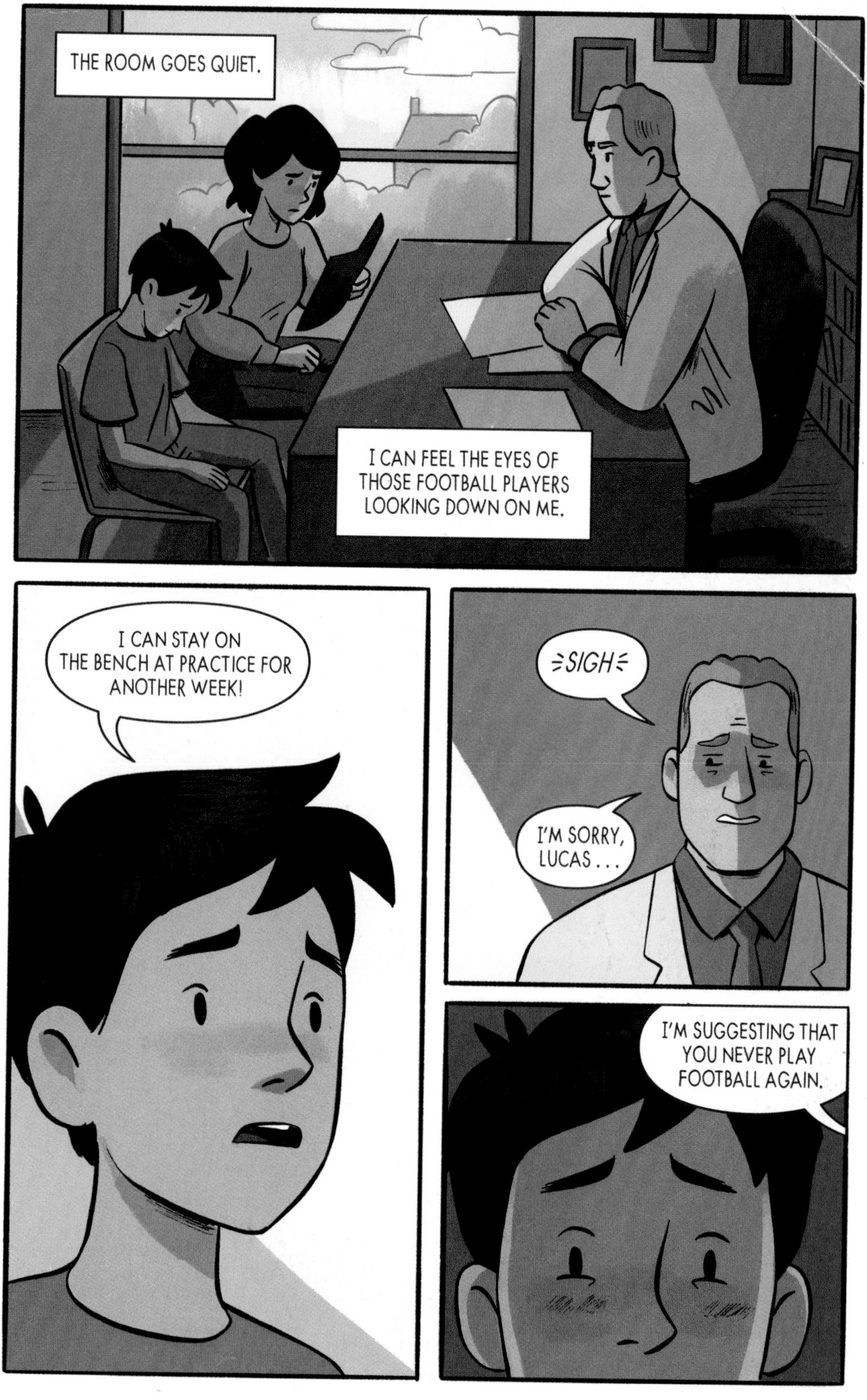
THE ROOM GOES QUIET.
I CAN FEEL THE EYES OF THOSE FOOTBALL PLAYERS LOOKING DOWN ON ME.
I CAN STAY ON THE BENCH AT PRACTICE FOR ANOTHER WEEK!
SIGH
I'M SORRY, LUCAS . . .
I'M SUGGESTING THAT YOU NEVER PLAY FOOTBALL AGAIN.

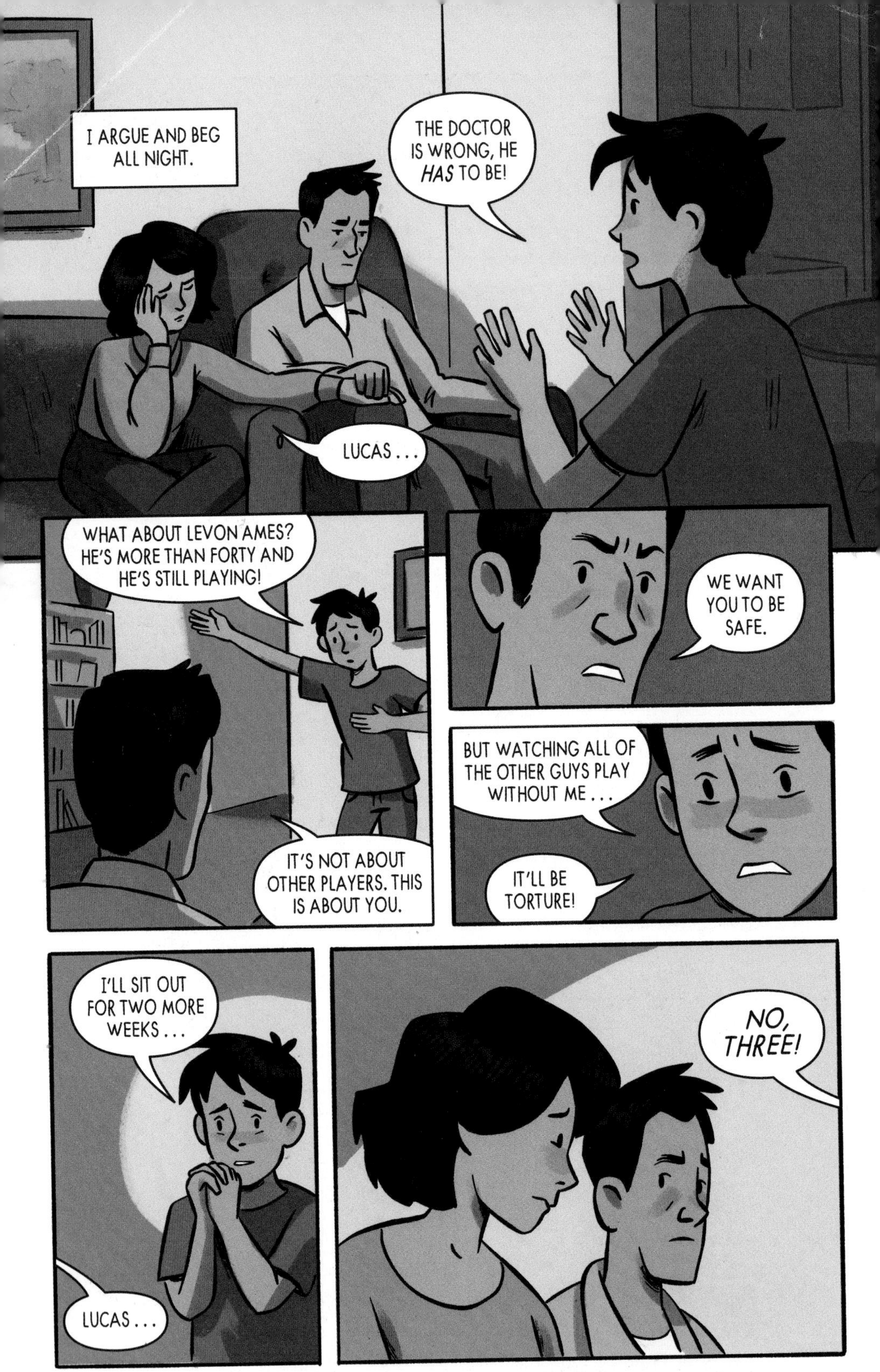
I ARGUE AND BEG ALL NIGHT.
THE DOCTOR IS WRONG, HE *HAS* TO BE!
LUCAS . . .
WHAT ABOUT LEVON AMES? HE'S MORE THAN FORTY AND HE'S STILL PLAYING!
IT'S NOT ABOUT OTHER PLAYERS. THIS IS ABOUT YOU.
WE WANT YOU TO BE SAFE.
BUT WATCHING ALL OF THE OTHER GUYS PLAY WITHOUT ME . . .
IT'LL BE TORTURE!
I'LL SIT OUT FOR TWO MORE WEEKS . . .
LUCAS . . .
NO, THREE!

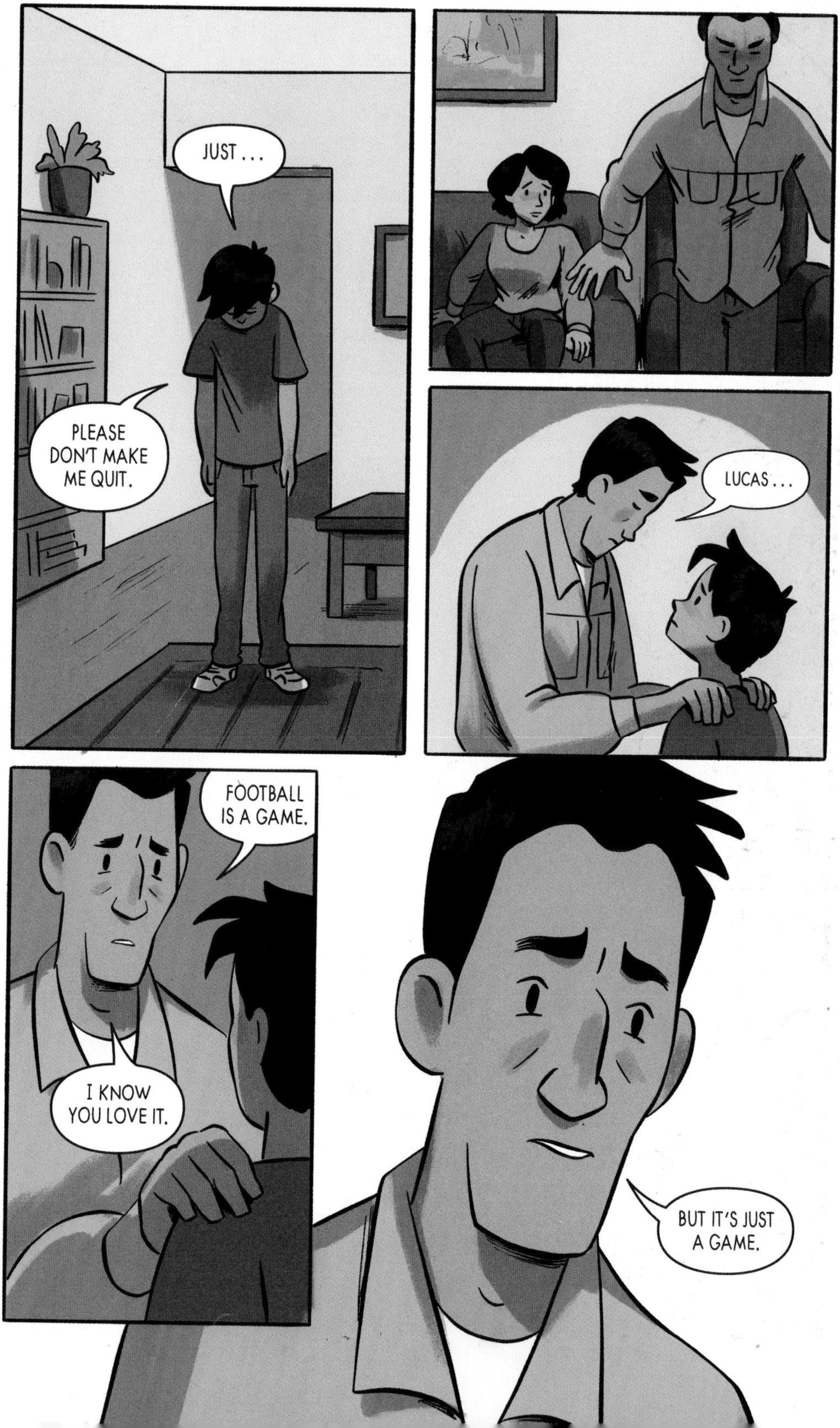
JUST . . .
PLEASE DON'T MAKE ME QUIT.
LUCAS . . .
FOOTBALL IS A GAME.
I KNOW YOU LOVE IT.
BUT IT'S JUST A GAME.

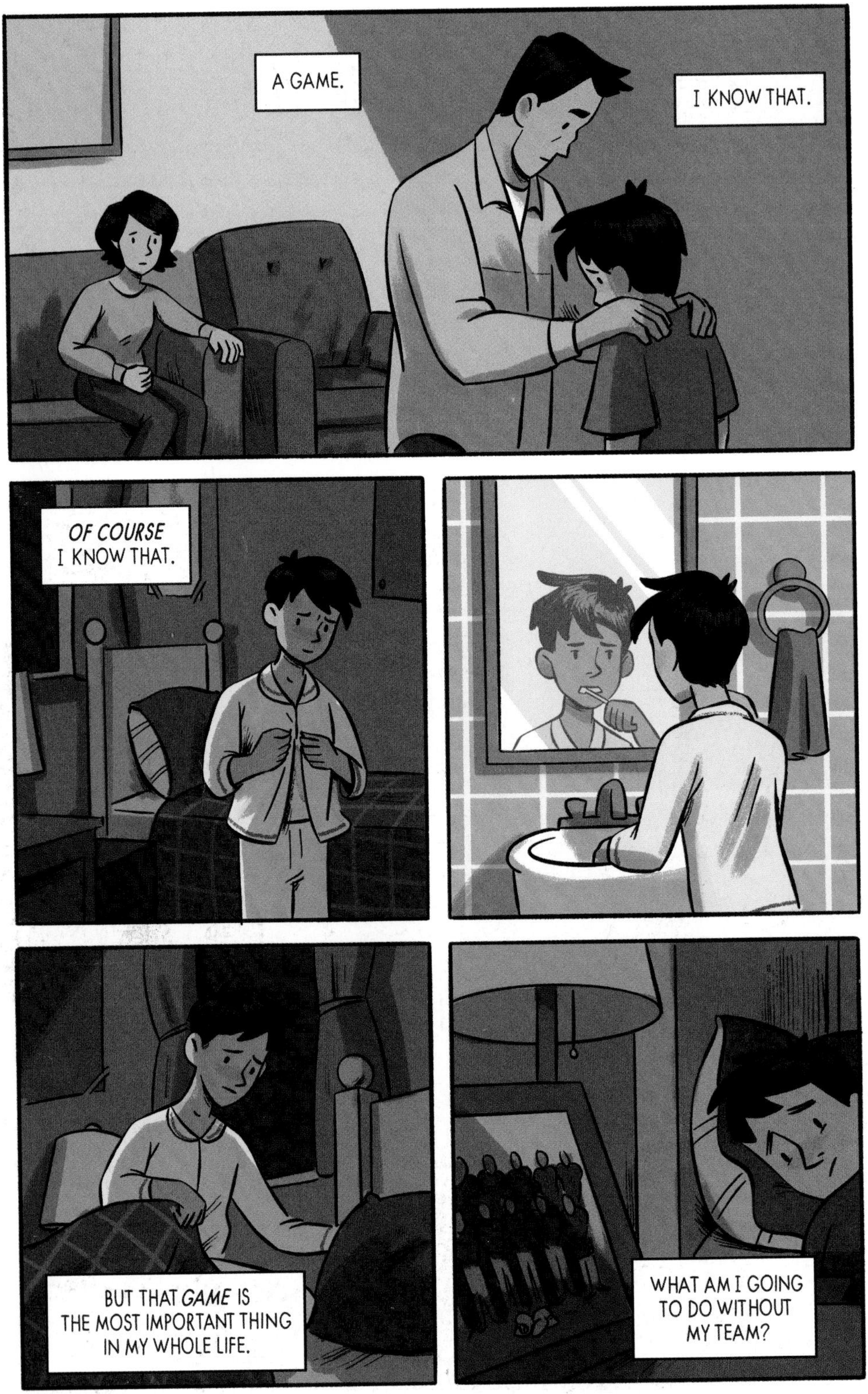
A GAME.
I KNOW THAT.
OF COURSE I KNOW THAT.
BUT THAT *GAME* IS THE MOST IMPORTANT THING IN MY WHOLE LIFE.
WHAT AM I GOING TO DO WITHOUT MY TEAM?

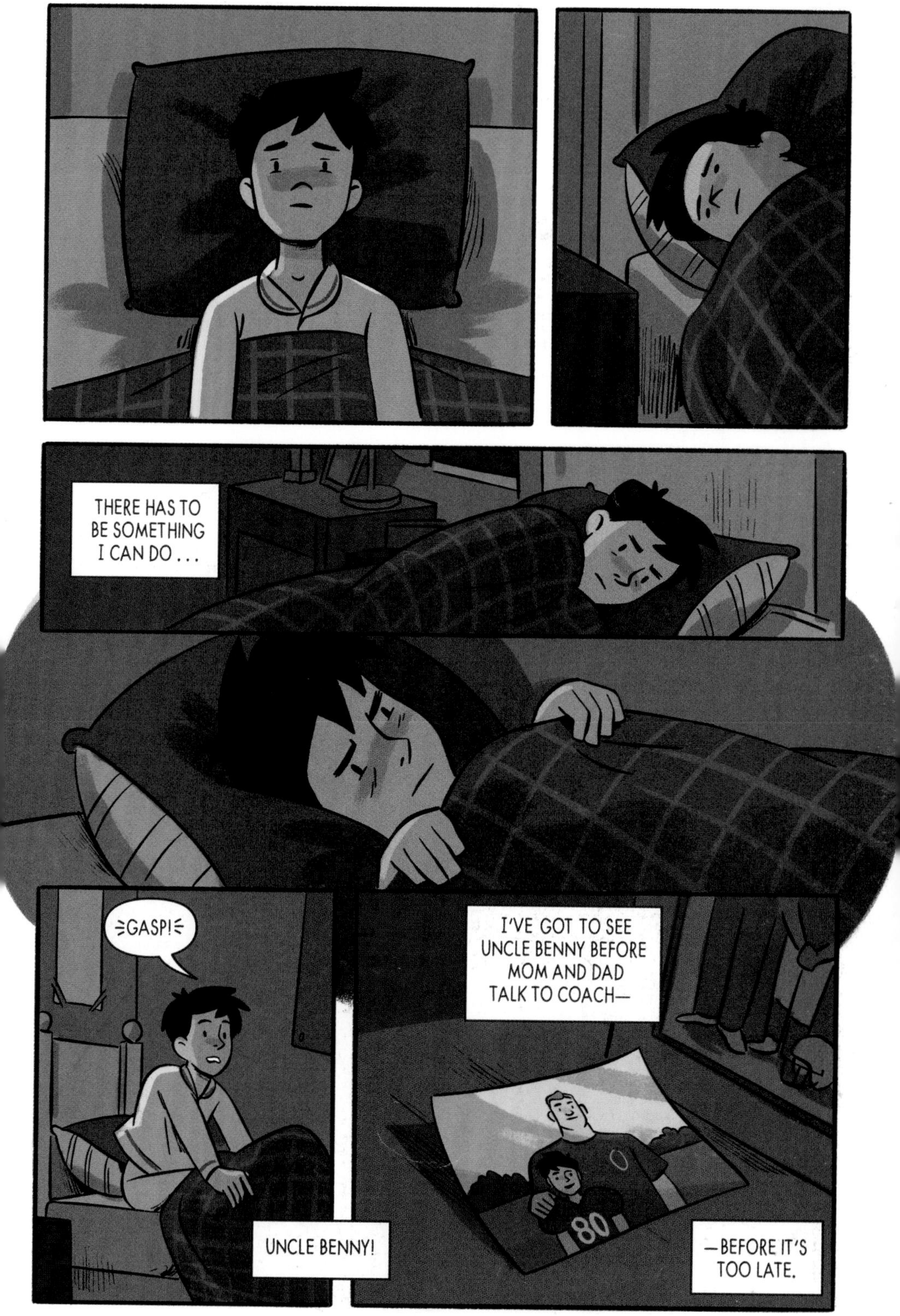
THERE HAS TO BE SOMETHING I CAN DO . . .
≶GASP!≶
UNCLE BENNY!
I'VE GOT TO SEE UNCLE BENNY BEFORE MOM AND DAD TALK TO COACH—
—BEFORE IT'S TOO LATE.

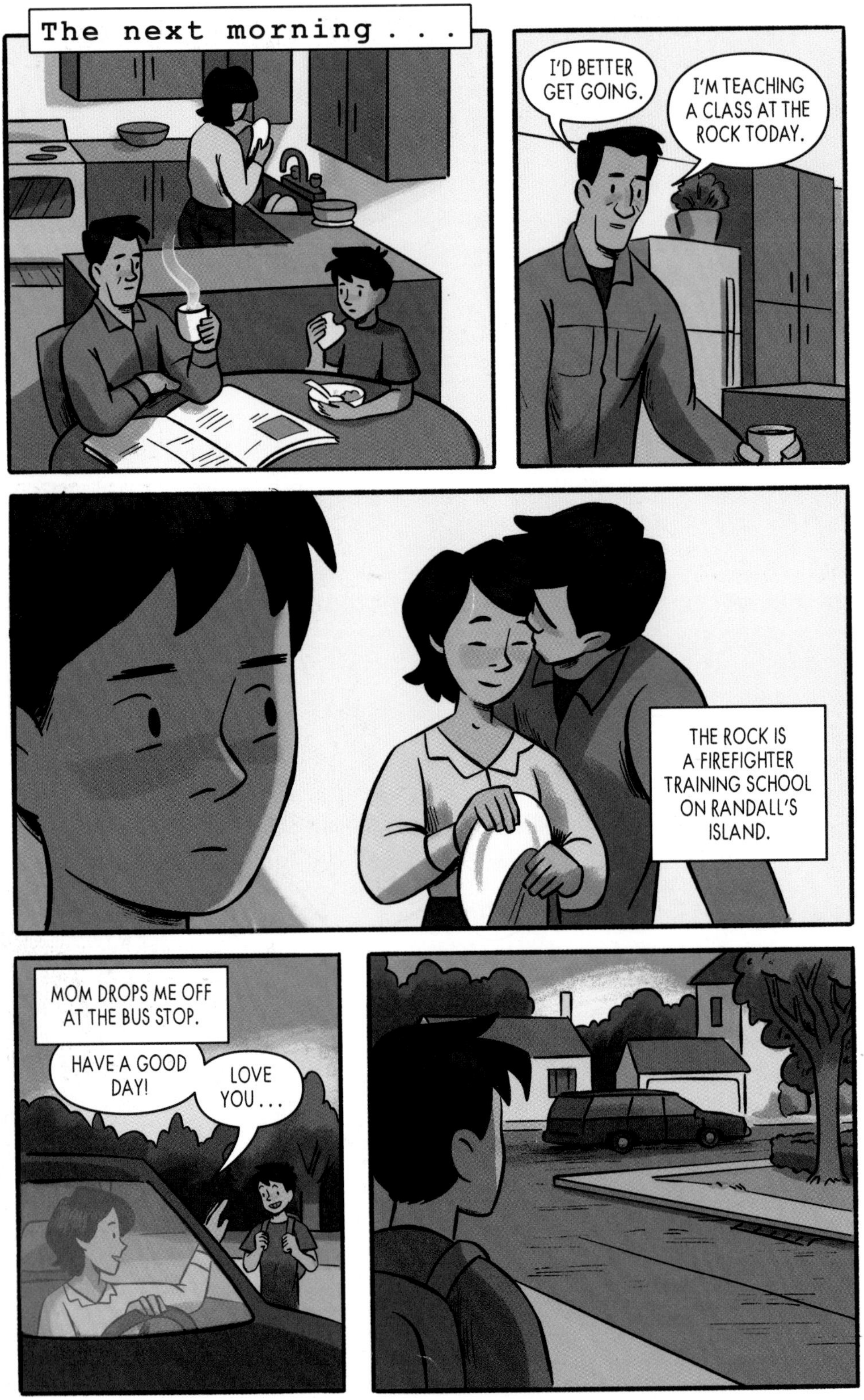

The next morning . . .
I'D BETTER GET GOING.
I'M TEACHING A CLASS AT THE ROCK TODAY.
THE ROCK IS A FIREFIGHTER TRAINING SCHOOL ON RANDALL'S ISLAND.
MOM DROPS ME OFF AT THE BUS STOP.
HAVE A GOOD DAY!
LOVE YOU . . .

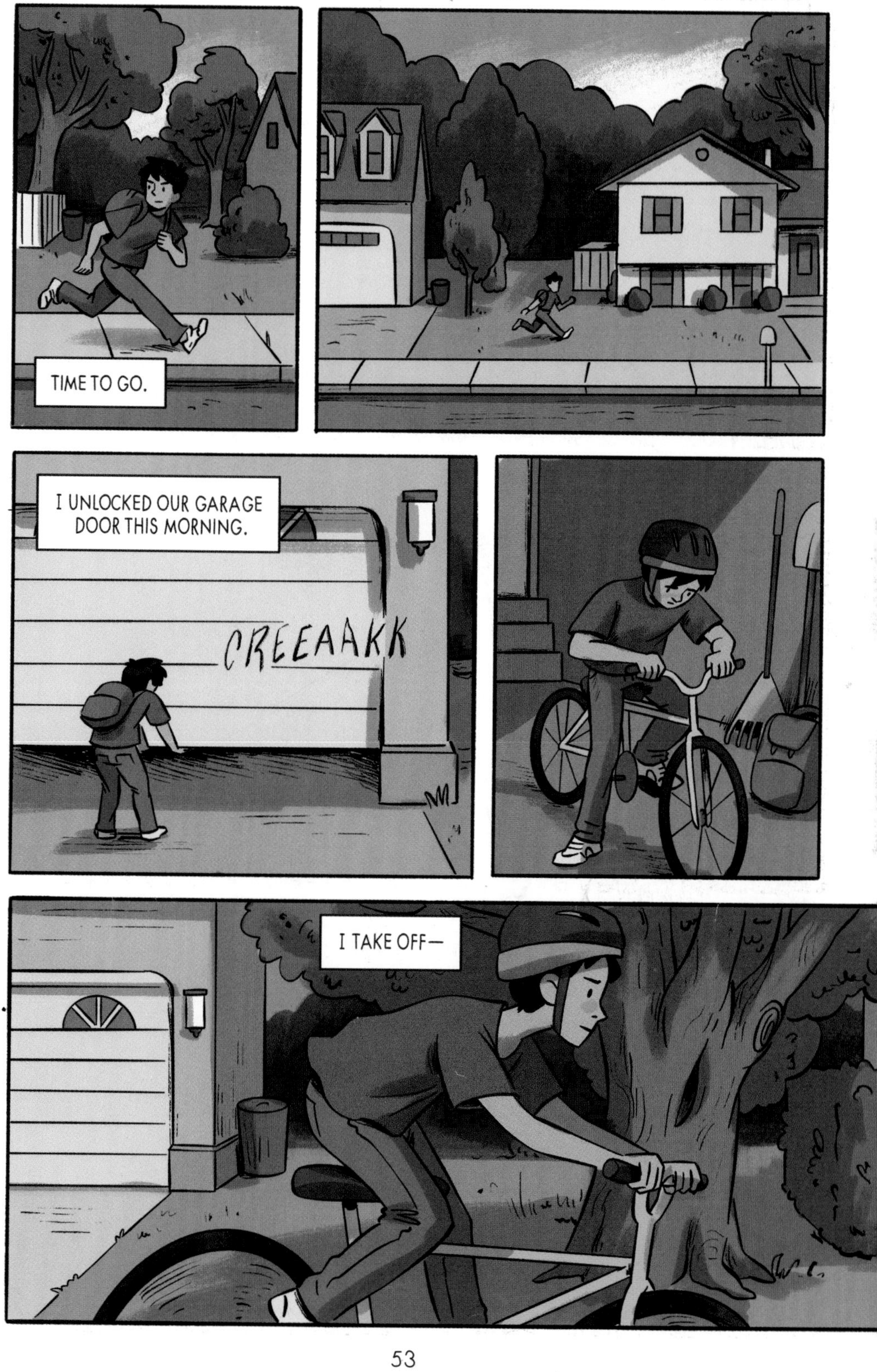
TIME TO GO.
I UNLOCKED OUR GARAGE DOOR THIS MORNING.
CREEAAKK
I TAKE OFF—

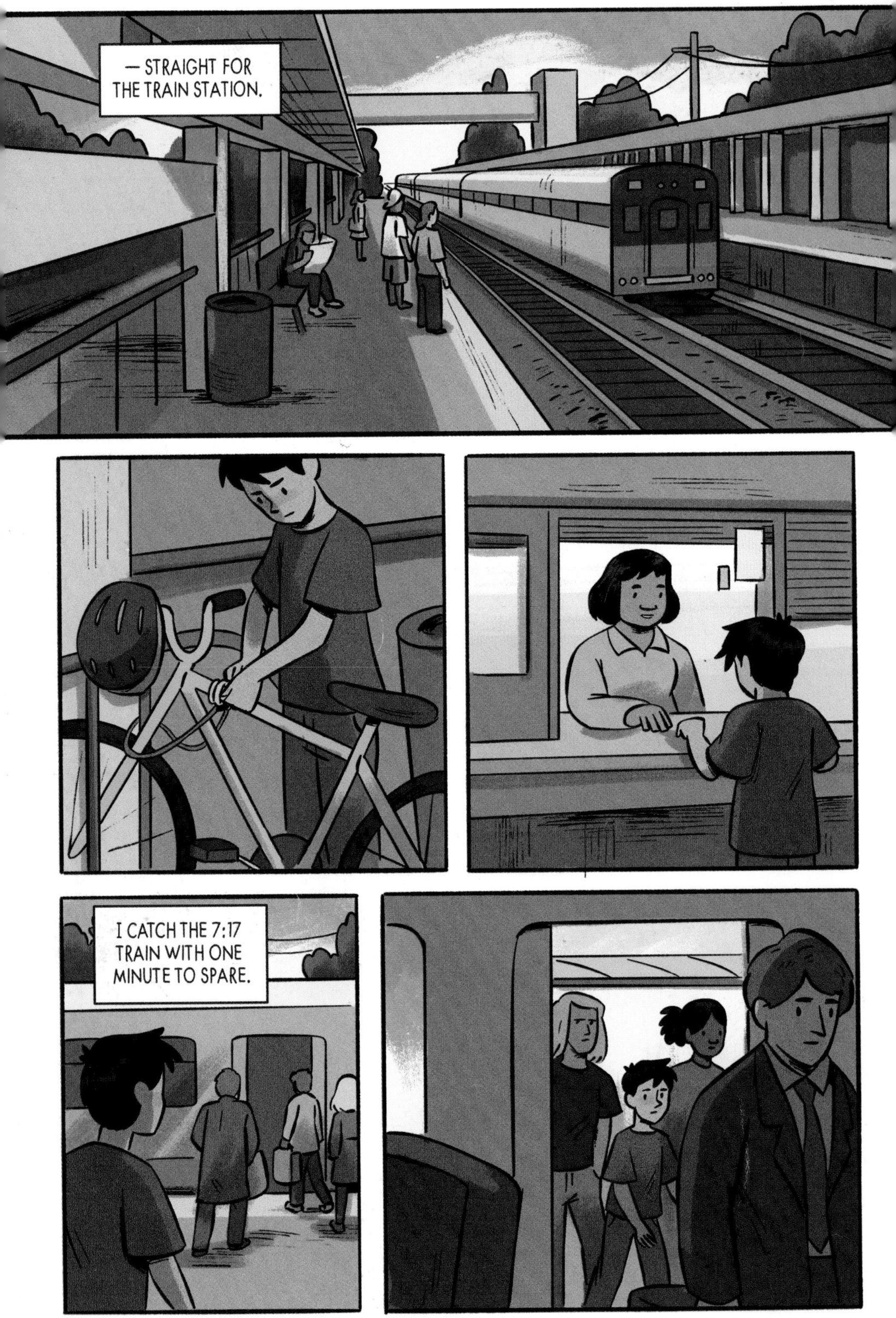
— STRAIGHT FOR THE TRAIN STATION.
I CATCH THE 7:17 TRAIN WITH ONE MINUTE TO SPARE.

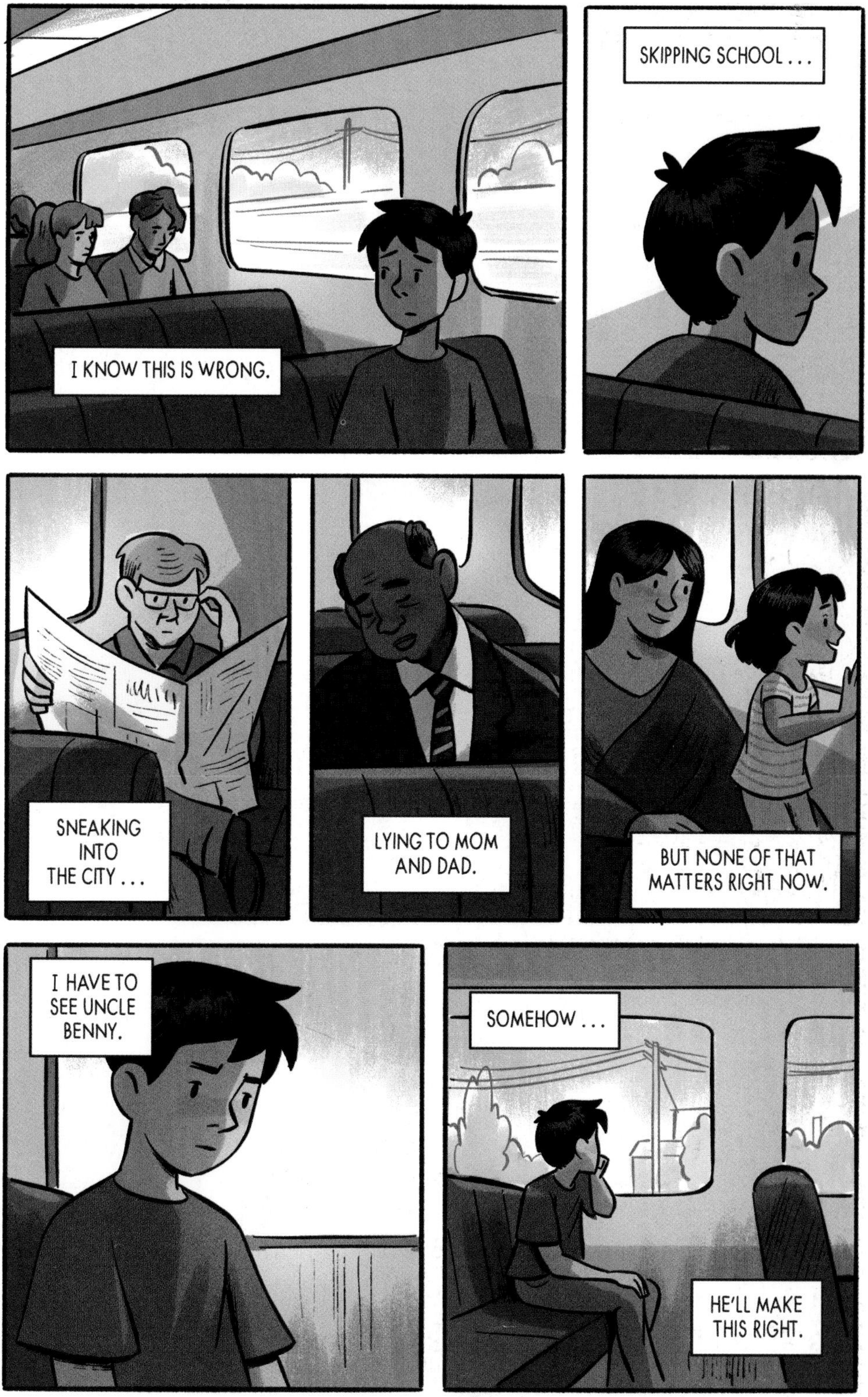
I KNOW THIS IS WRONG.
SKIPPING SCHOOL . . .
SNEAKING INTO THE CITY . . .
LYING TO MOM AND DAD.
BUT NONE OF THAT MATTERS RIGHT NOW.
I HAVE TO SEE UNCLE BENNY.
SOMEHOW . . .
HE'LL MAKE THIS RIGHT.

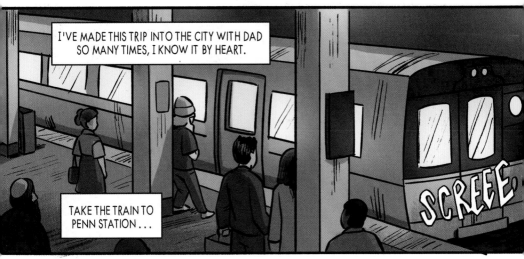

I'VE MADE THIS TRIP INTO THE CITY WITH DAD SO MANY TIMES, I KNOW IT BY HEART.

TAKE THE TRAIN TO PENN STATION...

SCREEE

TAKE THE SUBWAY DOWNTOWN TO CANAL STREET.

Ⓐ Downtown & Bklyn

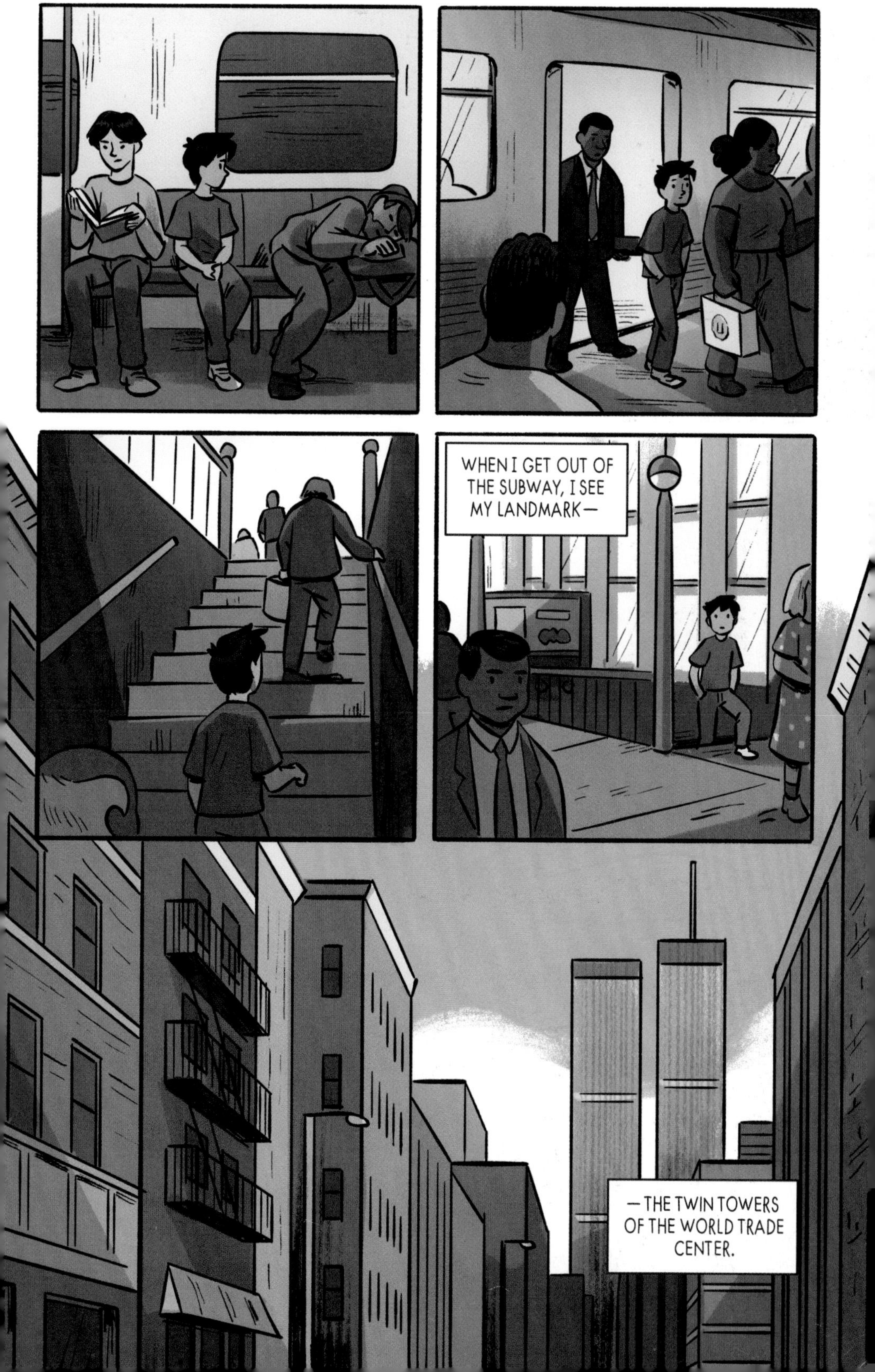
WHEN I GET OUT OF THE SUBWAY, I SEE MY LANDMARK—
—THE TWIN TOWERS OF THE WORLD TRADE CENTER.

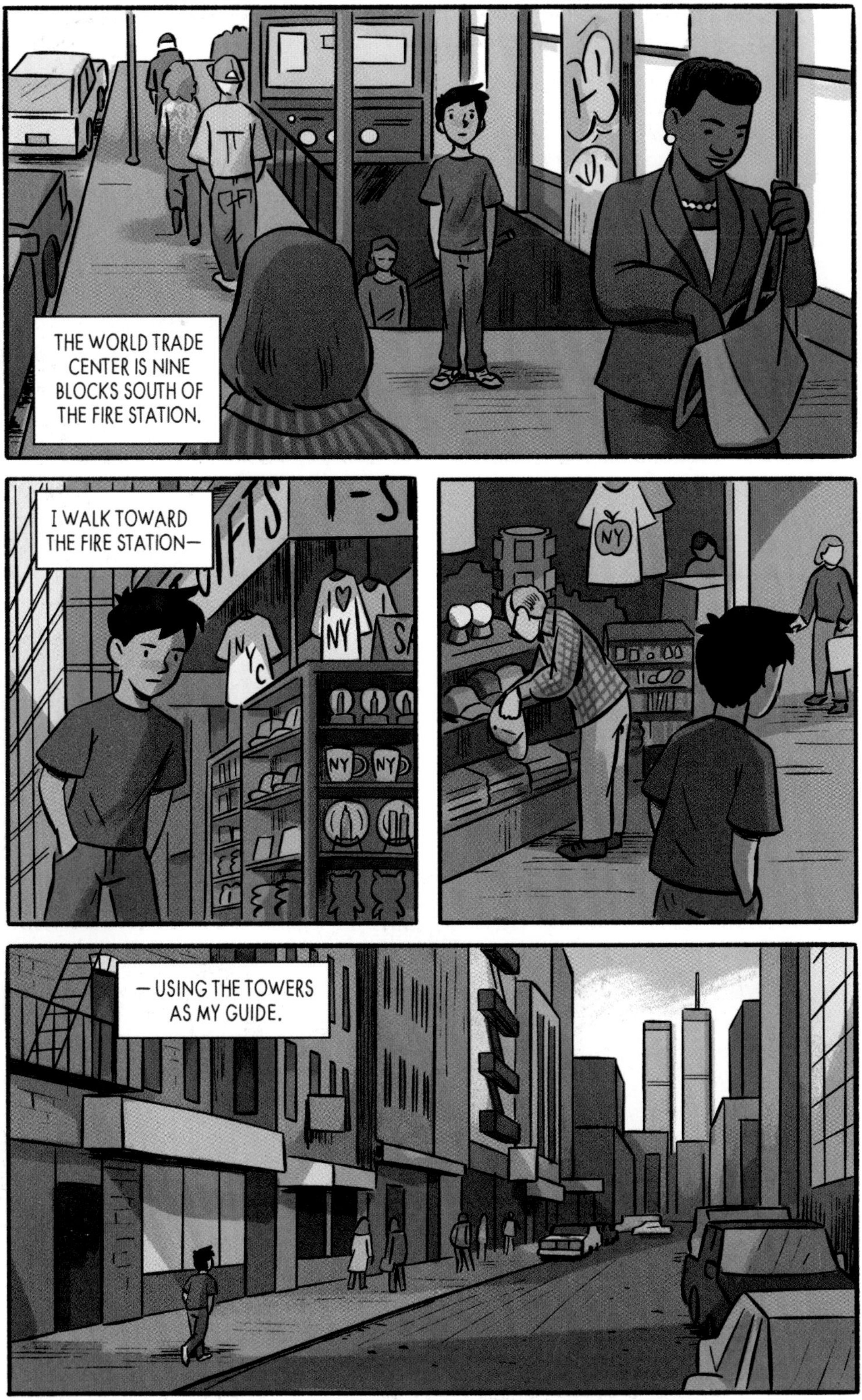
THE WORLD TRADE CENTER IS NINE BLOCKS SOUTH OF THE FIRE STATION.
I WALK TOWARD THE FIRE STATION—
— USING THE TOWERS AS MY GUIDE.

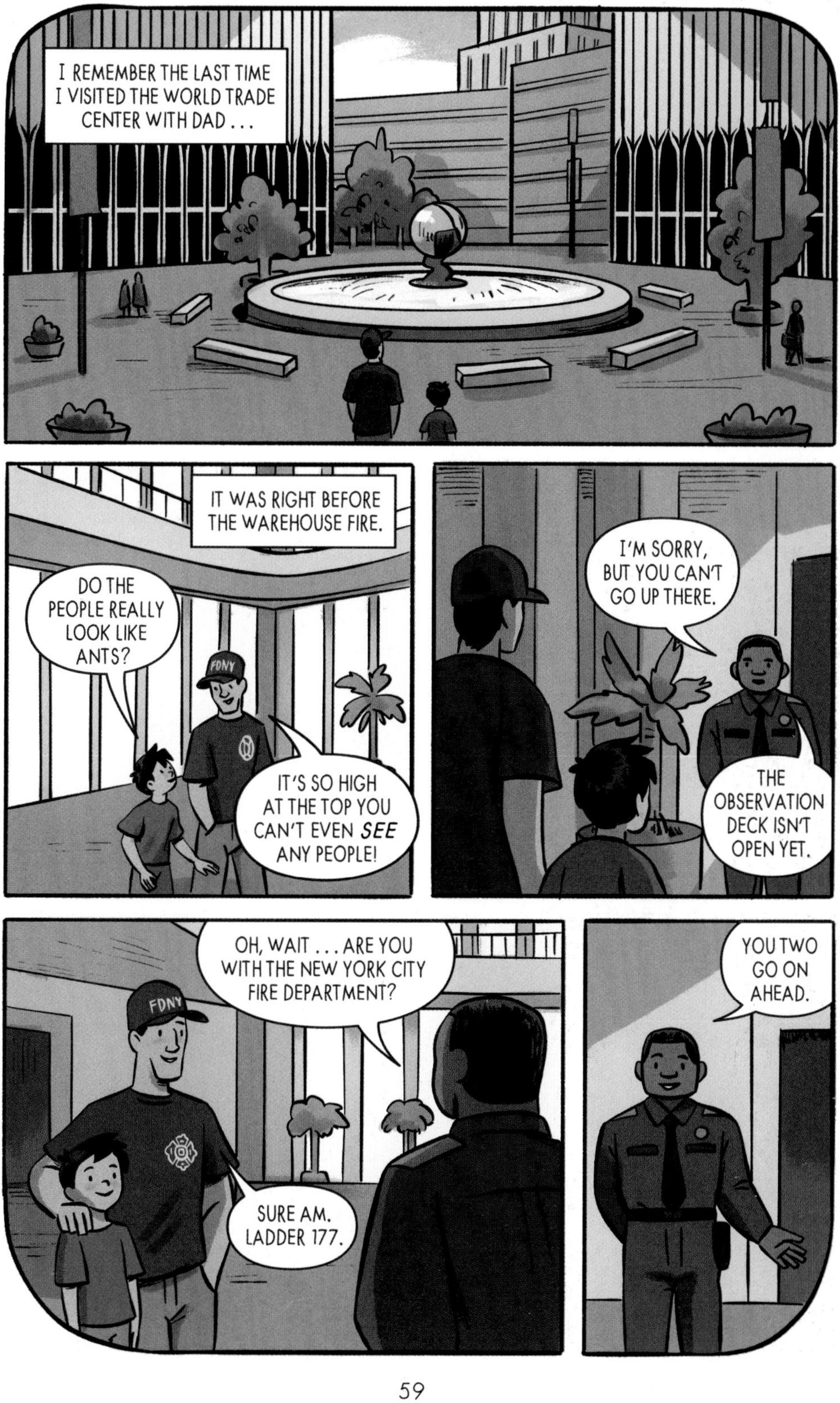
I REMEMBER THE LAST TIME I VISITED THE WORLD TRADE CENTER WITH DAD . . .
IT WAS RIGHT BEFORE THE WAREHOUSE FIRE.
DO THE PEOPLE REALLY LOOK LIKE ANTS?
FDNY
IT'S SO HIGH AT THE TOP YOU CAN'T EVEN *SEE* ANY PEOPLE!
I'M SORRY, BUT YOU CAN'T GO UP THERE.
THE OBSERVATION DECK ISN'T OPEN YET.
OH, WAIT . . . ARE YOU WITH THE NEW YORK CITY FIRE DEPARTMENT?
FDNY
SURE AM. LADDER 177.
YOU TWO GO ON AHEAD.

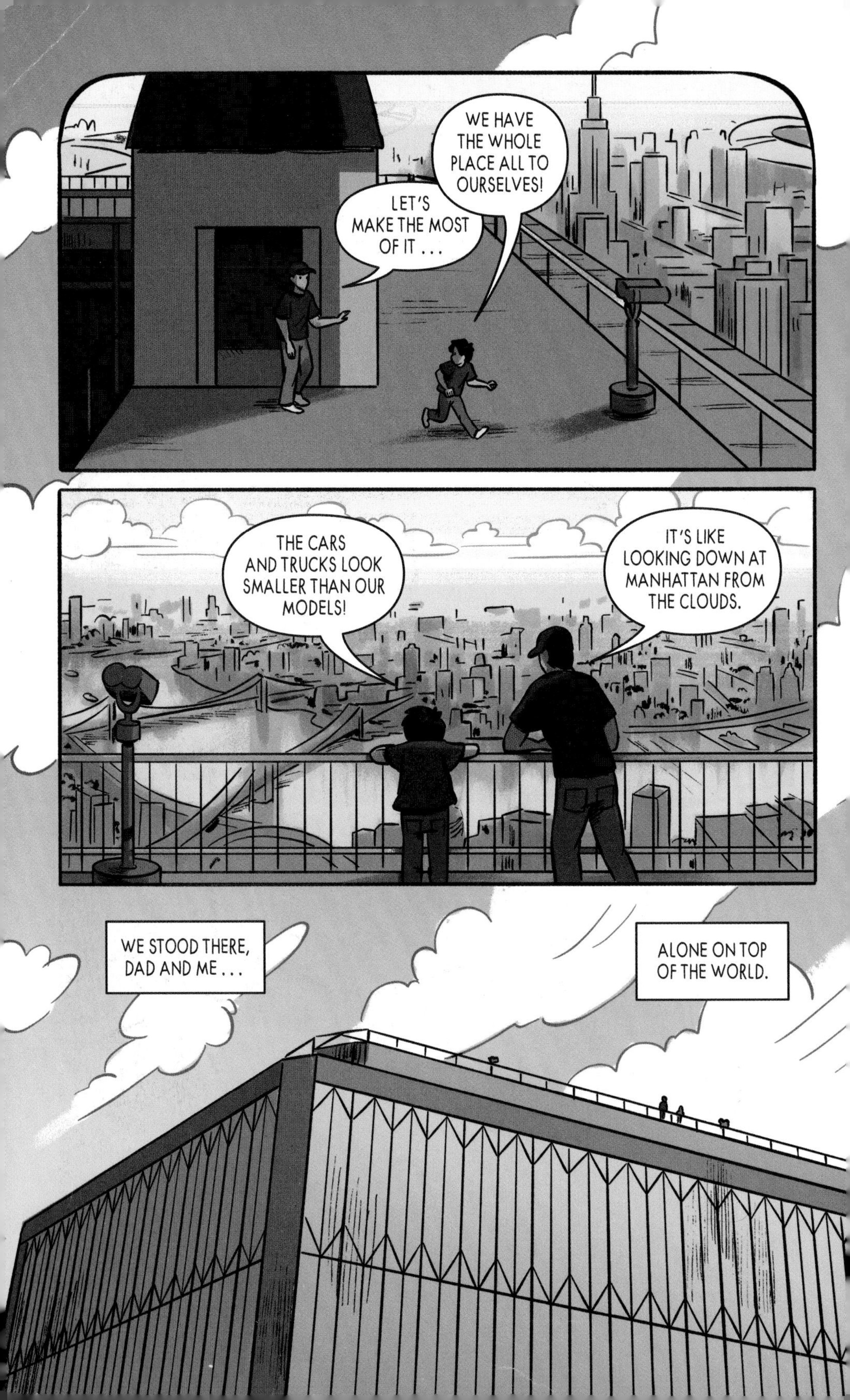
WE HAVE THE WHOLE PLACE ALL TO OURSELVES!
LET'S MAKE THE MOST OF IT . . .
THE CARS AND TRUCKS LOOK SMALLER THAN OUR MODELS!
IT'S LIKE LOOKING DOWN AT MANHATTAN FROM THE CLOUDS.
WE STOOD THERE, DAD AND ME . . .
ALONE ON TOP OF THE WORLD.

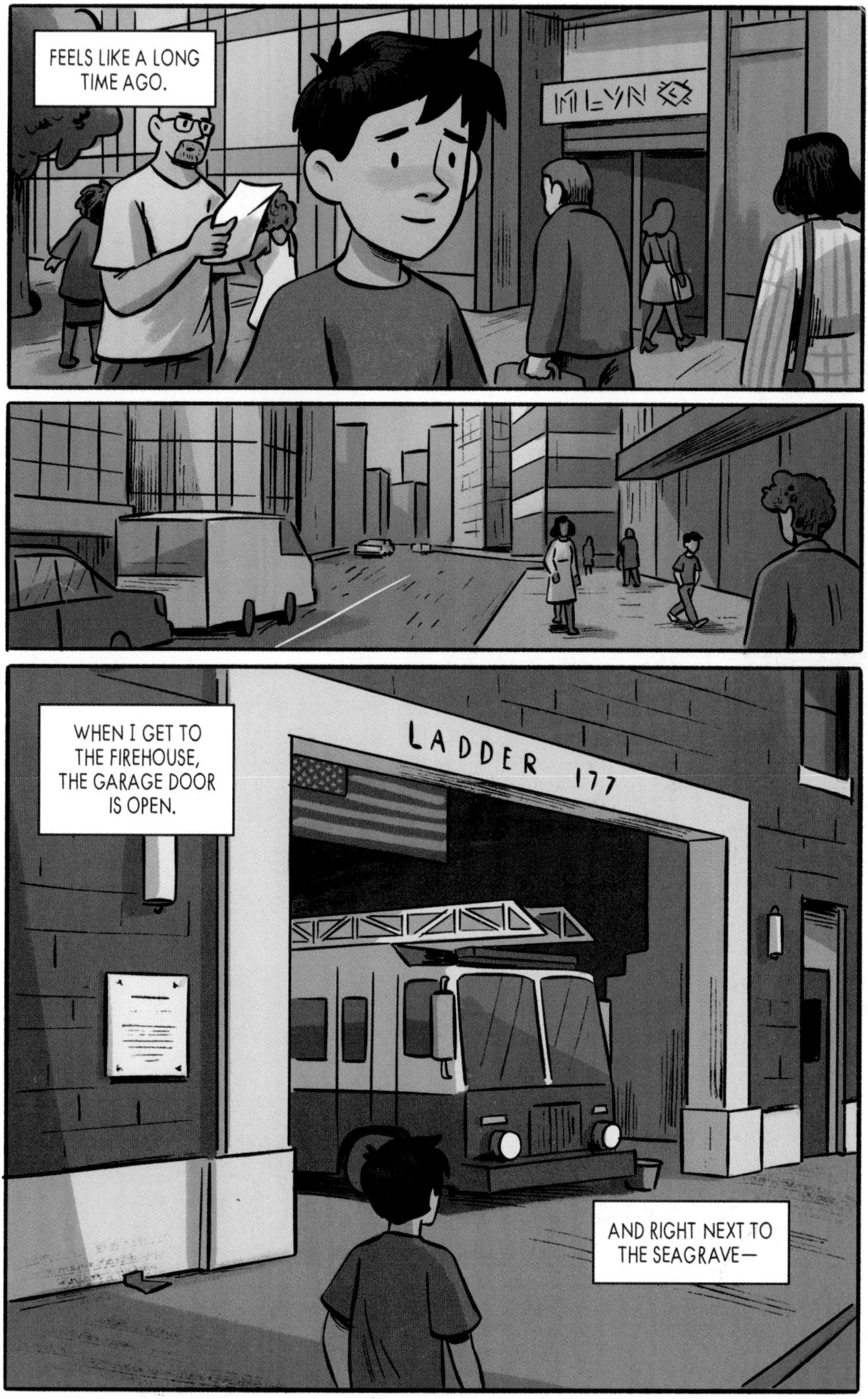
FEELS LIKE A LONG TIME AGO.
WHEN I GET TO THE FIREHOUSE, THE GARAGE DOOR IS OPEN.
LADDER 177
AND RIGHT NEXT TO THE SEAGRAVE—

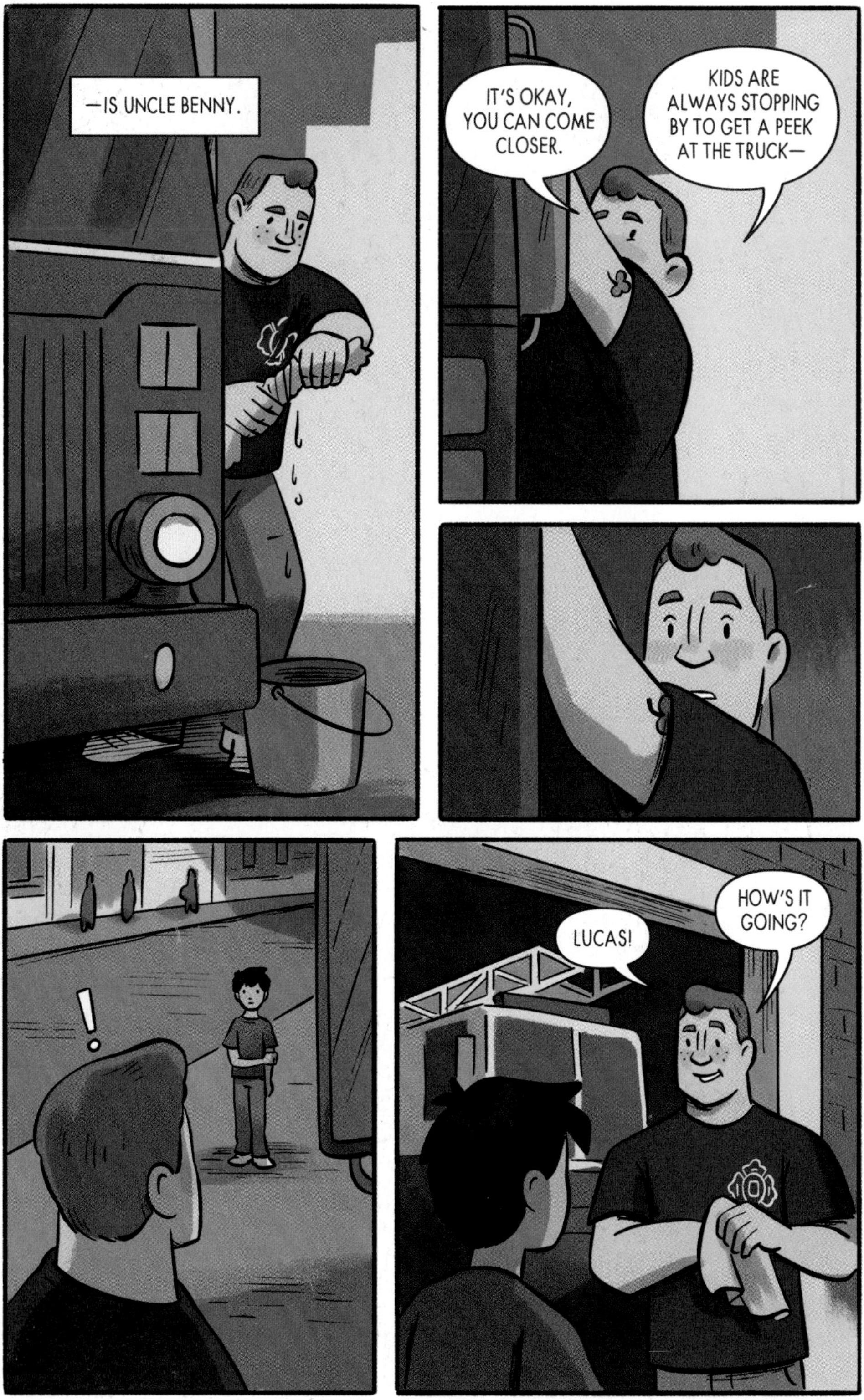
—IS UNCLE BENNY.
IT'S OKAY, YOU CAN COME CLOSER.
KIDS ARE ALWAYS STOPPING BY TO GET A PEEK AT THE TRUCK—
!
LUCAS!
HOW'S IT GOING?

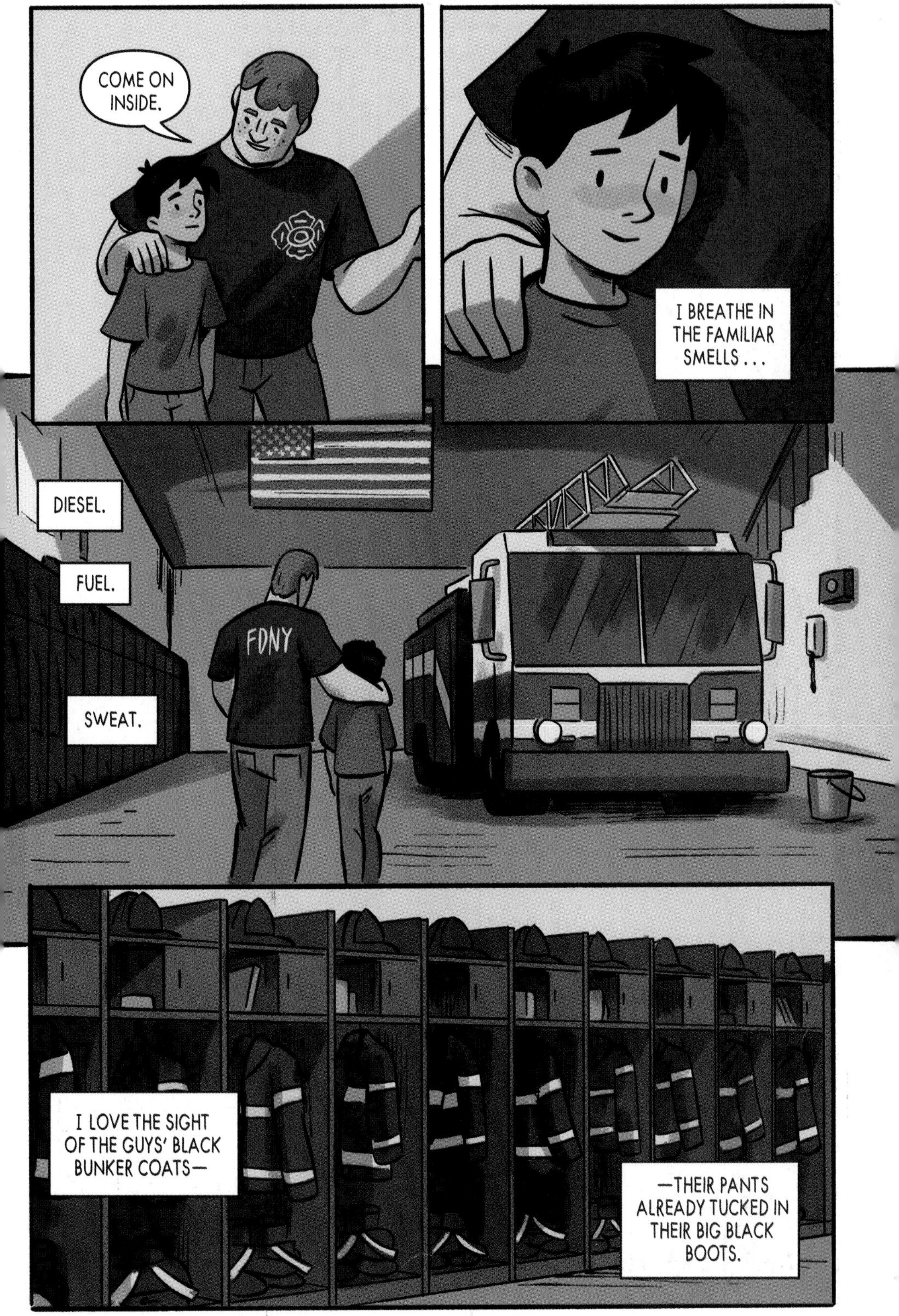
COME ON INSIDE.
I BREATHE IN THE FAMILIAR SMELLS . . .
DIESEL.
FUEL.
FDNY
SWEAT.
I LOVE THE SIGHT OF THE GUYS' BLACK BUNKER COATS—
—THEIR PANTS ALREADY TUCKED IN THEIR BIG BLACK BOOTS.

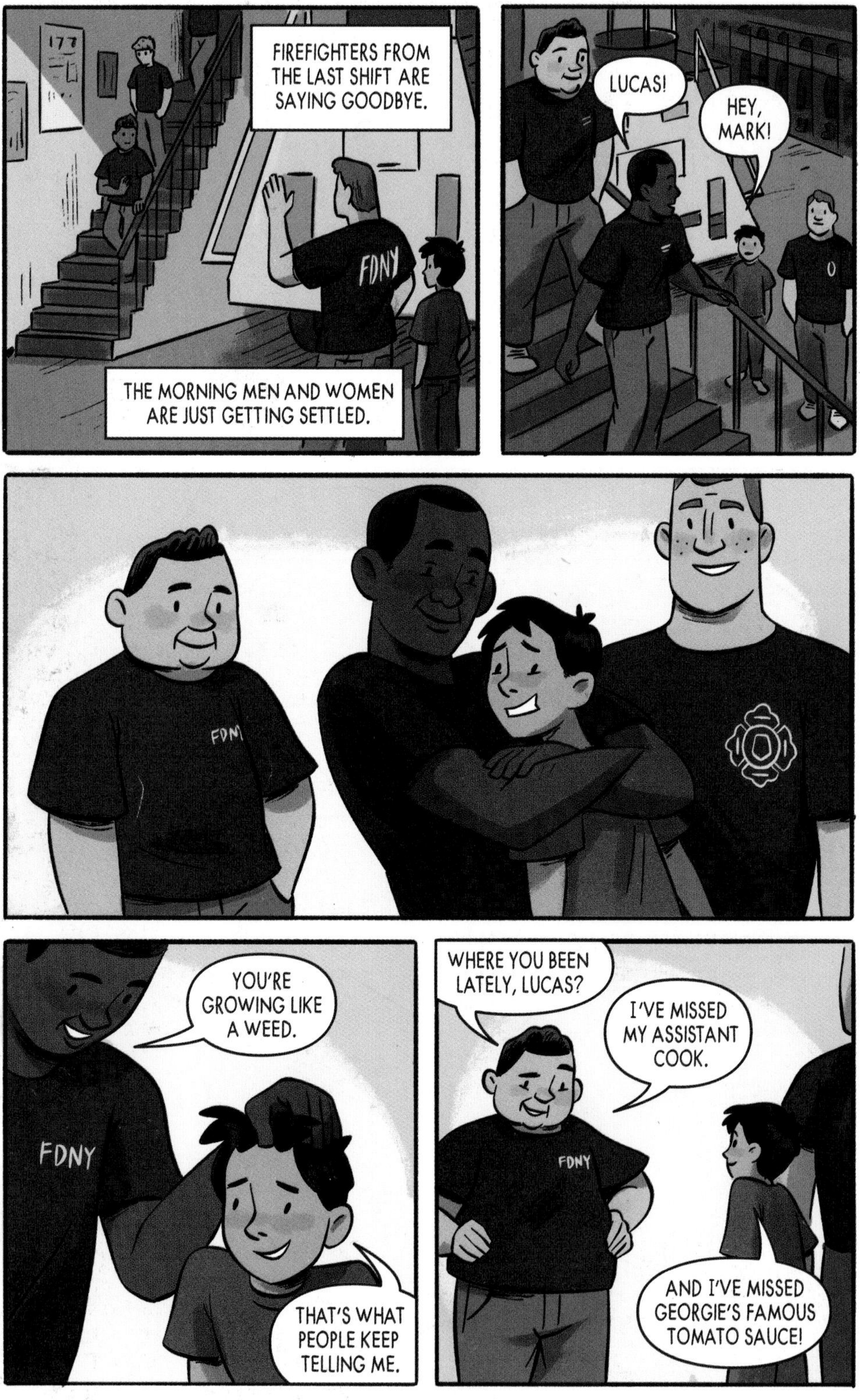
FIREFIGHTERS FROM THE LAST SHIFT ARE SAYING GOODBYE.
THE MORNING MEN AND WOMEN ARE JUST GETTING SETTLED.
LUCAS!
HEY, MARK!
FDNY
YOU'RE GROWING LIKE A WEED.
THAT'S WHAT PEOPLE KEEP TELLING ME.
WHERE YOU BEEN LATELY, LUCAS?
I'VE MISSED MY ASSISTANT COOK.
AND I'VE MISSED GEORGIE'S FAMOUS TOMATO SAUCE!

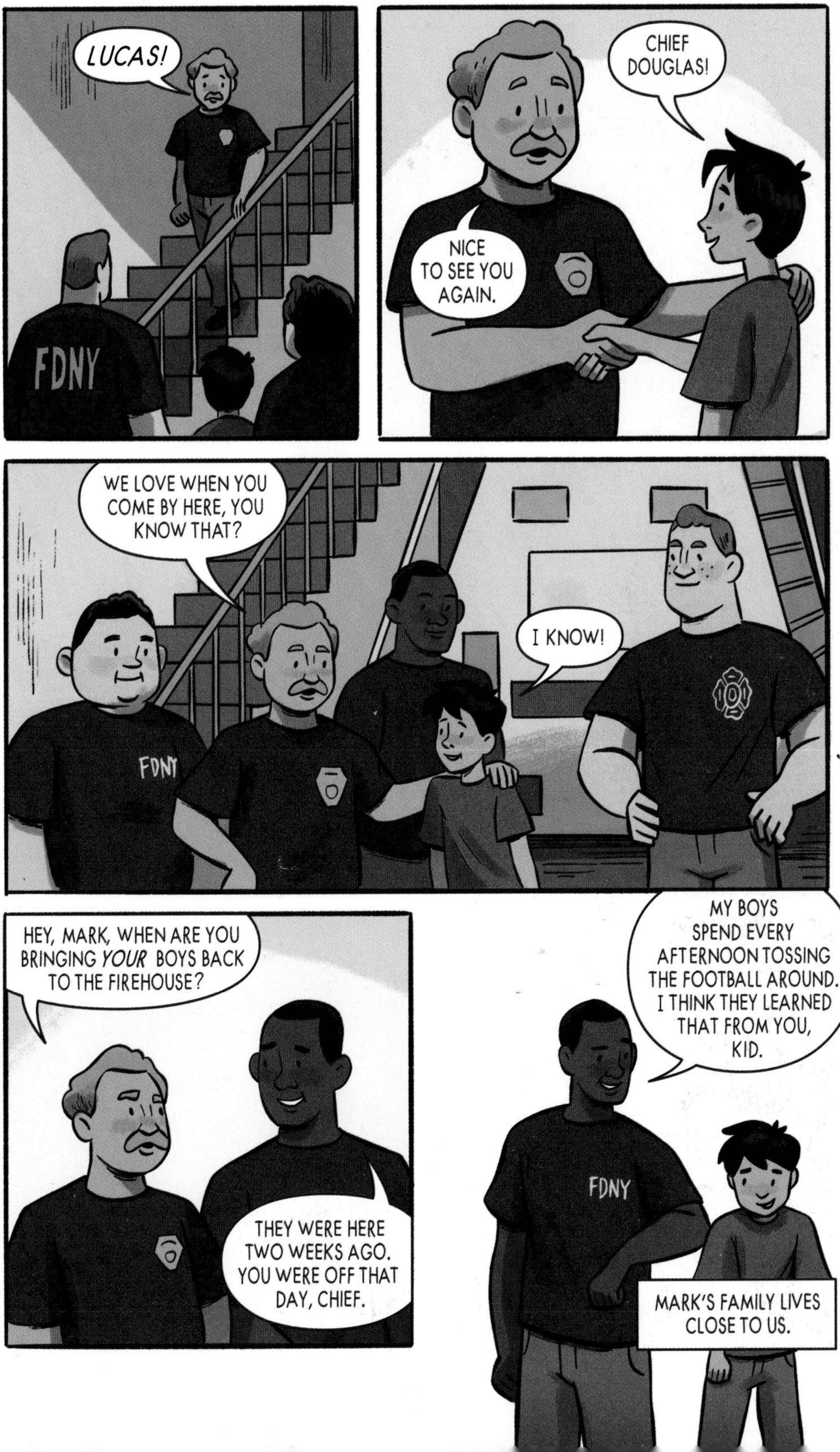
LUCAS!
CHIEF DOUGLAS!
NICE TO SEE YOU AGAIN.
FDNY
WE LOVE WHEN YOU COME BY HERE, YOU KNOW THAT?
I KNOW!
FDNY
HEY, MARK, WHEN ARE YOU BRINGING *YOUR* BOYS BACK TO THE FIREHOUSE?
THEY WERE HERE TWO WEEKS AGO. YOU WERE OFF THAT DAY, CHIEF.
MY BOYS SPEND EVERY AFTERNOON TOSSING THE FOOTBALL AROUND. I THINK THEY LEARNED THAT FROM YOU, KID.
FDNY
MARK'S FAMILY LIVES CLOSE TO US.

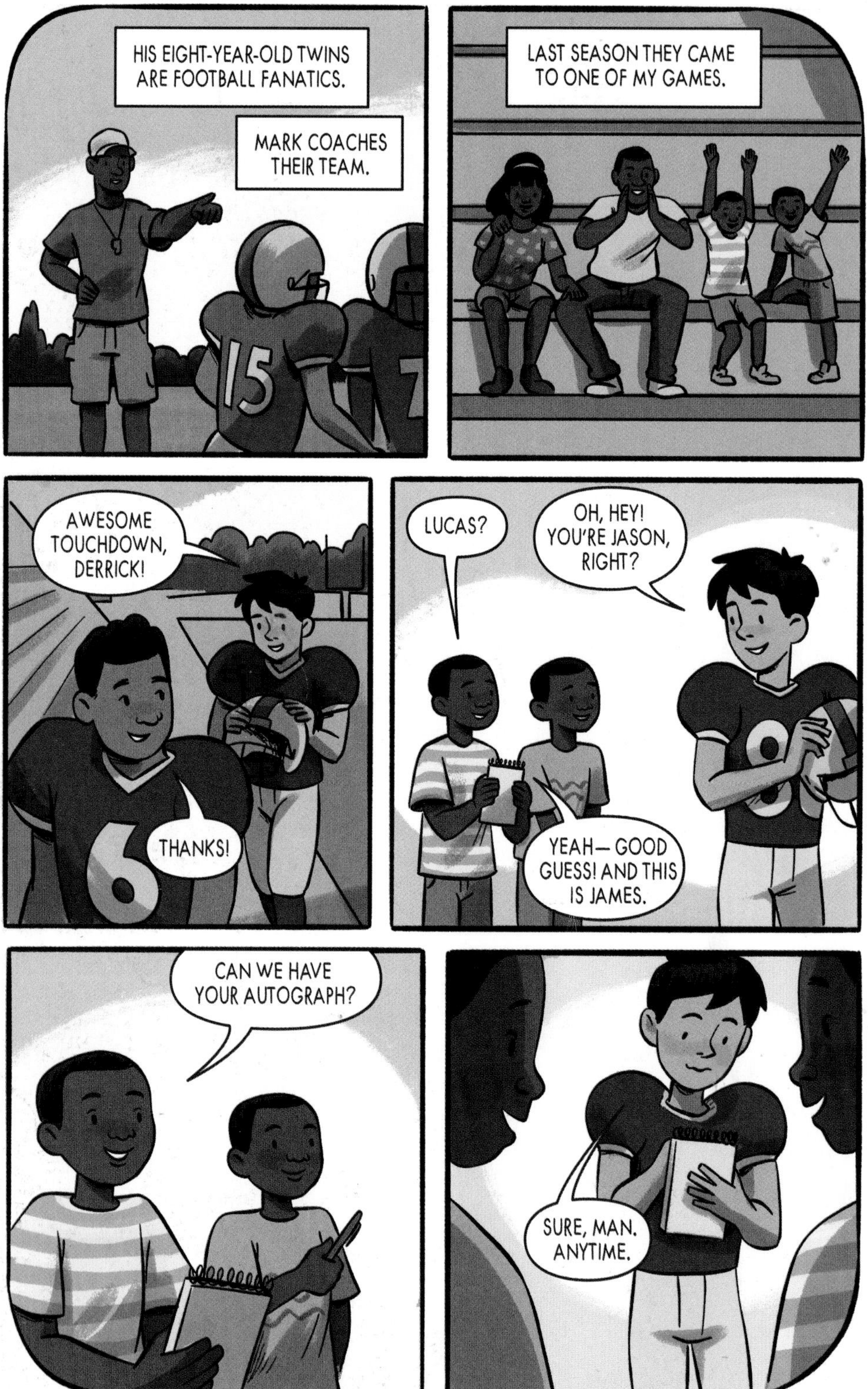
HIS EIGHT-YEAR-OLD TWINS ARE FOOTBALL FANATICS.
MARK COACHES THEIR TEAM.
15
LAST SEASON THEY CAME TO ONE OF MY GAMES.
AWESOME TOUCHDOWN, DERRICK!
THANKS!
6
LUCAS?
OH, HEY! YOU'RE JASON, RIGHT?
YEAH— GOOD GUESS! AND THIS IS JAMES.
CAN WE HAVE YOUR AUTOGRAPH?
SURE, MAN. ANYTIME.

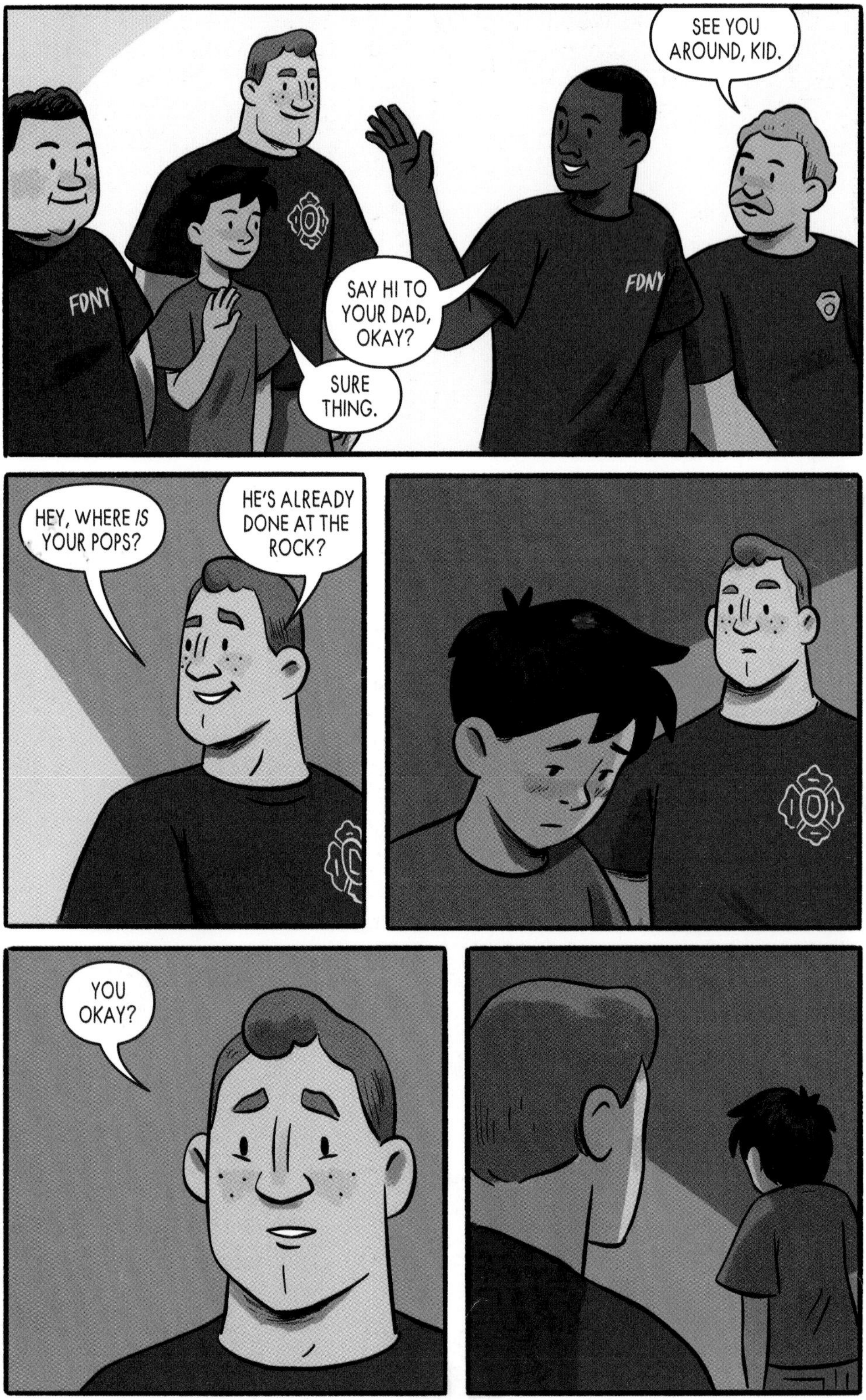
SEE YOU AROUND, KID.
SAY HI TO YOUR DAD, OKAY?
SURE THING.
FDNY
FDNY
HEY, WHERE *IS* YOUR POPS?
HE'S ALREADY DONE AT THE ROCK?
YOU OKAY?

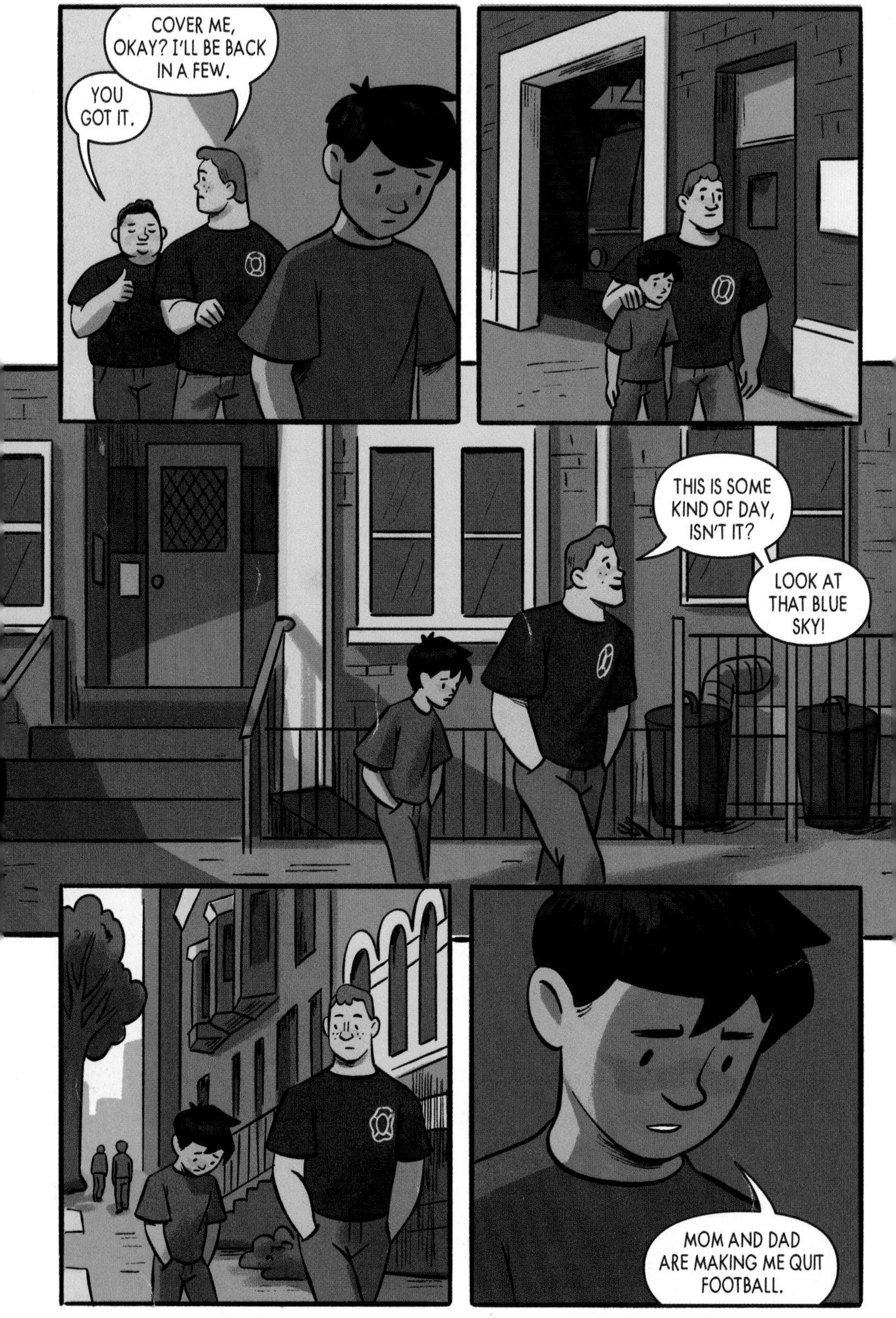
COVER ME, OKAY? I'LL BE BACK IN A FEW.
YOU GOT IT.
THIS IS SOME KIND OF DAY, ISN'T IT?
LOOK AT THAT BLUE SKY!
MOM AND DAD ARE MAKING ME QUIT FOOTBALL.

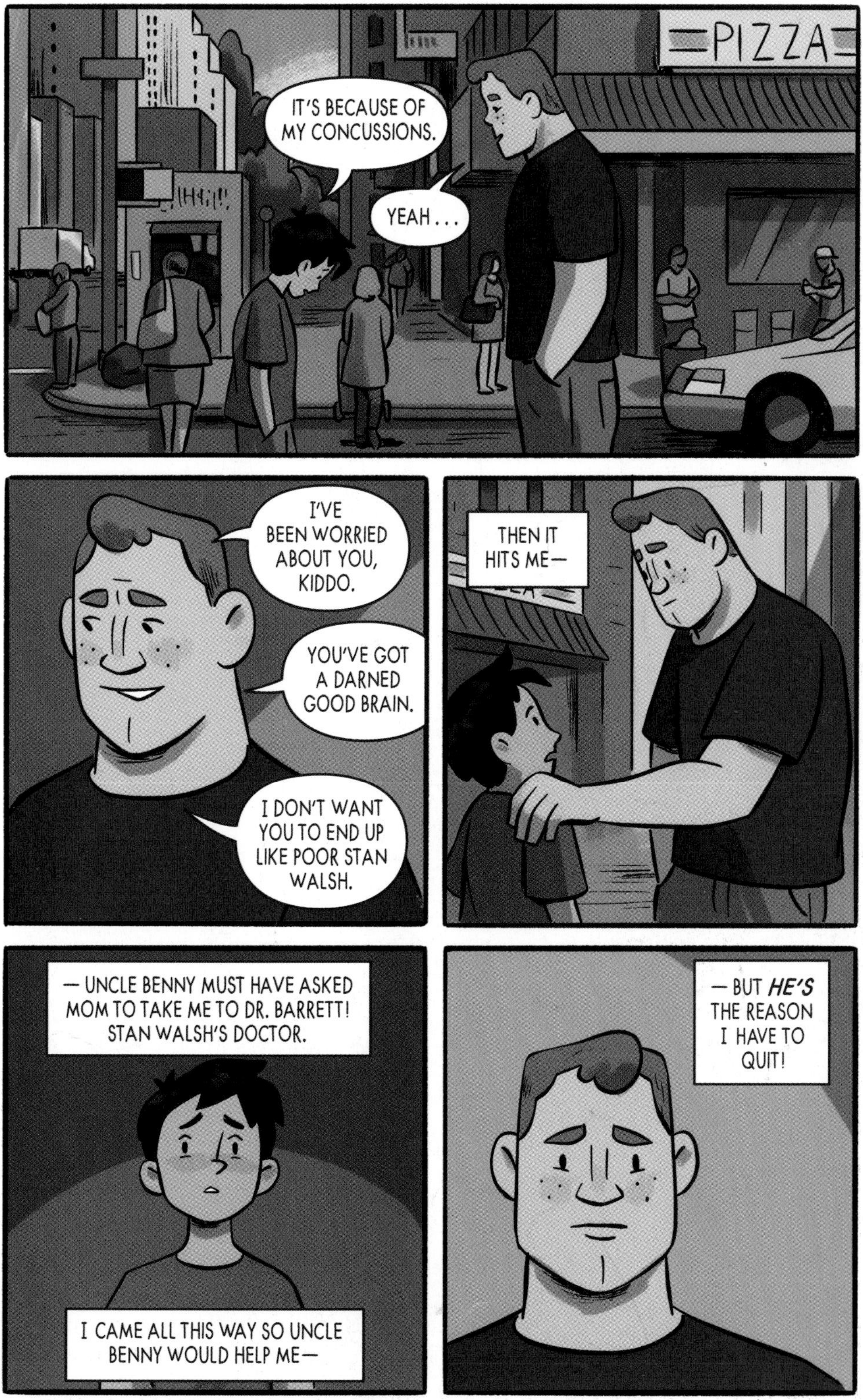
PIZZA
IT'S BECAUSE OF MY CONCUSSIONS.
YEAH . . .
I'VE BEEN WORRIED ABOUT YOU, KIDDO.
YOU'VE GOT A DARNED GOOD BRAIN.
I DON'T WANT YOU TO END UP LIKE POOR STAN WALSH.
THEN IT HITS ME—
— UNCLE BENNY MUST HAVE ASKED MOM TO TAKE ME TO DR. BARRETT! STAN WALSH'S DOCTOR.
I CAME ALL THIS WAY SO UNCLE BENNY WOULD HELP ME—
— BUT *HE'S* THE REASON I HAVE TO QUIT!

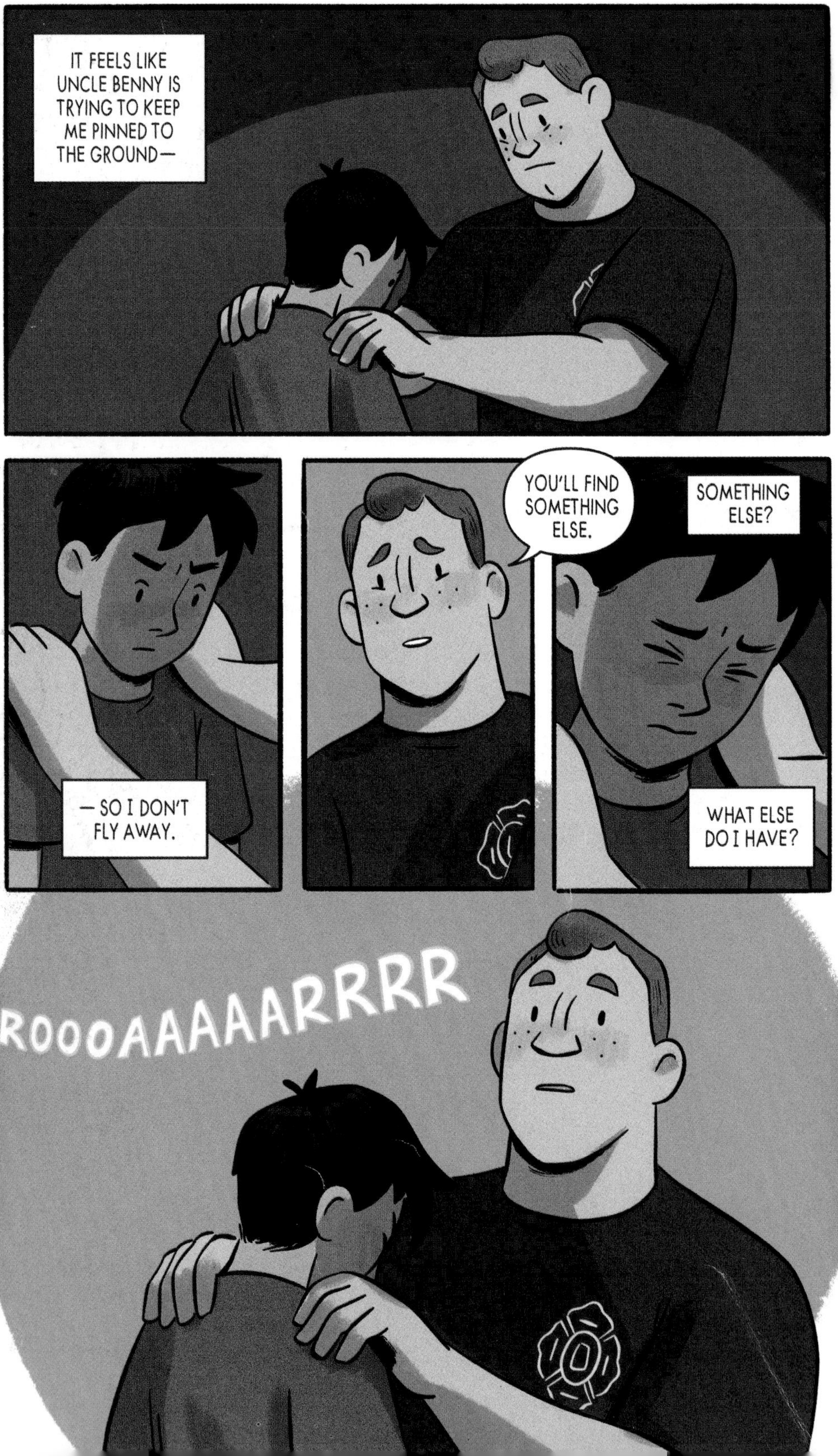
IT FEELS LIKE UNCLE BENNY IS TRYING TO KEEP ME PINNED TO THE GROUND—
— SO I DON'T FLY AWAY.
YOU'LL FIND SOMETHING ELSE.
SOMETHING ELSE?
WHAT ELSE DO I HAVE?
ROOOAAAAARRRR

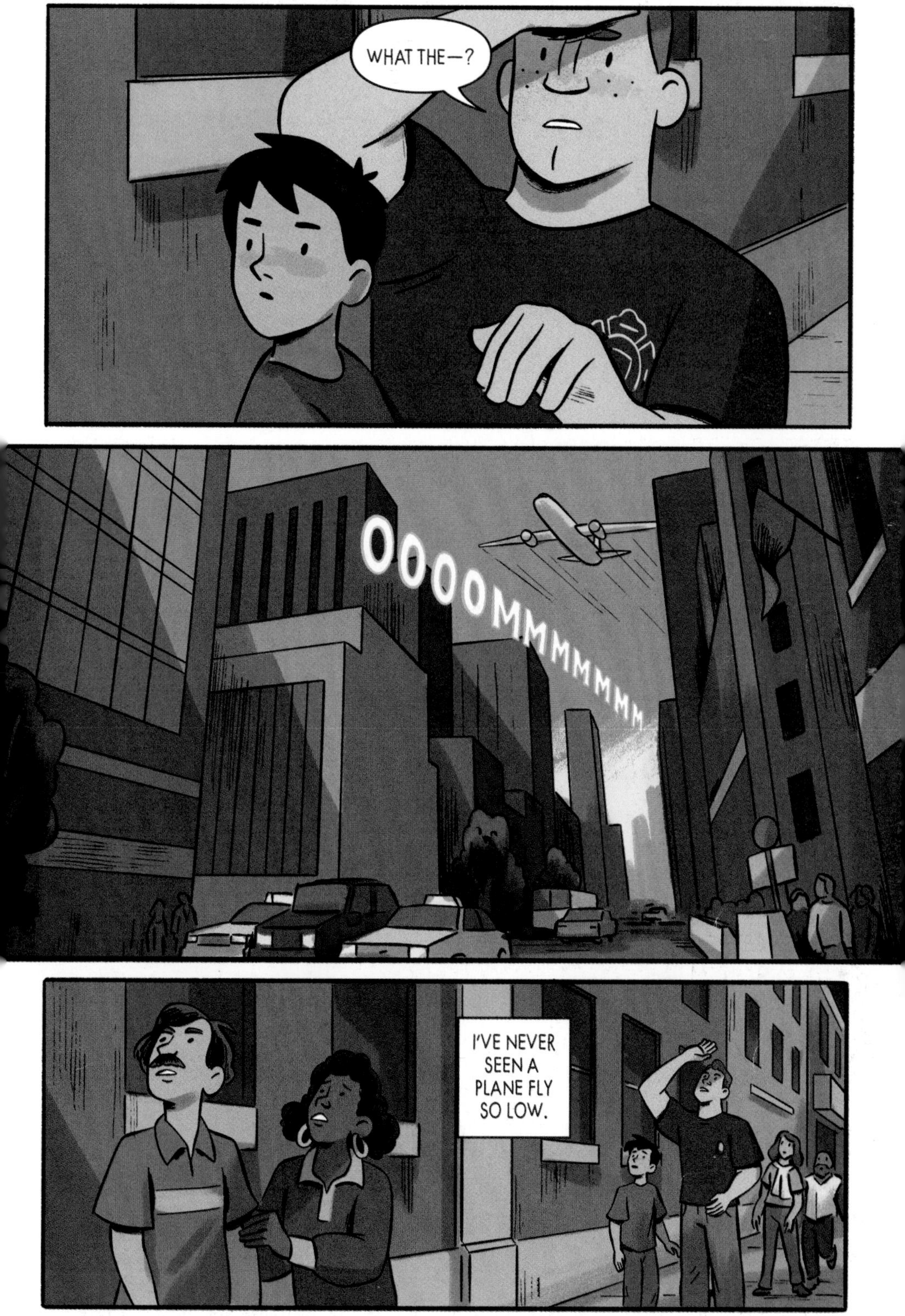
WHAT THE—?
OOOOMMMMMMMM
I'VE NEVER SEEN A PLANE FLY SO LOW.

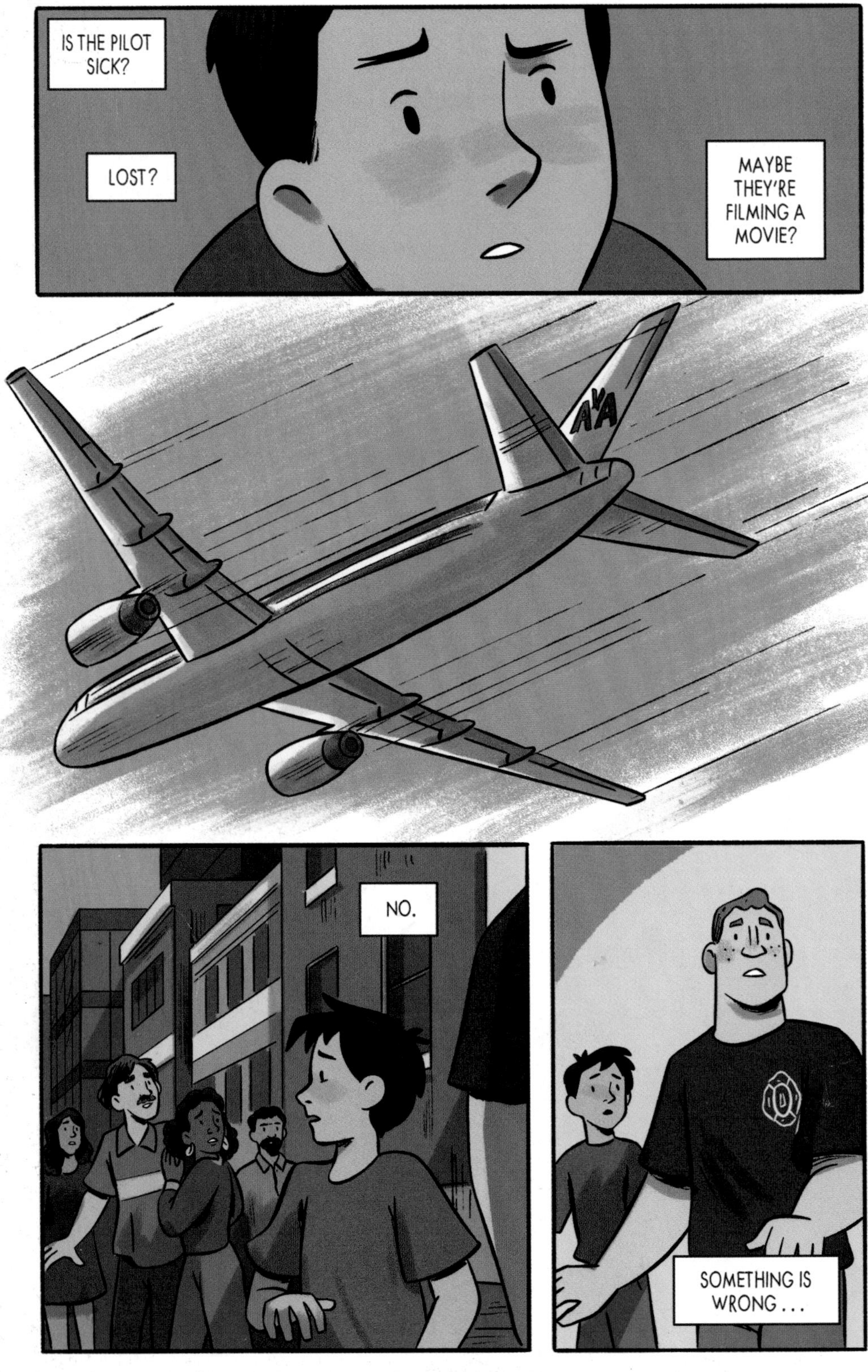
IS THE PILOT SICK?
LOST?
MAYBE THEY'RE FILMING A MOVIE?
AA
NO.
SOMETHING IS WRONG . . .

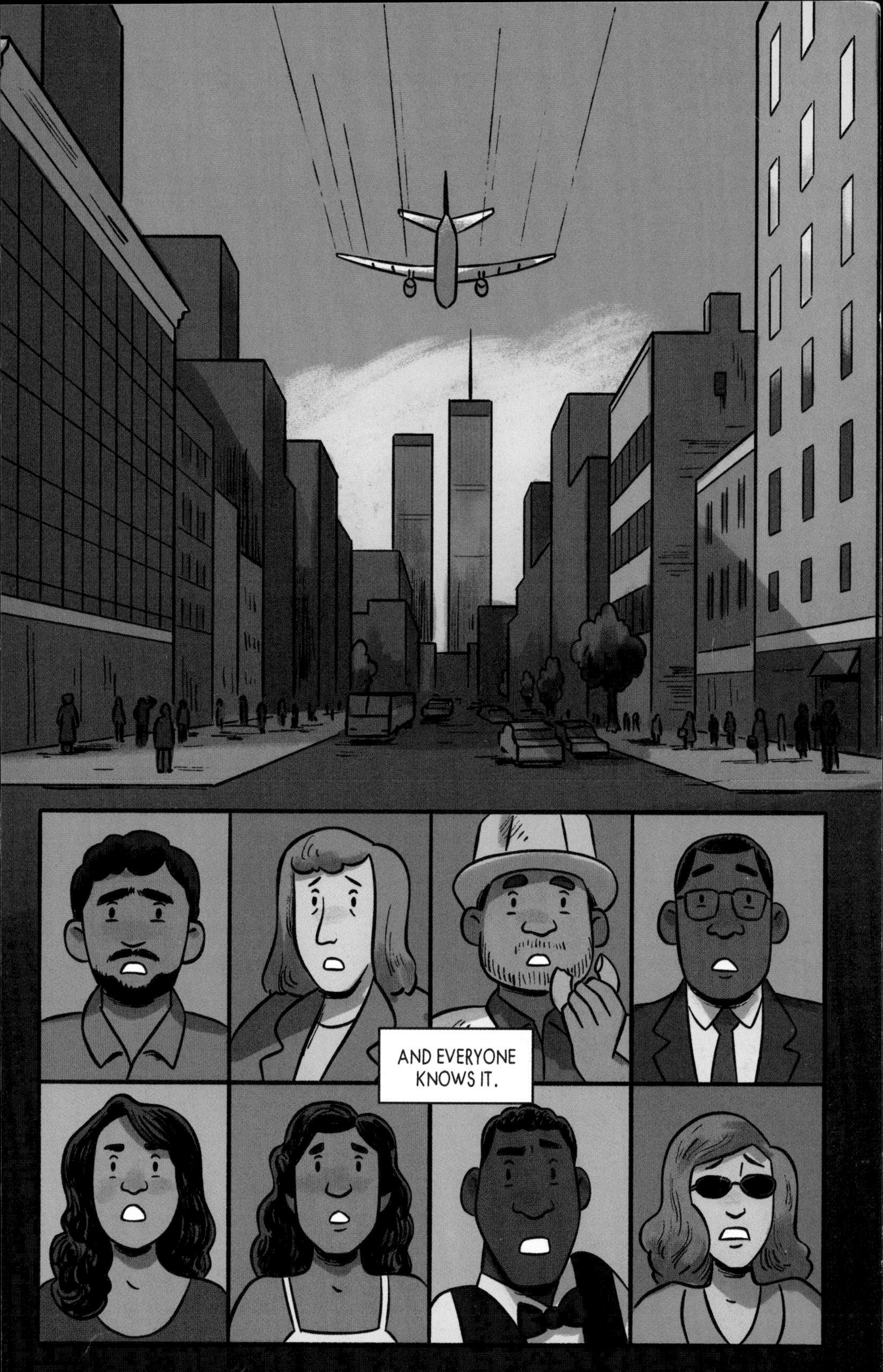
AND EVERYONE KNOWS IT.

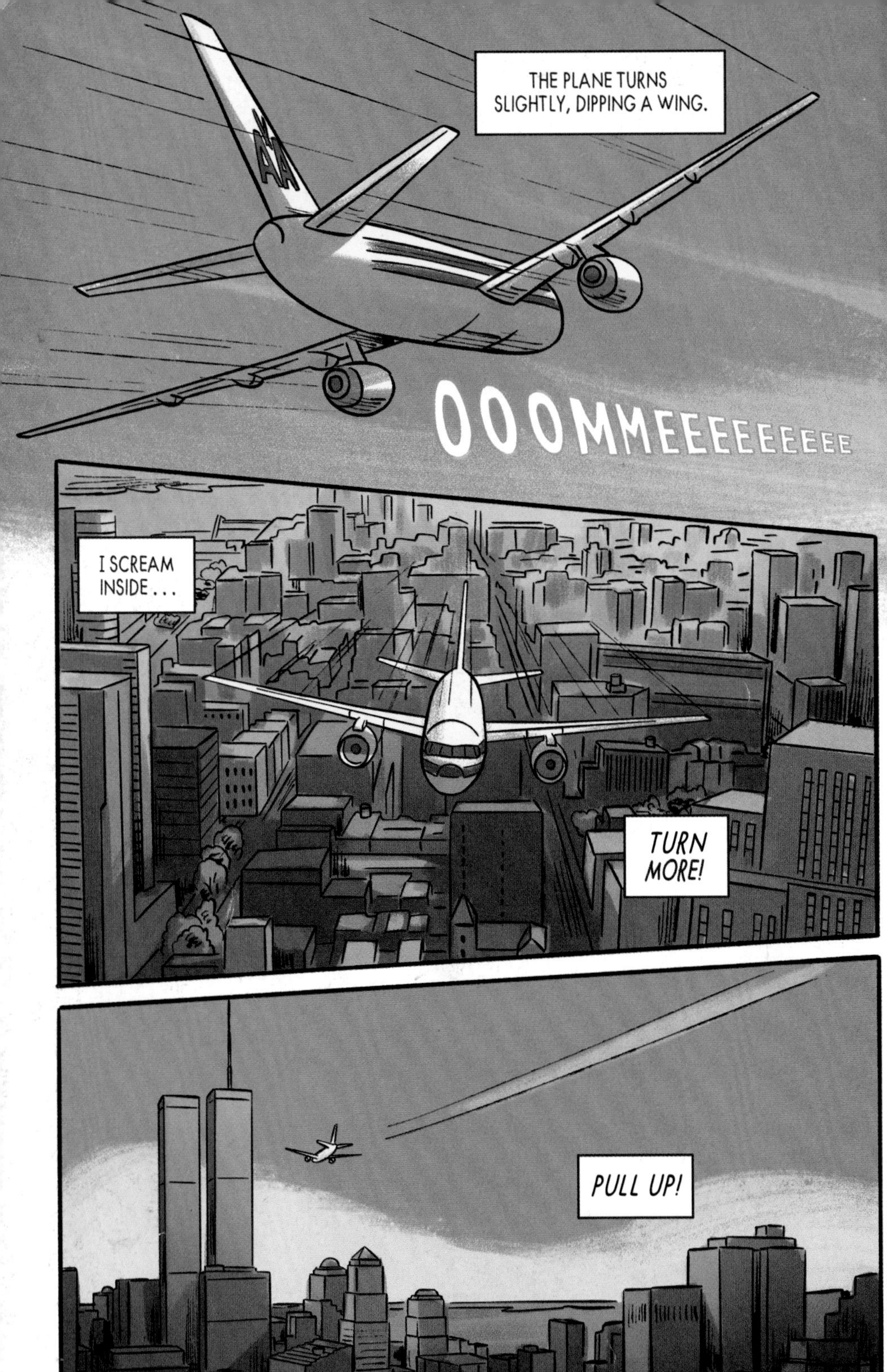
THE PLANE TURNS SLIGHTLY, DIPPING A WING.
OOOMMEEEEEEEEE
I SCREAM INSIDE . . .
TURN MORE!
PULL UP!

BUT IT DOESN'T.
EEERRRNCHHH
I HALF EXPECT IT TO FLY OUT THE OTHER SIDE . . .

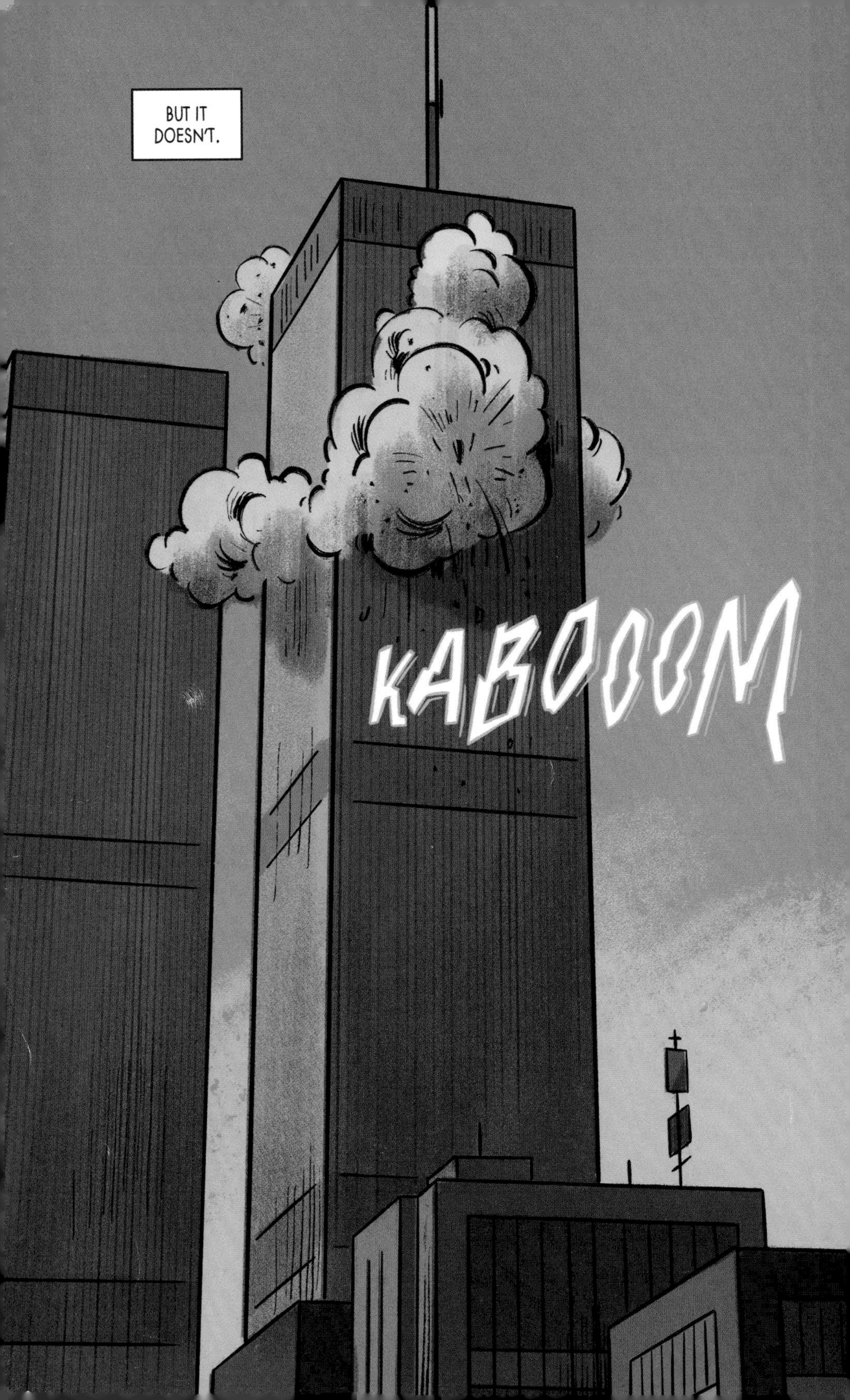
BUT IT DOESN'T.
KABOOOM

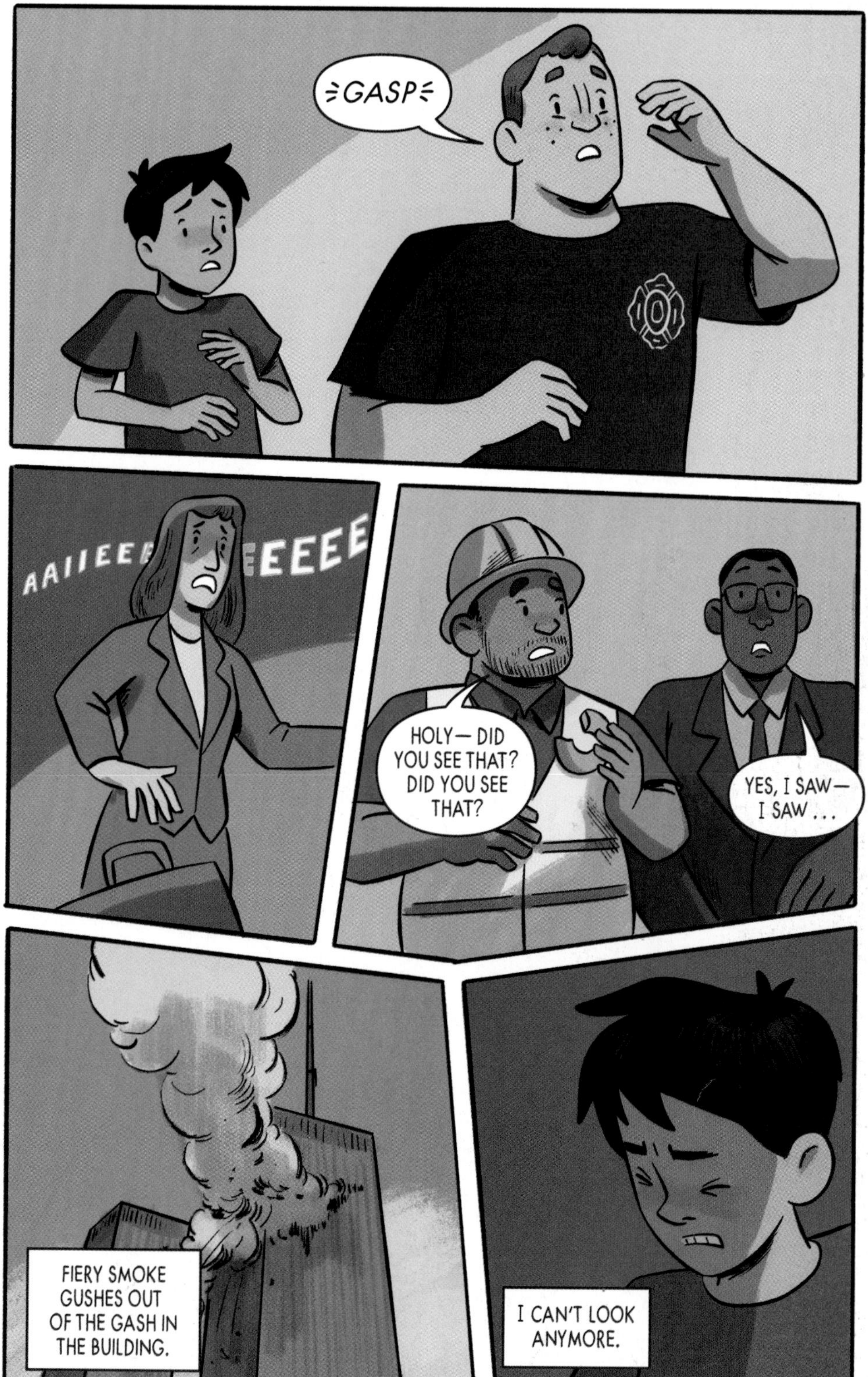

GASP
AAIIEEEEEEEE
HOLY— DID YOU SEE THAT? DID YOU SEE THAT?
YES, I SAW— I SAW . . .
FIERY SMOKE GUSHES OUT OF THE GASH IN THE BUILDING.
I CAN'T LOOK ANYMORE.

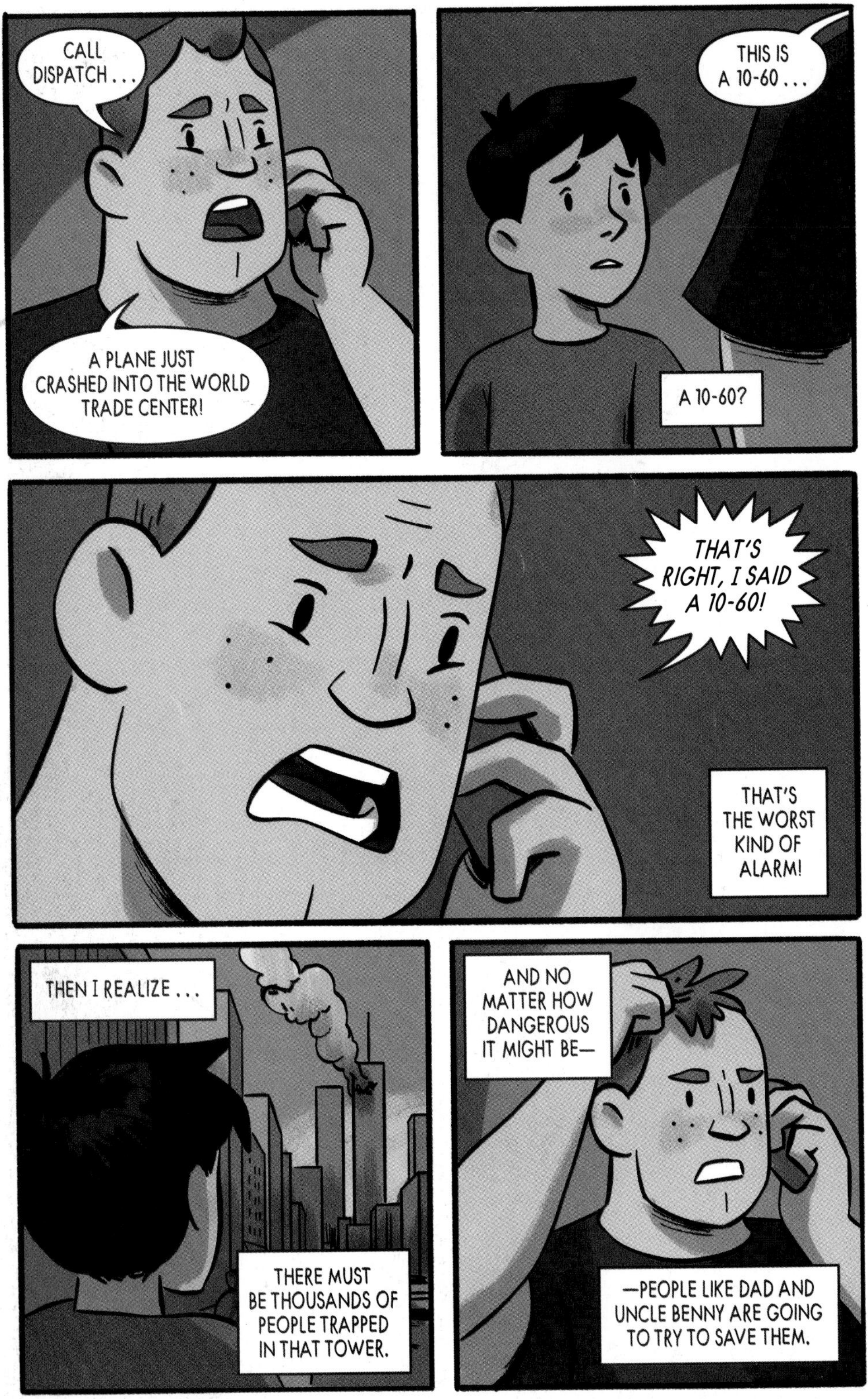
CALL DISPATCH . . .
A PLANE JUST CRASHED INTO THE WORLD TRADE CENTER!
THIS IS A 10-60 . . .
A 10-60?
THAT'S RIGHT, I SAID A 10-60!
THAT'S THE WORST KIND OF ALARM!
THEN I REALIZE . . .
THERE MUST BE THOUSANDS OF PEOPLE TRAPPED IN THAT TOWER.
AND NO MATTER HOW DANGEROUS IT MIGHT BE—
—PEOPLE LIKE DAD AND UNCLE BENNY ARE GOING TO TRY TO SAVE THEM.

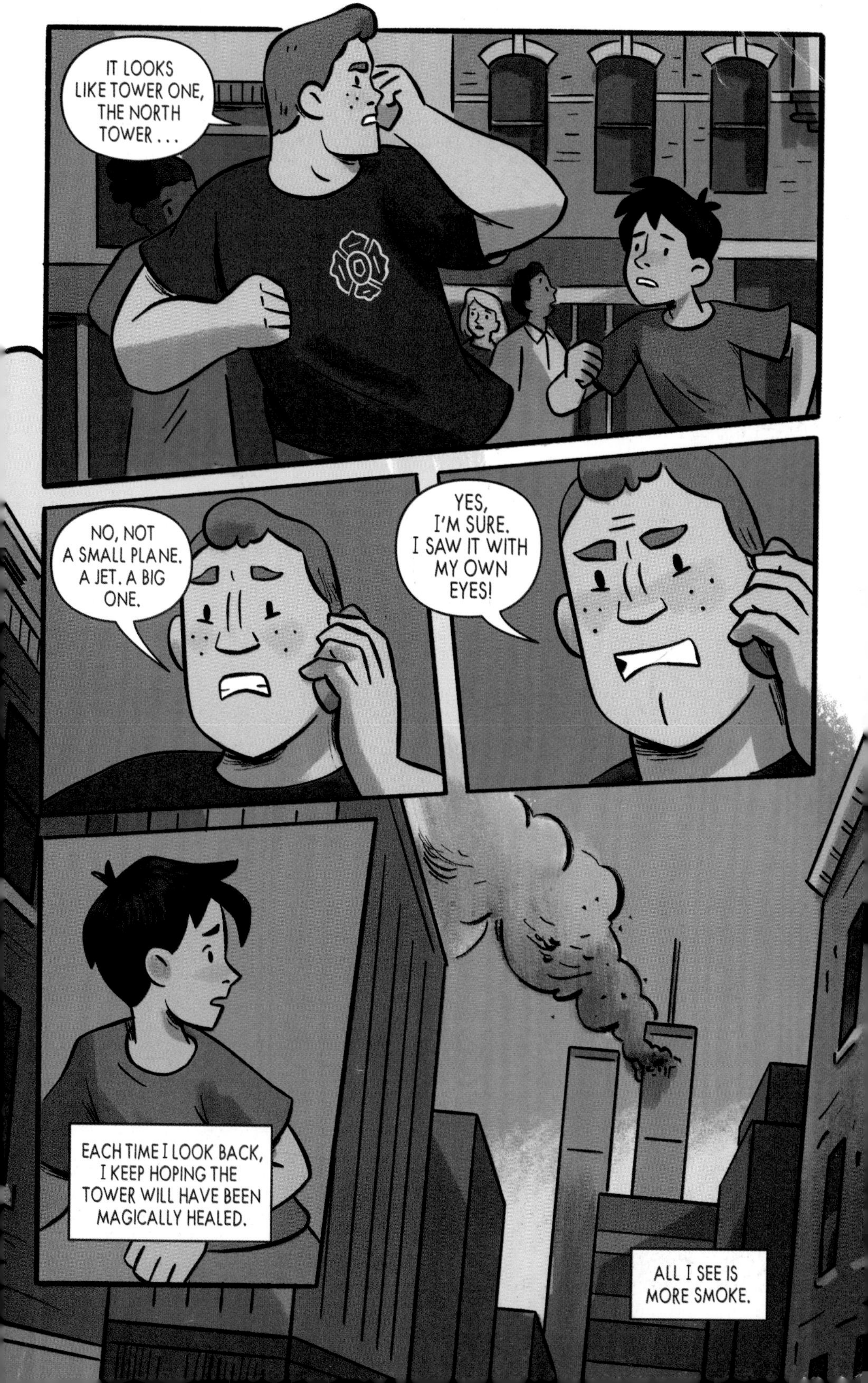
IT LOOKS LIKE TOWER ONE, THE NORTH TOWER . . .
NO, NOT A SMALL PLANE. A JET. A BIG ONE.
YES, I'M SURE. I SAW IT WITH MY OWN EYES!
EACH TIME I LOOK BACK, I KEEP HOPING THE TOWER WILL HAVE BEEN MAGICALLY HEALED.
ALL I SEE IS MORE SMOKE.

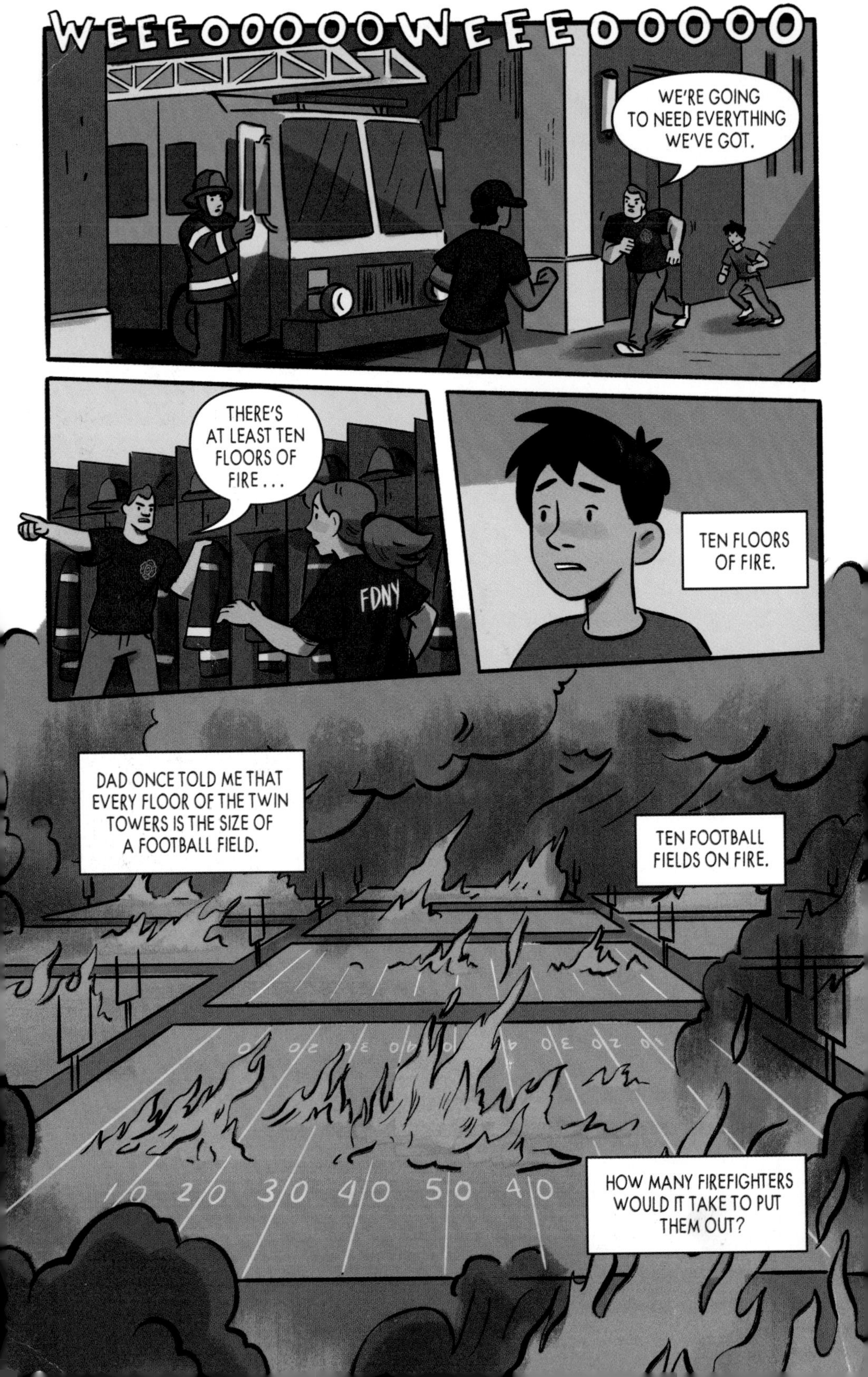
WEEEOOOOOWEEEOOOOO
WE'RE GOING TO NEED EVERYTHING WE'VE GOT.
THERE'S AT LEAST TEN FLOORS OF FIRE . . .
FDNY
TEN FLOORS OF FIRE.
DAD ONCE TOLD ME THAT EVERY FLOOR OF THE TWIN TOWERS IS THE SIZE OF A FOOTBALL FIELD.
TEN FOOTBALL FIELDS ON FIRE.
HOW MANY FIREFIGHTERS WOULD IT TAKE TO PUT THEM OUT?

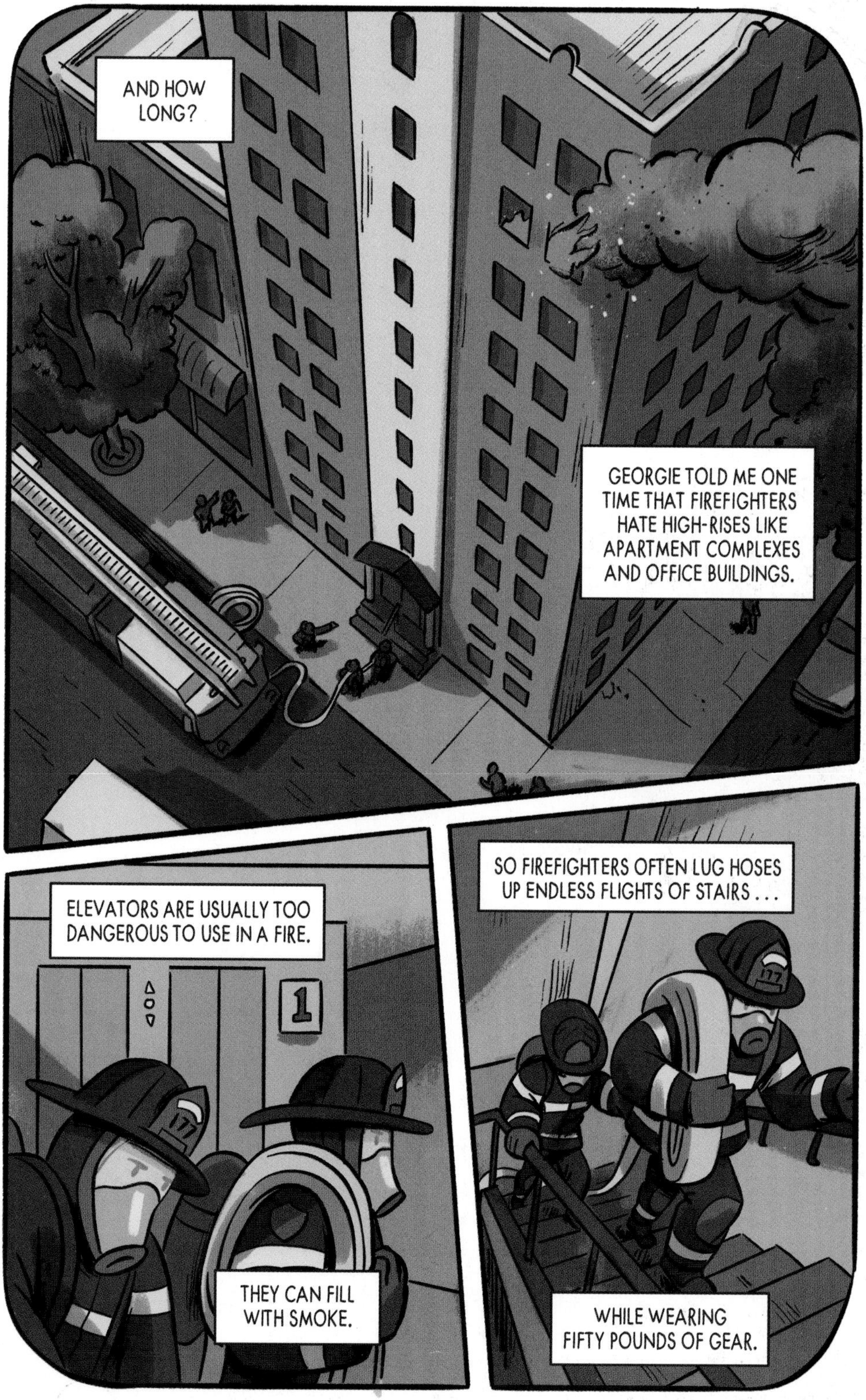
AND HOW LONG?
GEORGIE TOLD ME ONE TIME THAT FIREFIGHTERS HATE HIGH-RISES LIKE APARTMENT COMPLEXES AND OFFICE BUILDINGS.
ELEVATORS ARE USUALLY TOO DANGEROUS TO USE IN A FIRE.
1
THEY CAN FILL WITH SMOKE.
SO FIREFIGHTERS OFTEN LUG HOSES UP ENDLESS FLIGHTS OF STAIRS . . .
WHILE WEARING FIFTY POUNDS OF GEAR.

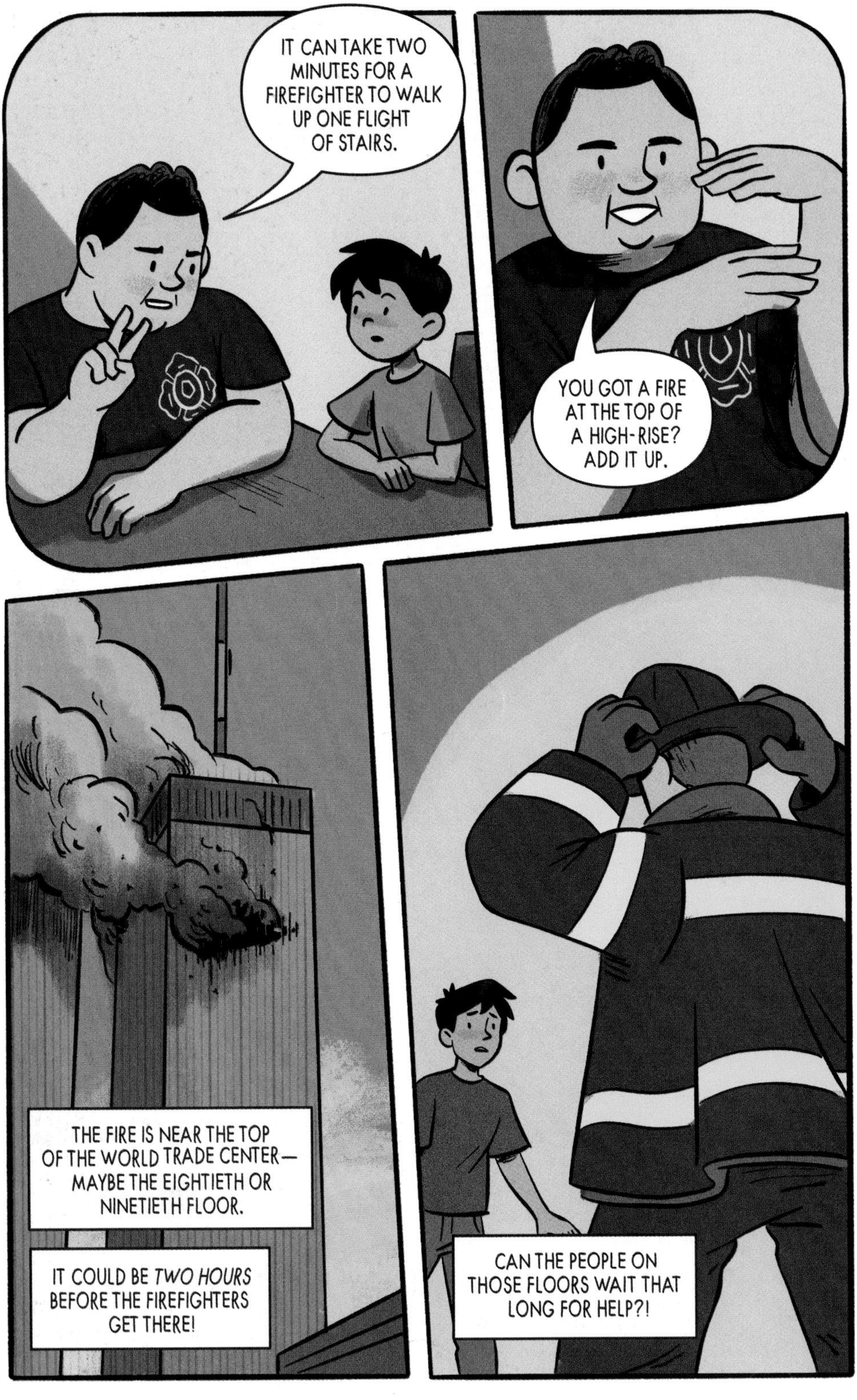
IT CAN TAKE TWO MINUTES FOR A FIREFIGHTER TO WALK UP ONE FLIGHT OF STAIRS.
YOU GOT A FIRE AT THE TOP OF A HIGH-RISE? ADD IT UP.
THE FIRE IS NEAR THE TOP OF THE WORLD TRADE CENTER— MAYBE THE EIGHTIETH OR NINETIETH FLOOR.
IT COULD BE *TWO HOURS* BEFORE THE FIREFIGHTERS GET THERE!
CAN THE PEOPLE ON THOSE FLOORS WAIT THAT LONG FOR HELP?!

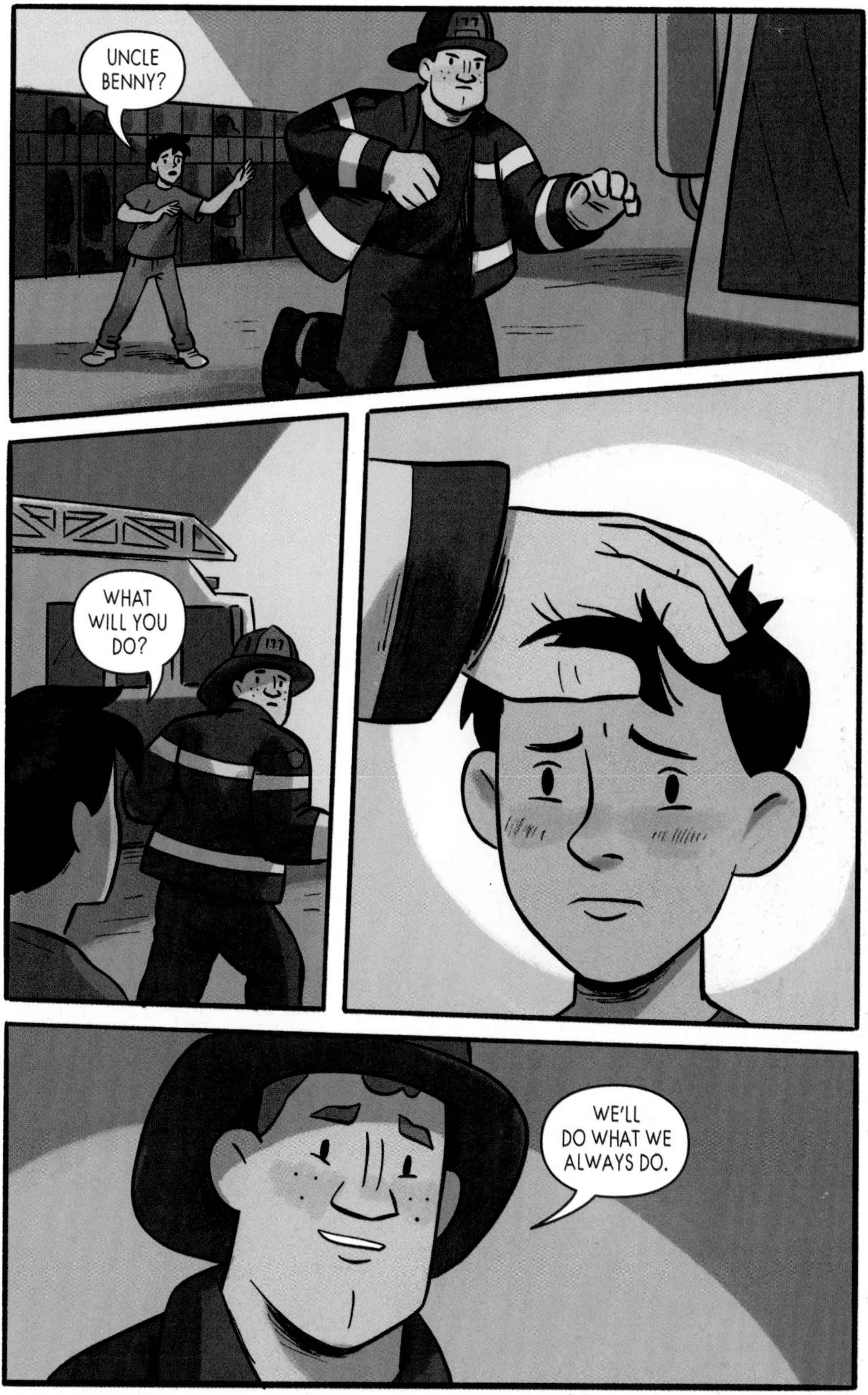
UNCLE BENNY?
WHAT WILL YOU DO?
WE'LL DO WHAT WE ALWAYS DO.

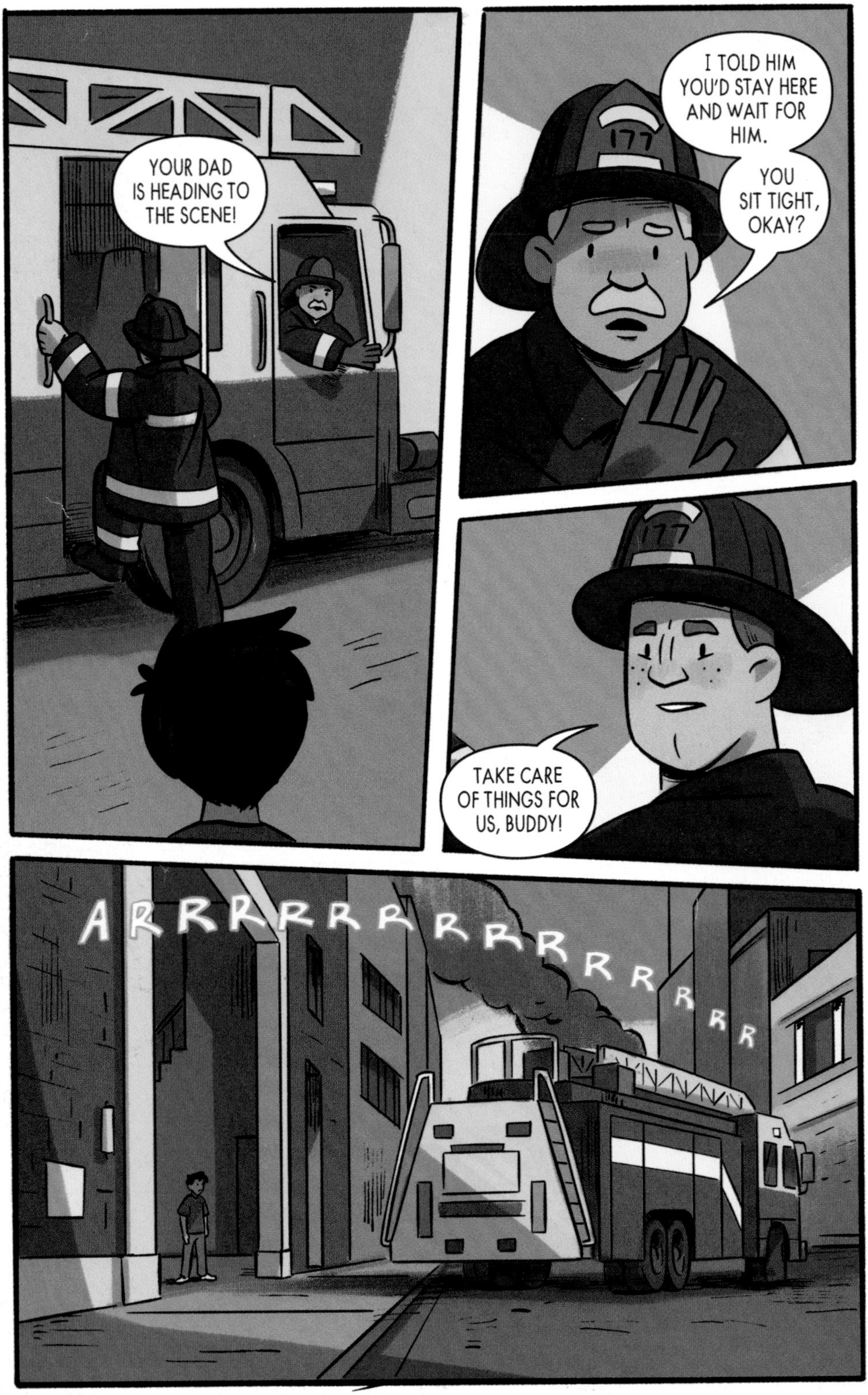
YOUR DAD IS HEADING TO THE SCENE!
I TOLD HIM YOU'D STAY HERE AND WAIT FOR HIM.
YOU SIT TIGHT, OKAY?
TAKE CARE OF THINGS FOR US, BUDDY!
ARRRRRRRRRRRRRRR

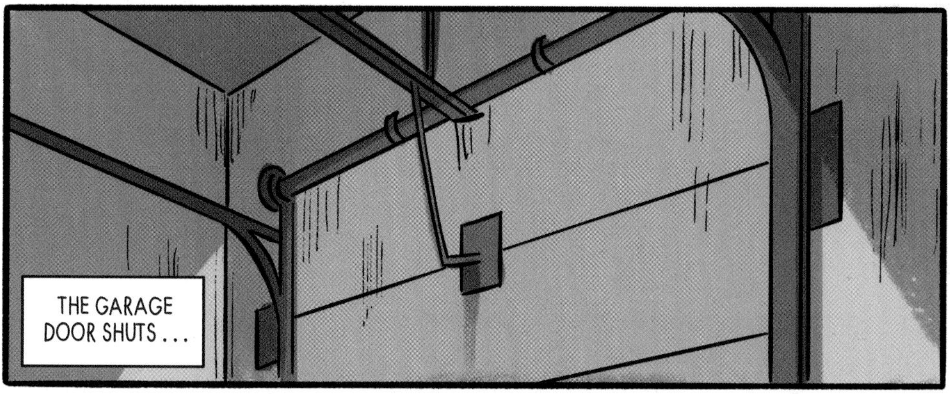
THE GARAGE DOOR SHUTS . . .

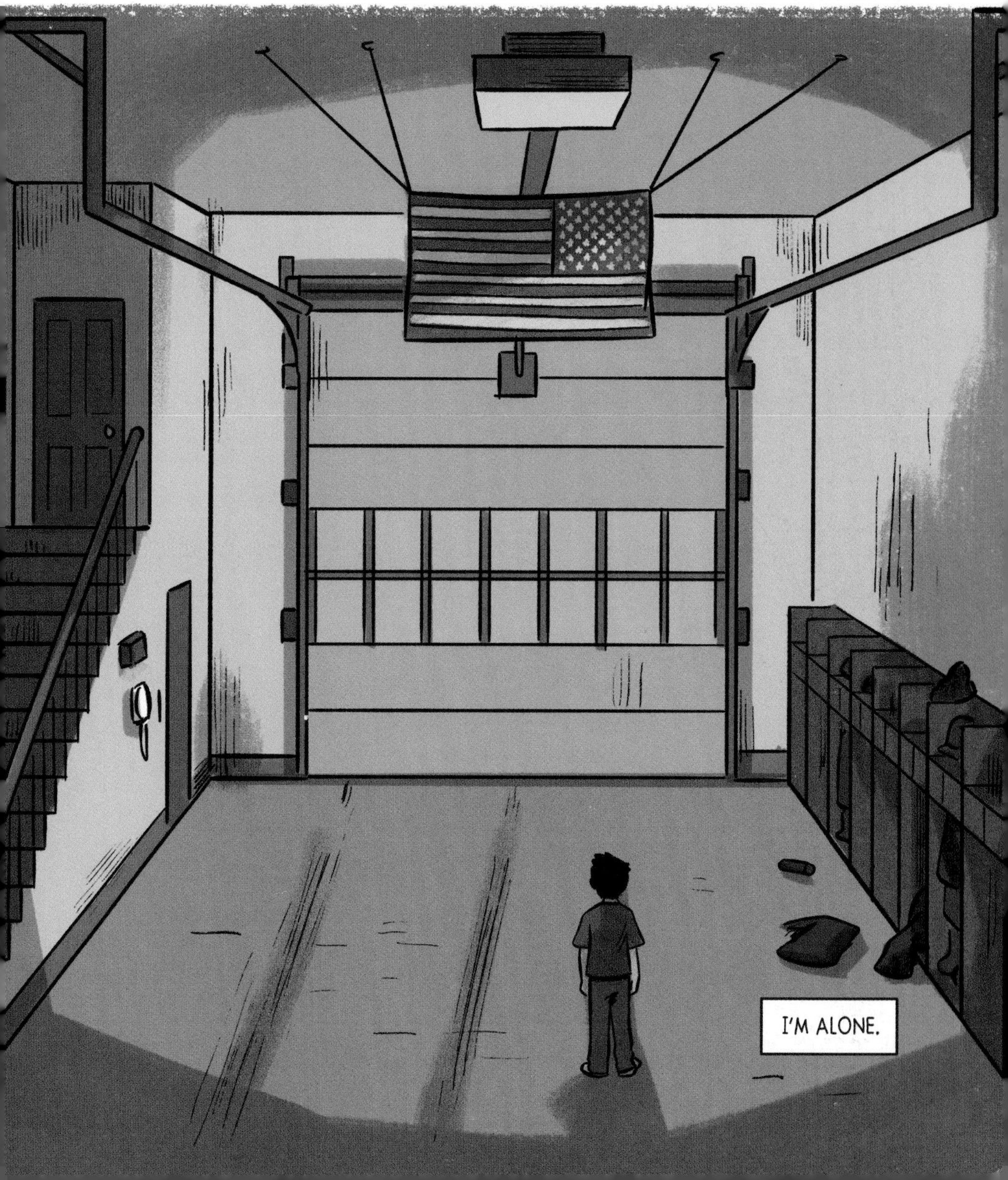
I'M ALONE.

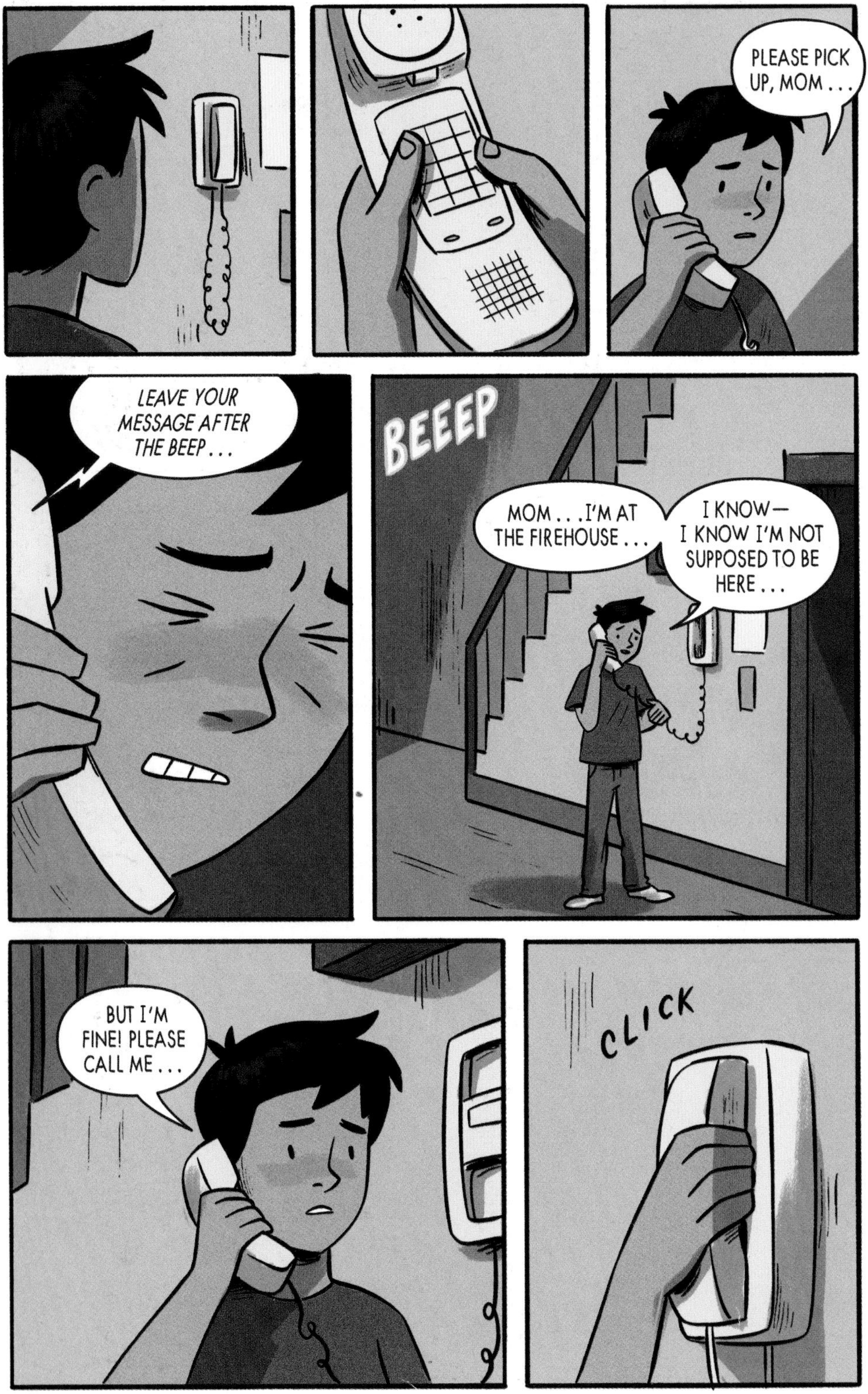
PLEASE PICK UP, MOM . . .
LEAVE YOUR MESSAGE AFTER THE BEEP . . .
BEEEP
MOM . . . I'M AT THE FIREHOUSE . . .
I KNOW— I KNOW I'M NOT SUPPOSED TO BE HERE . . .
BUT I'M FINE! PLEASE CALL ME . . .
CLICK

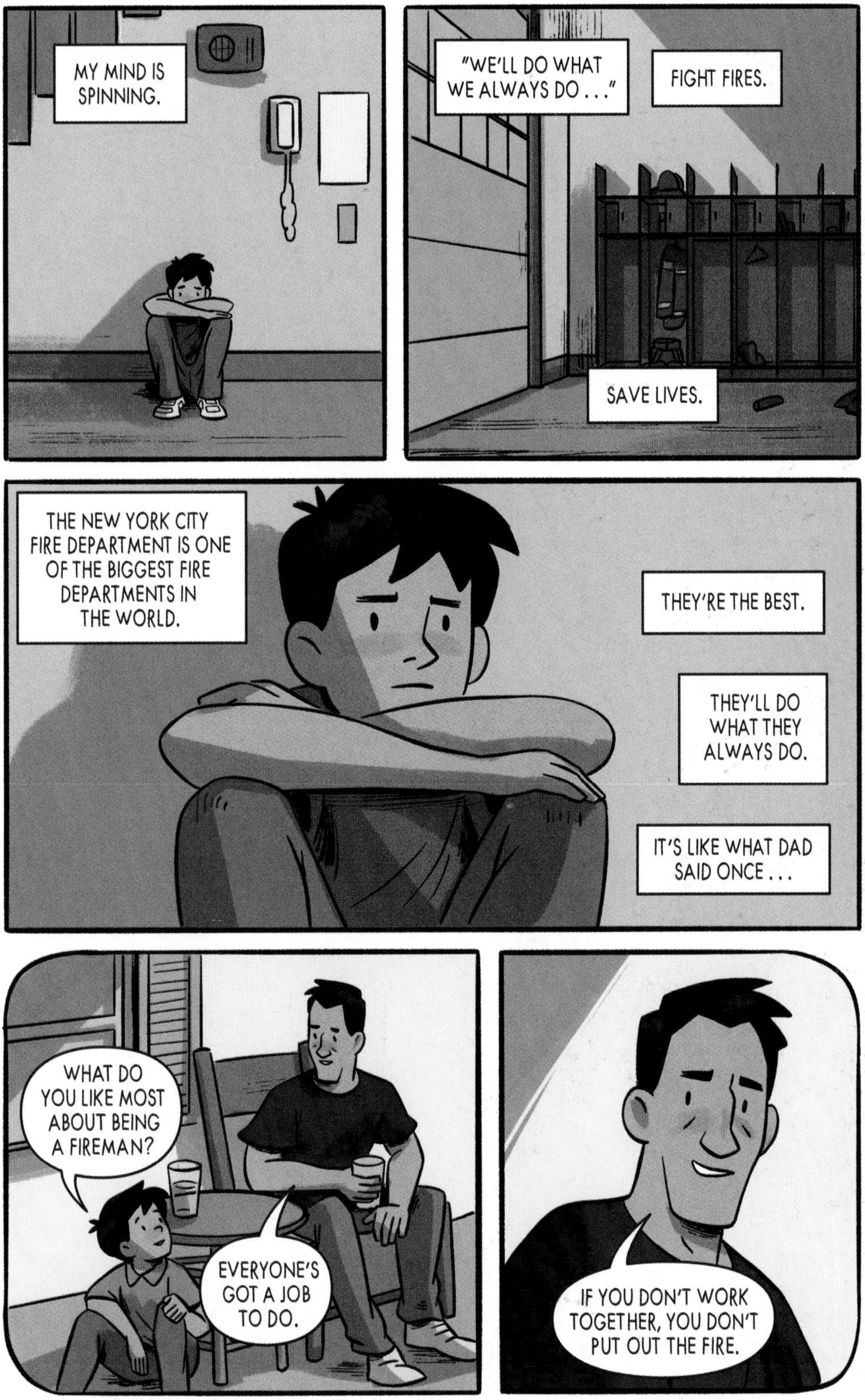
MY MIND IS SPINNING.
"WE'LL DO WHAT WE ALWAYS DO . . ."
FIGHT FIRES.
SAVE LIVES.
THE NEW YORK CITY FIRE DEPARTMENT IS ONE OF THE BIGGEST FIRE DEPARTMENTS IN THE WORLD.
THEY'RE THE BEST.
THEY'LL DO WHAT THEY ALWAYS DO.
IT'S LIKE WHAT DAD SAID ONCE . . .
WHAT DO YOU LIKE MOST ABOUT BEING A FIREMAN?
EVERYONE'S GOT A JOB TO DO.
IF YOU DON'T WORK TOGETHER, YOU DON'T PUT OUT THE FIRE.

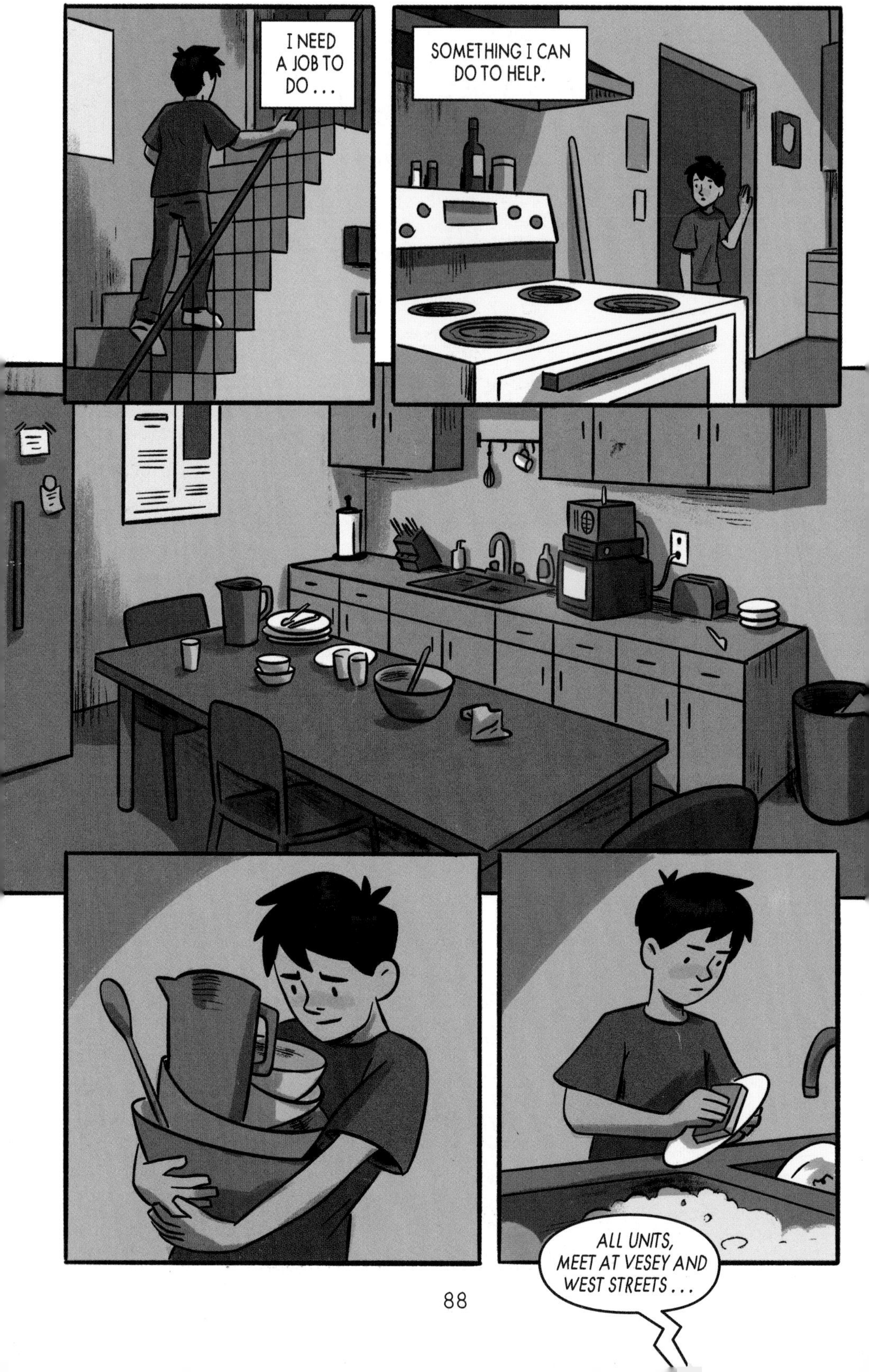
I NEED A JOB TO DO . . .
SOMETHING I CAN DO TO HELP.
ALL UNITS, MEET AT VESEY AND WEST STREETS . . .

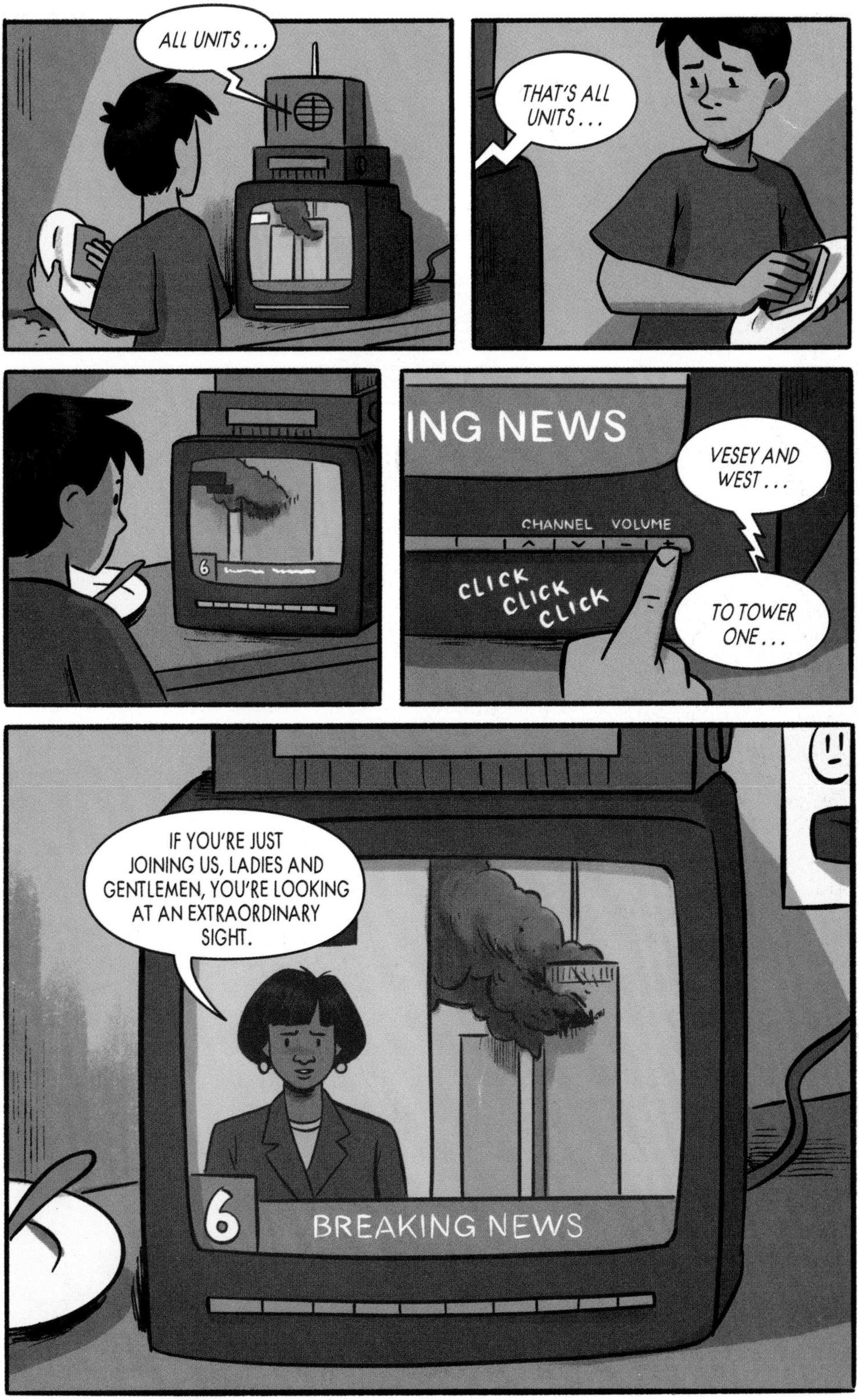
ALL UNITS . . .
THAT'S ALL UNITS . . .
ING NEWS
CHANNEL VOLUME
CLICK CLICK CLICK
VESEY AND WEST . . .
TO TOWER ONE . . .
IF YOU'RE JUST JOINING US, LADIES AND GENTLEMEN, YOU'RE LOOKING AT AN EXTRAORDINARY SIGHT.
6
BREAKING NEWS

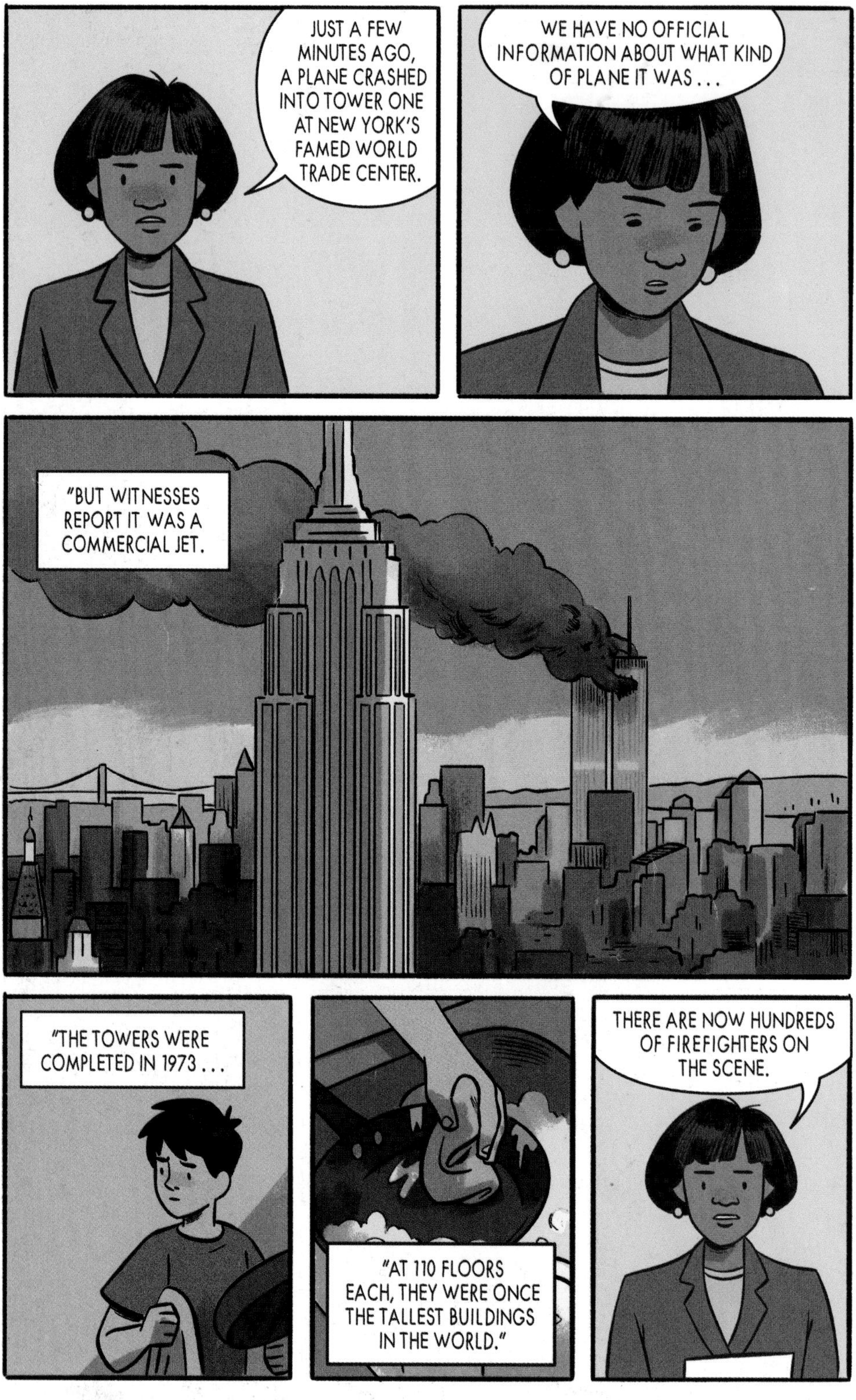
JUST A FEW MINUTES AGO, A PLANE CRASHED INTO TOWER ONE AT NEW YORK'S FAMED WORLD TRADE CENTER.
WE HAVE NO OFFICIAL INFORMATION ABOUT WHAT KIND OF PLANE IT WAS . . .
"BUT WITNESSES REPORT IT WAS A COMMERCIAL JET.
"THE TOWERS WERE COMPLETED IN 1973 . . .
"AT 110 FLOORS EACH, THEY WERE ONCE THE TALLEST BUILDINGS IN THE WORLD."
THERE ARE NOW HUNDREDS OF FIREFIGHTERS ON THE SCENE.

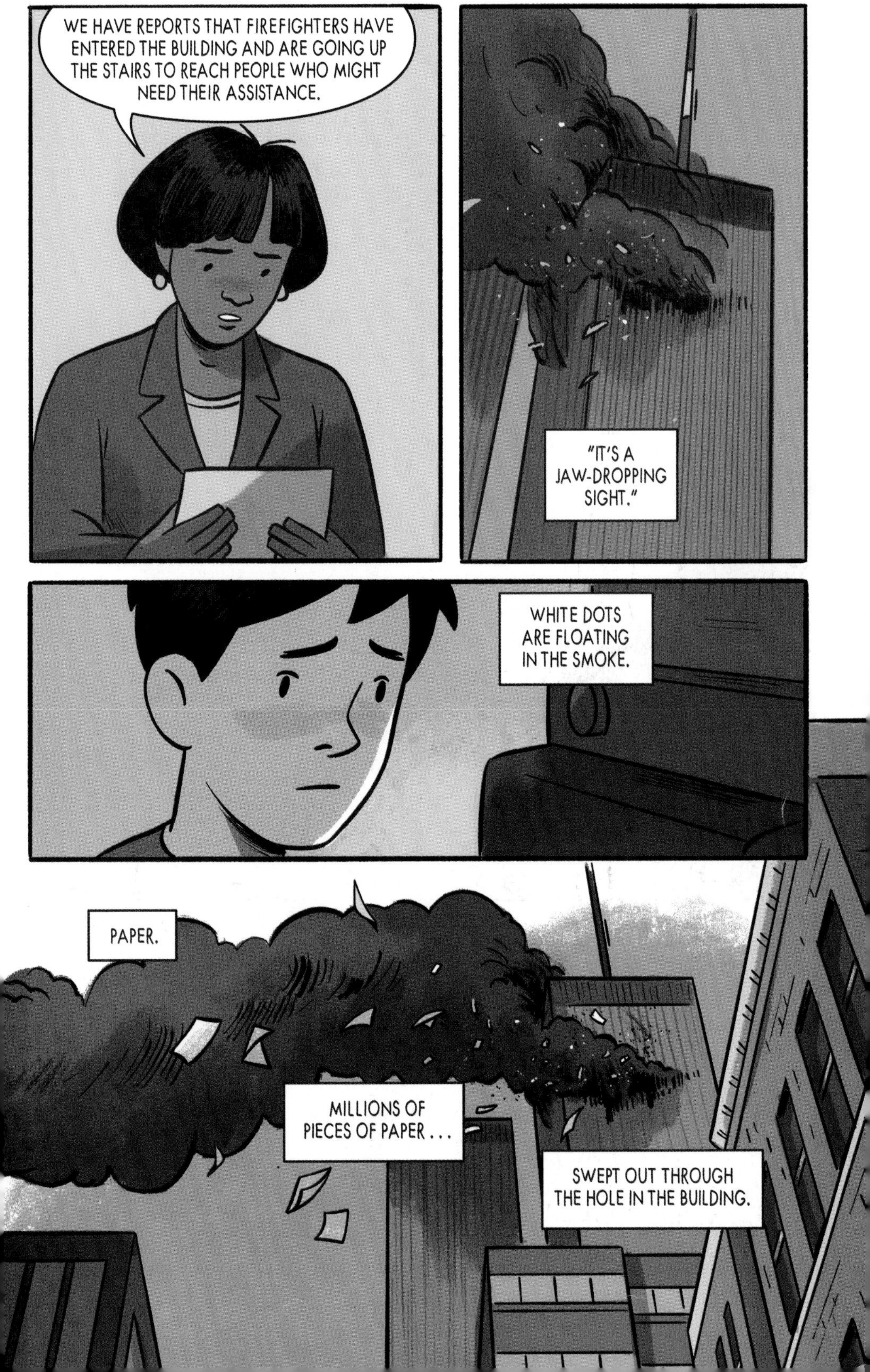
WE HAVE REPORTS THAT FIREFIGHTERS HAVE ENTERED THE BUILDING AND ARE GOING UP THE STAIRS TO REACH PEOPLE WHO MIGHT NEED THEIR ASSISTANCE.
"IT'S A JAW-DROPPING SIGHT."
WHITE DOTS ARE FLOATING IN THE SMOKE.
PAPER.
MILLIONS OF PIECES OF PAPER . . .
SWEPT OUT THROUGH THE HOLE IN THE BUILDING.

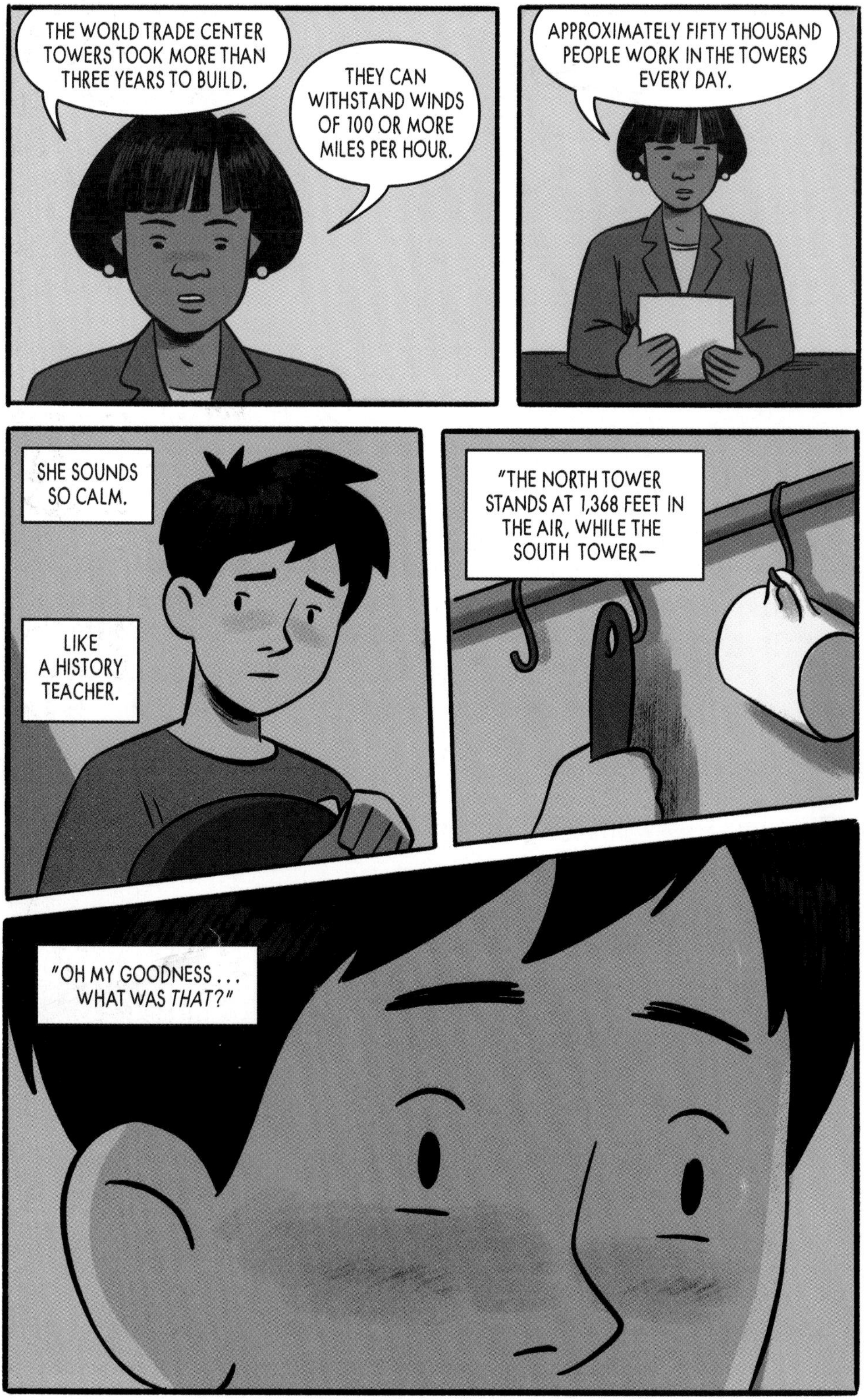
THE WORLD TRADE CENTER TOWERS TOOK MORE THAN THREE YEARS TO BUILD.
THEY CAN WITHSTAND WINDS OF 100 OR MORE MILES PER HOUR.
APPROXIMATELY FIFTY THOUSAND PEOPLE WORK IN THE TOWERS EVERY DAY.
SHE SOUNDS SO CALM.
LIKE A HISTORY TEACHER.
"THE NORTH TOWER STANDS AT 1,368 FEET IN THE AIR, WHILE THE SOUTH TOWER—
"OH MY GOODNESS . . . WHAT WAS *THAT*?"

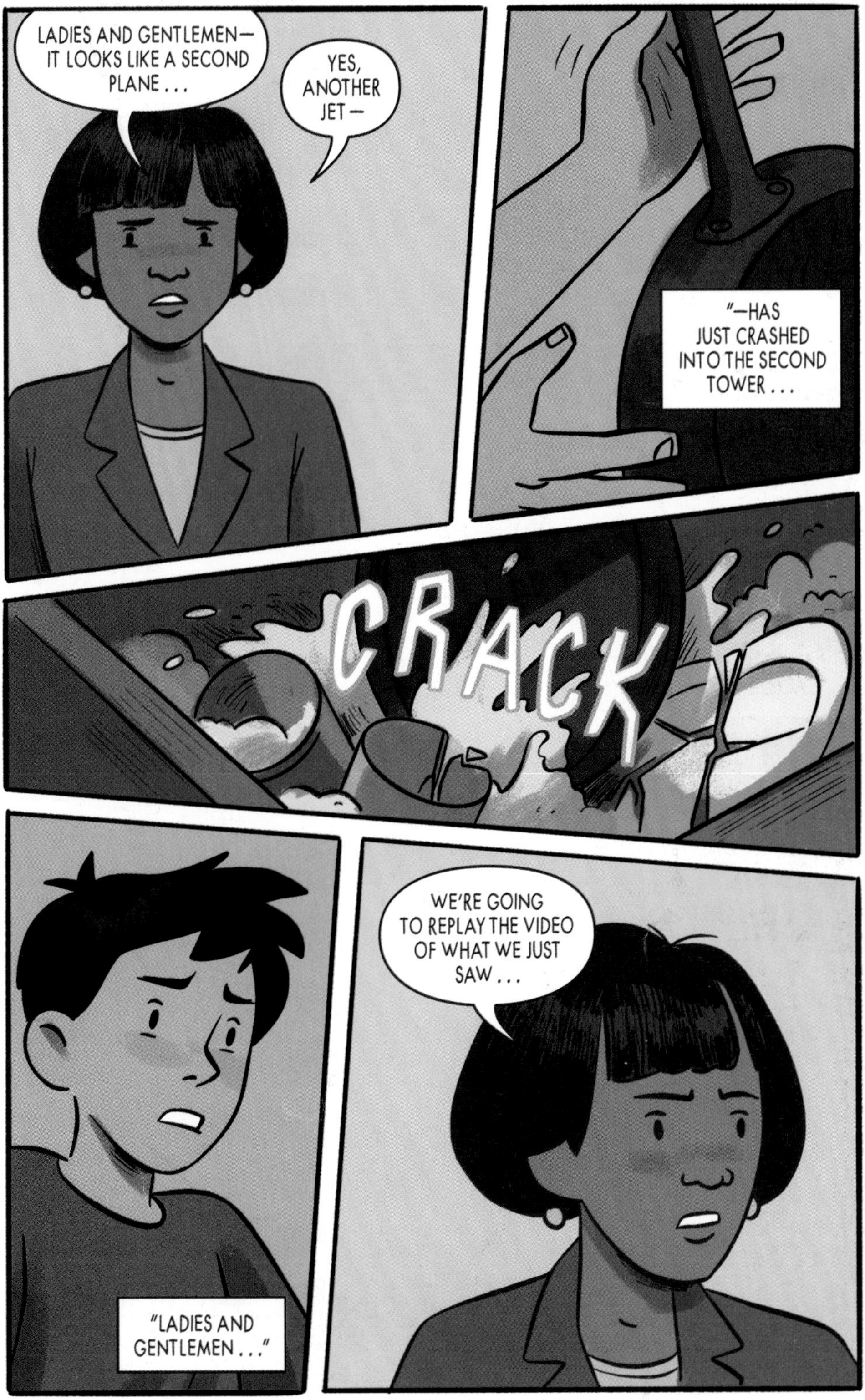
LADIES AND GENTLEMEN—IT LOOKS LIKE A SECOND PLANE . . .
YES, ANOTHER JET —
"—HAS JUST CRASHED INTO THE SECOND TOWER . . .
CRACK
"LADIES AND GENTLEMEN . . ."
WE'RE GOING TO REPLAY THE VIDEO OF WHAT WE JUST SAW . . .

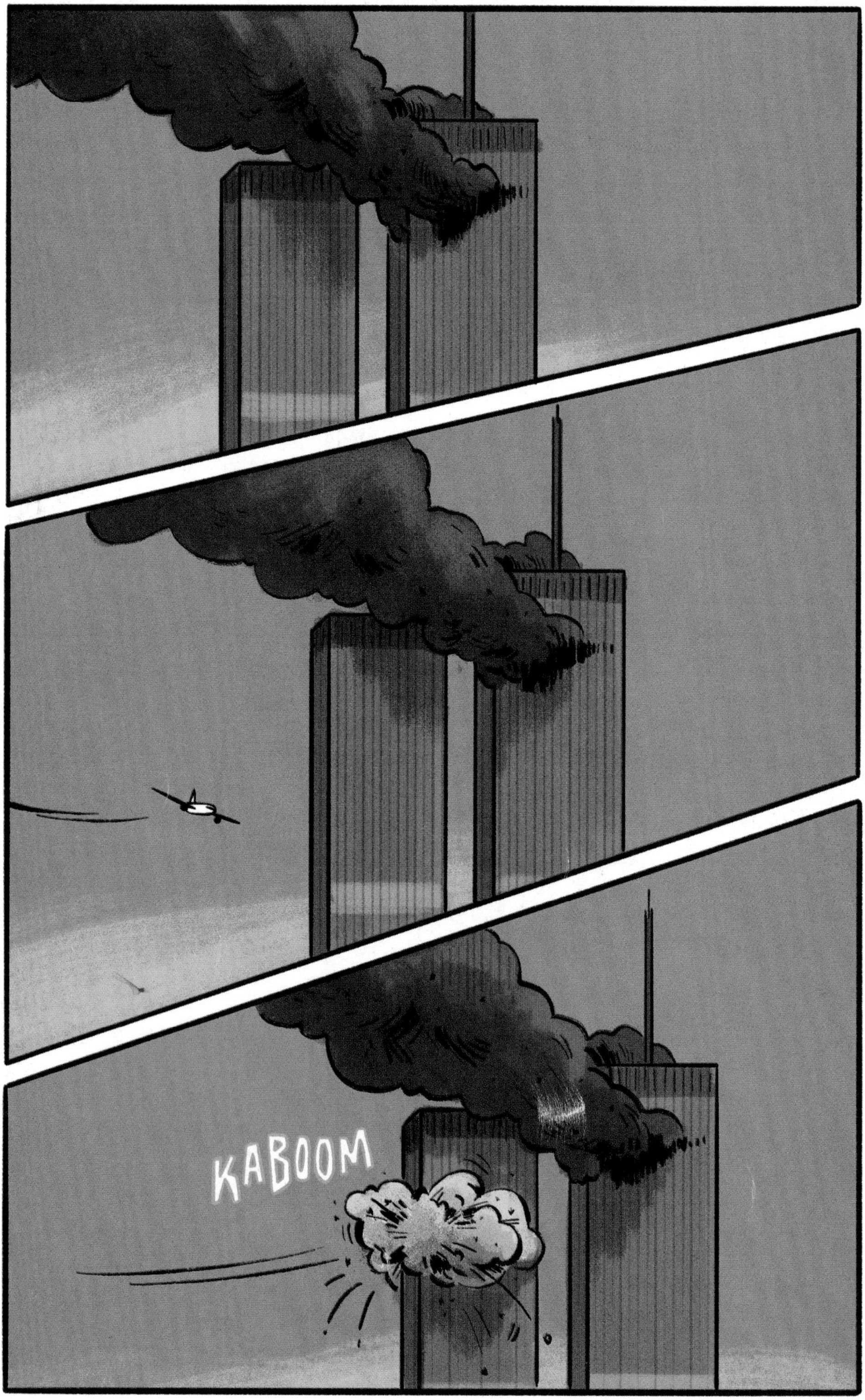
KABOOM

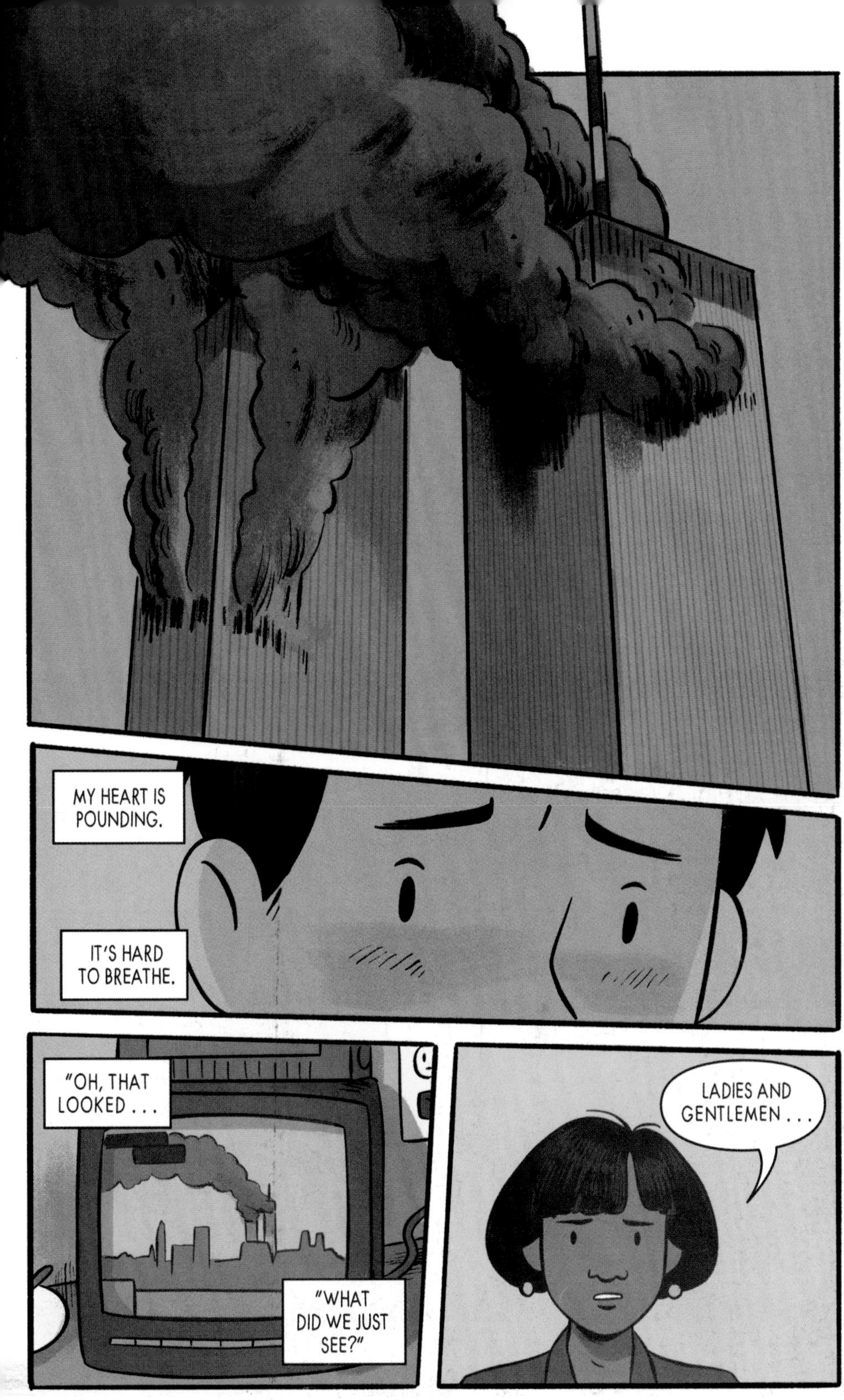
MY HEART IS POUNDING.
IT'S HARD TO BREATHE.
"OH, THAT LOOKED . . .
"WHAT DID WE JUST SEE?"
LADIES AND GENTLEMEN . . .

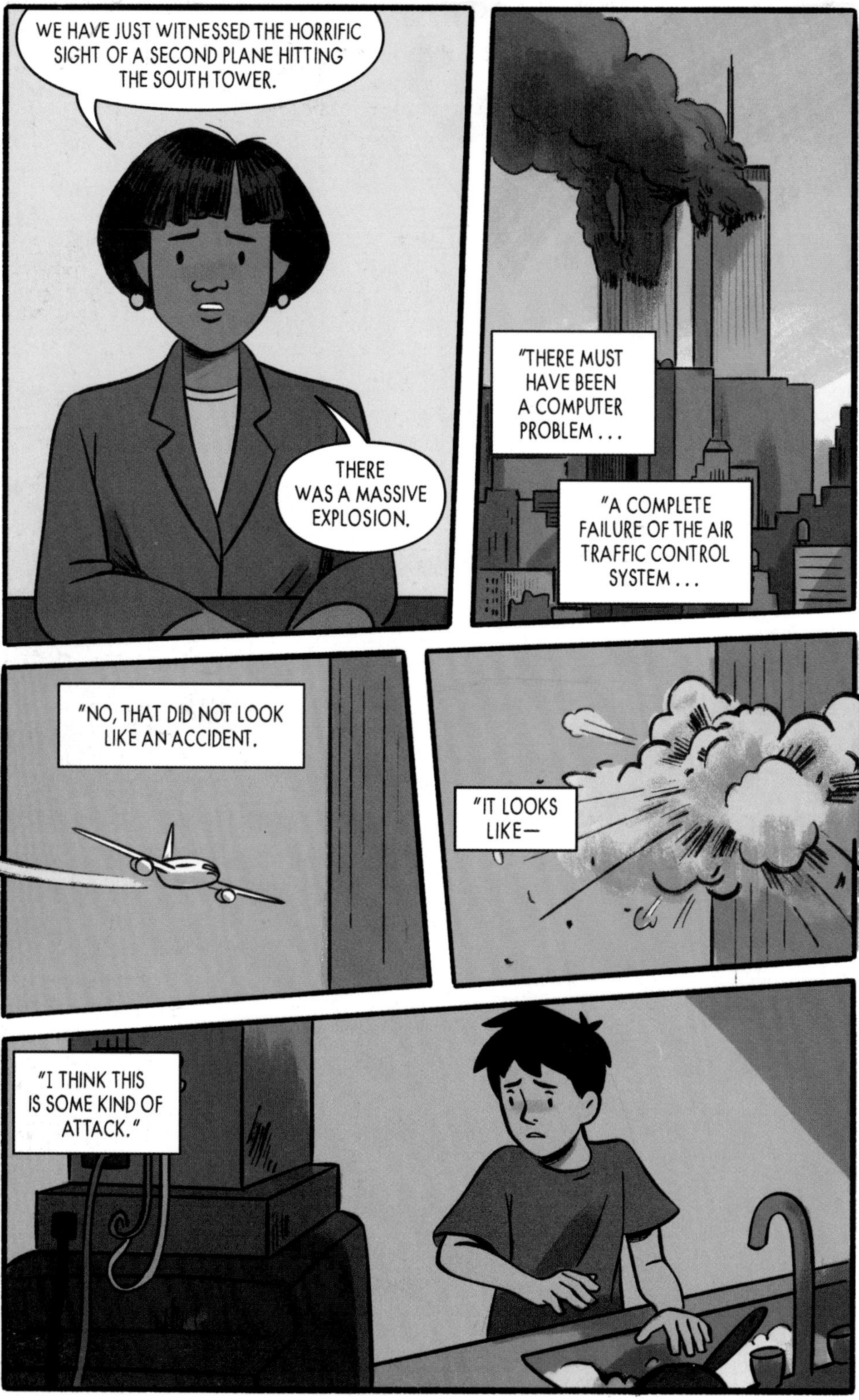
WE HAVE JUST WITNESSED THE HORRIFIC SIGHT OF A SECOND PLANE HITTING THE SOUTH TOWER.
THERE WAS A MASSIVE EXPLOSION.
"THERE MUST HAVE BEEN A COMPUTER PROBLEM . . .
"A COMPLETE FAILURE OF THE AIR TRAFFIC CONTROL SYSTEM . . .
"NO, THAT DID NOT LOOK LIKE AN ACCIDENT.
"IT LOOKS LIKE—
"I THINK THIS IS SOME KIND OF ATTACK."

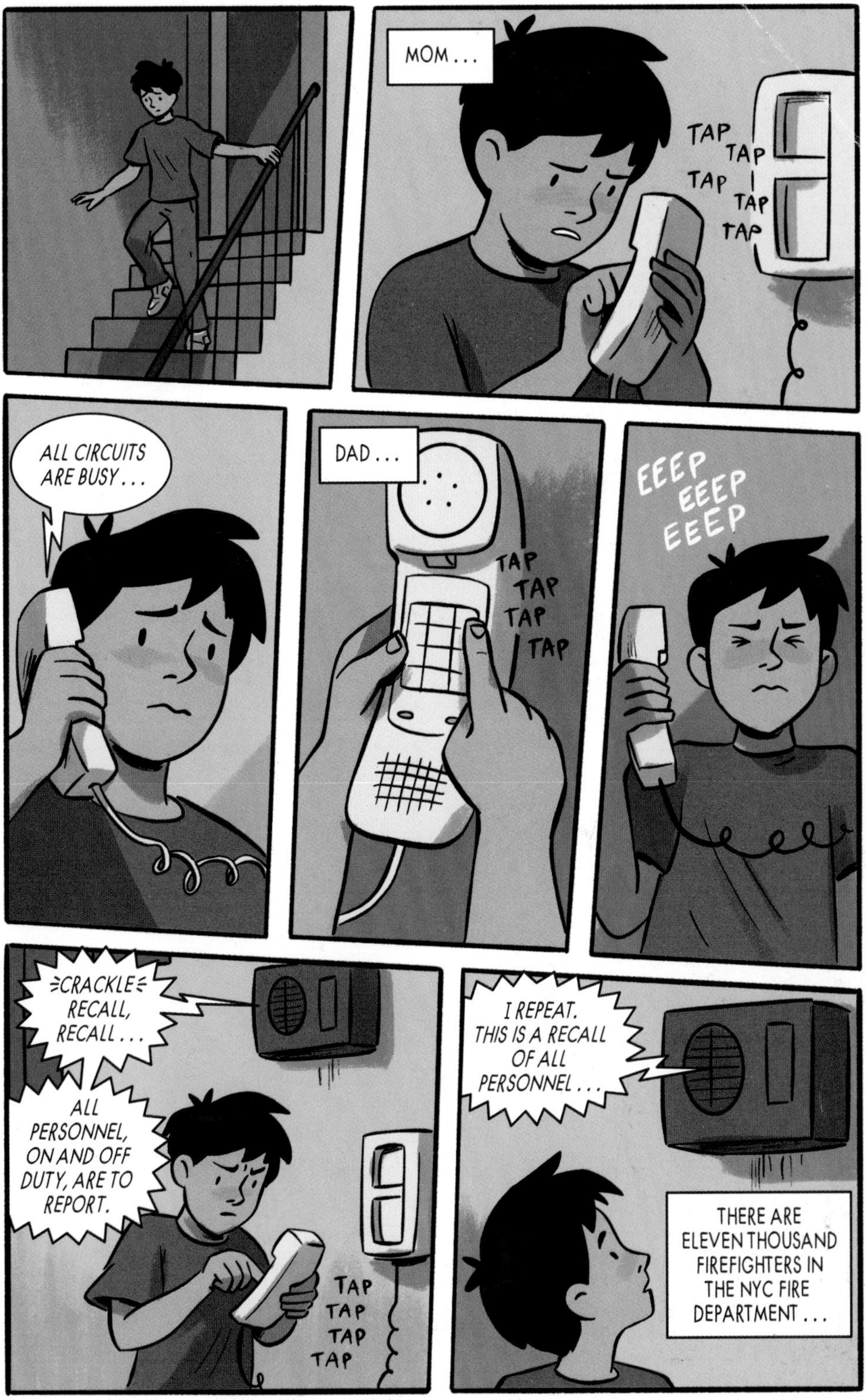
MOM . . .
TAP TAP TAP TAP TAP
ALL CIRCUITS ARE BUSY . . .
DAD . . .
TAP TAP TAP TAP
EEEP EEEP EEEP
CRACKLE RECALL, RECALL . . .
ALL PERSONNEL, ON AND OFF DUTY, ARE TO REPORT.
TAP TAP TAP TAP
I REPEAT. THIS IS A RECALL OF ALL PERSONNEL . . .
THERE ARE ELEVEN THOUSAND FIREFIGHTERS IN THE NYC FIRE DEPARTMENT . . .

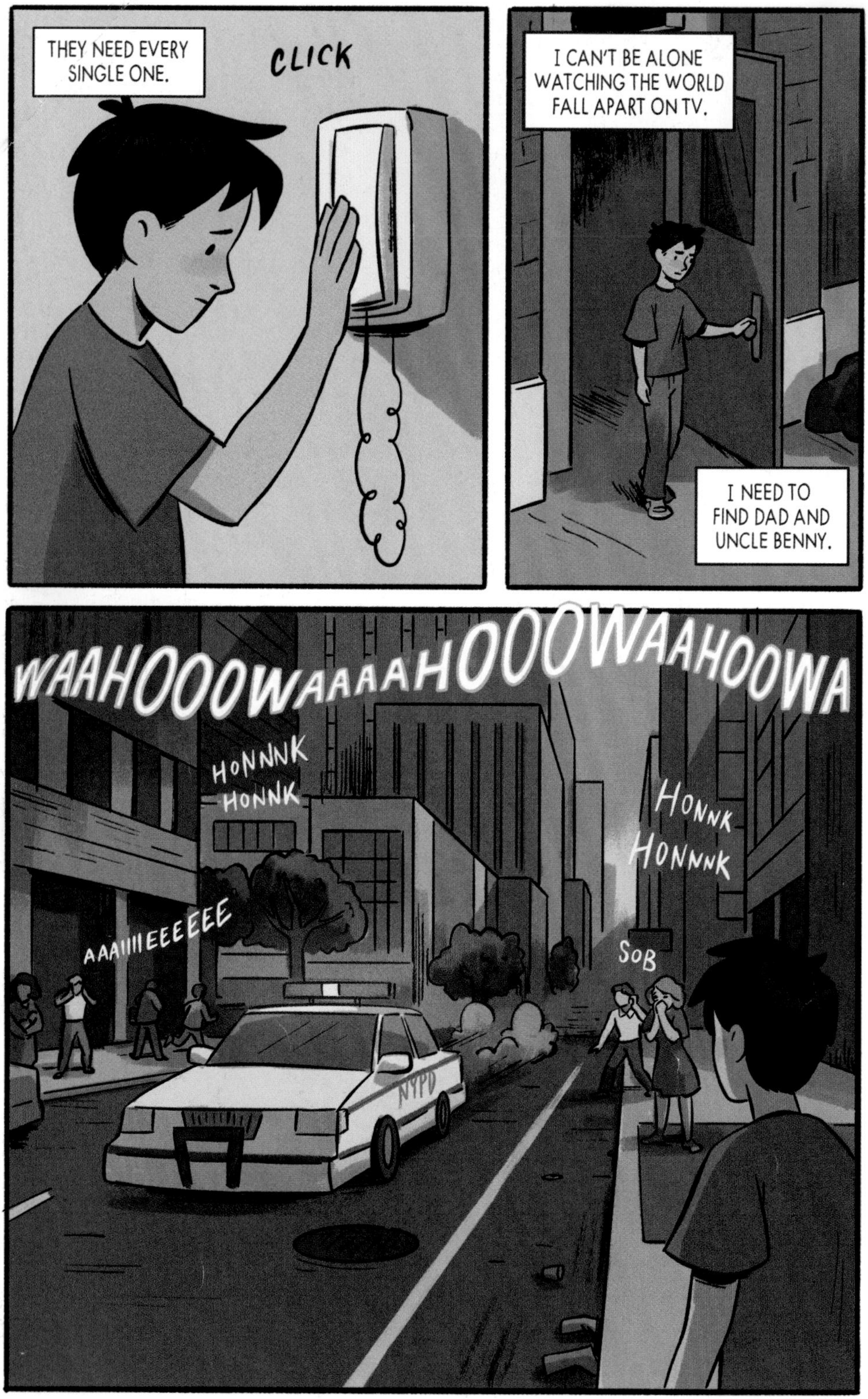
THEY NEED EVERY SINGLE ONE.
CLICK
I CAN'T BE ALONE WATCHING THE WORLD FALL APART ON TV.
I NEED TO FIND DAD AND UNCLE BENNY.
WAAHOOOWAAAAHOOOOWAAHOOWA
HONNNK HONNK
HONNK HONNNK
AAAIIIIEEEEEE
SOB
NYPD

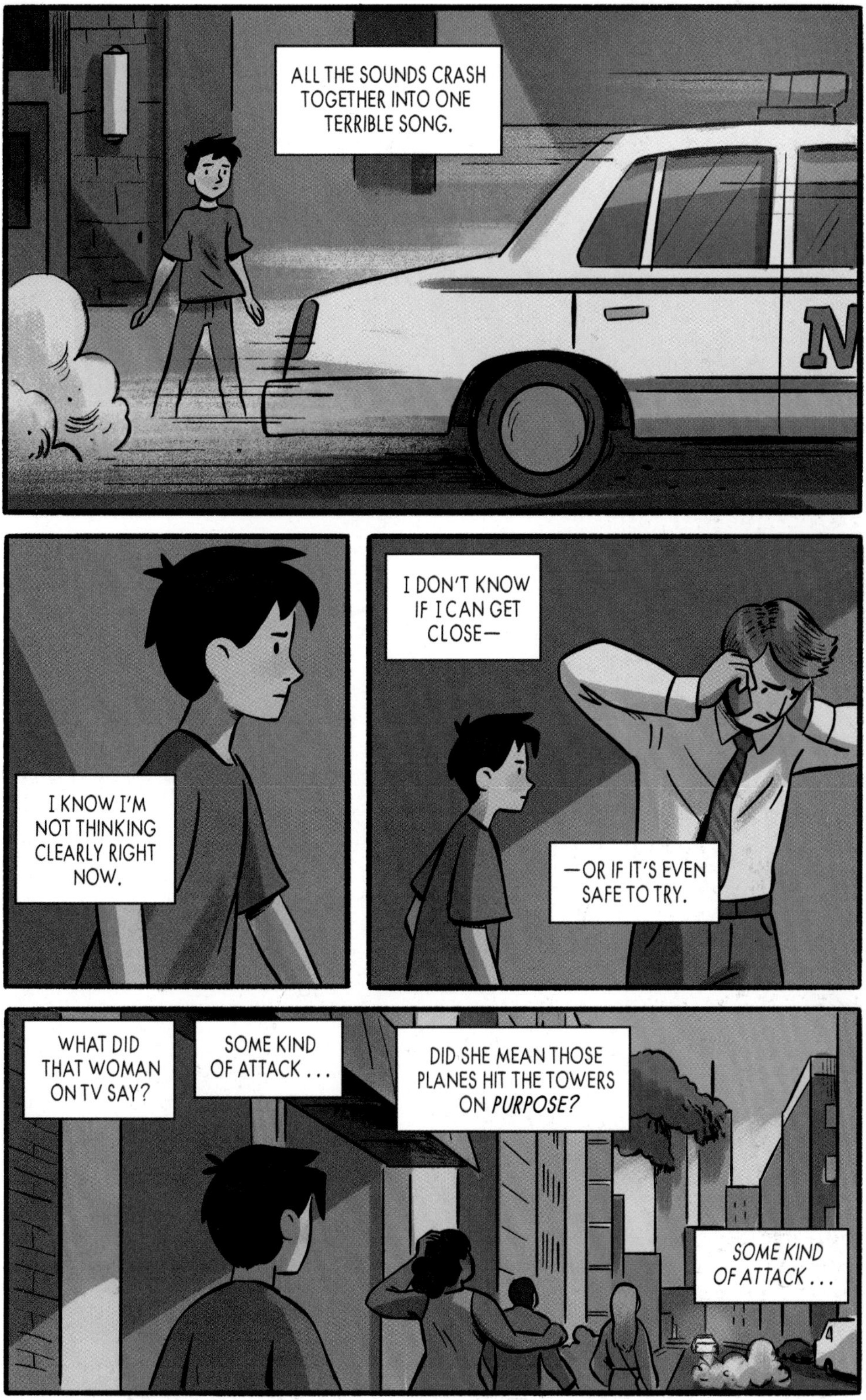
ALL THE SOUNDS CRASH TOGETHER INTO ONE TERRIBLE SONG.
I KNOW I'M NOT THINKING CLEARLY RIGHT NOW.
I DON'T KNOW IF I CAN GET CLOSE—
—OR IF IT'S EVEN SAFE TO TRY.
WHAT DID THAT WOMAN ON TV SAY?
SOME KIND OF ATTACK . . .
DID SHE MEAN THOSE PLANES HIT THE TOWERS ON *PURPOSE?*
SOME KIND OF ATTACK . . .

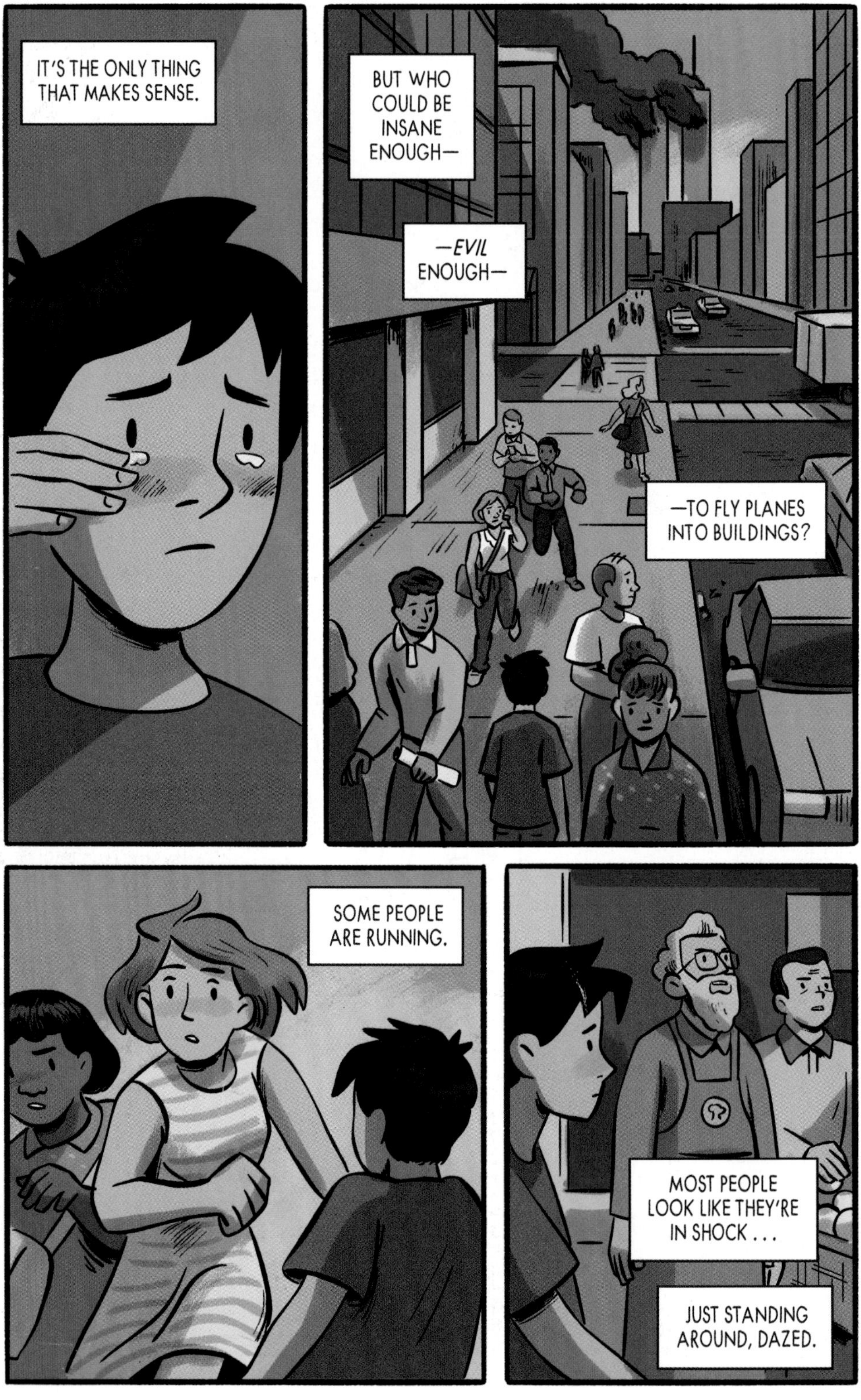
IT'S THE ONLY THING THAT MAKES SENSE.
BUT WHO COULD BE INSANE ENOUGH—
—EVIL ENOUGH—
—TO FLY PLANES INTO BUILDINGS?
SOME PEOPLE ARE RUNNING.
MOST PEOPLE LOOK LIKE THEY'RE IN SHOCK . . .
JUST STANDING AROUND, DAZED.

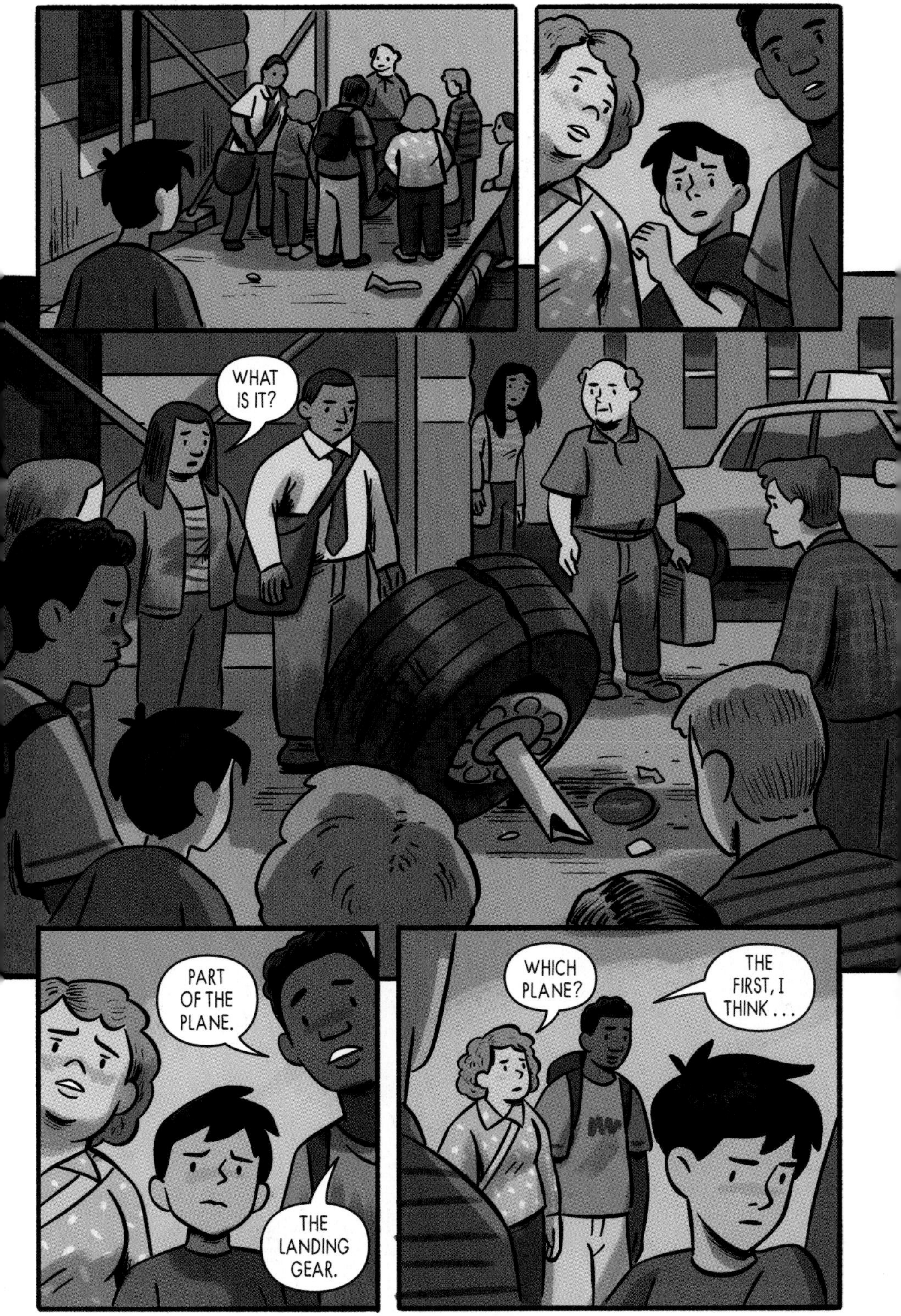
WHAT IS IT?
PART OF THE PLANE.
THE LANDING GEAR.
WHICH PLANE?
THE FIRST, I THINK . . .

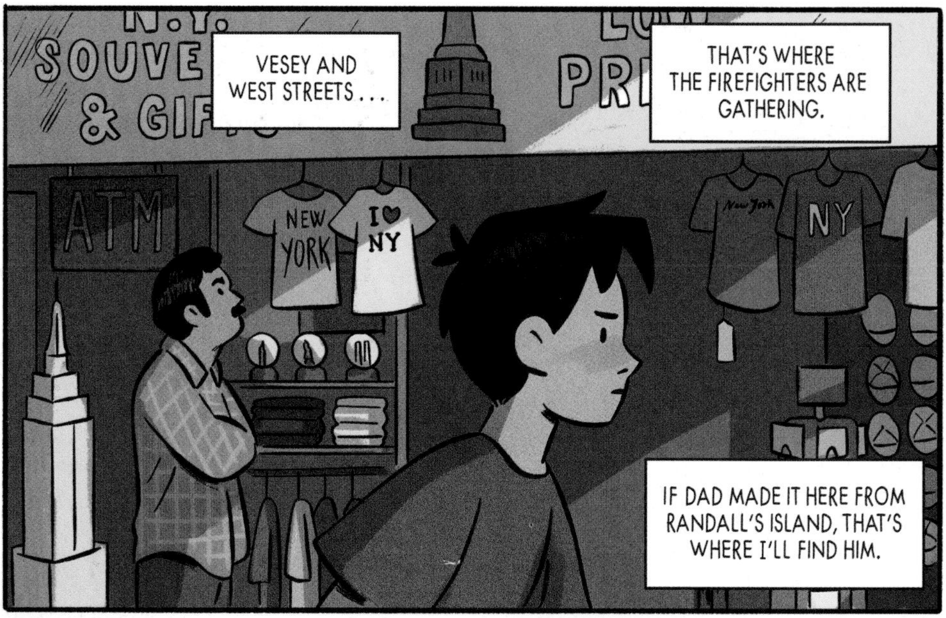
VESEY AND WEST STREETS . . .
THAT'S WHERE THE FIREFIGHTERS ARE GATHERING.
IF DAD MADE IT HERE FROM RANDALL'S ISLAND, THAT'S WHERE I'LL FIND HIM.
N.Y. SOUVE
& GIF
ATM
NEW YORK
I ♥ NY
NY

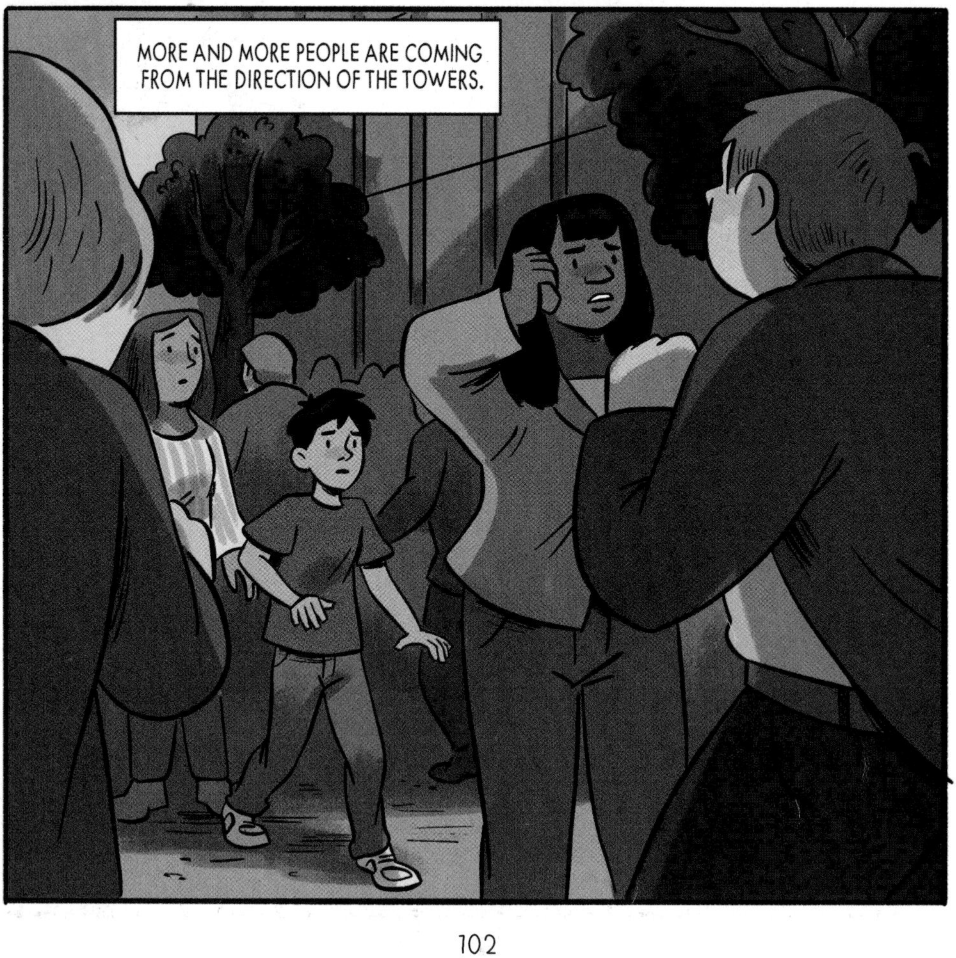
MORE AND MORE PEOPLE ARE COMING FROM THE DIRECTION OF THE TOWERS.

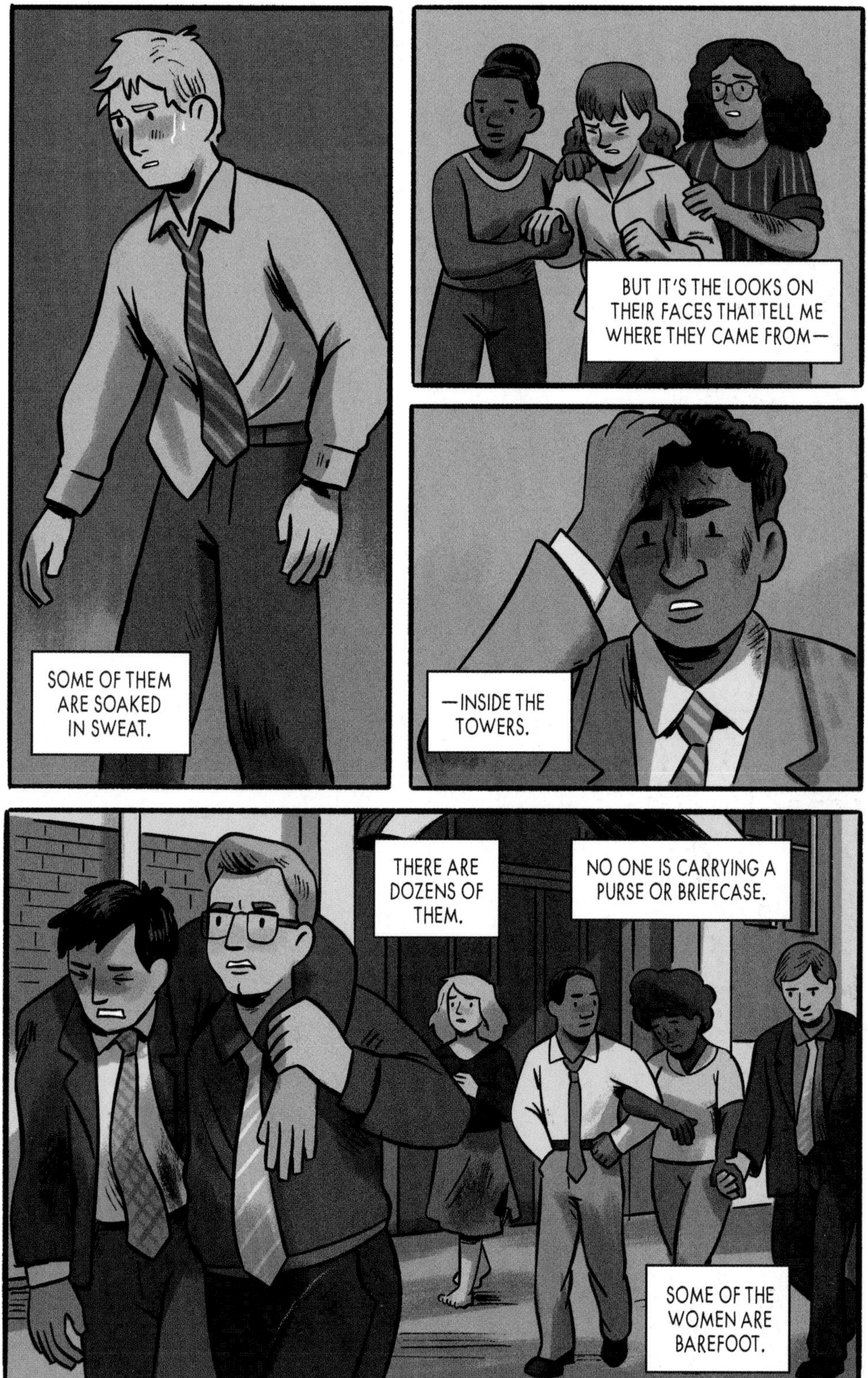
SOME OF THEM ARE SOAKED IN SWEAT.
BUT IT'S THE LOOKS ON THEIR FACES THAT TELL ME WHERE THEY CAME FROM—
—INSIDE THE TOWERS.
THERE ARE DOZENS OF THEM.
NO ONE IS CARRYING A PURSE OR BRIEFCASE.
SOME OF THE WOMEN ARE BAREFOOT.

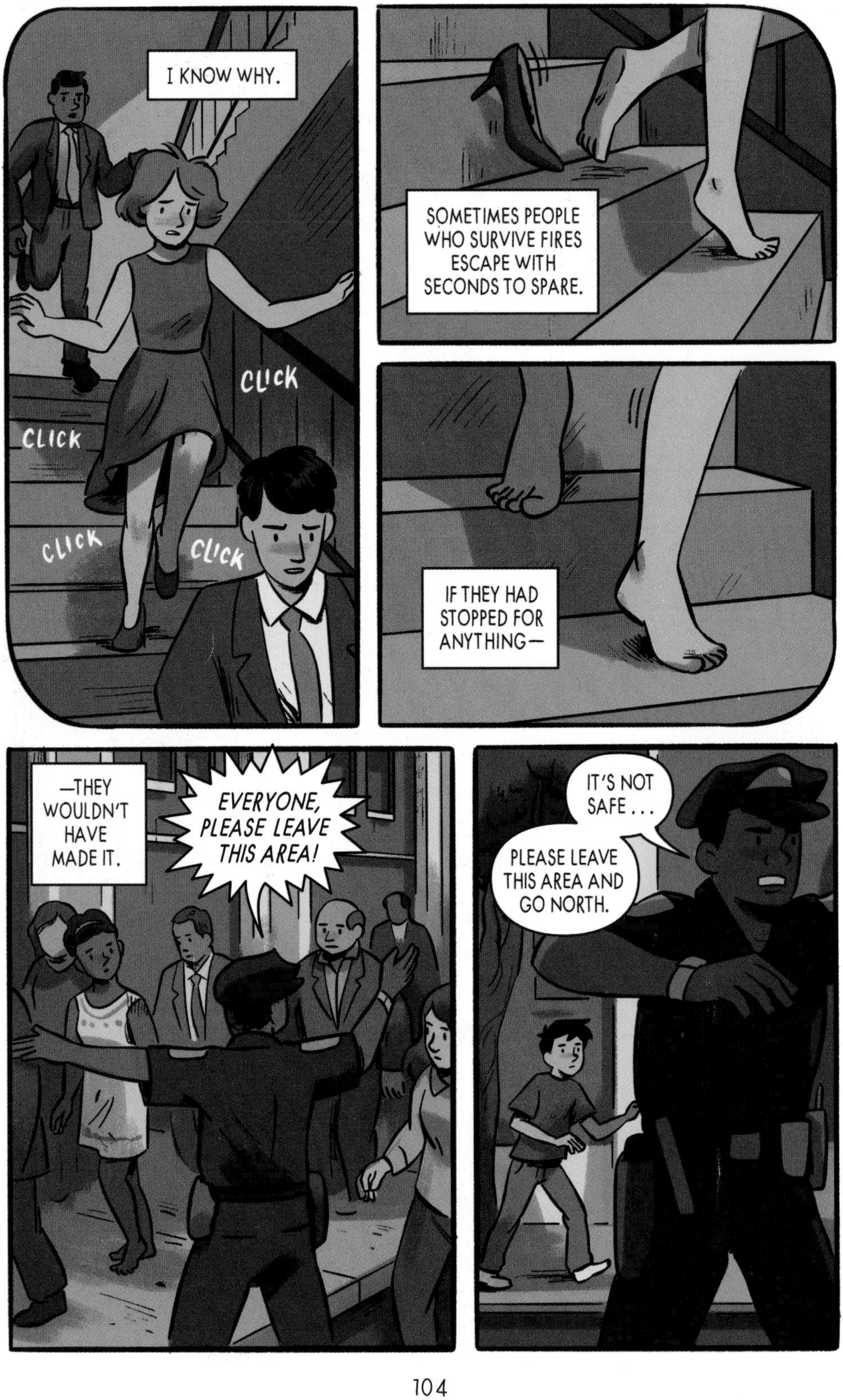

I KNOW WHY.
CLICK
CLICK
CLICK
CLICK
SOMETIMES PEOPLE WHO SURVIVE FIRES ESCAPE WITH SECONDS TO SPARE.
IF THEY HAD STOPPED FOR ANYTHING—
—THEY WOULDN'T HAVE MADE IT.
EVERYONE, PLEASE LEAVE THIS AREA!
IT'S NOT SAFE . . .
PLEASE LEAVE THIS AREA AND GO NORTH.

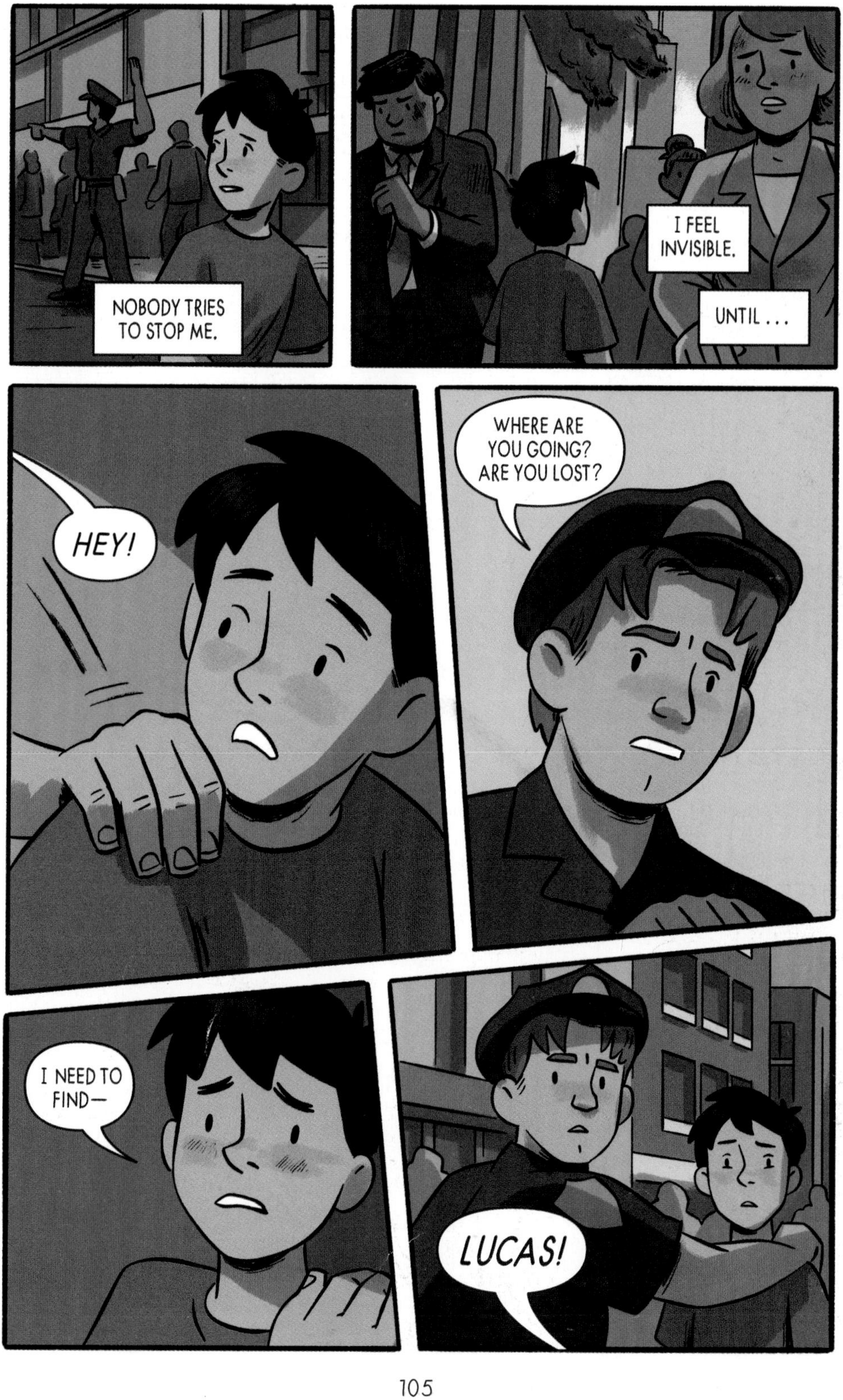
NOBODY TRIES
TO STOP ME.
I FEEL
INVISIBLE.
UNTIL . . .
HEY!
WHERE ARE
YOU GOING?
ARE YOU LOST?
I NEED TO
FIND—
LUCAS!

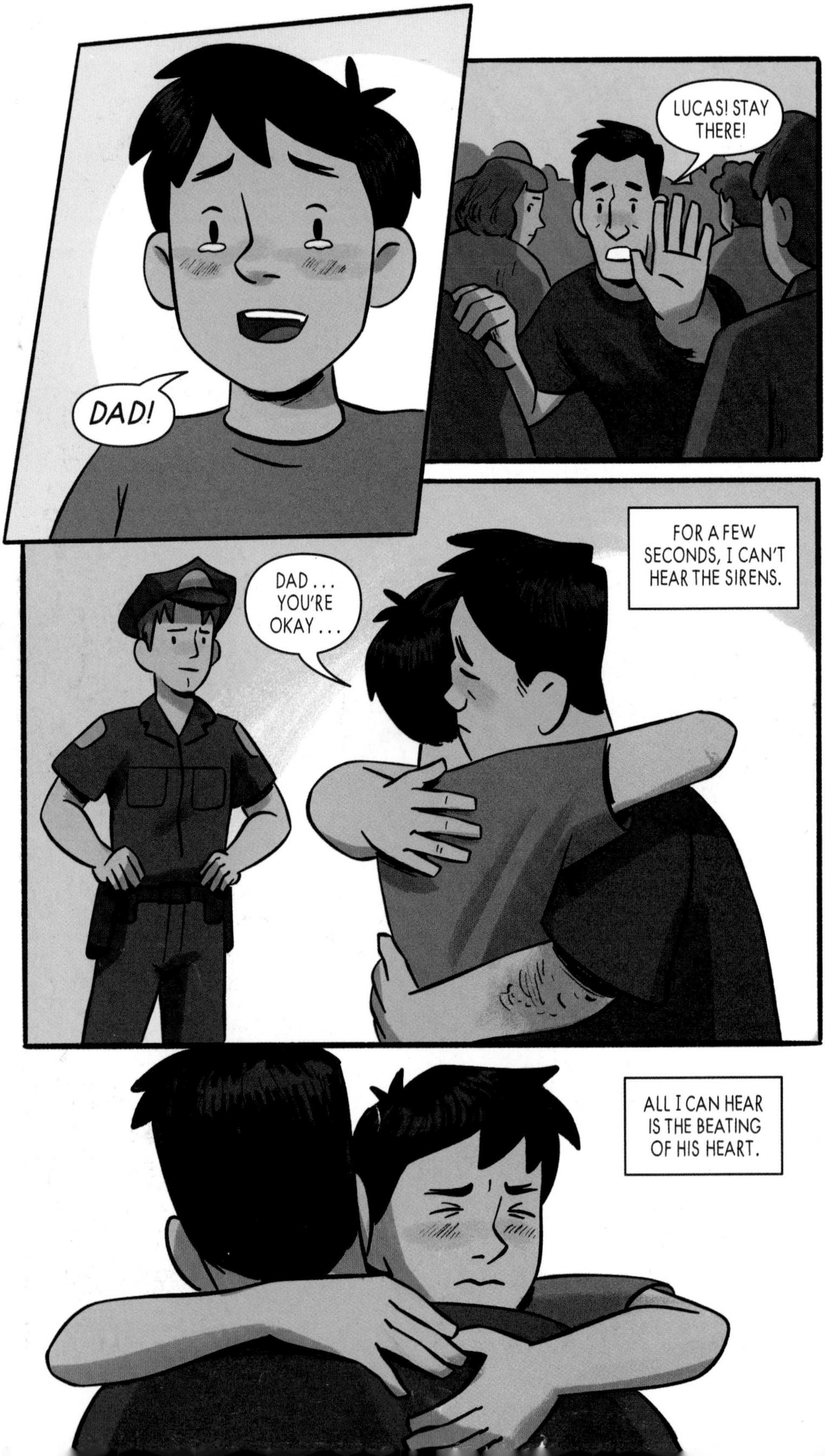
DAD!
LUCAS! STAY THERE!
FOR A FEW SECONDS, I CAN'T HEAR THE SIRENS.
DAD... YOU'RE OKAY...
ALL I CAN HEAR IS THE BEATING OF HIS HEART.

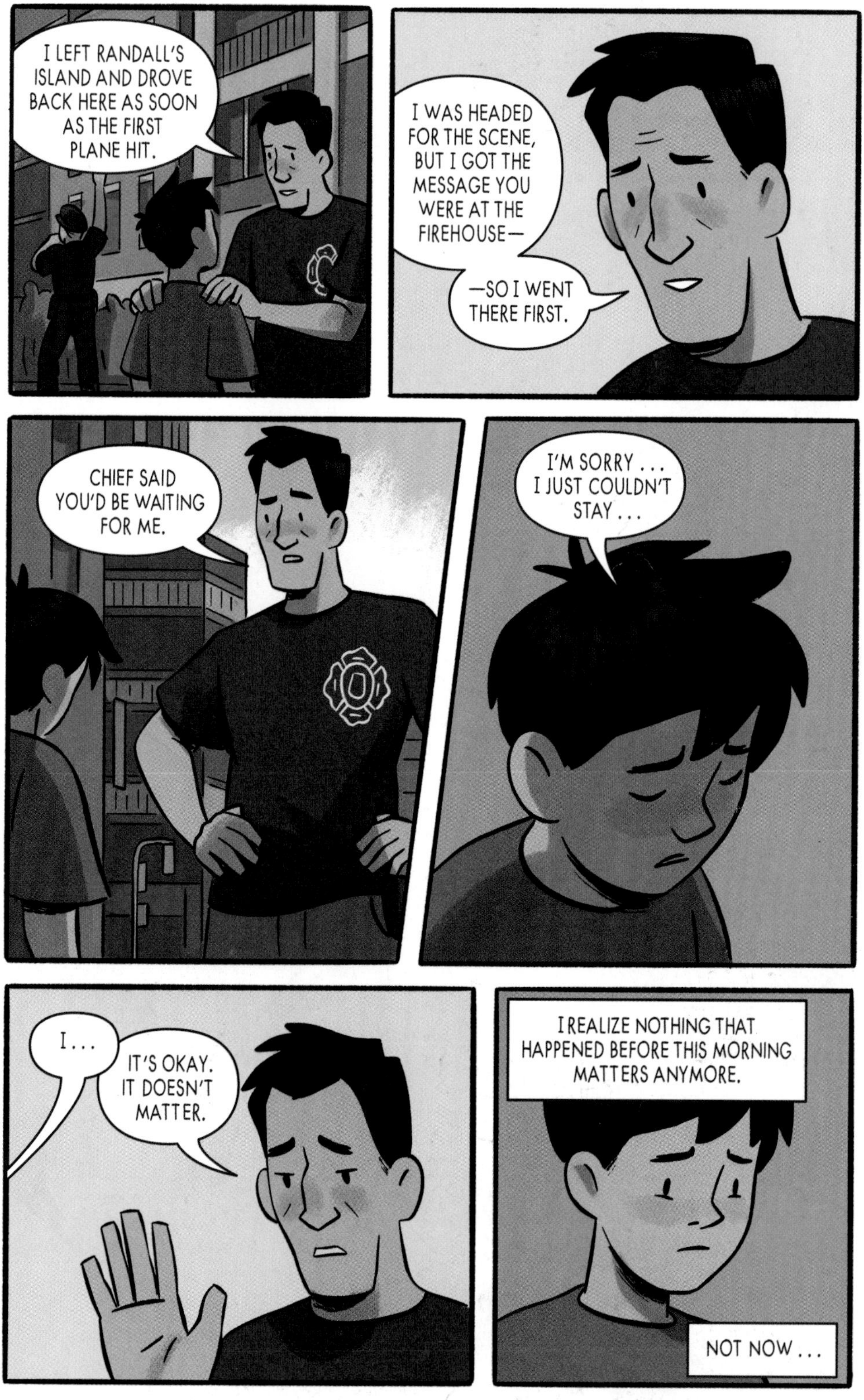
I LEFT RANDALL'S ISLAND AND DROVE BACK HERE AS SOON AS THE FIRST PLANE HIT.
I WAS HEADED FOR THE SCENE, BUT I GOT THE MESSAGE YOU WERE AT THE FIREHOUSE—
—SO I WENT THERE FIRST.
CHIEF SAID YOU'D BE WAITING FOR ME.
I'M SORRY . . . I JUST COULDN'T STAY . . .
I . . .
IT'S OKAY. IT DOESN'T MATTER.
I REALIZE NOTHING THAT HAPPENED BEFORE THIS MORNING MATTERS ANYMORE.
NOT NOW . . .

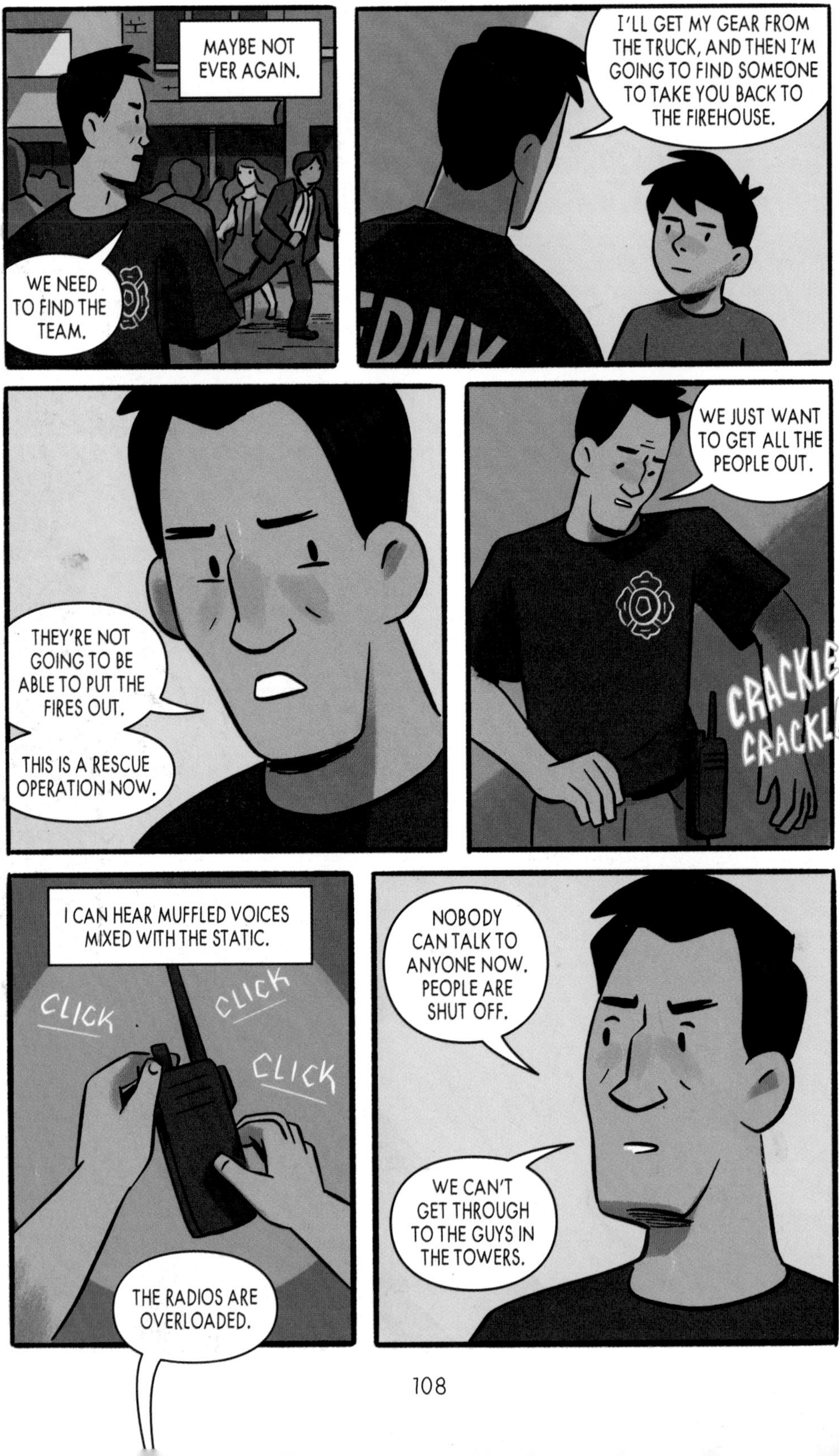
MAYBE NOT EVER AGAIN.
WE NEED TO FIND THE TEAM.
I'LL GET MY GEAR FROM THE TRUCK, AND THEN I'M GOING TO FIND SOMEONE TO TAKE YOU BACK TO THE FIREHOUSE.
FDNY
THEY'RE NOT GOING TO BE ABLE TO PUT THE FIRES OUT.
THIS IS A RESCUE OPERATION NOW.
WE JUST WANT TO GET ALL THE PEOPLE OUT.
CRACKLE
CRACKLE
I CAN HEAR MUFFLED VOICES MIXED WITH THE STATIC.
CLICK
CLICK
CLICK
THE RADIOS ARE OVERLOADED.
NOBODY CAN TALK TO ANYONE NOW. PEOPLE ARE SHUT OFF.
WE CAN'T GET THROUGH TO THE GUYS IN THE TOWERS.

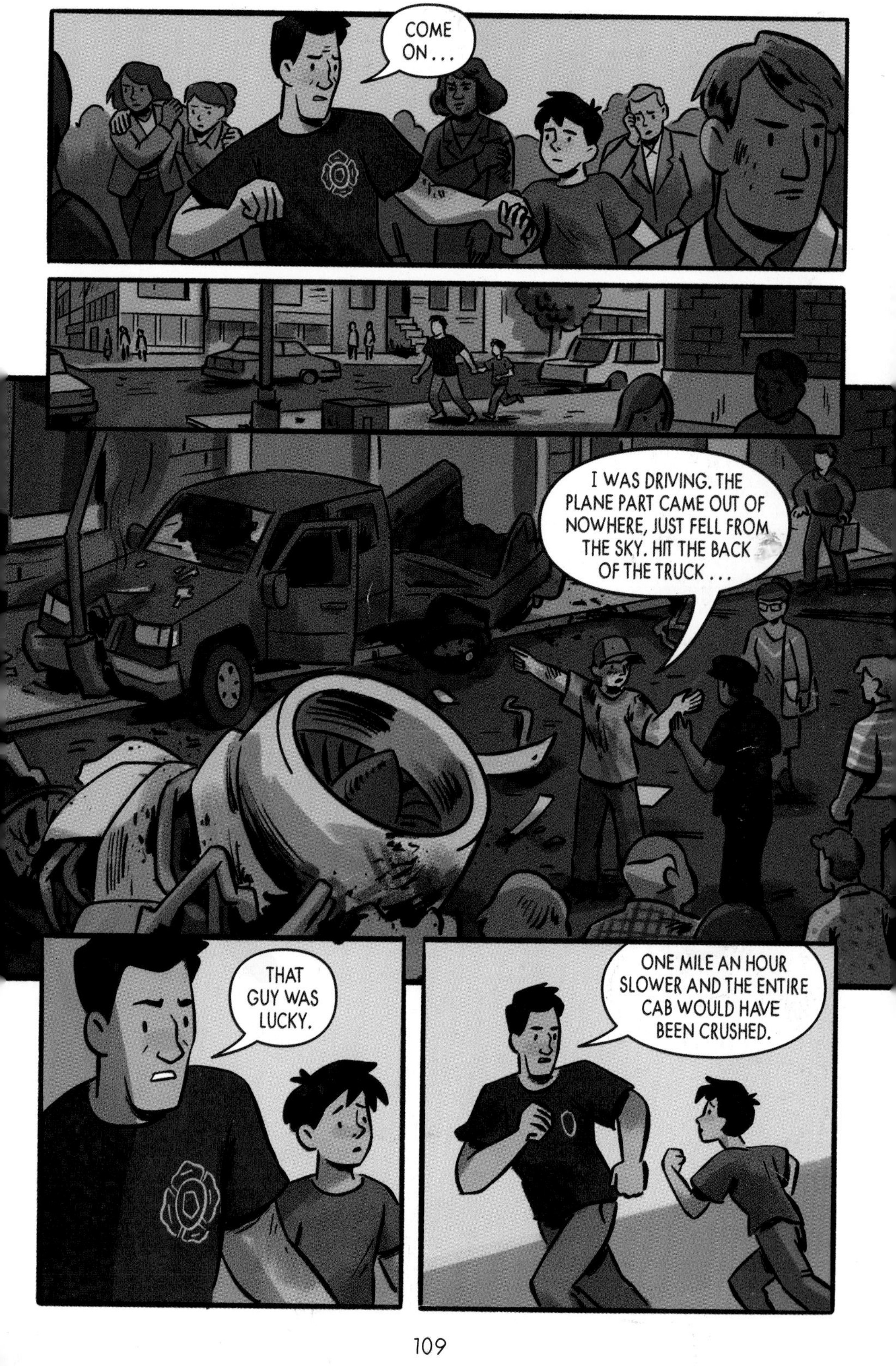
COME ON...
I WAS DRIVING. THE PLANE PART CAME OUT OF NOWHERE, JUST FELL FROM THE SKY. HIT THE BACK OF THE TRUCK...
THAT GUY WAS LUCKY.
ONE MILE AN HOUR SLOWER AND THE ENTIRE CAB WOULD HAVE BEEN CRUSHED.

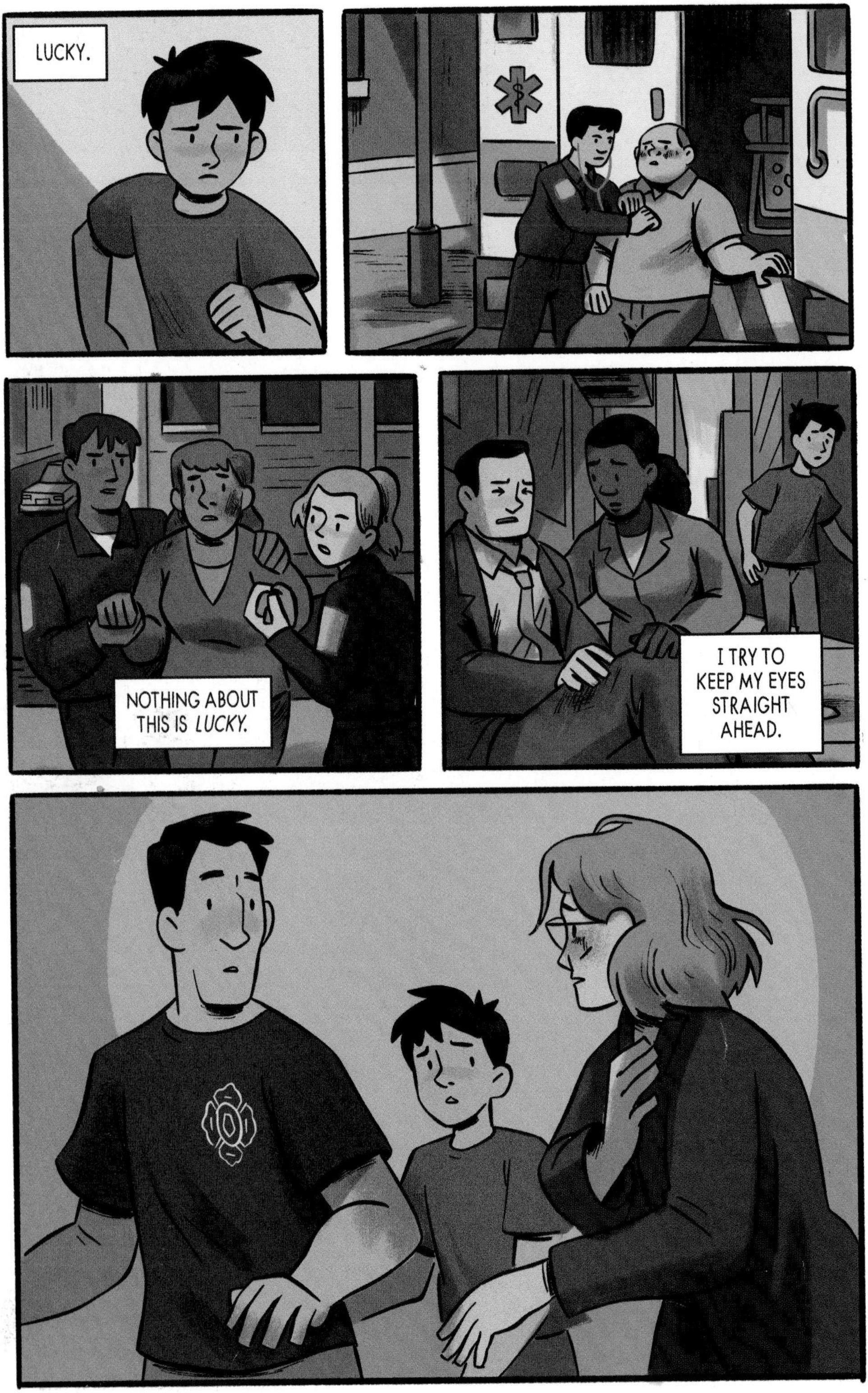
LUCKY.
NOTHING ABOUT THIS IS *LUCKY.*
I TRY TO KEEP MY EYES STRAIGHT AHEAD.

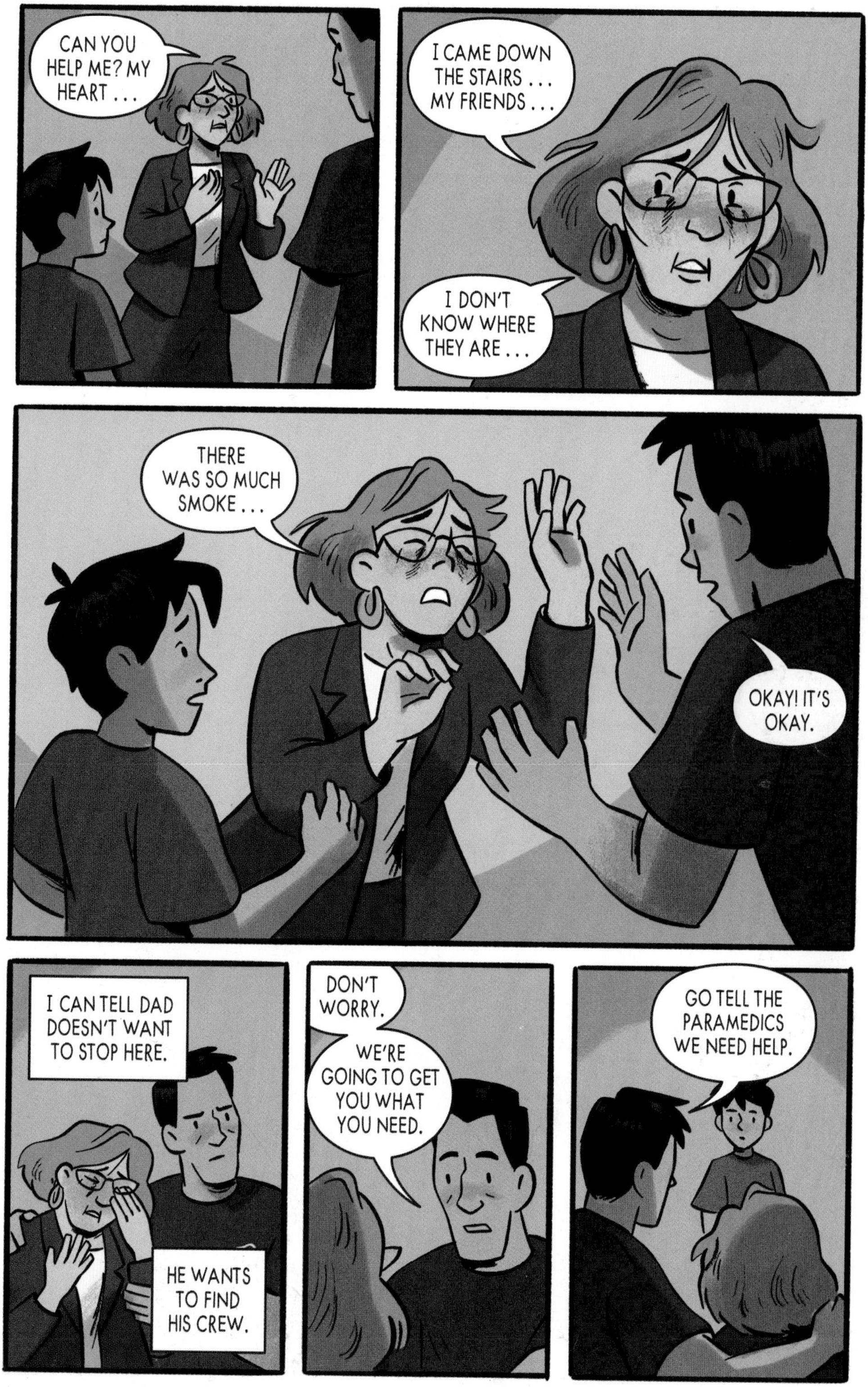
CAN YOU HELP ME? MY HEART . . .
I CAME DOWN THE STAIRS . . . MY FRIENDS . . .
I DON'T KNOW WHERE THEY ARE . . .
THERE WAS SO MUCH SMOKE . . .
OKAY! IT'S OKAY.
I CAN TELL DAD DOESN'T WANT TO STOP HERE.
HE WANTS TO FIND HIS CREW.
DON'T WORRY.
WE'RE GOING TO GET YOU WHAT YOU NEED.
GO TELL THE PARAMEDICS WE NEED HELP.

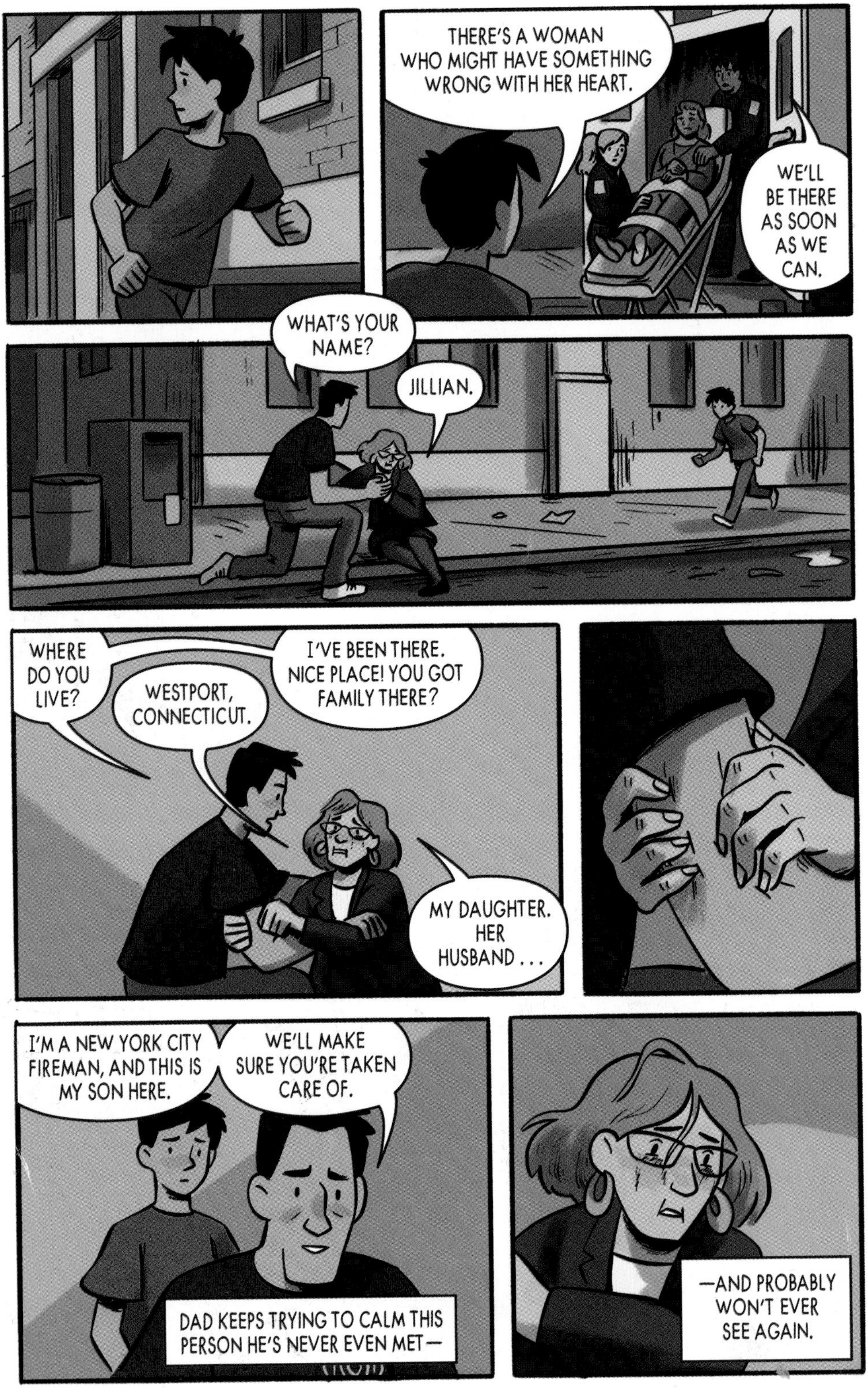
THERE'S A WOMAN WHO MIGHT HAVE SOMETHING WRONG WITH HER HEART.
WE'LL BE THERE AS SOON AS WE CAN.
WHAT'S YOUR NAME?
JILLIAN.
WHERE DO YOU LIVE?
WESTPORT, CONNECTICUT.
I'VE BEEN THERE. NICE PLACE! YOU GOT FAMILY THERE?
MY DAUGHTER. HER HUSBAND . . .
I'M A NEW YORK CITY FIREMAN, AND THIS IS MY SON HERE.
WE'LL MAKE SURE YOU'RE TAKEN CARE OF.
DAD KEEPS TRYING TO CALM THIS PERSON HE'S NEVER EVEN MET—
—AND PROBABLY WON'T EVER SEE AGAIN.

MA'AM? WE'RE HERE TO HELP.

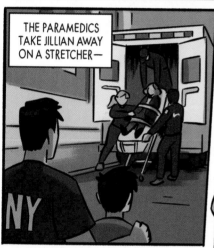

THE PARAMEDICS TAKE JILLIAN AWAY ON A STRETCHER—

RUMBLE RUMBLE RUMBLE RUMBLE

WAIT . . .

—AND WE CAN GET BACK TO FINDING THE CREW.

LET'S GO.

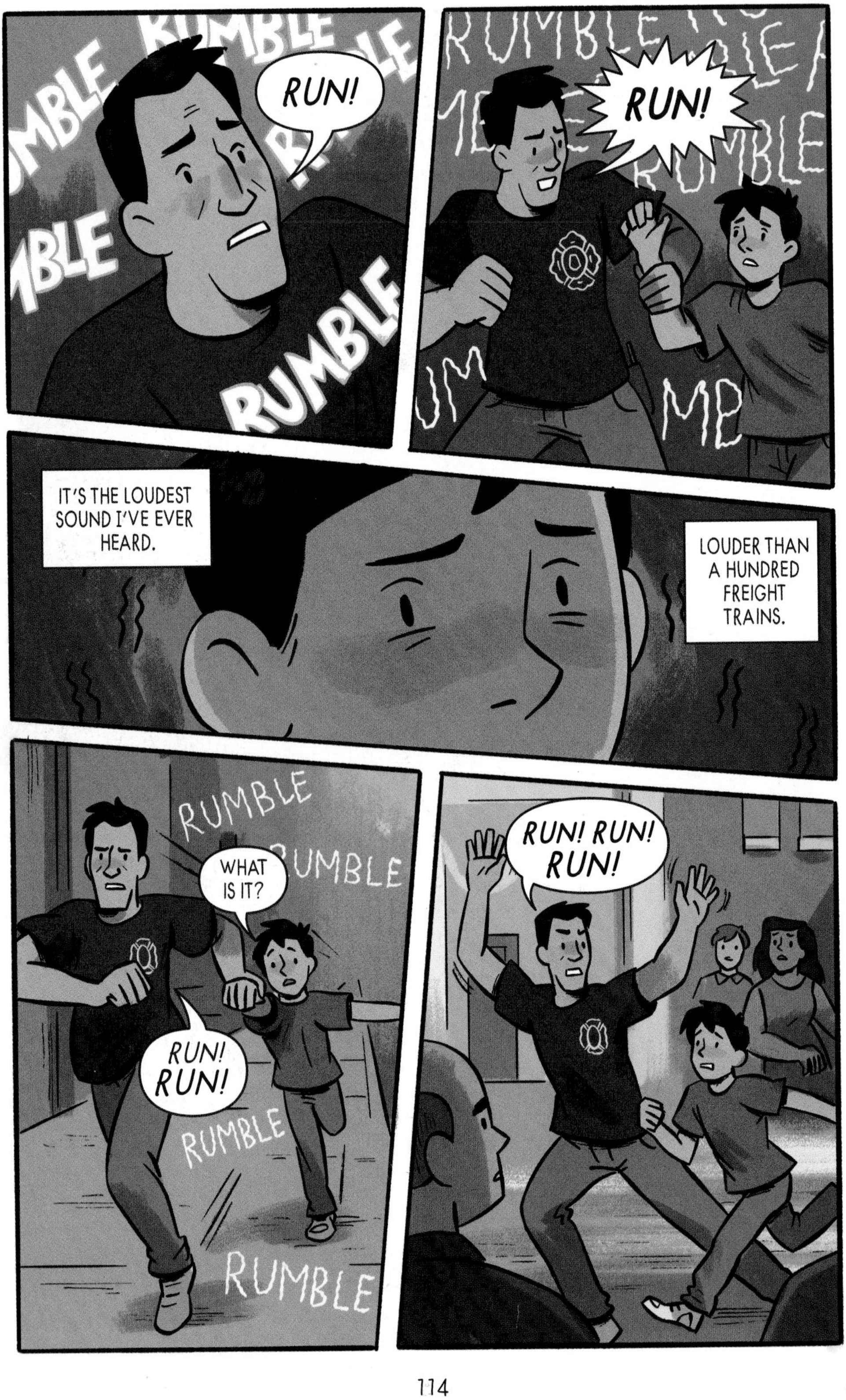
RUMBLE
RUMBLE
RUN!
RUMBLE
RUMBLE
RUMBLE
RUN!
RUMBLE
IT'S THE LOUDEST SOUND I'VE EVER HEARD.
LOUDER THAN A HUNDRED FREIGHT TRAINS.
RUMBLE
WHAT IS IT?
RUMBLE
RUN! RUN!
RUMBLE
RUMBLE
RUN! RUN! RUN!

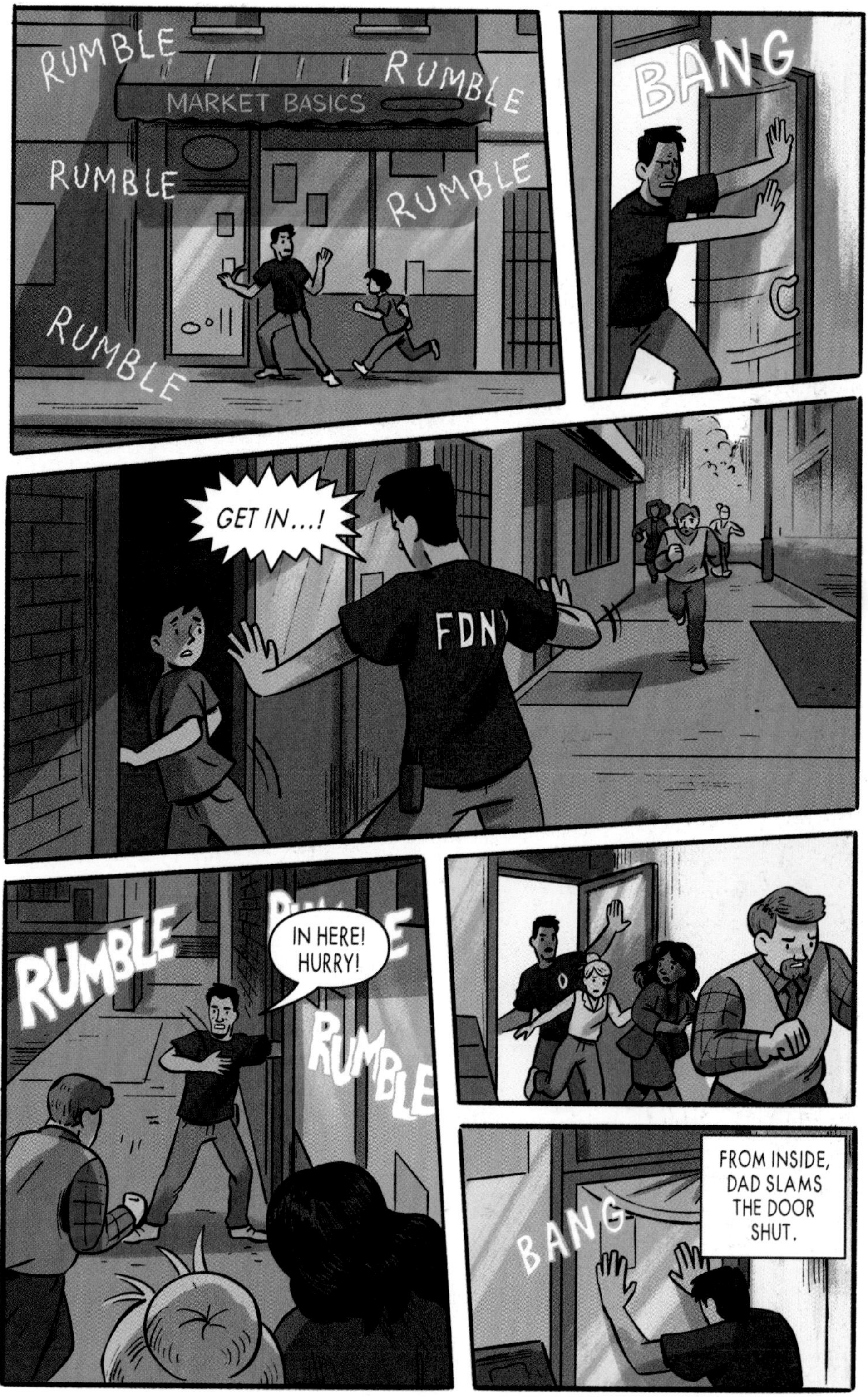
RUMBLE
MARKET BASICS
RUMBLE
RUMBLE
RUMBLE
RUMBLE
BANG
GET IN...!
FDNY
RUMBLE
IN HERE!
HURRY!
RUMBLE
BANG
FROM INSIDE,
DAD SLAMS
THE DOOR
SHUT.

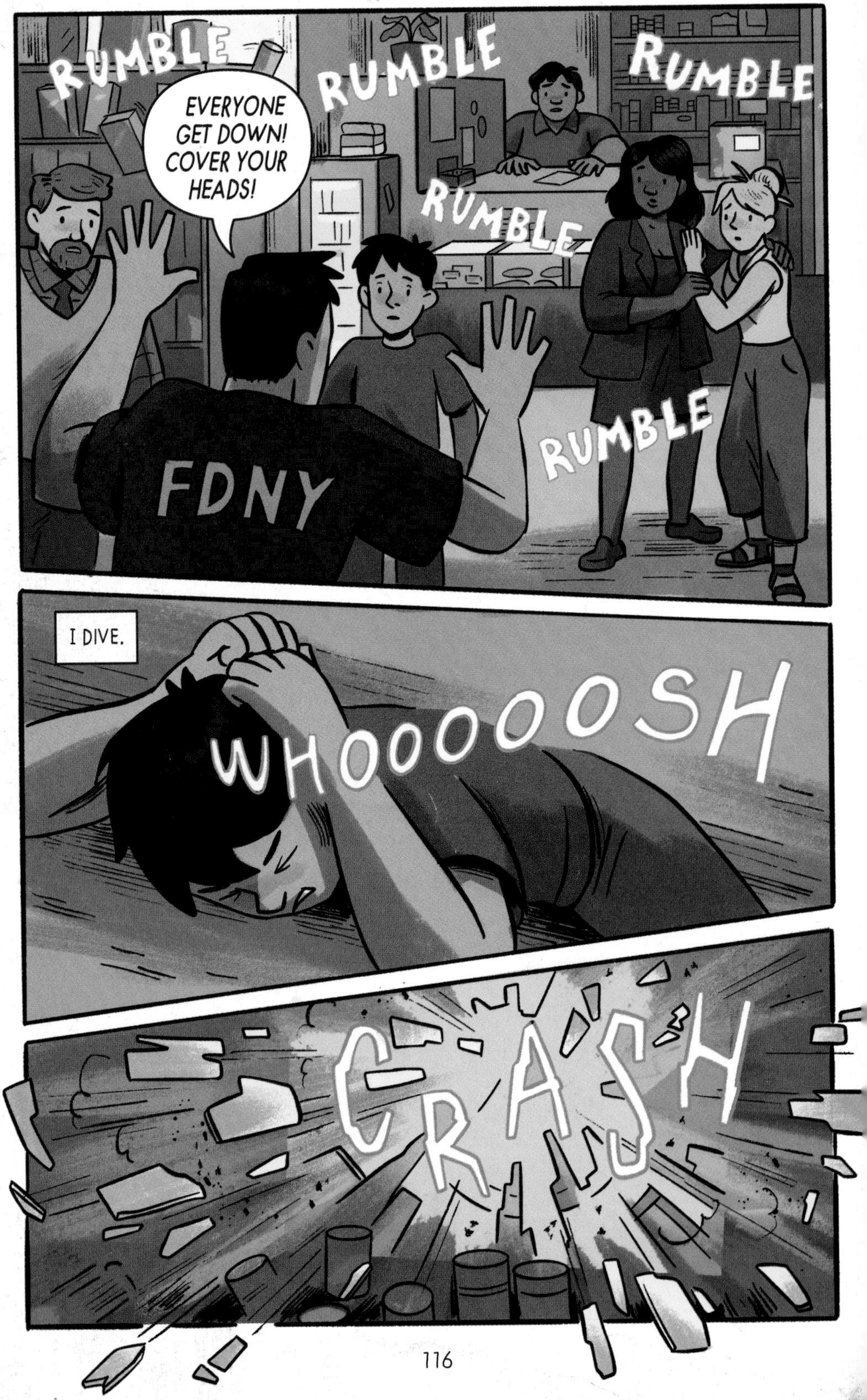
RUMBLE
RUMBLE
RUMBLE
EVERYONE GET DOWN! COVER YOUR HEADS!
RUMBLE
FDNY
RUMBLE
I DIVE.
WHOOOOOOSH
CRASH

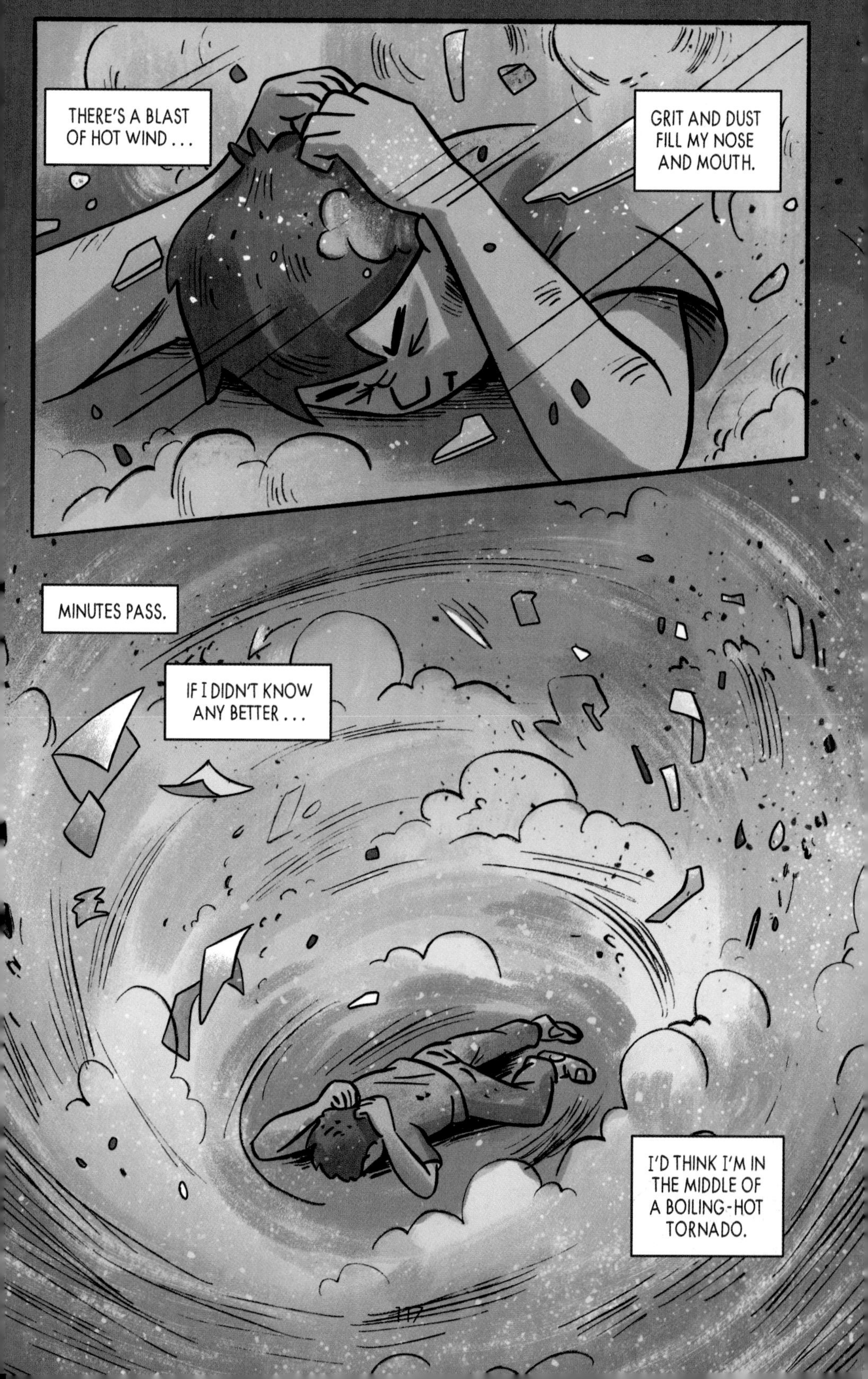
THERE'S A BLAST OF HOT WIND . . .
GRIT AND DUST FILL MY NOSE AND MOUTH.
MINUTES PASS.
IF I DIDN'T KNOW ANY BETTER . . .
I'D THINK I'M IN THE MIDDLE OF A BOILING-HOT TORNADO.

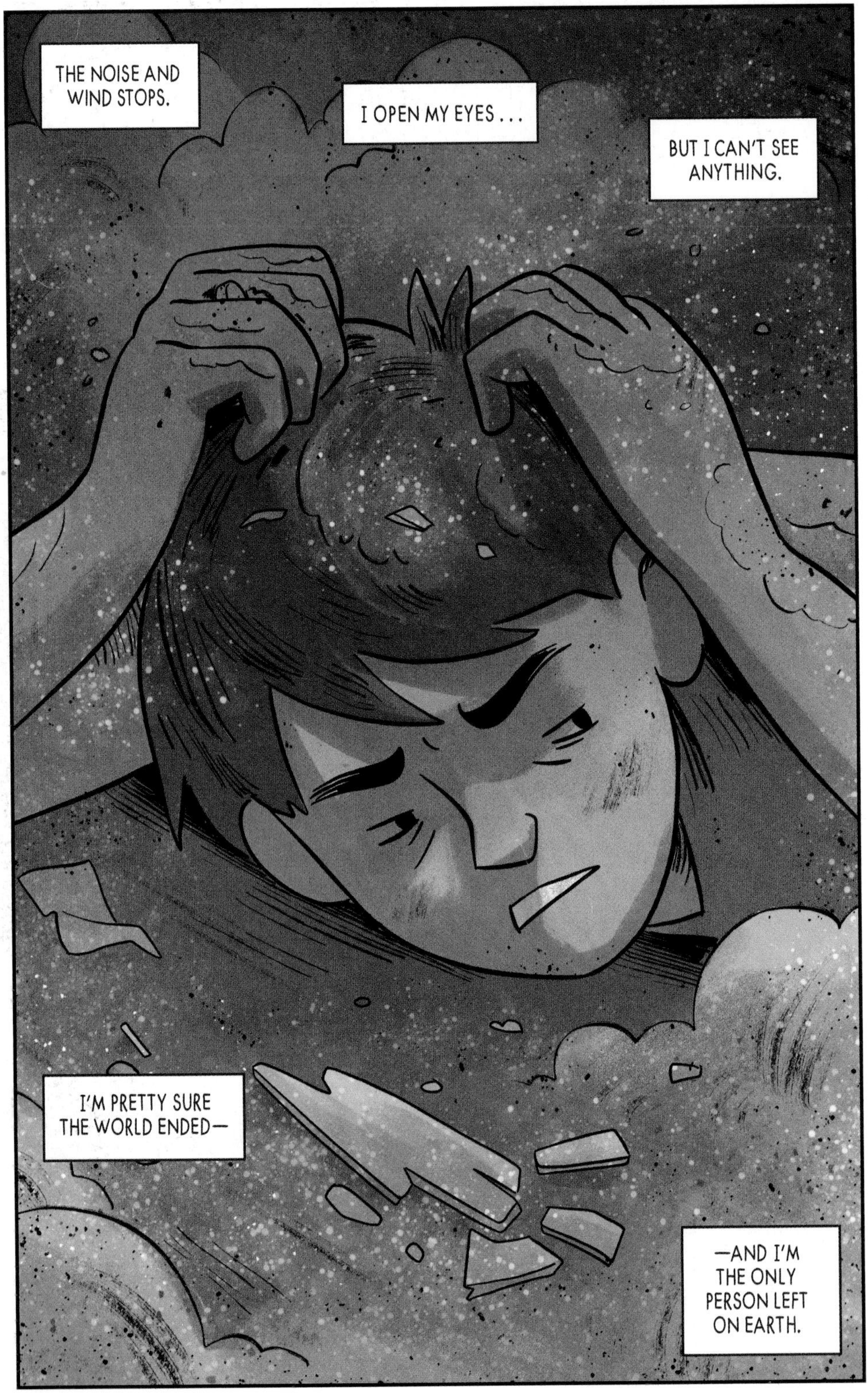
THE NOISE AND WIND STOPS.
I OPEN MY EYES . . .
BUT I CAN'T SEE ANYTHING.
I'M PRETTY SURE THE WORLD ENDED—
—AND I'M THE ONLY PERSON LEFT ON EARTH.

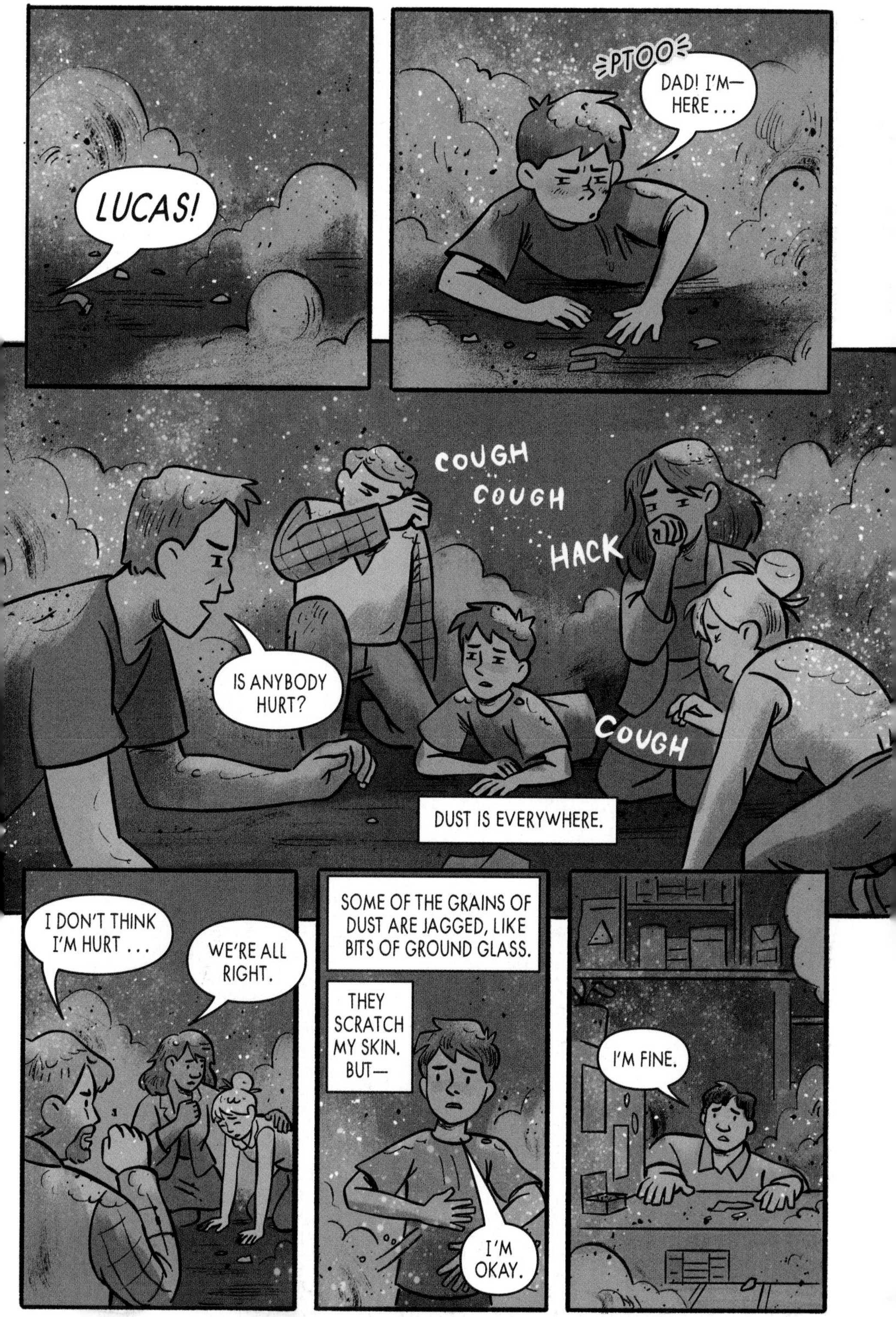
LUCAS!
PTOO
DAD! I'M—
HERE . . .
IS ANYBODY HURT?
COUGH
COUGH
HACK
COUGH
DUST IS EVERYWHERE.
I DON'T THINK I'M HURT . . .
WE'RE ALL RIGHT.
SOME OF THE GRAINS OF DUST ARE JAGGED, LIKE BITS OF GROUND GLASS.
THEY SCRATCH MY SKIN. BUT—
I'M OKAY.
I'M FINE.

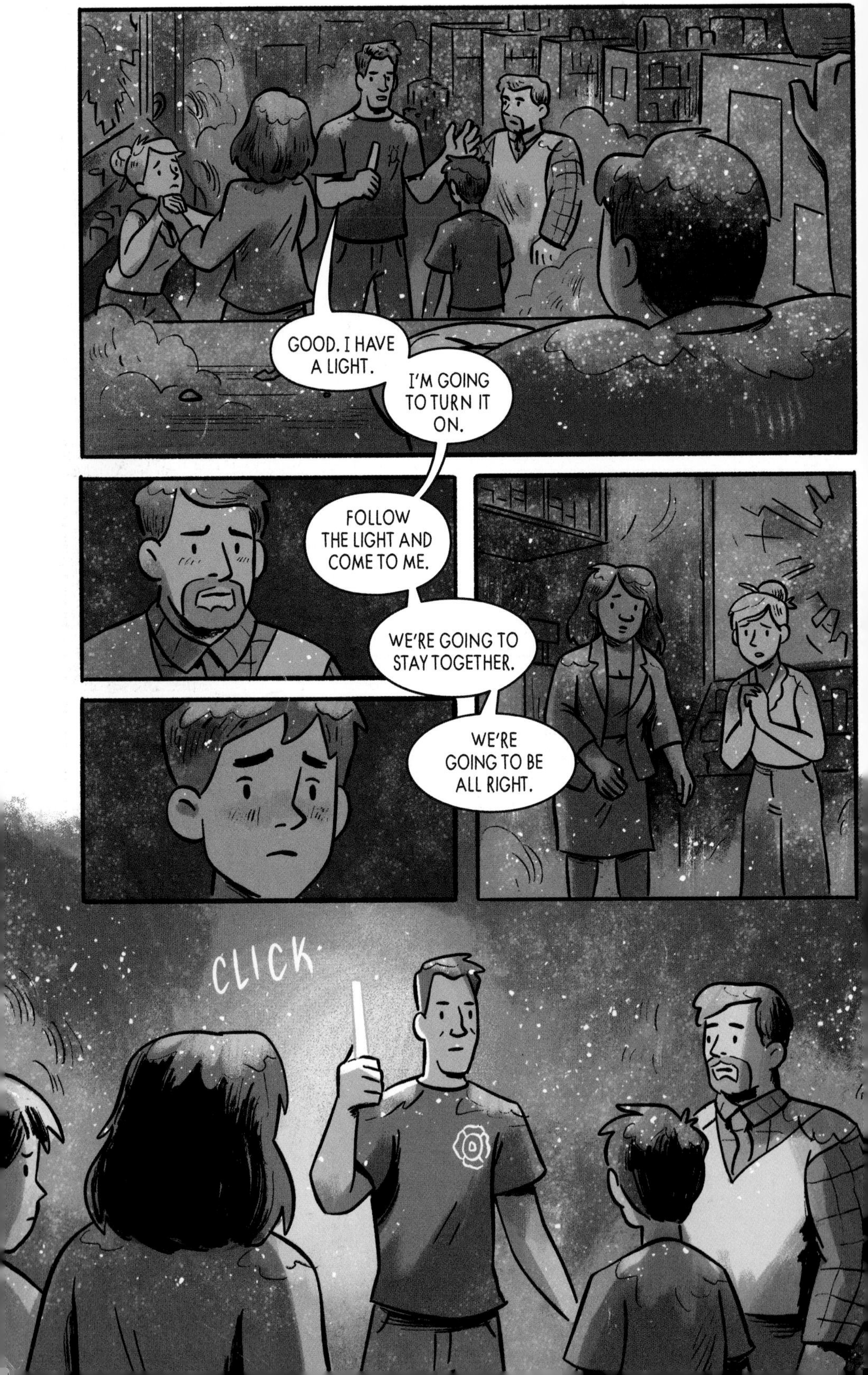
GOOD. I HAVE A LIGHT.
I'M GOING TO TURN IT ON.
FOLLOW THE LIGHT AND COME TO ME.
WE'RE GOING TO STAY TOGETHER.
WE'RE GOING TO BE ALL RIGHT.
CLICK

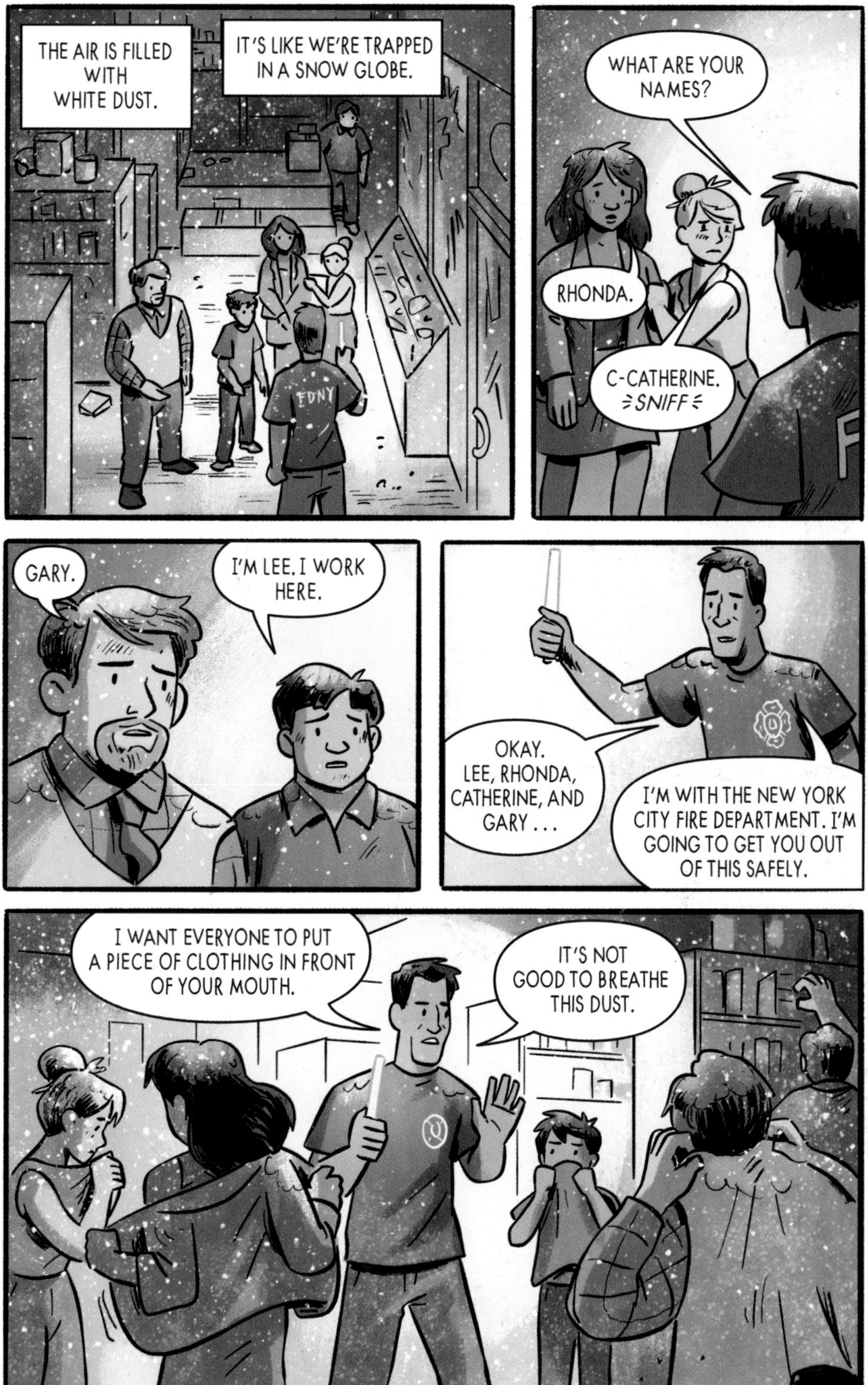
THE AIR IS FILLED WITH WHITE DUST.
IT'S LIKE WE'RE TRAPPED IN A SNOW GLOBE.
FDNY
WHAT ARE YOUR NAMES?
RHONDA.
C-CATHERINE. SNIFF
GARY.
I'M LEE. I WORK HERE.
OKAY. LEE, RHONDA, CATHERINE, AND GARY . . .
I'M WITH THE NEW YORK CITY FIRE DEPARTMENT. I'M GOING TO GET YOU OUT OF THIS SAFELY.
I WANT EVERYONE TO PUT A PIECE OF CLOTHING IN FRONT OF YOUR MOUTH.
IT'S NOT GOOD TO BREATHE THIS DUST.

LEE GRABS SOME WATER AND PAPER TOWELS.

TAKE THESE.

THANK YOU!

WHAT *WAS* THAT?

ANOTHER PLANE?

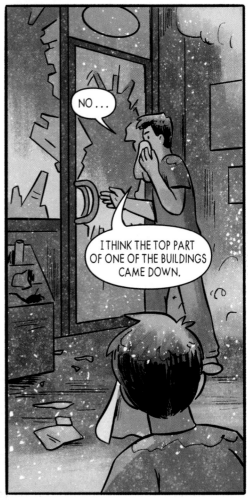

NO . . .

I THINK THE TOP PART OF ONE OF THE BUILDINGS CAME DOWN.

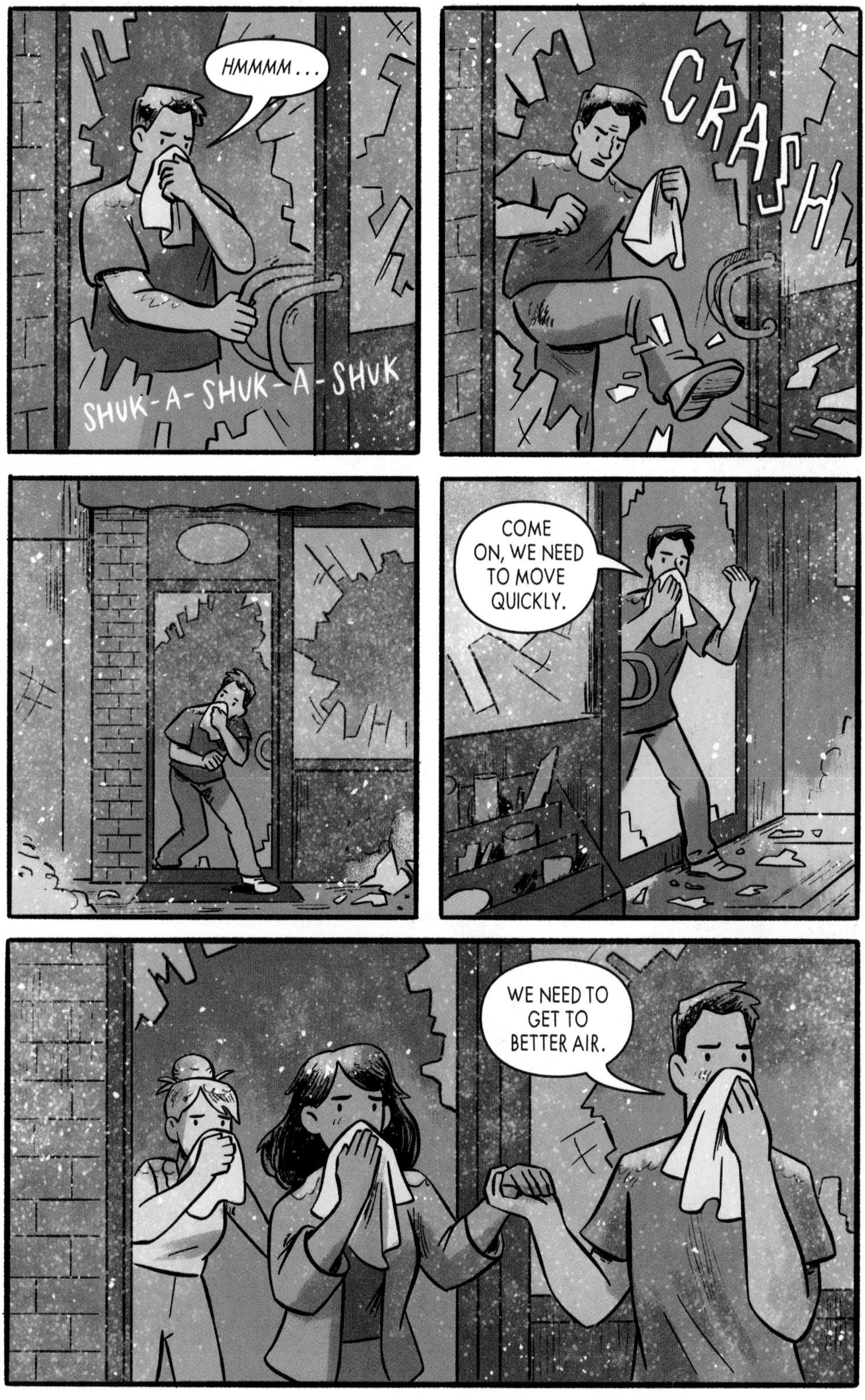
HMMMM...
SHUK-A-SHUK-A-SHUK
CRASH
COME ON, WE NEED TO MOVE QUICKLY.
WE NEED TO GET TO BETTER AIR.

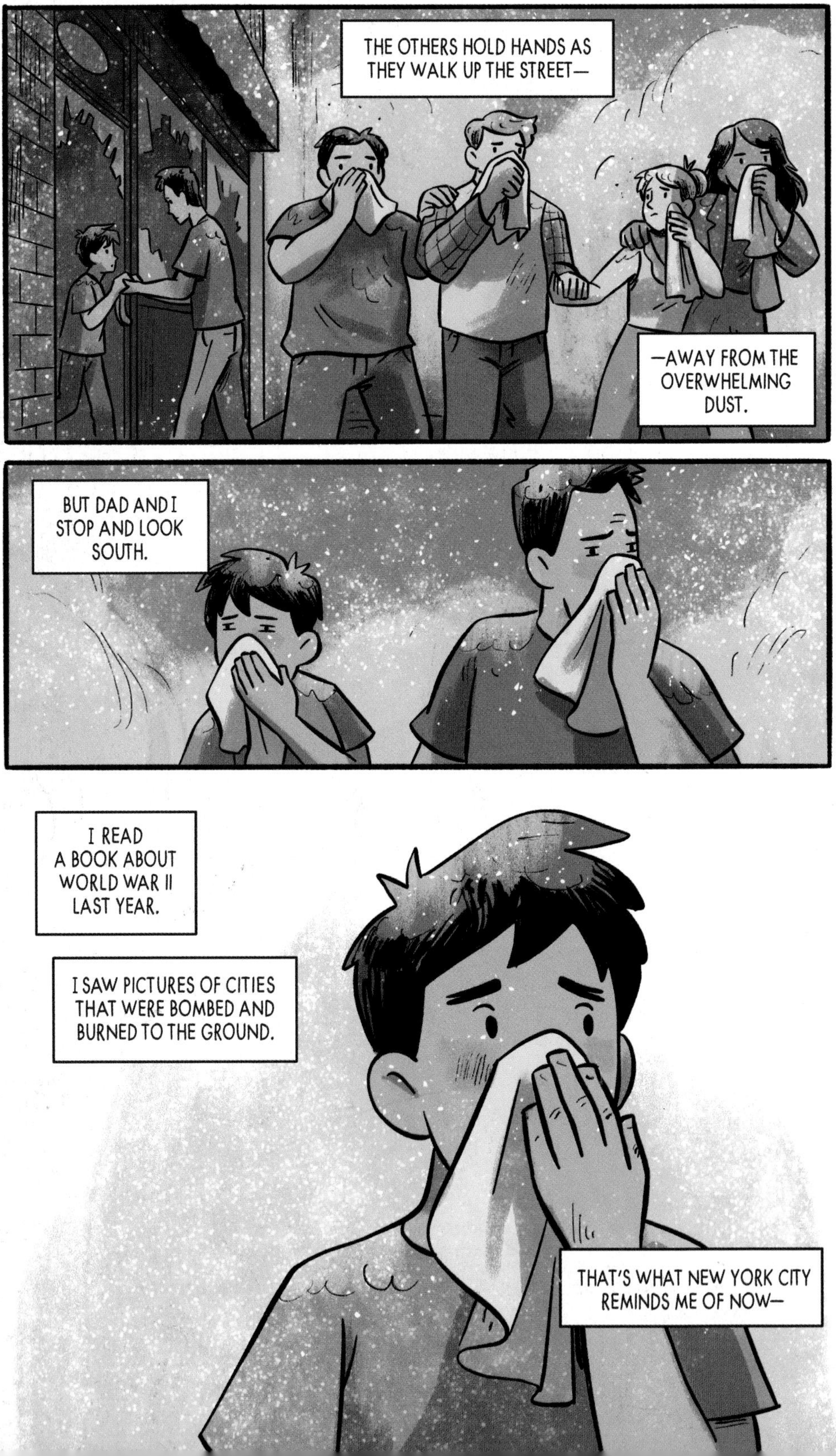
THE OTHERS HOLD HANDS AS THEY WALK UP THE STREET—
—AWAY FROM THE OVERWHELMING DUST.
BUT DAD AND I STOP AND LOOK SOUTH.
I READ A BOOK ABOUT WORLD WAR II LAST YEAR.
I SAW PICTURES OF CITIES THAT WERE BOMBED AND BURNED TO THE GROUND.
THAT'S WHAT NEW YORK CITY REMINDS ME OF NOW—

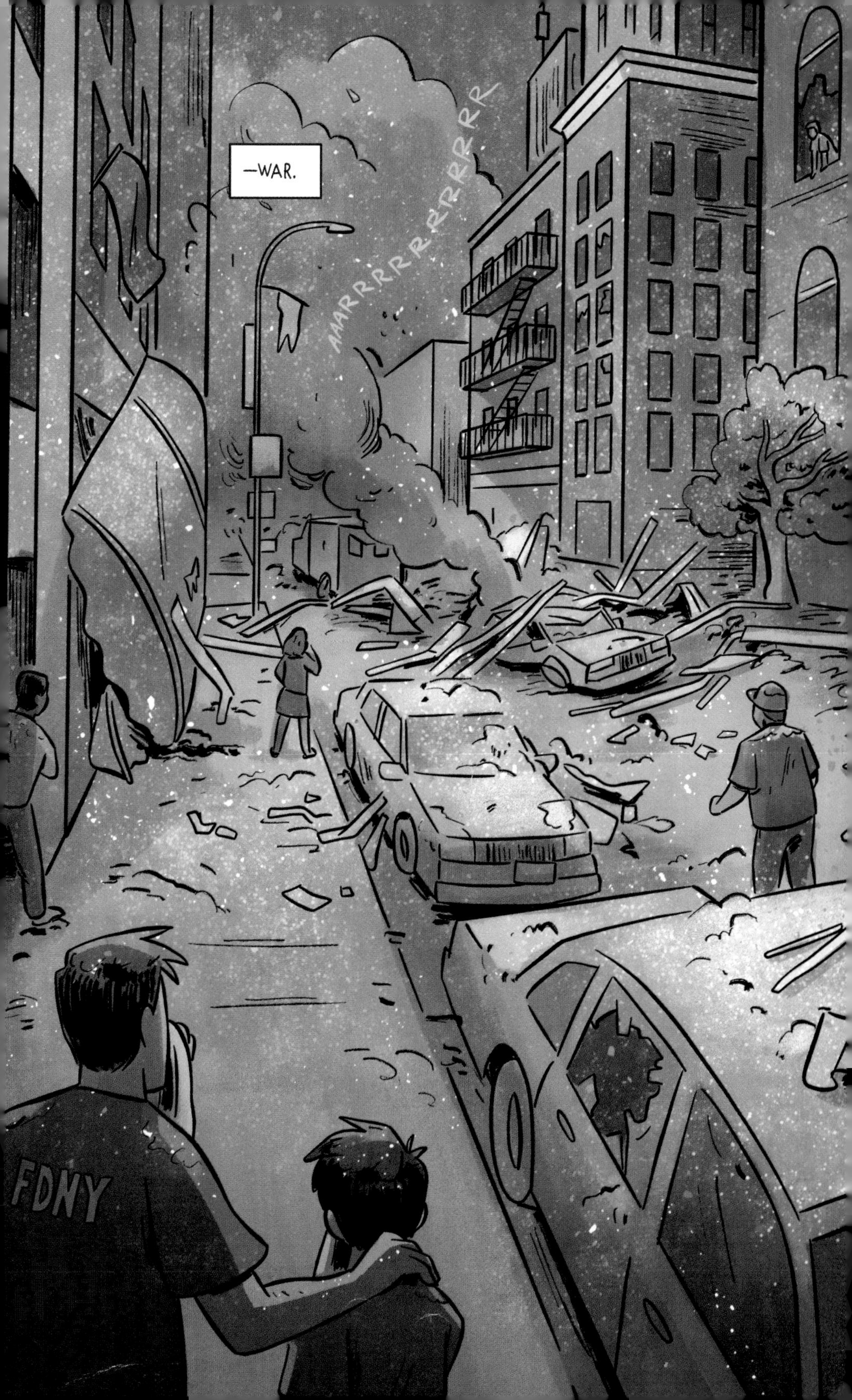
—WAR.
AAARRRRRRRRRRRRRRR
FDNY

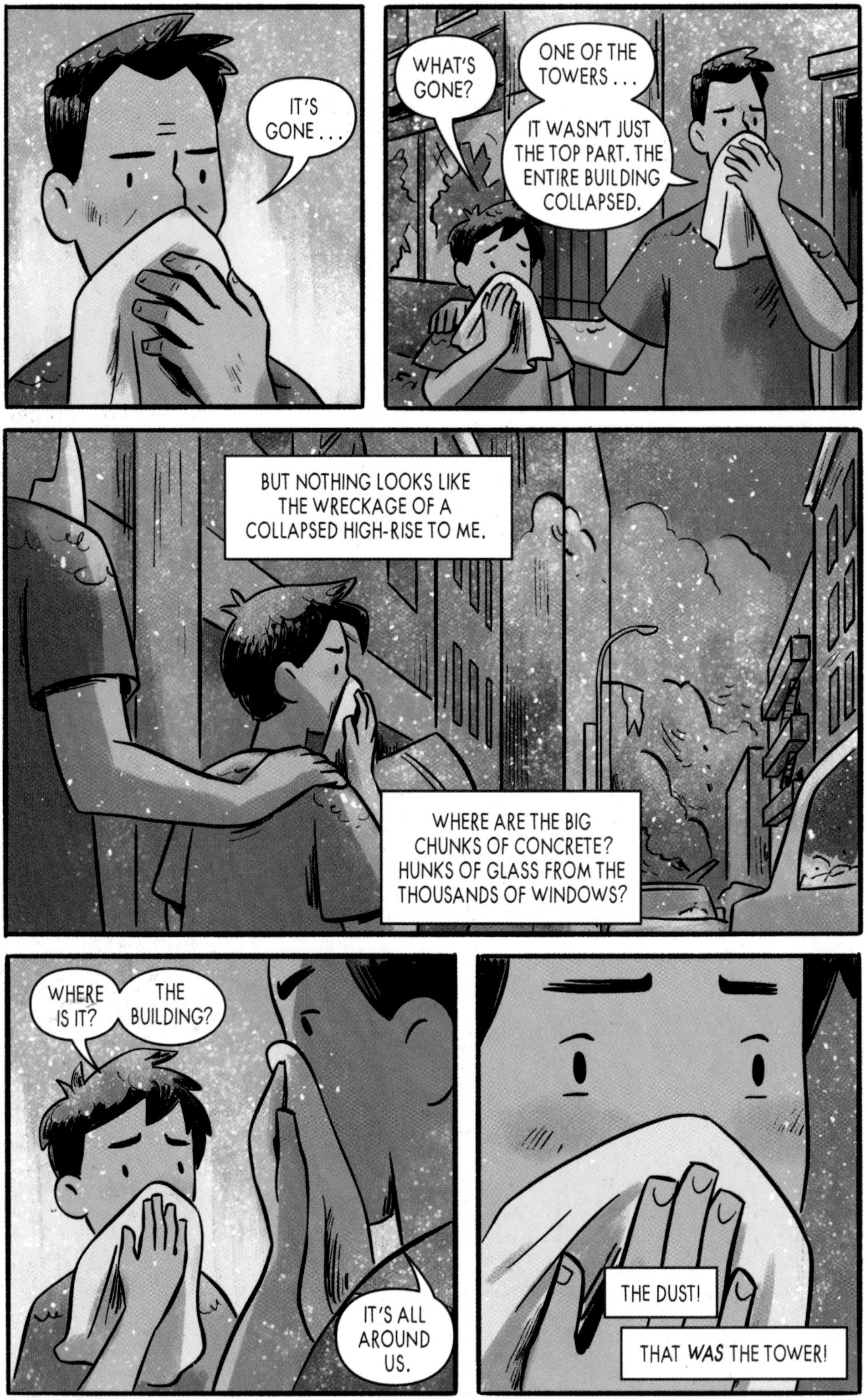
IT'S GONE . . .
WHAT'S GONE?
ONE OF THE TOWERS . . .
IT WASN'T JUST THE TOP PART. THE ENTIRE BUILDING COLLAPSED.
BUT NOTHING LOOKS LIKE THE WRECKAGE OF A COLLAPSED HIGH-RISE TO ME.
WHERE ARE THE BIG CHUNKS OF CONCRETE? HUNKS OF GLASS FROM THE THOUSANDS OF WINDOWS?
WHERE IS IT?
THE BUILDING?
IT'S ALL AROUND US.
THE DUST!
THAT *WAS* THE TOWER!

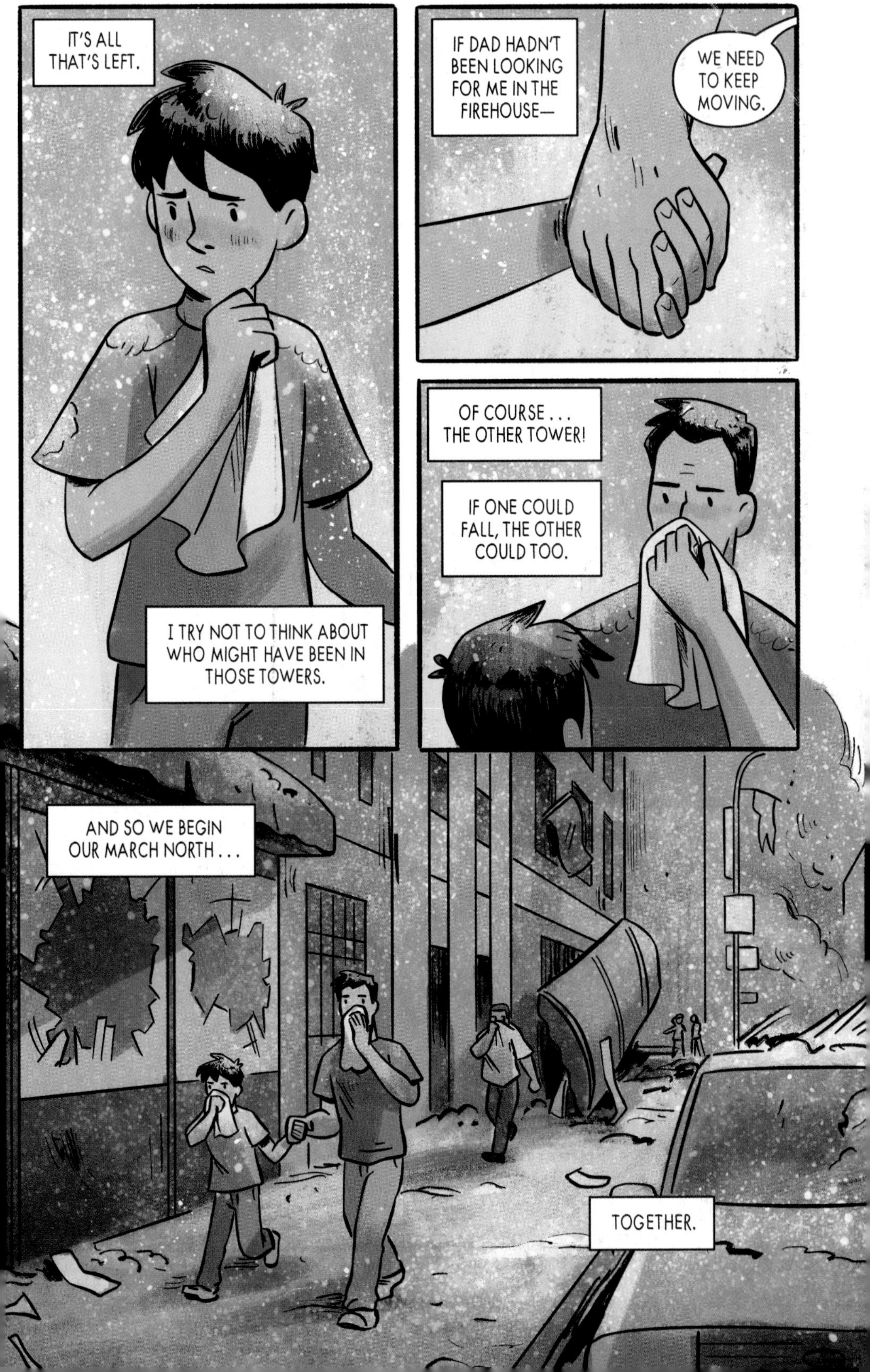
IT'S ALL THAT'S LEFT.
I TRY NOT TO THINK ABOUT WHO MIGHT HAVE BEEN IN THOSE TOWERS.
IF DAD HADN'T BEEN LOOKING FOR ME IN THE FIREHOUSE—
WE NEED TO KEEP MOVING.
OF COURSE . . . THE OTHER TOWER!
IF ONE COULD FALL, THE OTHER COULD TOO.
AND SO WE BEGIN OUR MARCH NORTH . . .
TOGETHER.

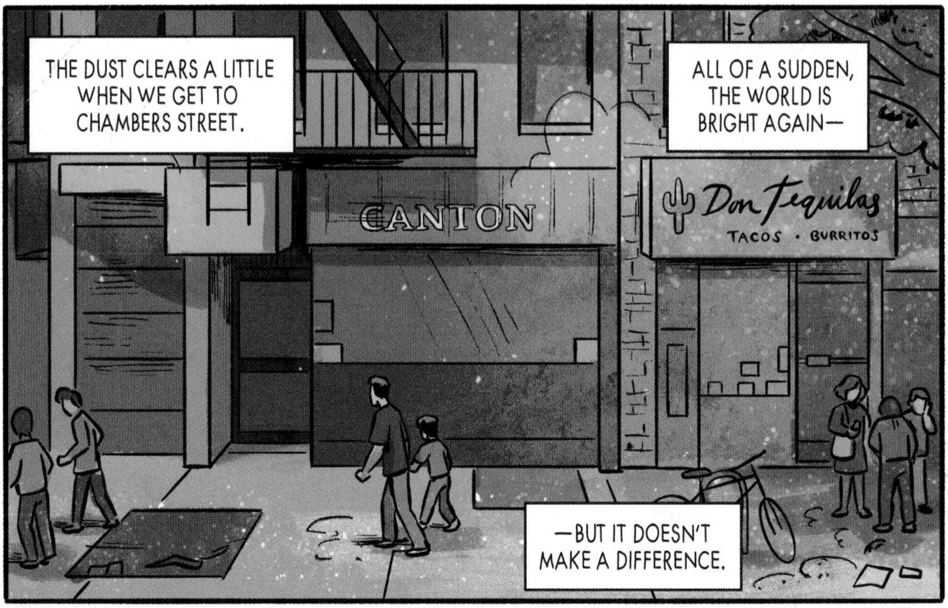
THE DUST CLEARS A LITTLE WHEN WE GET TO CHAMBERS STREET.
CANTON
Don Tequilas
TACOS • BURRITOS
ALL OF A SUDDEN, THE WORLD IS BRIGHT AGAIN—
—BUT IT DOESN'T MAKE A DIFFERENCE.

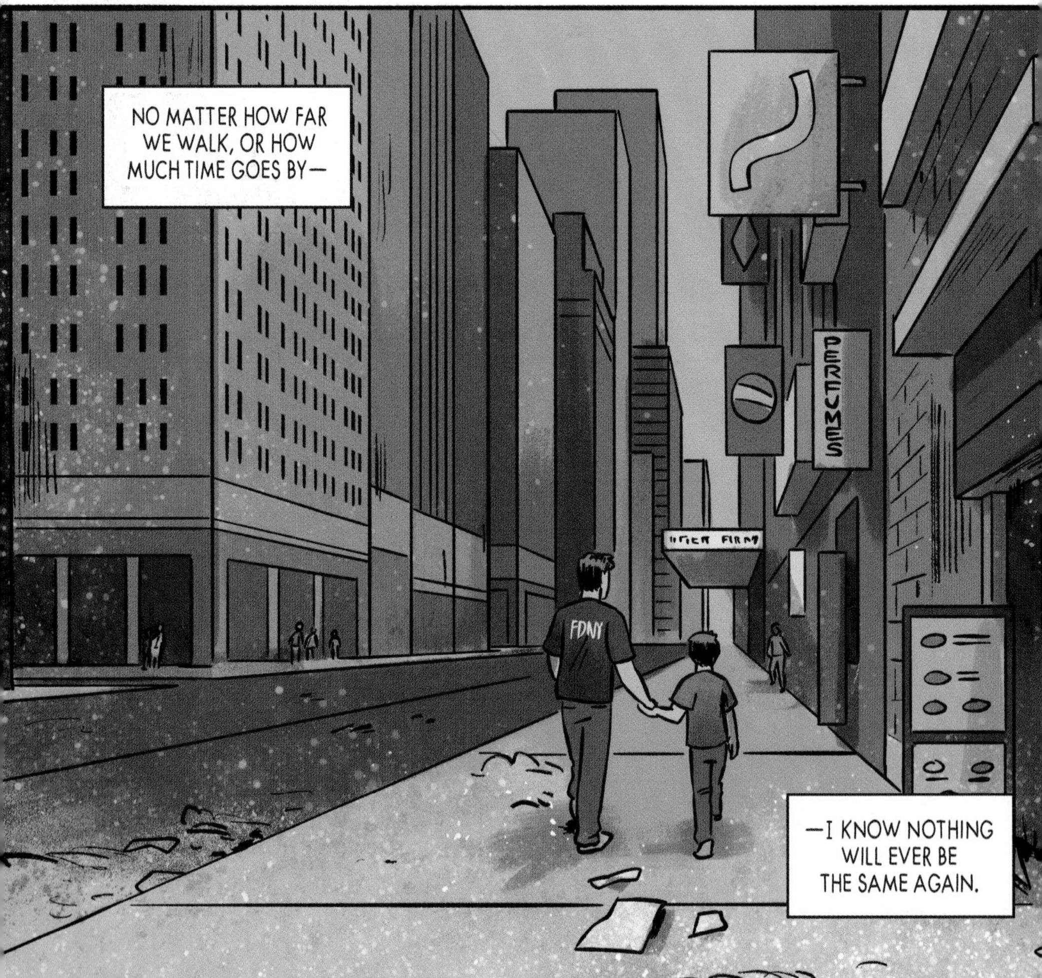
NO MATTER HOW FAR WE WALK, OR HOW MUCH TIME GOES BY—
PERFUMES
FDNY
—I KNOW NOTHING WILL EVER BE THE SAME AGAIN.

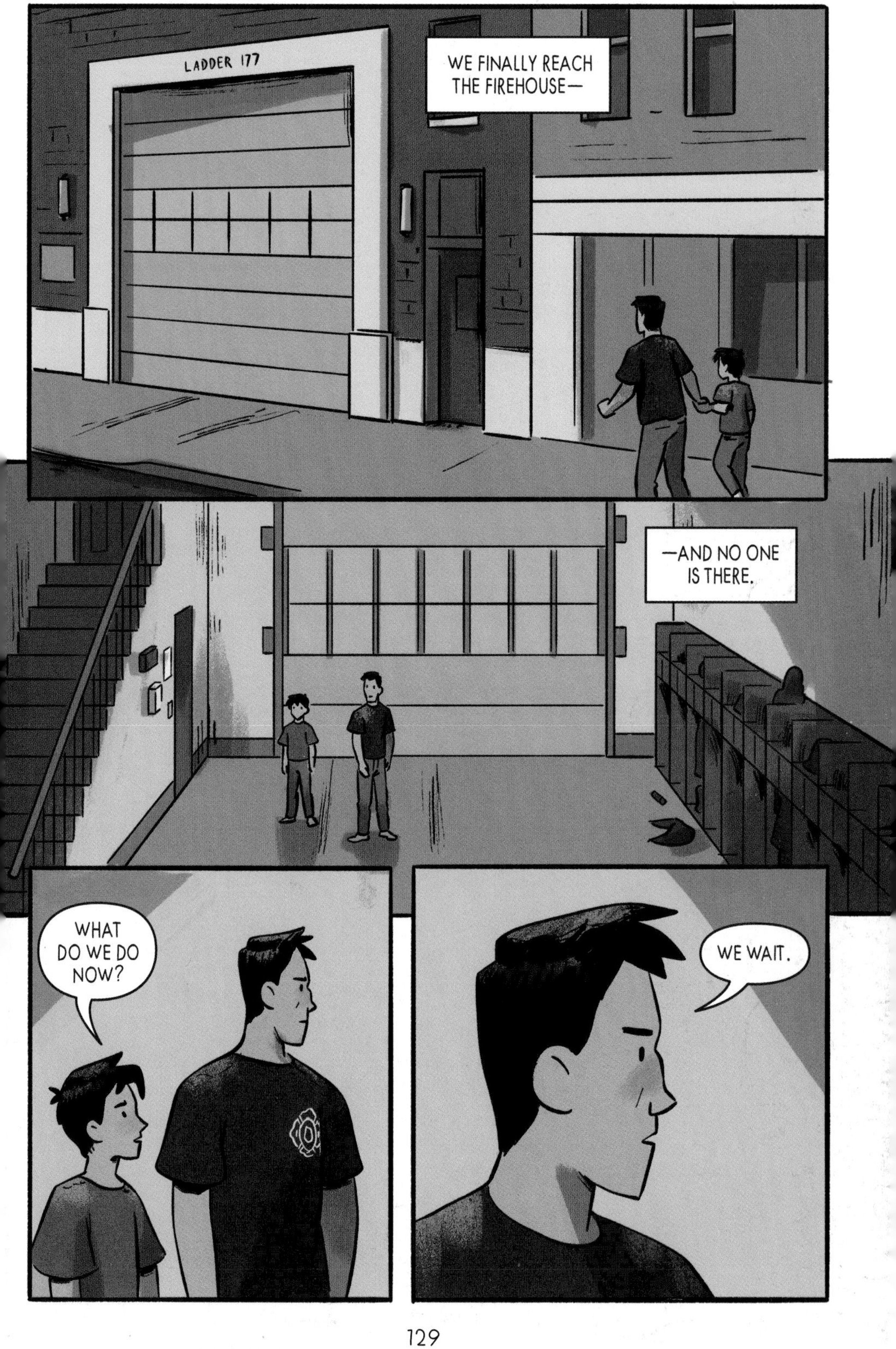
LADDER 177
WE FINALLY REACH THE FIREHOUSE—
—AND NO ONE IS THERE.
WHAT DO WE DO NOW?
WE WAIT.

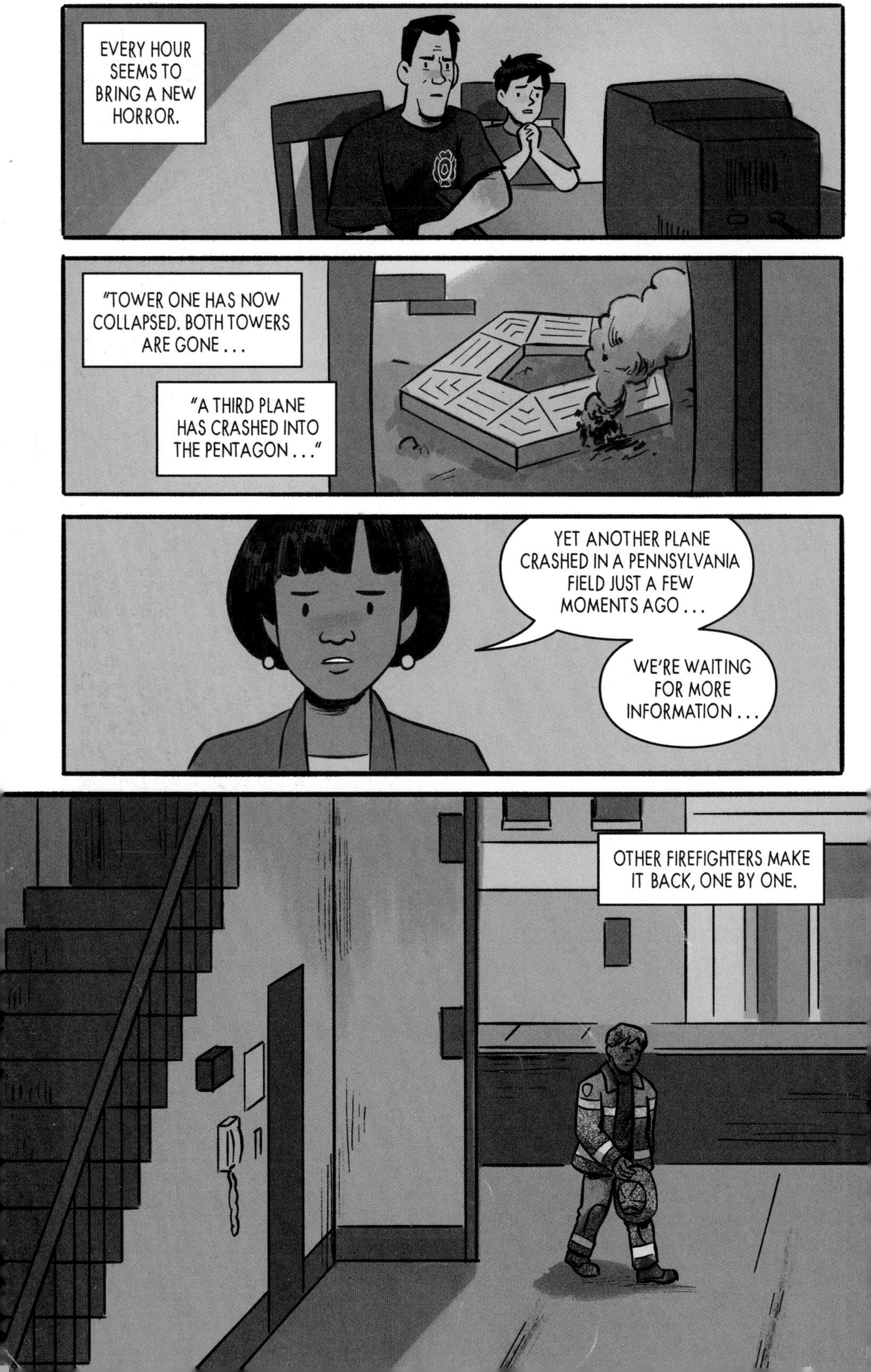
EVERY HOUR SEEMS TO BRING A NEW HORROR.
"TOWER ONE HAS NOW COLLAPSED. BOTH TOWERS ARE GONE . . .
"A THIRD PLANE HAS CRASHED INTO THE PENTAGON . . ."
YET ANOTHER PLANE CRASHED IN A PENNSYLVANIA FIELD JUST A FEW MOMENTS AGO . . .
WE'RE WAITING FOR MORE INFORMATION . . .
OTHER FIREFIGHTERS MAKE IT BACK, ONE BY ONE.

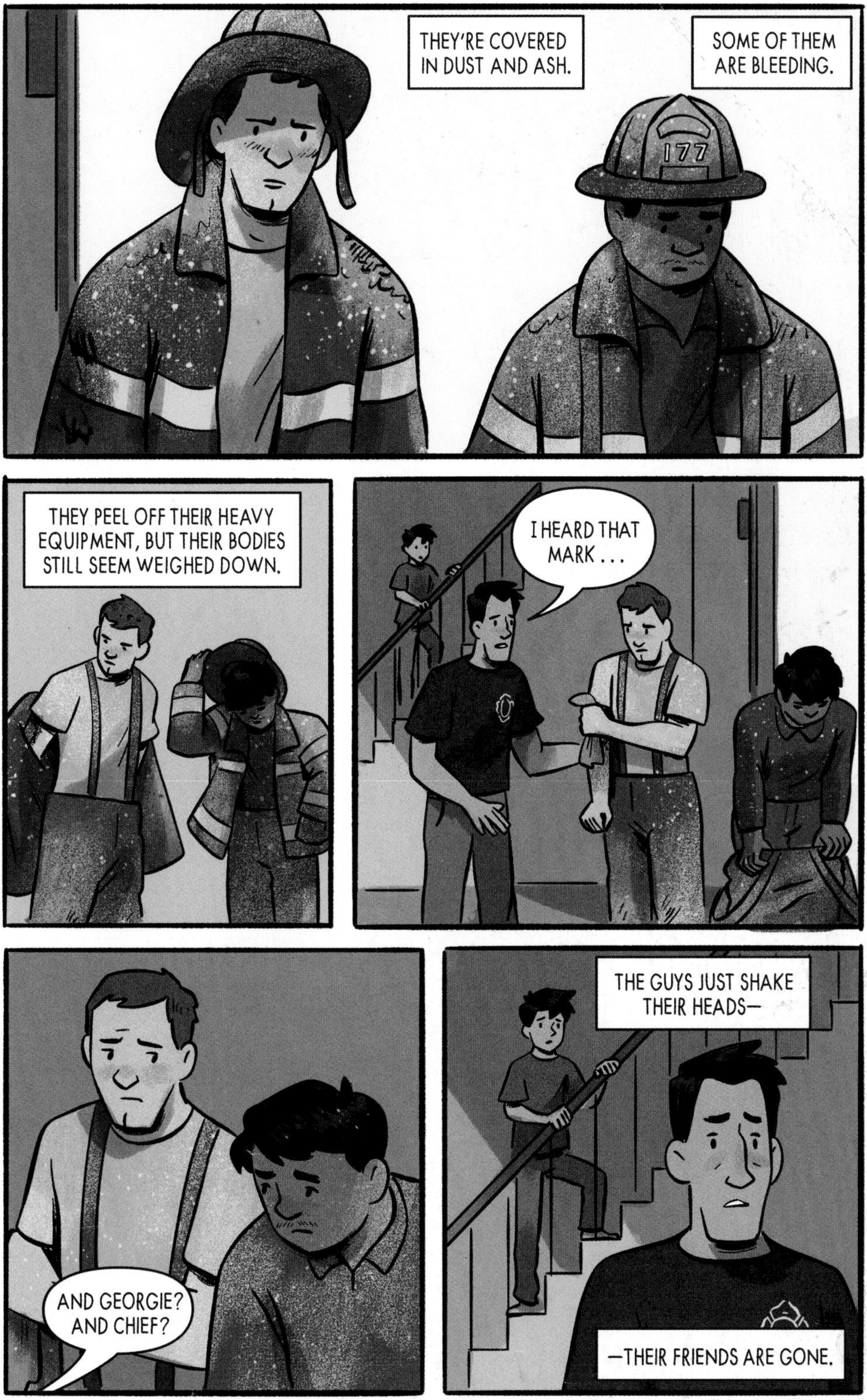
THEY'RE COVERED IN DUST AND ASH.
SOME OF THEM ARE BLEEDING.
177
THEY PEEL OFF THEIR HEAVY EQUIPMENT, BUT THEIR BODIES STILL SEEM WEIGHED DOWN.
I HEARD THAT MARK . . .
AND GEORGIE? AND CHIEF?
THE GUYS JUST SHAKE THEIR HEADS—
—THEIR FRIENDS ARE GONE.

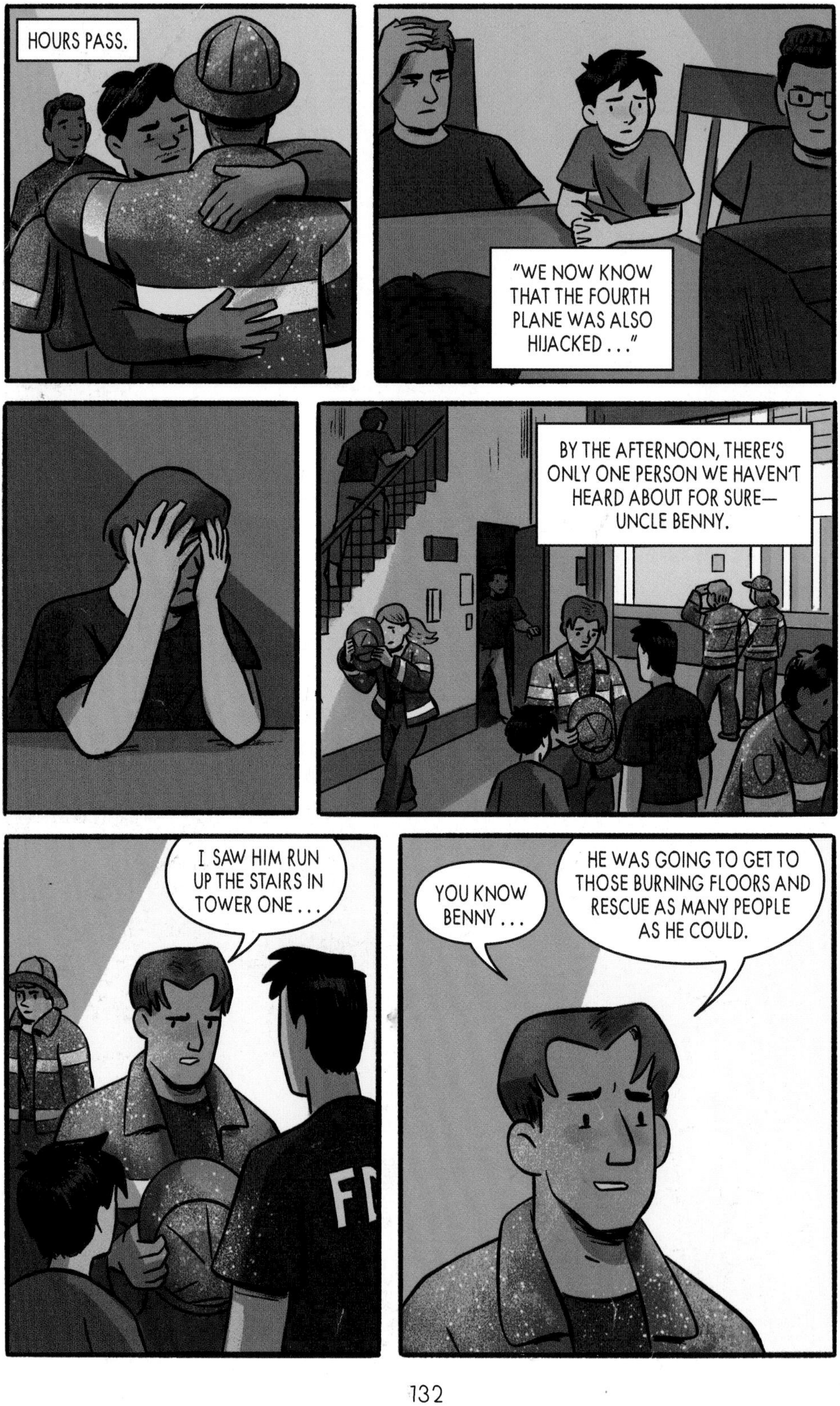
HOURS PASS.
"WE NOW KNOW THAT THE FOURTH PLANE WAS ALSO HIJACKED . . ."
BY THE AFTERNOON, THERE'S ONLY ONE PERSON WE HAVEN'T HEARD ABOUT FOR SURE— UNCLE BENNY.
I SAW HIM RUN UP THE STAIRS IN TOWER ONE . . .
FD
YOU KNOW BENNY . . .
HE WAS GOING TO GET TO THOSE BURNING FLOORS AND RESCUE AS MANY PEOPLE AS HE COULD.

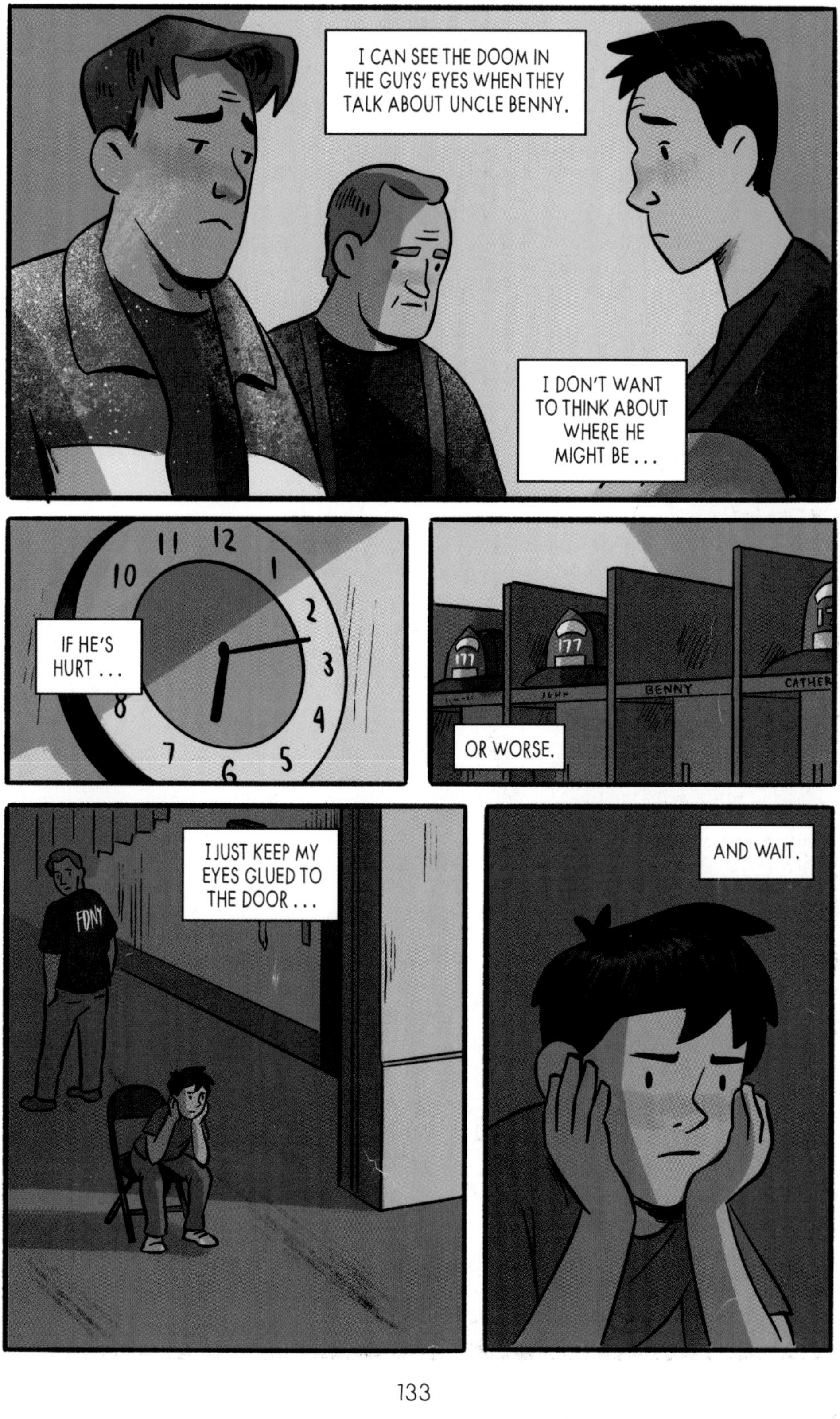
I CAN SEE THE DOOM IN THE GUYS' EYES WHEN THEY TALK ABOUT UNCLE BENNY.
I DON'T WANT TO THINK ABOUT WHERE HE MIGHT BE . . .
IF HE'S HURT . . .
177
177
BENNY
OR WORSE.
I JUST KEEP MY EYES GLUED TO THE DOOR . . .
FDNY
AND WAIT.

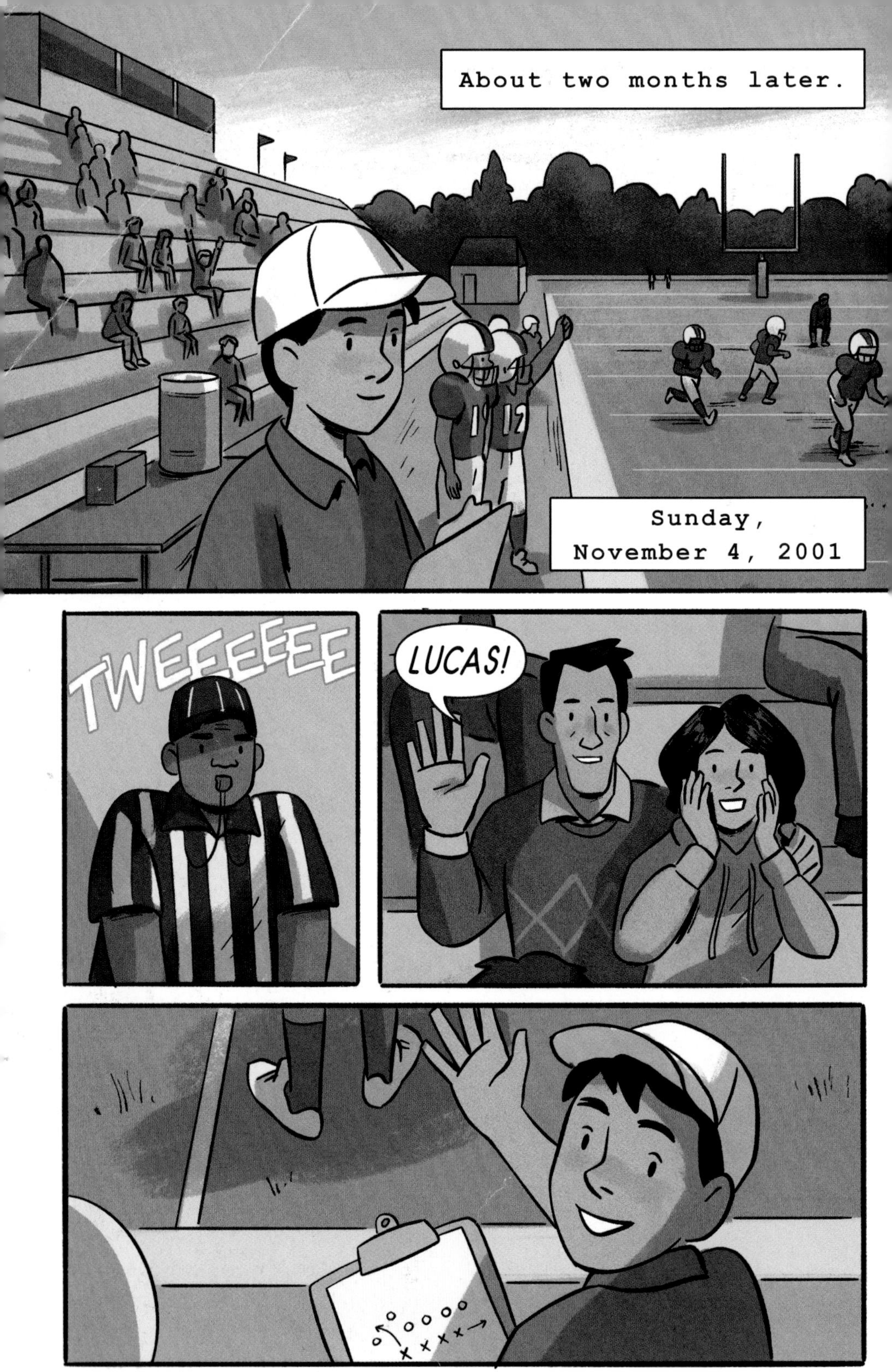
About two months later.
Sunday,
November 4, 2001
TWEEEEEE
LUCAS!

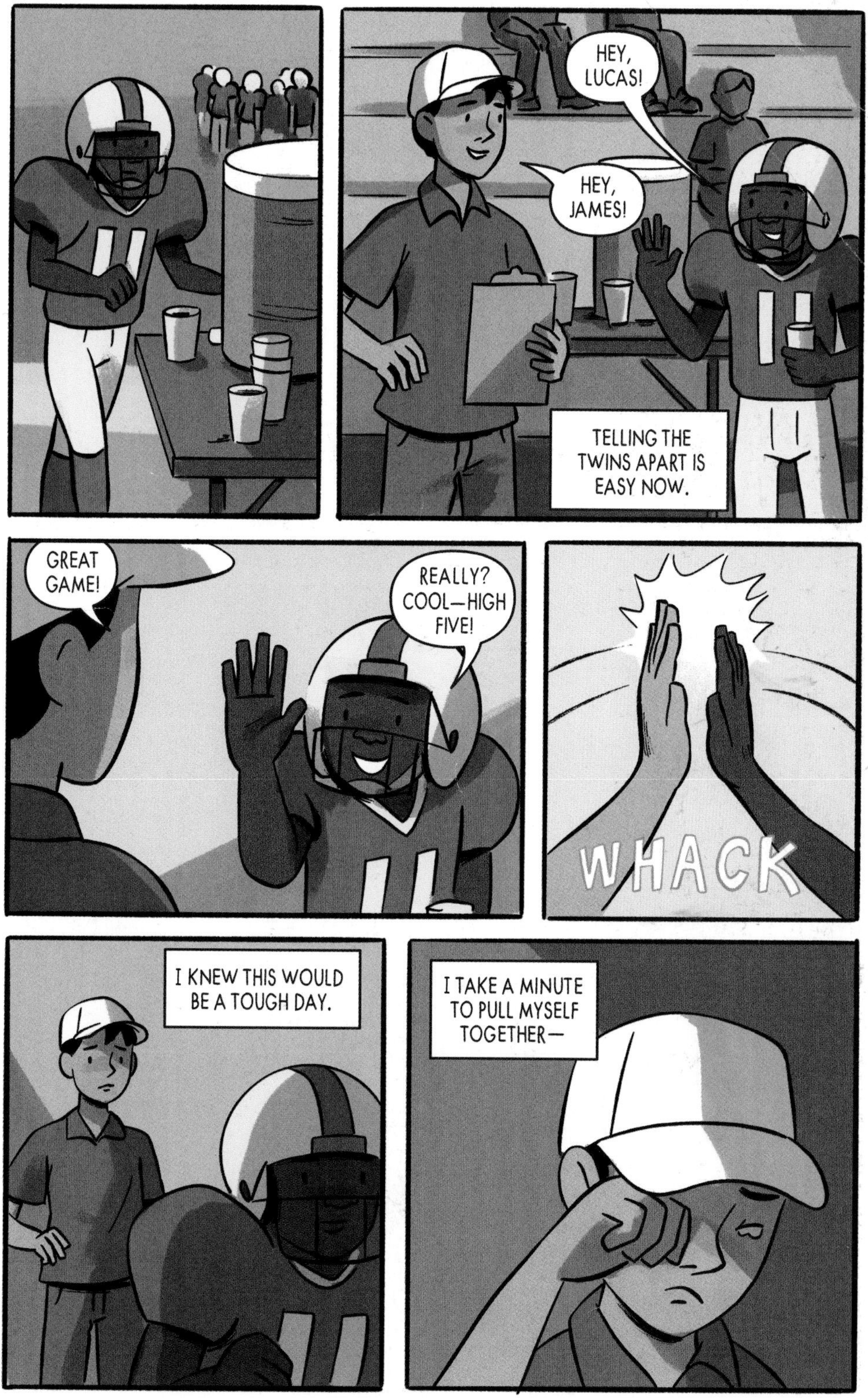
HEY, LUCAS!
HEY, JAMES!
TELLING THE TWINS APART IS EASY NOW.
GREAT GAME!
REALLY? COOL—HIGH FIVE!
WHACK
I KNEW THIS WOULD BE A TOUGH DAY.
I TAKE A MINUTE TO PULL MYSELF TOGETHER—

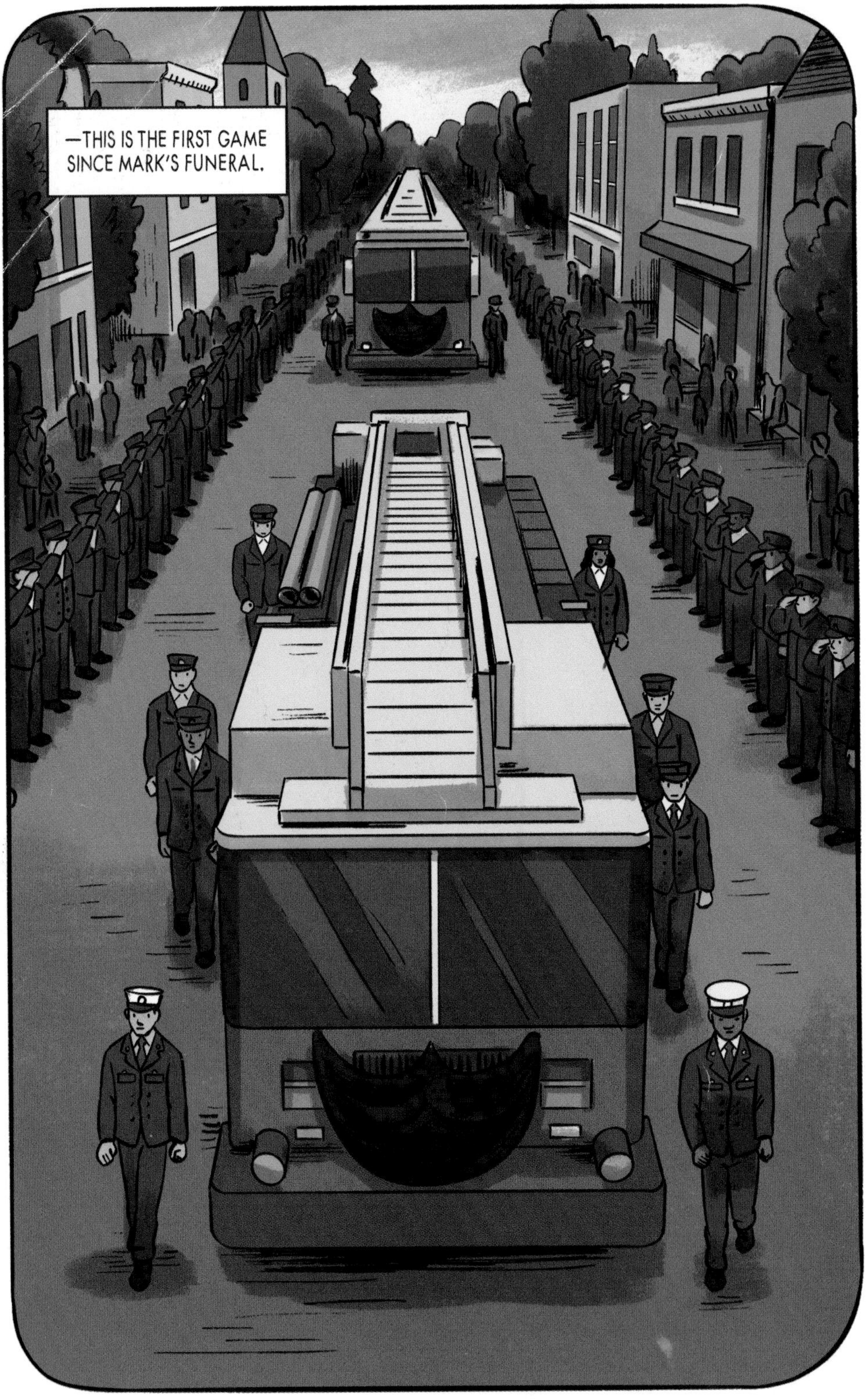
—THIS IS THE FIRST GAME SINCE MARK'S FUNERAL.

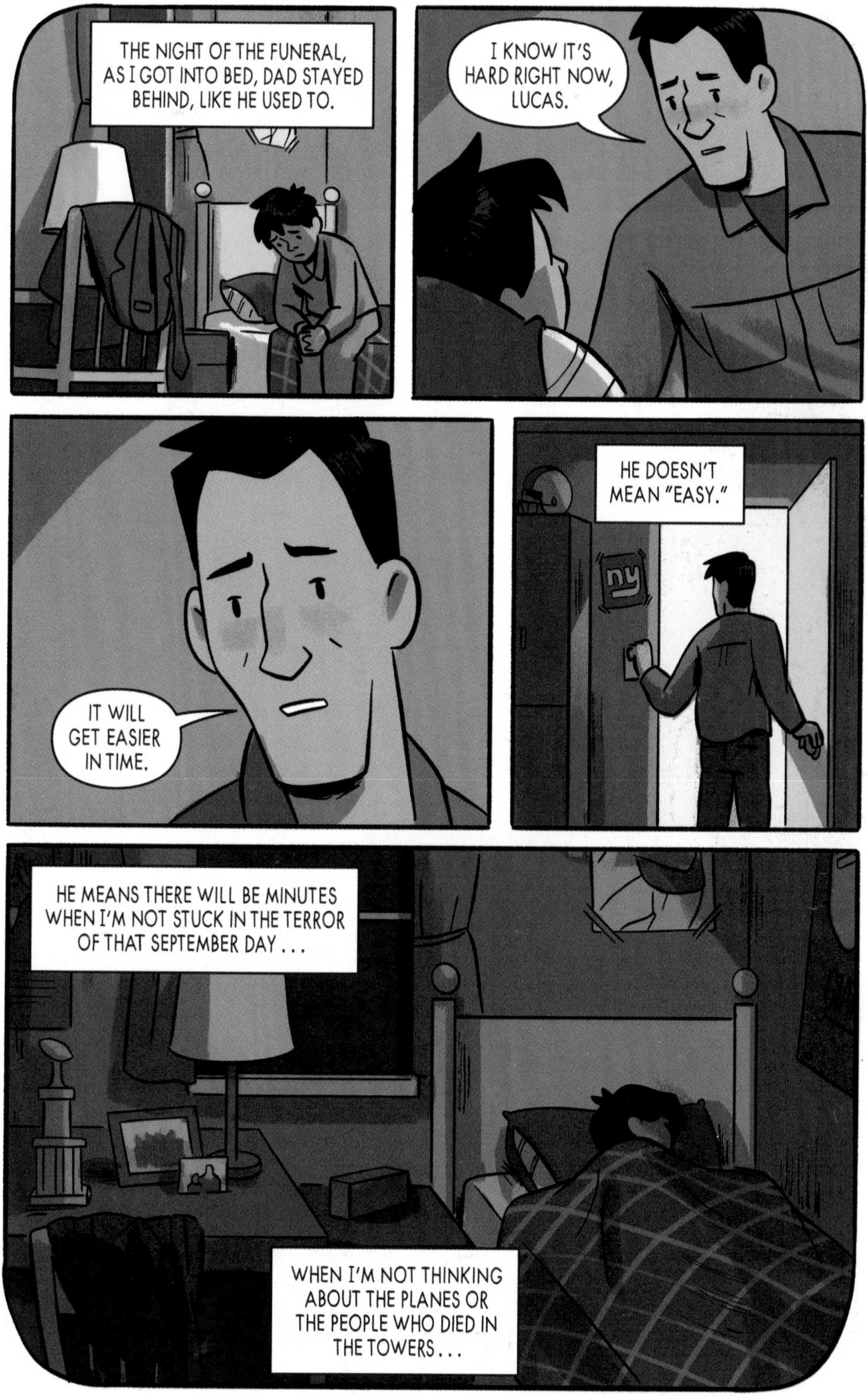
THE NIGHT OF THE FUNERAL, AS I GOT INTO BED, DAD STAYED BEHIND, LIKE HE USED TO.
I KNOW IT'S HARD RIGHT NOW, LUCAS.
IT WILL GET EASIER IN TIME.
HE DOESN'T MEAN "EASY."
HE MEANS THERE WILL BE MINUTES WHEN I'M NOT STUCK IN THE TERROR OF THAT SEPTEMBER DAY . . .
WHEN I'M NOT THINKING ABOUT THE PLANES OR THE PEOPLE WHO DIED IN THE TOWERS . . .

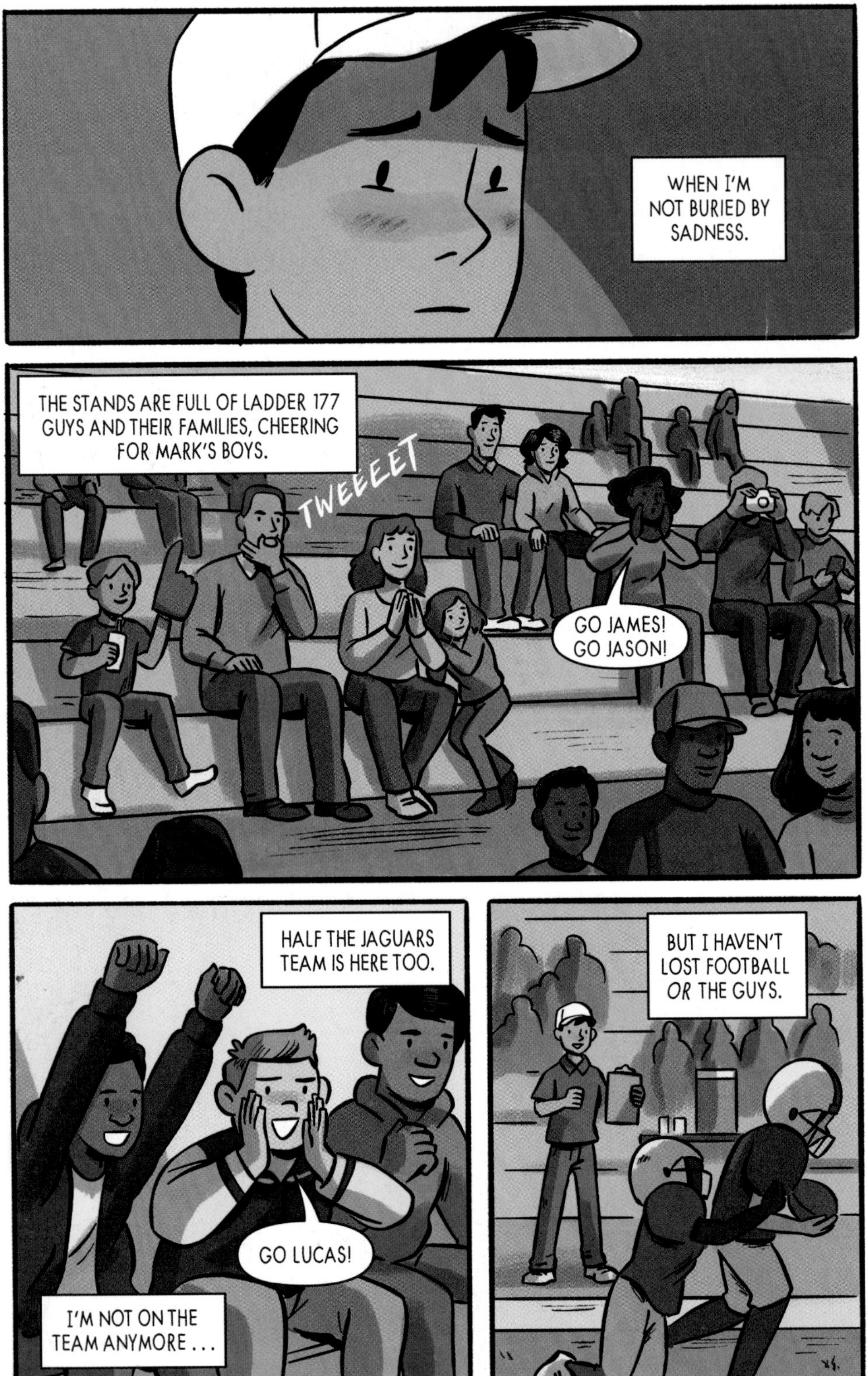
WHEN I'M NOT BURIED BY SADNESS.
THE STANDS ARE FULL OF LADDER 177 GUYS AND THEIR FAMILIES, CHEERING FOR MARK'S BOYS.
TWEEEET
GO JAMES! GO JASON!
HALF THE JAGUARS TEAM IS HERE TOO.
GO LUCAS!
I'M NOT ON THE TEAM ANYMORE . . .
BUT I HAVEN'T LOST FOOTBALL *OR* THE GUYS.

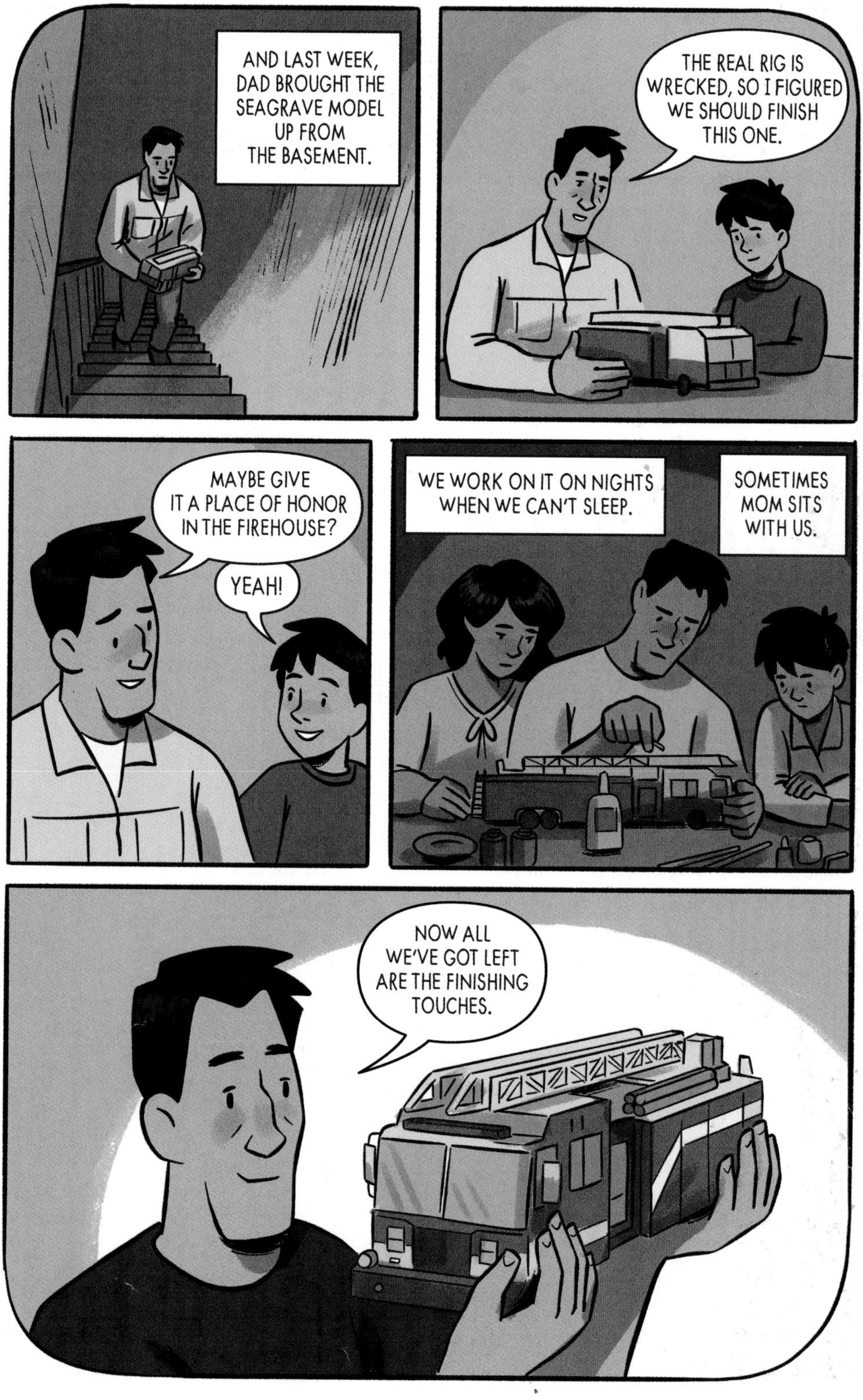
AND LAST WEEK, DAD BROUGHT THE SEAGRAVE MODEL UP FROM THE BASEMENT.
THE REAL RIG IS WRECKED, SO I FIGURED WE SHOULD FINISH THIS ONE.
MAYBE GIVE IT A PLACE OF HONOR IN THE FIREHOUSE?
YEAH!
WE WORK ON IT ON NIGHTS WHEN WE CAN'T SLEEP.
SOMETIMES MOM SITS WITH US.
NOW ALL WE'VE GOT LEFT ARE THE FINISHING TOUCHES.

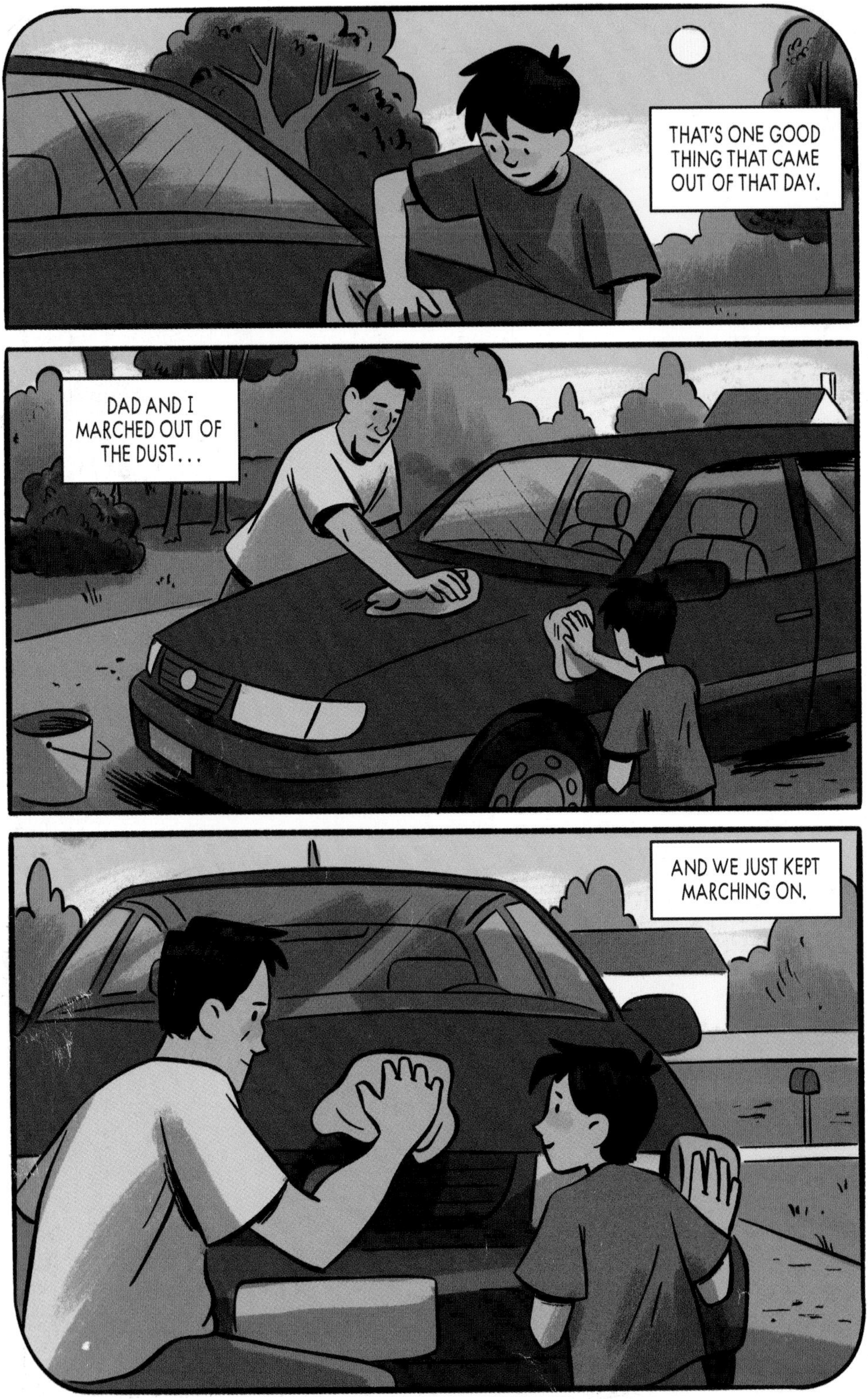
THAT'S ONE GOOD THING THAT CAME OUT OF THAT DAY.
DAD AND I MARCHED OUT OF THE DUST. . .
AND WE JUST KEPT MARCHING ON.

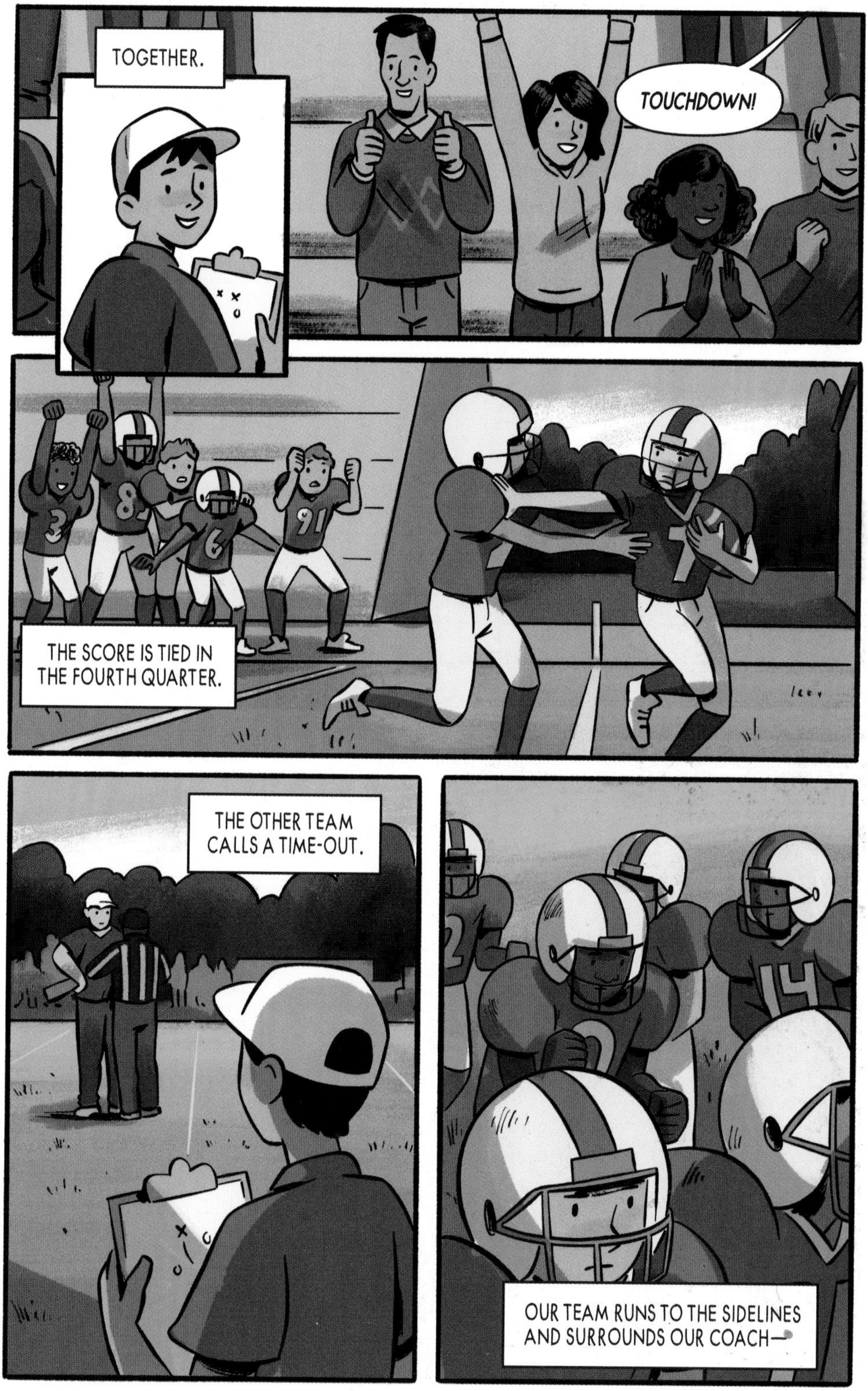
TOGETHER.
TOUCHDOWN!
THE SCORE IS TIED IN THE FOURTH QUARTER.
THE OTHER TEAM CALLS A TIME-OUT.
OUR TEAM RUNS TO THE SIDELINES AND SURROUNDS OUR COACH—

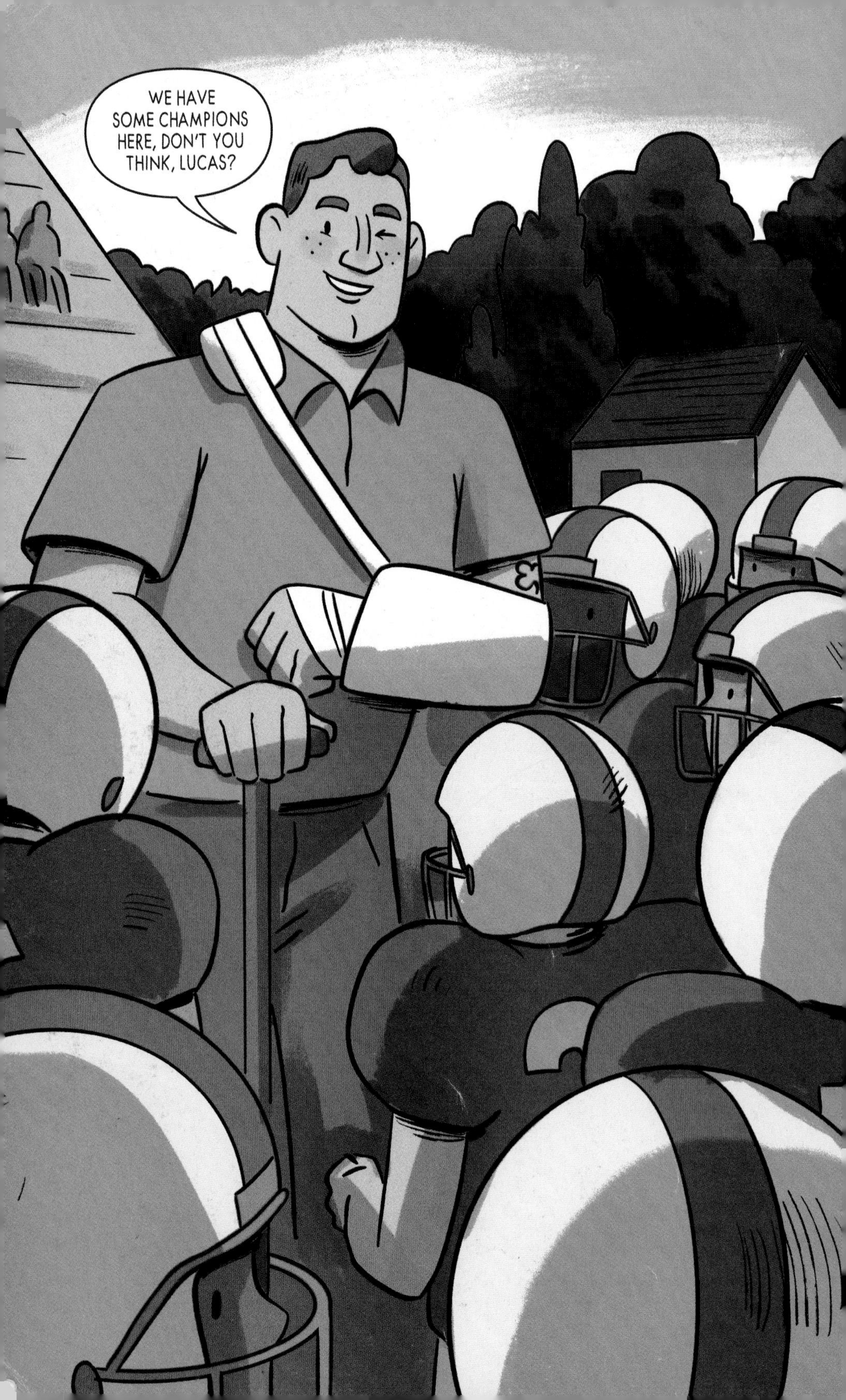
WE HAVE SOME CHAMPIONS HERE, DON'T YOU THINK, LUCAS?

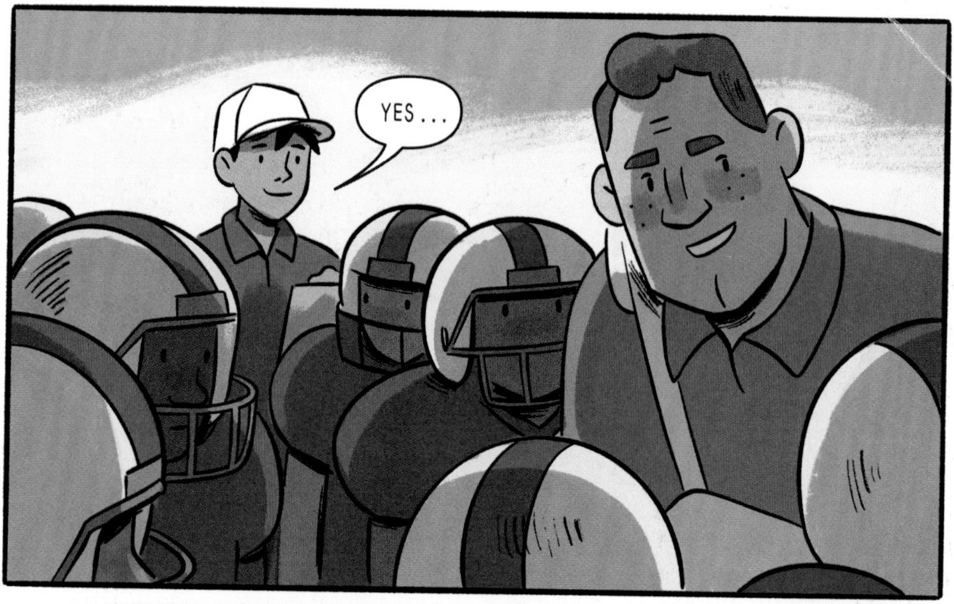
YES . . .

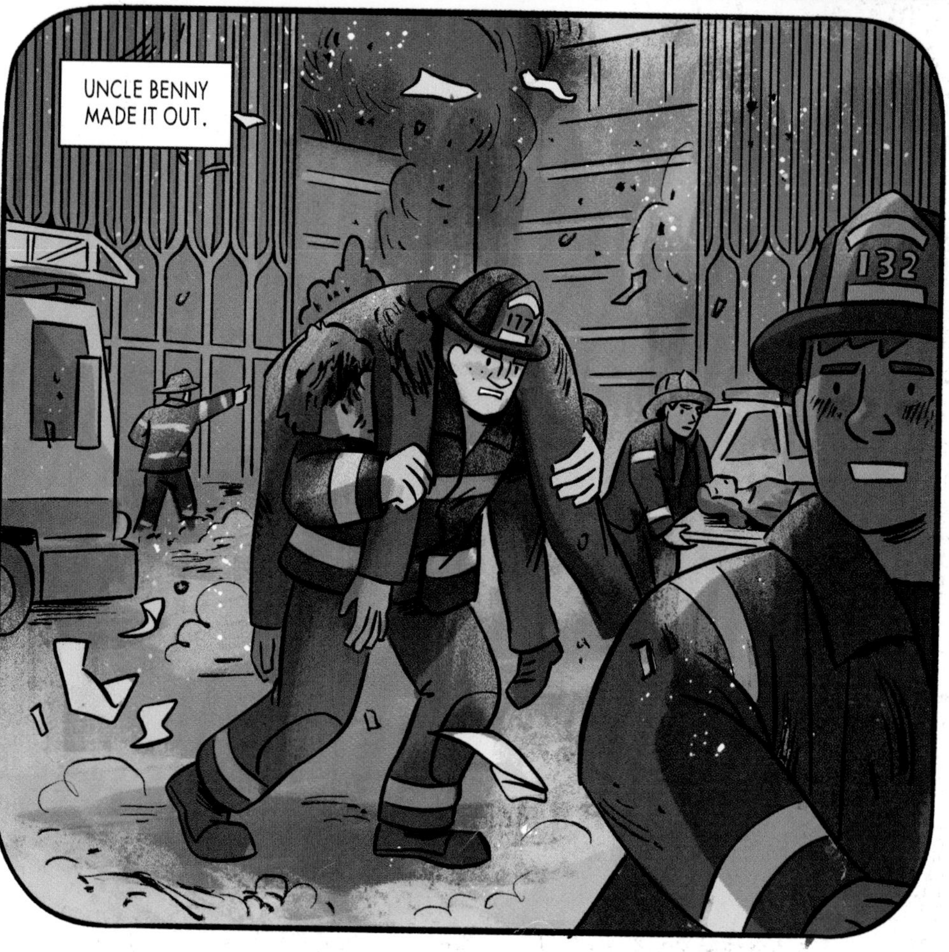
UNCLE BENNY MADE IT OUT.
177
132

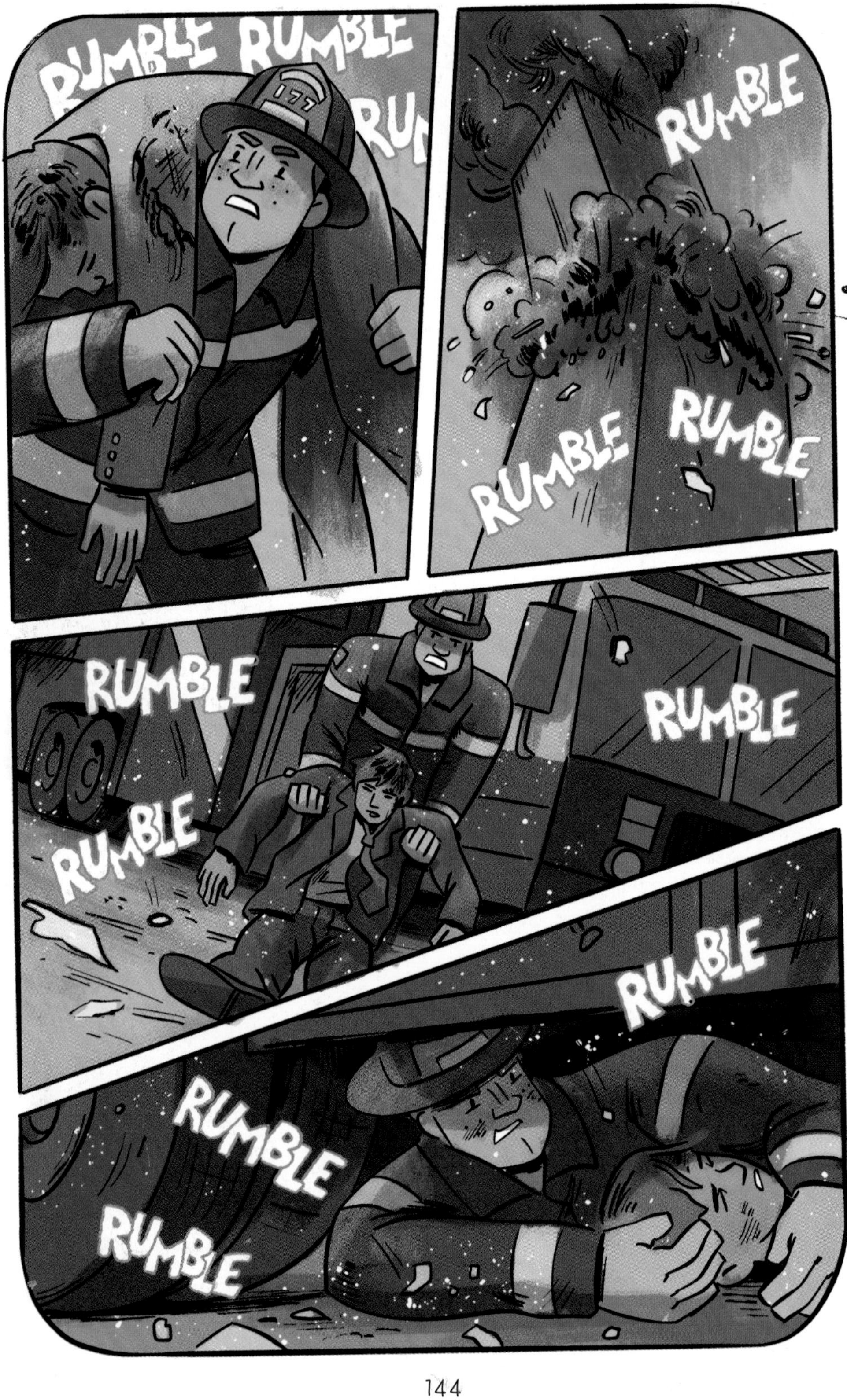
RUMBLE RUMBLE
RU
RUMBLE
RUMBLE
RUMBLE
RUMBLE
RUMBLE
RUMBLE
RUMBLE
RUMBLE
RUMBLE

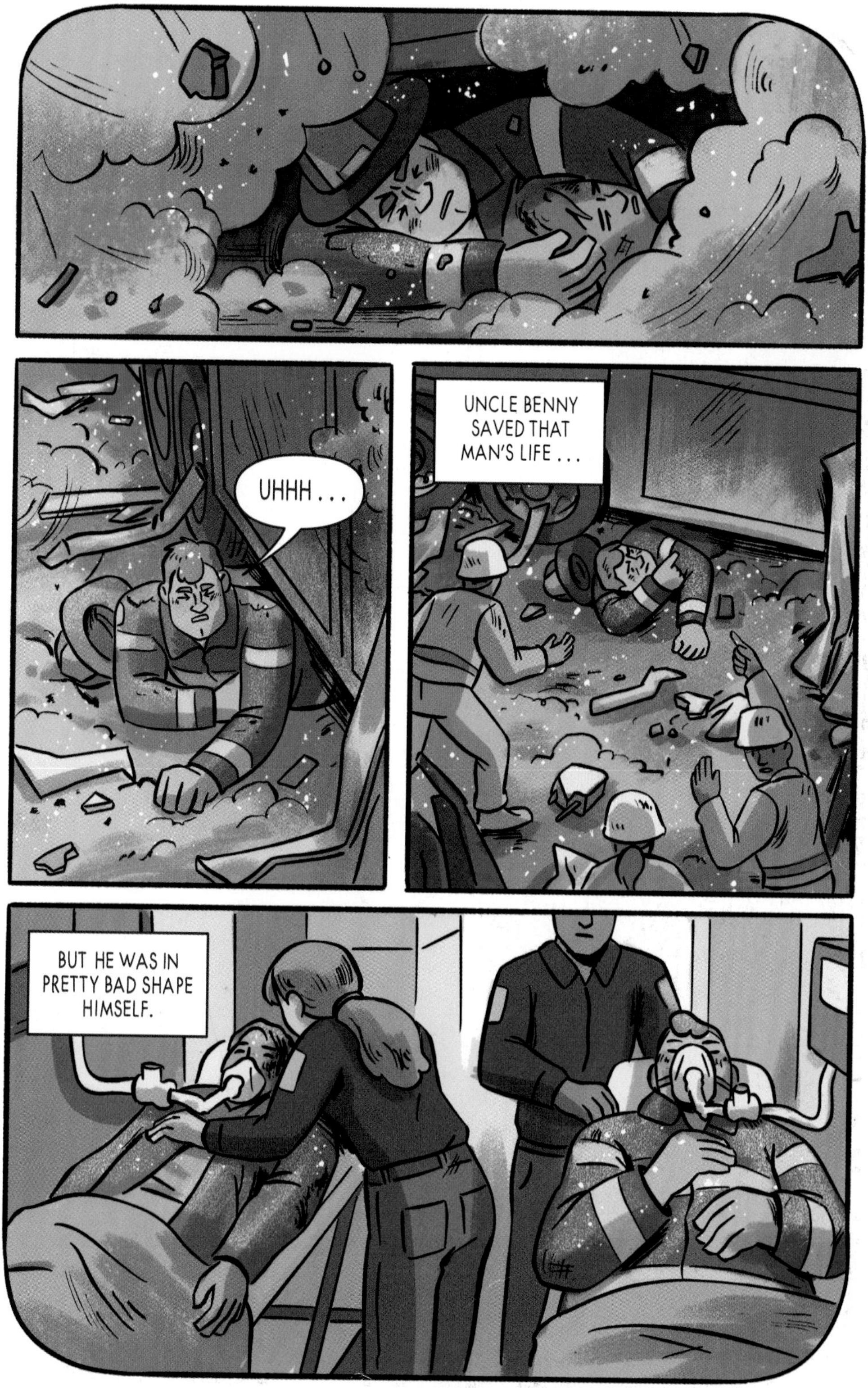
UHHH . . .
UNCLE BENNY SAVED THAT MAN'S LIFE . . .
BUT HE WAS IN PRETTY BAD SHAPE HIMSELF.

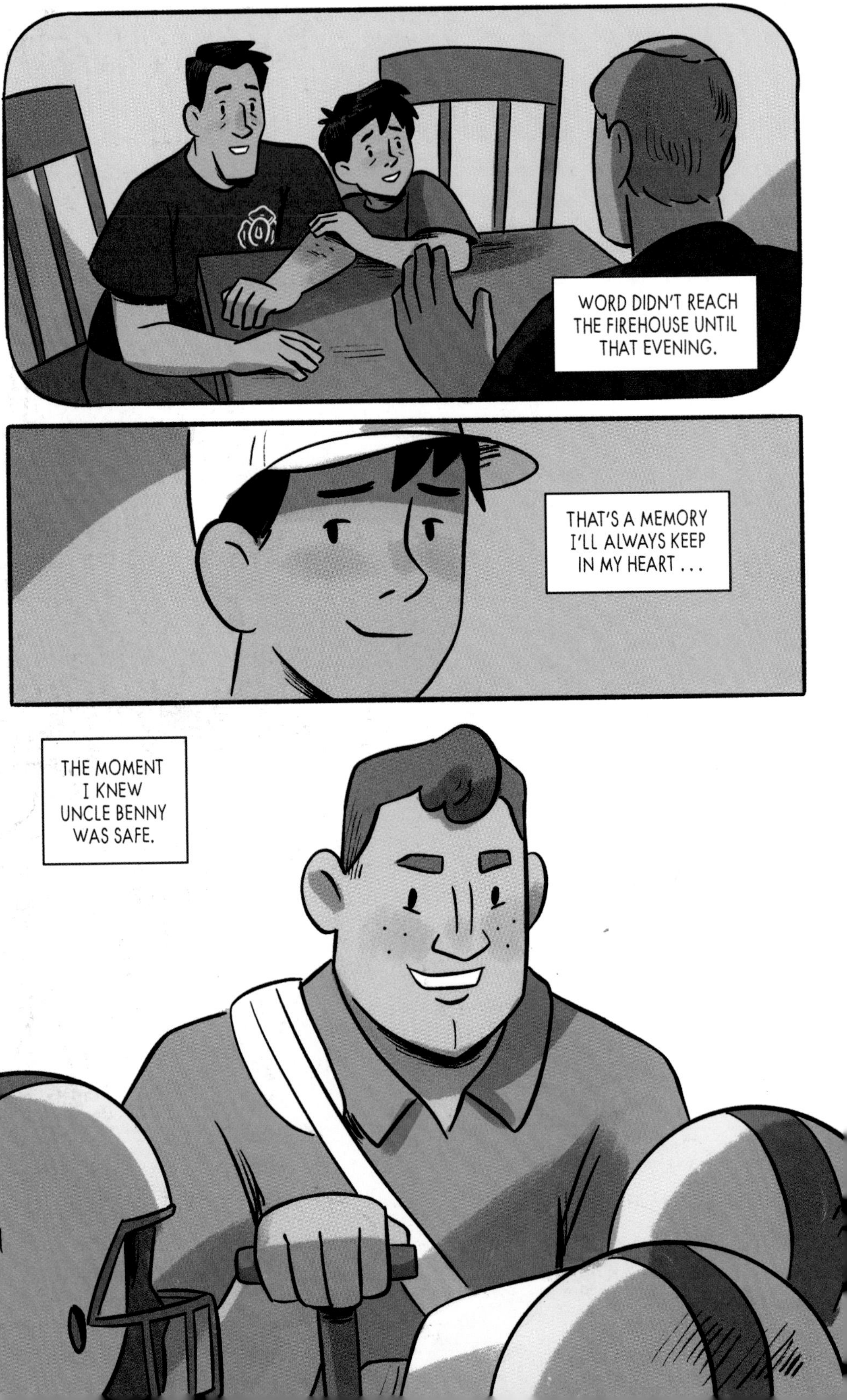
WORD DIDN'T REACH THE FIREHOUSE UNTIL THAT EVENING.
THAT'S A MEMORY I'LL ALWAYS KEEP IN MY HEART . . .
THE MOMENT I KNEW UNCLE BENNY WAS SAFE.

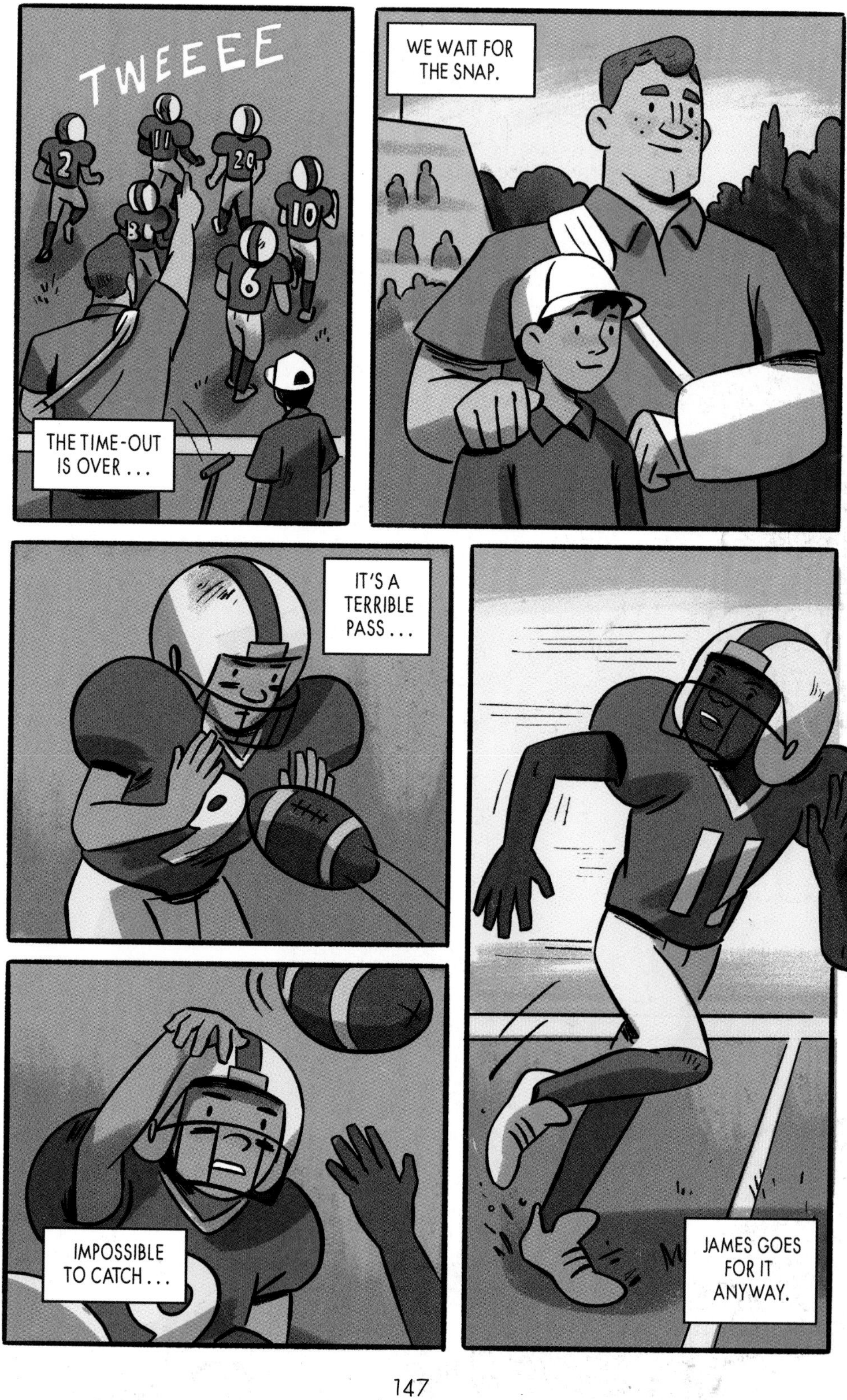
TWEEEE
THE TIME-OUT IS OVER . . .
WE WAIT FOR THE SNAP.
IT'S A TERRIBLE PASS . . .
IMPOSSIBLE TO CATCH . . .
JAMES GOES FOR IT ANYWAY.

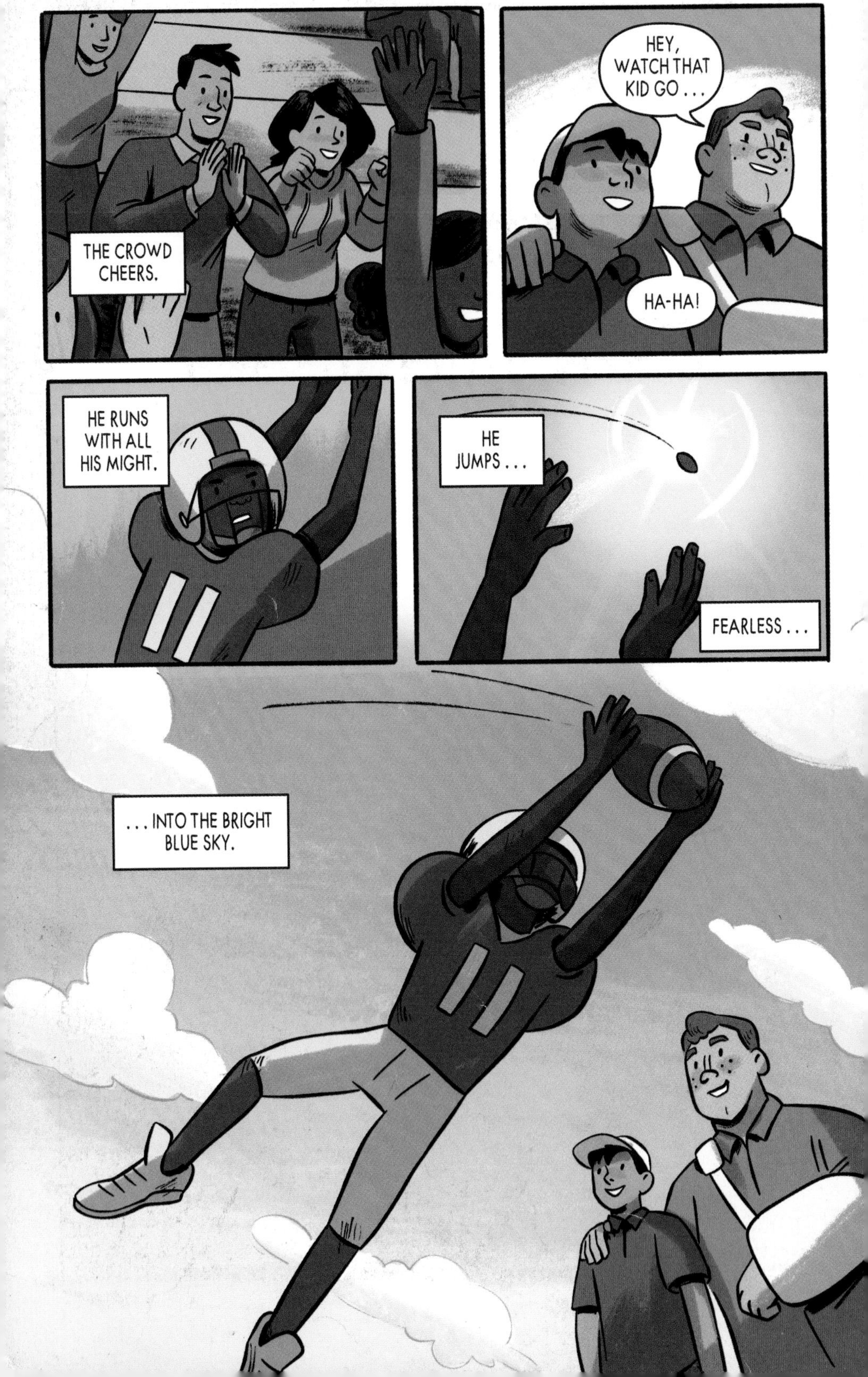

THE CROWD CHEERS.
HEY, WATCH THAT KID GO . . .
HA-HA!
HE RUNS WITH ALL HIS MIGHT.
HE JUMPS . . .
FEARLESS . . .
. . . INTO THE BRIGHT BLUE SKY.

TURN THE PAGE
TO READ MORE ABOUT
THE REAL-LIFE EVENTS OF
SEPTEMBER II, 2001

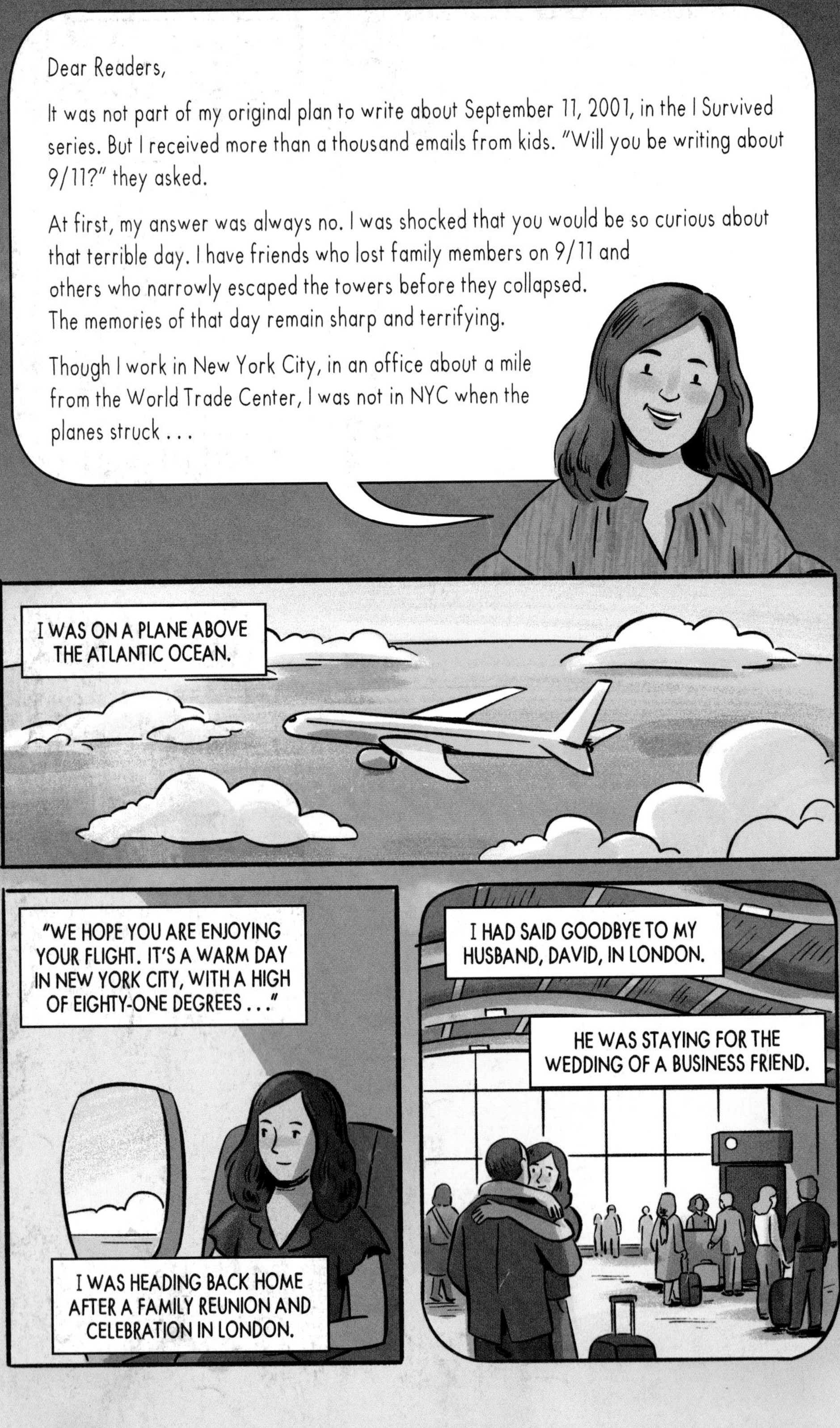
Dear Readers,
It was not part of my original plan to write about September 11, 2001, in the I Survived series. But I received more than a thousand emails from kids. "Will you be writing about 9/11?" they asked.
At first, my answer was always no. I was shocked that you would be so curious about that terrible day. I have friends who lost family members on 9/11 and others who narrowly escaped the towers before they collapsed. The memories of that day remain sharp and terrifying.
Though I work in New York City, in an office about a mile from the World Trade Center, I was not in NYC when the planes struck . . .
I WAS ON A PLANE ABOVE THE ATLANTIC OCEAN.
"WE HOPE YOU ARE ENJOYING YOUR FLIGHT. IT'S A WARM DAY IN NEW YORK CITY, WITH A HIGH OF EIGHTY-ONE DEGREES . . ."
I WAS HEADING BACK HOME AFTER A FAMILY REUNION AND CELEBRATION IN LONDON.
I HAD SAID GOODBYE TO MY HUSBAND, DAVID, IN LONDON.
HE WAS STAYING FOR THE WEDDING OF A BUSINESS FRIEND.

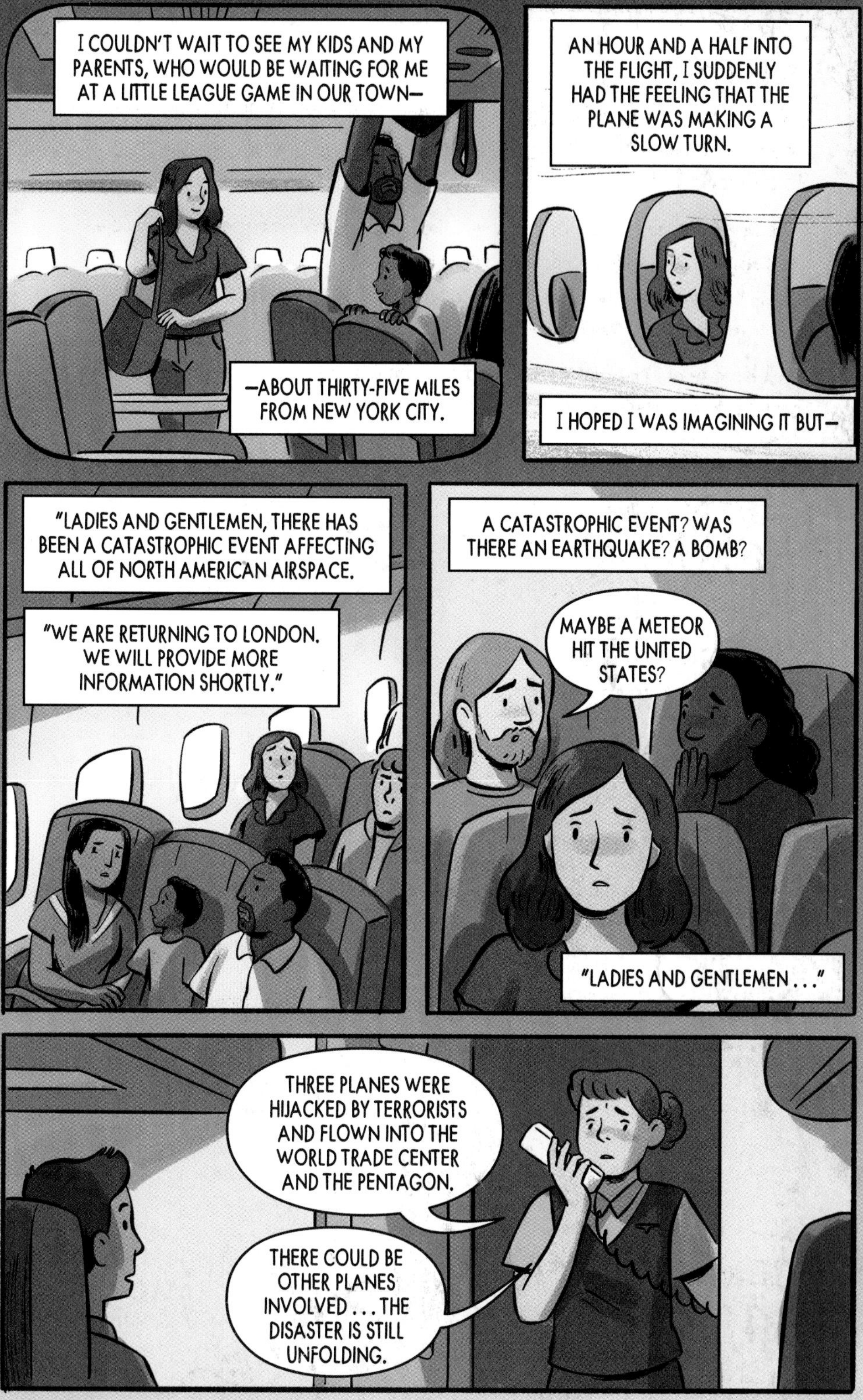
I COULDN'T WAIT TO SEE MY KIDS AND MY PARENTS, WHO WOULD BE WAITING FOR ME AT A LITTLE LEAGUE GAME IN OUR TOWN—
—ABOUT THIRTY-FIVE MILES FROM NEW YORK CITY.
AN HOUR AND A HALF INTO THE FLIGHT, I SUDDENLY HAD THE FEELING THAT THE PLANE WAS MAKING A SLOW TURN.
I HOPED I WAS IMAGINING IT BUT—
"LADIES AND GENTLEMEN, THERE HAS BEEN A CATASTROPHIC EVENT AFFECTING ALL OF NORTH AMERICAN AIRSPACE.
"WE ARE RETURNING TO LONDON. WE WILL PROVIDE MORE INFORMATION SHORTLY."
A CATASTROPHIC EVENT? WAS THERE AN EARTHQUAKE? A BOMB?
MAYBE A METEOR HIT THE UNITED STATES?
"LADIES AND GENTLEMEN . . ."
THREE PLANES WERE HIJACKED BY TERRORISTS AND FLOWN INTO THE WORLD TRADE CENTER AND THE PENTAGON.
THERE COULD BE OTHER PLANES INVOLVED . . . THE DISASTER IS STILL UNFOLDING.

WHEN WE LANDED IN LONDON, POLICE ESCORTED US INTO THE CHAOTIC AIRPORT.

I DIDN'T HAVE ANY MONEY, BUT A NICE TAXI DRIVER TOOK ME TO MY HUSBAND'S HOTEL.

WE BOTH CRIED THE WHOLE WAY.

DAVID AND I WEREN'T ABLE TO GET A CALL THROUGH TO OUR KIDS UNTIL LATE THAT NIGHT.

IT WAS FOUR MORE DAYS BEFORE PLANES BEGAN FLYING TO THE UNITED STATES AGAIN—

—AND WE COULD GET HOME TO OUR FAMILY.

I'D NEVER HUGGED THEM SO TIGHT.

The city slowly came back to life. Today, while the horrors of that day still linger, people have done their best to move forward.

So why did I write this book? Because after talking to many of you, I began to understand: 9/11 shaped the world you were born into. It's only natural that you would be curious about it. I hope my story gives you a sense of that day—the fear and the courage, the sense of horror and shock.

I will admit that in my plans for this story, Uncle Benny did not survive. I had it in my mind that he charged up the stairs of Tower One with fifty pounds of gear on his back. Lucas waited for him to return to the firehouse, but he never did.

But as I wrote the last page with Lucas on the football field, suddenly there was Uncle Benny. He just appeared. I could picture him so clearly, still banged up, but his eyes sparkling, looking at me as if to say, "Come on, there was so much sadness that day. Could you please give Lucas's story a happy ending?" And so I did.

Keep reading to learn more about 9/11 and the heroes who risked everything to help their fellow New Yorkers, with Lucas, Uncle Benny, Dad, and Mom to guide you.

TIMELINE

SEPTEMBER 11, 2001

8:46 A.M.	A commercial jet, **AMERICAN AIRLINES FLIGHT 11**, crashes into the North Tower (Tower One) of the World Trade Center.
9:03 A.M.	Another jet, **UNITED AIRLINES FLIGHT 175**, crashes into the South Tower (Tower Two) of the World Trade Center.
9:25 A.M.	United States airspace begins shutting down. No planes are allowed to take off.
9:37 A.M.	**AMERICAN AIRLINES FLIGHT 77** crashes into the Pentagon, the headquarters of the United States military, in Arlington County, Virginia.
9:59 A.M.	The **SOUTH TOWER** of the World Trade Center begins to collapse. People from around the country and the world watch it on TV.
10:03 A.M.	A fourth and final jet, **UNITED AIRLINES FLIGHT 93**, crashes into a field near Shanksville, Pennsylvania. It is later learned that Flight 93 was intended for either the United States Capitol building or the White House in Washington, DC. Passengers on that plane had learned of the crashes at the World Trade Center and the Pentagon. They stormed the cockpit and tried to regain control of the plane from the terrorists.
10:28 A.M.	The **NORTH TOWER** of the World Trade Center collapses.

WHEN THE BUILDINGS COLLAPSED, THE DUST REACHED THE EMPIRE STATE BUILDING, ALMOST THREE MILES AWAY.

THE FIRST RESPONDERS

IN THE MINUTES, HOURS, AND DAYS AFTER THE TOWERS COLLAPSED, THOUSANDS OF **FIREFIGHTERS AND OTHER RESCUE WORKERS** SWARMED THE SIXTEEN-ACRE DISASTER ZONE, SEARCHING FOR SURVIVORS.

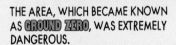

MANY CAME BECAUSE THEY WERE CALLED BY THEIR DEPARTMENTS, BUT OTHER INDIVIDUALS SIMPLY SHOWED UP, HELPING HOWEVER THEY COULD.

THE AREA, WHICH BECAME KNOWN AS **GROUND ZERO**, WAS EXTREMELY DANGEROUS.

UNDERGROUND FIRES SMOLDERED, AND THE SMOKE WAS A **TOXIC** MIX OF MELTED PLASTIC, STEEL, LEAD, AND MANY OTHER POISONOUS CHEMICALS.

AFTER BREATHING IN THESE TOXINS, MANY FIRST RESPONDERS AND VOLUNTEERS BECAME SICK WITH **CANCER OR OTHER ILLNESSES**.

IN RESPONSE TO THIS, THE U.S. GOVERNMENT CREATED THE **SEPTEMBER 11TH VICTIMS COMPENSATION FUND**. IT HELPS THOSE WHO GOT SICK PAY THEIR MEDICAL BILLS. BUT MANY FAMILIES ARE STILL FEELING THE EFFECTS OF THAT DAY, EVEN TWENTY YEARS LATER.

IN THE FRIGHTENING AND UNCERTAIN DAYS AFTER 9/11, THE FIRST RESPONDERS AND OTHER VOLUNTEERS BROUGHT THE AMERICAN PEOPLE **HOPE**.

AFTER THE ATTACKS

A TEAM OF MEN ORGANIZED THE ATTACK. BUT THE MAN MOST RESPONSIBLE WAS **OSAMA BIN LADEN**. HE WAS THE LEADER OF A TERRORIST GROUP CALLED AL QAEDA (AL-**KYE**-DUH). THE GROUP'S HEADQUARTERS WAS IN THE COUNTRY OF AFGHANISTAN (AF-**GAN**-IH-STAN).

TURKMENISTAN
UZBEKISTAN
DUSHANBE
TAJIKISTAN
CHINA
RAN
KABUL
AFGHANISTAN
Peshawar
ISLAMABAD
Srinagar
INDIA
Jammu
Gujranwala
Lahore
Faisalabad
Kandahar
Punjab
Ludhiana
Quetta
Multan
PAKISTAN
Delhi
NEW DELHI
IRAN
Jaipur
INDIA
Hyderabad
Karachi
ARABIAN SEA

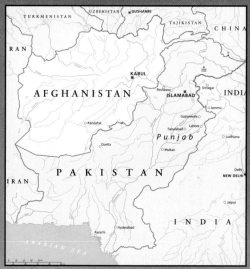

PRESIDENT GEORGE W. BUSH DEMANDED THAT AFGHANISTAN'S GOVERNMENT CAPTURE BIN LADEN AND HAND HIM OVER TO THE UNITED STATES. THE GOVERNMENT OF AFGHANISTAN, THEN CONTROLLED BY A GROUP CALLED THE TALIBAN, REFUSED.

ON OCTOBER 7, 2001, THE UNITED STATES, JOINED BY FORCES FROM OTHER COUNTRIES, DECLARED **WAR ON AFGHANISTAN**. THESE FORCES TOPPLED THE TALIBAN GOVERNMENT AND CAPTURED OR KILLED MANY MEMBERS OF AL QAEDA. BUT OSAMA BIN LADEN REMAINED ON THE RUN.

AFTER A TEN-YEAR MANHUNT, OSAMA BIN LADEN WAS DISCOVERED TO BE HIDING IN THE COUNTRY OF PAKISTAN. ON A TOP-SECRET MISSION ON MAY 2, 2011, BIN LADEN WAS KILLED BY MEMBERS OF A SPECIAL OPERATIONS UNIT OF THE UNITED STATES NAVY— **SEAL TEAM 6**.

"NAVY SEALS" IS A NICKNAME FOR THE U.S. NAVY SEA, AIR, AND LAND TEAMS. SEALS GO ON SECRET MISSIONS AROUND THE WORLD.

THE WAR IN AFGHANISTAN DRAGGED ON FOR MANY YEARS, COSTING THE LIVES OF APPROXIMATELY 16,000 AFGHANI PEOPLE AND 2,400 AMERICAN TROOPS. AS OF 2021, AFTER **TWENTY YEARS OF CONFLICT**, THERE ARE PLANS TO WITHDRAW AMERICAN TROOPS FROM AFGHANISTAN.

HONORING THOSE WE LOST

A TOTAL OF **2,977 PEOPLE DIED** AS A RESULT OF THE 9/11 ATTACKS: **2,753** AT THE WORLD TRADE CENTER (OF WHICH **412** WERE NEW YORK CITY FIRST RESPONDERS); **184** PEOPLE AT THE PENTAGON; AND **40** PEOPLE WHEN THE FOURTH HIJACKED PLANE CRASHED IN SHANKSVILLE, PENNSYLVANIA.

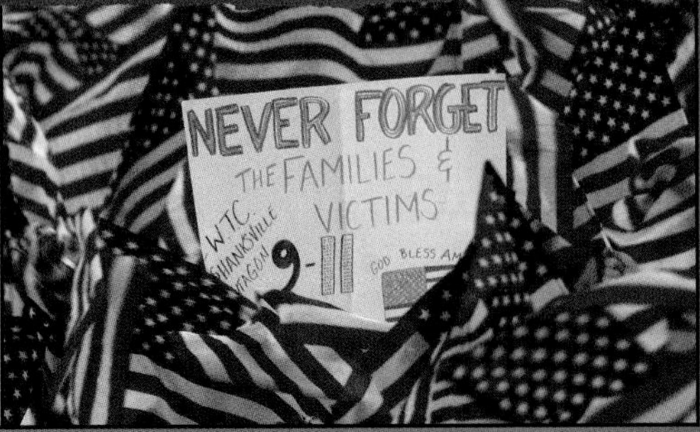
NEVER FORGET
THE FAMILIES &
VICTIMS
W.T.C.
SHANKSVILLE
9-11

THE **NATIONAL SEPTEMBER 11 MEMORIAL** OPENED IN SEPTEMBER OF 2011. WHERE THE TWIN TOWERS ONCE STOOD, THERE ARE NOW TWO ENORMOUS REFLECTING POOLS SURROUNDED BY TWO OF THE LARGEST WATERFALLS IN NORTH AMERICA. THE NAMES OF ALL THE VICTIMS ARE CARVED INTO BRONZE PANELS CIRCLING THE MEMORIAL POOLS.

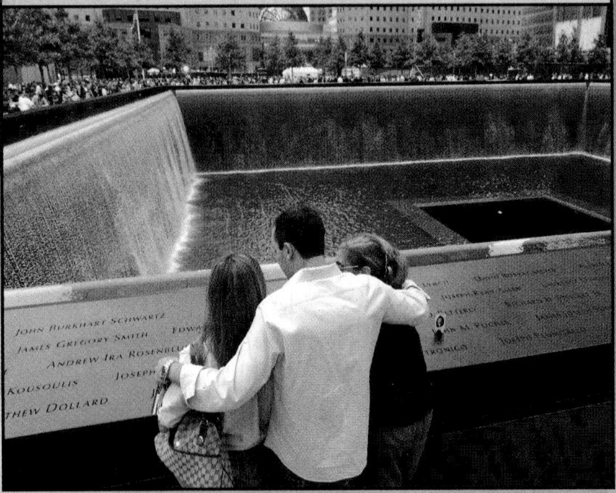
JOHN BURKHART SCHWARTZ
JAMES GREGORY SMITH

UNDERNEATH THE MEMORIAL IS THE **NATIONAL 9/11 MEMORIAL MUSEUM**, WHICH IS DEDICATED TO EXPLORING BOTH THE EVENTS OF 9/11 AND THE LASTING IMPACT.

EVERY YEAR ON SEPTEMBER 11, AN ART PIECE CALLED **TRIBUTE IN LIGHT** ILLUMINATES THE SKY IN REMEMBRANCE. IT IS MADE UP OF 88 SEARCHLIGHTS ARRANGED IN TWO GIANT SQUARES.

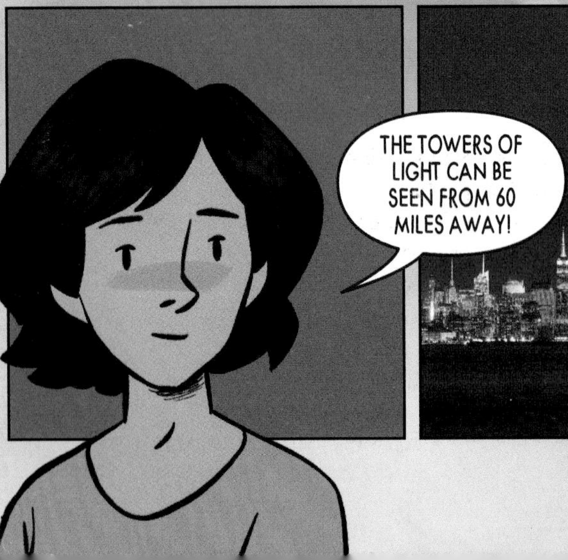
THE TOWERS OF LIGHT CAN BE SEEN FROM 60 MILES AWAY!

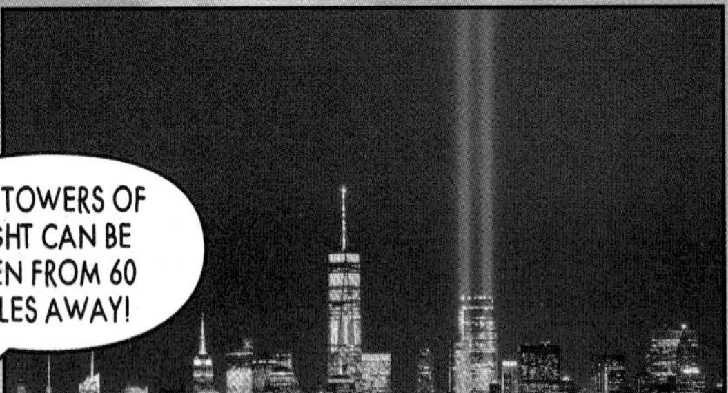

NEW YORK CITY, THEN AND NOW

WHEN THE **TWIN TOWERS** WERE COMPLETED IN 1973, THEY WERE THE TALLEST BUILDINGS IN THE MANHATTAN SKYLINE.

THE TOWER BUILT AFTER THE ATTACK, **ONE WORLD TRADE CENTER**, OPENED IN 2014.

MORE 9/11 BOOKS TO EXPLORE

Baskin, Nora Raleigh. *Nine, Ten: A September 11 Story.*
New York: Atheneum, 2016.

Gratz, Alan. *Ground Zero.* New York: Scholastic, 2021.

Rhodes, Jewel Parker. *Towers Falling.*
New York: Little, Brown, 2016.

SELECTED BIBLIOGRAPHY

Coe, Andrew. *FDNY: An Illustrated History of the Fire Department of New York City.*
Hong Kong: Odyssey Books and Maps, 2003.

Dwyer, Jim, and Kevin Flynn. *102 Minutes: The Untold Story of the Fight to Survive Inside the Twin Towers.* New York: Henry Holt and Company, 2005.

Halberstam, David. *Firehouse.* New York: Hachette, 2002.

The National Commission on Terrorist Attacks Upon the United States. *The 9/11 Commission Report.* July 26, 2004.

Wright, Lawrence. *The Looming Tower.* New York: Knopf, 2006.

LAUREN TARSHIS'S

NEW YORK TIMES BESTSELLING I SURVIVED SERIES TELLS STORIES OF YOUNG PEOPLE AND THEIR RESILIENCE AND STRENGTH IN THE MIDST OF UNIMAGINABLE DISASTERS AND TIMES OF TURMOIL. LAUREN HAS BROUGHT HER SIGNATURE WARMTH, INTEGRITY, AND EXHAUSTIVE RESEARCH TO TOPICS SUCH AS THE BATTLE OF D-DAY, THE AMERICAN REVOLUTION, HURRICANE KATRINA, THE BOMBING OF PEARL HARBOR, AND OTHER WORLD EVENTS. LAUREN LIVES IN CONNECTICUT WITH HER FAMILY, AND CAN BE FOUND ONLINE AT LAURENTARSHIS.COM.

GEORGIA BALL

HAS WRITTEN COMICS FOR MANY OF HER FAVORITE CHILDHOOD CHARACTERS, INCLUDING STRAWBERRY SHORTCAKE, TRANSFORMERS, LITTLEST PET SHOP, MY LITTLE PONY, AND THE DISNEY PRINCESSES. IN ADDITION TO ADAPTING LAUREN TARSHIS'S I SURVIVED SERIES TO GRAPHIC NOVELS, GEORGIA WRITES ABOUT HISTORICAL EVENTS SUCH AS THE WORLD WAR II BATTLES OF KURSK AND GUADALCANAL. GEORGIA LIVES WITH HER HUSBAND, DAUGHTER, AND RAMBUNCTIOUS PETS IN FLORIDA. VISIT HER ONLINE AT GEORGIABALLAUTHOR.COM.

COREY EGBERT

LOVES ILLUSTRATING STORIES THAT EMPOWER AND INSPIRE YOUNG PEOPLE. THIS IS HIS FIRST GRAPHIC NOVEL. HE LIVES WITH HIS WIFE, SON, AND TWO CATS IN A LITTLE HOUSE BY THE WOODS IN VIRGINIA. YOU CAN SEE MORE OF HIS WORK AT COREYEGBERT.COM.

CHI NGO

IS A VIETNAMESE ILLUSTRATOR/ANIMATION ARTIST LOCATED IN LOS ANGELES. SHE HAS CONTRIBUTED TO BRANDS LIKE TRANSFORMERS AND CLIFFORD AND WORKED FOR CARTOON NETWORK, NETFLIX, HASBRO, AND BENTOBOX. YOU CAN SEE MORE OF HER WORK AT CHI-NGO.COM.